A WORDLESS DEATH

TAM MAY

A Wordless Death

Adele Gossling Mysteries: Book 2

Tam May

Published by Dreambook Press.

Click or visit:
https://www.tammayauthor.com

Cover Design © 2022 by Aries/100 Covers

ISBN: 9780998338569 (Print)
ISBN: 9780998338576 (ebook)

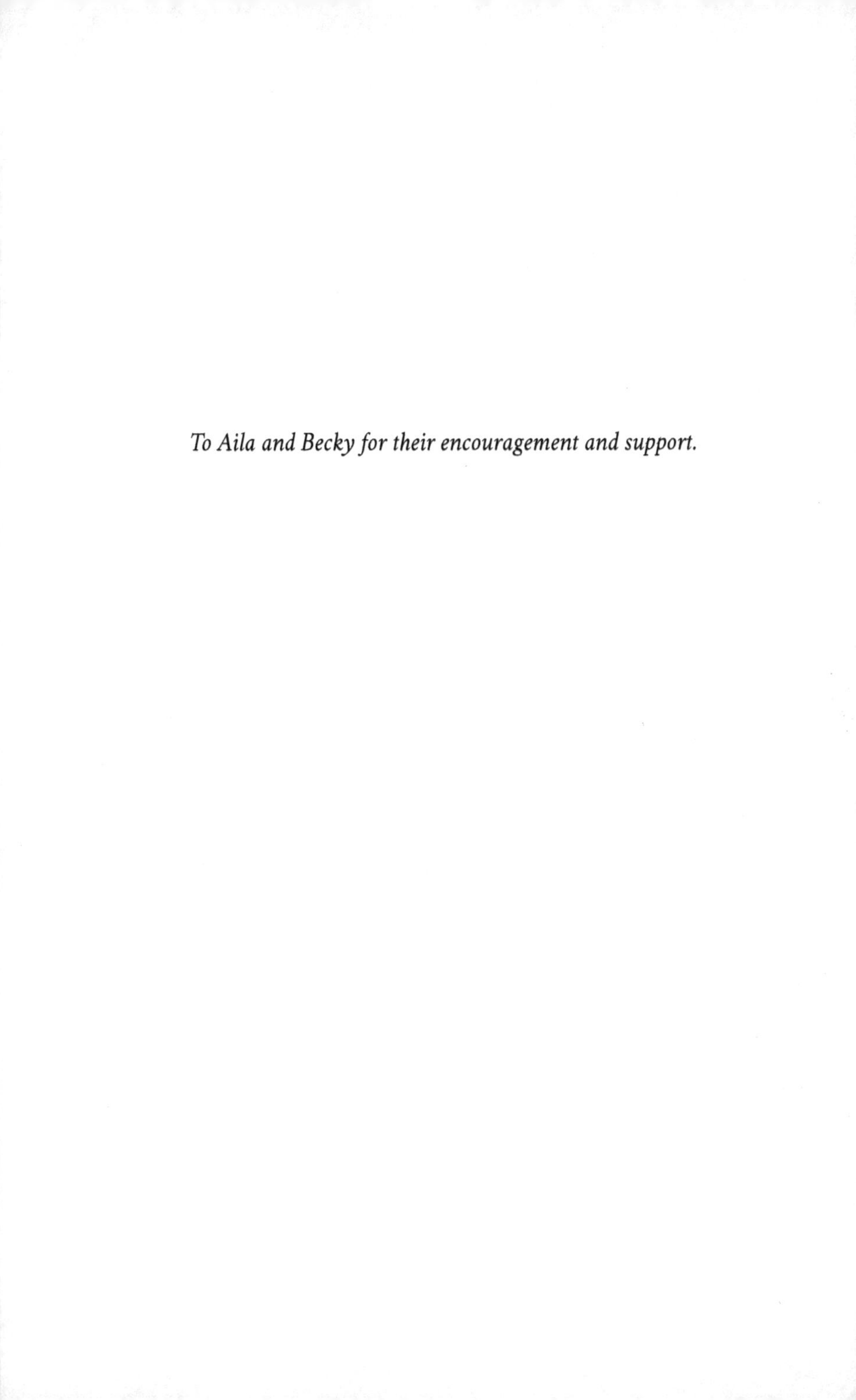

To Aila and Becky for their encouragement and support.

CHAPTER 1

If you're interested in reading more early 20th century mysteries, my free offer at the end of this book is for you! So don't forget to check that out when you get to the end. Happy reading!

The fall of 1903 came early in September, bringing with it a sweeping wind. Shopkeepers on Bridge Street closed early, anticipating few people out on the street once the storm hit. Adele Gossling followed suit, closing her stationery store at four o'clock in the afternoon. She persuaded her friend to accompany her to the post office.

"Auntie's companion promised she would write," she said.

"Have no fear," said Nin. "Your aunt will be all right."

Adele smiled. Nin had a special gift and could see and feel things no one else did. Her predictions were usually right.

The Arrojo Post Office was a small wooden house standing alongside the two-story buildings lining Bridge Street. Lyle Duncan, postmaster and telegraph operator, lived on the premises like many business people in Arrojo, but his resembled more a shack one would find in the more rural parts of town. He was more content putting his money into buying the latest Ford Model A than enhancing his modest accommodations.

Mr. Duncan greeted them with a cautious smiles. He laid aside the armful of envelopes he was sorting and handed Adele a small stack of telegrams and letters with her Caliber Lane address. "I hope the news is good, Miss Gossling."

"The news will be good," Nin said in a firm voice.

The man glanced at her for a moment, then turned back to the mail.

"Miss Gibbons says Auntie ought to be out of bed soon." Adele's breath eased. "She can even speak a little."

"Perhaps she shall find her voice when she sees your letter," Nin said as Adele handed the stamped envelope to Mr. Duncan.

Adele smiled and tore open another letter. "Elsie wants us to come to Sacramento."

"Whatever for?"

"They're going ahead with the protest." Adele folded the letter. "Outside the governor's mansion on the day he's giving a dinner party, no less. They need every able-bodied woman they can get."

"They might get arrested," Nin pointed out.

"That's what they want," Adele said. "She read about the work of the British suffragists, and she insists she may resort to that if the governor continues to treat our right to have a voice in the elections as an joke."

"Do you think he will?"

"Probably." Adele sighed. "I hope she doesn't do anything rash. Her father is with her and his health —"

Over the sound of Nin's reply came pounding feet. Dust floated around them.

"Has a letter come for me?"

"I would greatly appreciate it if you would shut the door," Mr. Duncan snapped. "Can't you see there's a dust storm?"

"I said, has a letter come for me?"

The voice, grated and demanding, showed the trying patience of one tasked with disciplining children. And, indeed, the woman was a teacher. Adele recognized her as Millie Gibb, the new English teacher at the Wrigley School for Girls.

Adele glanced at Nin. The girls at the school who ran errands for her now and again told her about Miss Gibb. Beatrice, in her usual outspoken way, called her Grammar Bobby with the twist in her jaw at the strange British word for the law officers who roamed the streets of London with their whistles whom she had seen the summer before when her parents took her to Europe.

"Well, has it?" The voice sounded like shaved ice.

Mr. Duncan set down the mail as if it were made of lace. "The evening mail will be delivered shortly," he said in a cold voice.

"Oh, for God's sake, if you could just *look*." Miss Gibb's face was red like a newly washed apple. Adele observed the uncommon pallor, its paleness replaced with a vibrance more disturbing than exuberant.

"Is it important?" she asked gently.

"I'll thank you to mind your own business!"

Nin's dark eyes narrowed and she gave the woman a sinister glare that made everyone think her gift more evil than good. Miss Gibb backed away, her mouse-gray eyes more anxious than before. Adele took hold of her friend's hand.

"No need to shout, miss," Mr. Duncan mumbled.

"I'm not shouting," Miss Gibb said. "I'm merely inquiring after a letter, and it's your duty as postmaster to give it to me."

"You're very precise," said Nin. Then, in a lower voice, she added, "Though perhaps not as precise as you want to believe."

"Words are my profession," Miss Gibb threw out but she was looking at Mr. Duncan. When she spoke again, her voice was composed. "I'm expecting a very important letter. Life-changing, to be *precise*." She glared at Nin. "I must have it, you see. I must have it *now*."

"Mr. Duncan, will you please see if you can find it, since it's so important to Miss Gibb?" Adele asked. "Surely, a few minutes of your time —"

The man bowed and shuffled through a stack of envelopes.

Rather than thank her, Miss Gibb gave Adele a cockeyed stare that mummified her skeletal frame. "Some women can get a man to do anything for them."

"When they are kind," Nin said in a sharp voice.

Something deflated Millie's whole countenance. "I was never like that," she said. "Never like that at all." She spoke almost to herself like someone who was used to speaking to empty rooms.

"No letters," Mr. Duncan said in a brisk voice.

"None at all?" Miss Gibb leaned into the wooden counter. "Can you look again, please? It would have a Sacramento address, I think—yes, Sacramento." She sounded uncertain.

Mr. Duncan raised his eyebrow at Adele, who nodded. He went back to his stack of envelopes but declared there was not so much as a postcard with a Sacramento address.

For a moment, Adele thought Miss Gibb was going to faint. The redness was gone from her face, replaced by an unusual marble shade, cold and listless. Miss Gibb's eyes wandered to the open doorway, looking at the Arrojo Hotel across the street.

"I'm sure it will come soon," Adele reassured her.

As if trying to muster enough courage to speak, Miss Gibb asked, "Any parcels for me, Mr. Duncan?"

Mr. Duncan handed her a wrapped package and a rolled-up magazine tied with string. Miss Gibb immediately began to flutter about, grasping the parcel with both hands. Her hold was so hard her knuckles almost tore through her skin. She looked down at it with a wide-eyed expression.

"It looks like a book," Nin remarked in a low voice.

Miss Gibb answered, "It is a book. A book of magic."

This clearly alarmed Mr. Duncan, as he coughed, but Miss Gibb seemed not to notice. She continued in her dreamy voice,

"In this book lies a key to unlock the way we are and not the way we must be. Do you understand what I mean, Miss Gossling?" She looked at Adele with her mouse eyes, making Adele realize how cold-blooded they really were. At the same time, brightness lit up her face, making it almost pretty, despite the premature lines forming at the corners of her mouth.

"There is magic even in the simplest things, Miss Gibb," said Adele. "I'm sure your students will realize this when you read to them from your book."

"My students!" The last word spit out on the dusty floor along with a sweeping wind crossing the threshold. "Those spoiled, insolent girls!"

Adele stiffened. She had great affection for the girls at the Wrigley School. They had been gathering information for her since her arrival in Arrojo. She felt like telling Miss Gibb of the sordid crime involving Lucy Blackstone that these girls, with their open eyes and ears, had helped to solve. But she was afraid Miss Gibb would tell Mrs. Wrigley and the school mistress, despite her friendly manner, was not one to tolerate a breach of what she considered the most girlish etiquette: to remain clean of life's sordid affairs.

"If you hate them so much, why did you take the job as English teacher?" Nin asked. It was never Nin's way to dance around a subject but spear it and hold it up for examination.

"I must earn my living, Miss Branch, the same as you and Miss Gossling," the woman sniffed. "I never had your opportunities. Soft ways and pretty hair always find opportunities." Her hand flew to her own hair which was wiry and coarse.

"May I ask what your book is about?" Adele inquired.

"The history to words," said the woman. "They don't appear out of the sky. Someone had to make them up. And in the case of the English language, many people put their hand in." Her eyes still on the invisible shine, she advanced a little, the red returning to her face. "One word can go through thousands of evolutions."

"You're a language Darwinist?" Nin asked with amusement.

Miss Gibb drew away. "I hardly expect *you* to understand. You're rather more of the spirit than the word, aren't you?"

Adele grabbed Nin's arm just in time before she flew at the woman. Nin's temper could be as stormy as the San Francisco Bay.

Oblivious to Nin's outburst, she announced, "I'm going to be a great etymologist someday."

"A what?" Mr. Duncan asked.

"I'm nothing now and there are people who want to keep me here. But I shall prevail. I shall prevail!" Her entire body was pointed like an arrow. "I'm about to embark on a new adventure, as a matter of fact."

"I imagine you haven't much time for reading with your work at the school," Nin remarked.

"Nonsense," Miss Gibb said. "I can read a book like this in two days."

"Indeed?" Adele glanced at the thick package.

"I stay up all night to read sometimes," she said. "When I'm excited — when I'm excited —" She stared at Adele. "I have nothing else, you see. Nothing else." She covered her mouth with her hand and rushed out of the post office.

CHAPTER 2

"*I* declare!" Mr. Duncan spoke first, but he seemed reluctant to declare anything after that. He turned back to his mail.

"The wind makes some people restless," Nin said.

"She's always been an odd one," the man said. "Don't think I'll give her any more mail outside of delivery hours."

The street was quieter now that most businesses were closed for the day. Dusk put lines of deep blue on the sky. Even though Adele had lived in Arrojo for over a year, she still found the clearness of the country sky invigorating. It was a relief to be away from the city fog and crowded streets. She had even imagined seeing figures shaped in the fog as she walked along the cobblestones. That was very soon after her father died, and some of the women in the settlement houses warned her many people saw the souls of the dearly departed in the fog.

"I think it was more than nerves," Adele said as she held her friend's arm. "People don't make intimate declarations to strangers unless —"

"Unless?"

"They think they will never speak to anyone again."

"Adele!" Nin stared at her. "Your brother shouldn't confide in you about his work. It puts death into your head."

Adele laughed. "You know that's the last thing Jackson would ever do."

"He has antiquated ideas about what constitutes appropriate conversation for women," Nin agreed.

"It does seem startling a woman like Miss Gibb would have such lofty ideas about her future," Adele continued.

"And rather arrogant ones," Nin added. "I don't even know what etymology is."

They reached the deeper end of Bridge Street where both of their shops stood, small wooden storefronts one right next to the other. Only last summer Adele convinced Nin to allow her to paint them both a pleasant faded peach that even the red dust could not coat.

"It is arrogant to boast about being something most people wouldn't know about," Adele agreed. "Perhaps her students would know."

"The insolent brats?" Nin had little warmth for the cackling bunch of girls Adele favored.

"She was rather critical of them," Adele said. "But one is critical of a life one doesn't want. I found fault in every picnic and ball I was dragged to when I was living in San Francisco."

"You had a higher sense of purpose," Nin insisted.

"Perhaps Miss Gibb does too," Adele said.

She bid her friend goodbye and watched Nin open the creaking side door leading to the second floor of the building where she lived. She always watched to make sure Nin reached the top of the rickety staircase in one piece. Only when she was safety inside did Adele close the door and lock it with the key Nin had given her.

She made her way down the windy street, pulling the veil from her hat over her face to shield the dust out of her eyes. Arrojo had surprisingly sturdy roots, and the building and vegetation did little more than sway in the storm. Like the people who had built the town, nothing, not even a split in the earth or the raging fires of hell would leave its mark.

The Arrojo Police Station was empty except for her brother Jackson who sat at the new desk Sheriff Hatfield had put in a few months before.

"Did Edison go home for his dinner?" she asked as she peeled off her gloves. They felt grainy from the dust.

Her brother nodded. "That boy is afraid of storms. Believes evil spirits will rise from the ground. Such nonsense!"

"Nin said the wind brings strange behavior." Out of habit, she examined the papers lying on the desk with the magnifying glass she always wore around her neck.

"She ought to know," Jackson said. There was silence for a time. Adele felt he was watching her. "Well?"

"Auntie is doing better," she said.

"Perhaps we ought to go down there." His eyebrows peaked.

She kissed his cheek. "Miss Gibbons is quite capable of managing things."

"Apoplexy is serious, Del." He leaned back. "It's lucky she has such a loyal companion like Miss Gibbons. Still, companions aren't family."

Adele nodded. "It's different when one has family about. I don't know what I would have done if you hadn't taken the deputy sheriff position when Hatfield offered it to you."

Jackson smiled. "Hatfield is a hard man to refuse."

The door swung open and the sheriff entered. He was a massive man both vertically and horizontally, though his largeness was more in figure than girth. He had a pleasant, almost boyish face despite his fifty-odd years. He saw her and immediately his countenance became almost that of a shy boy.

"Good evening, Adele." They had been in familiar terms with one another since the Blackstone murder case the year before.

"Good evening, Sheriff," she said just as kindly.

"Any news about your aunt from Santa Barbara?" he asked.

She nodded. "And news from Elsie in Sacramento."

Jackson eyed her. "And what is she doing in Sacramento?"

"On one of her suffragist missions, no doubt." Hatfield shook the red dust off his shoulders. Somehow, he always managed to get something caught in the grooves of the heavy jacket he wore.

"She wants to coax the governor into a meeting about the vote for women," she said.

"I've no doubt she'll succeed," the sheriff said.

"Elsie could coax a California grizzly back into its cave," her brother snorted. "If only by the sheer fright of her severe face."

"You needn't be severe yourself because she once had designs on you," Adele said.

"My dear sister, I'm only as severe as necessary toward one who is determined to pull my sister into her shenanigans."

The bone that dug between his sister's chestnut eyebrows lurched forward. "Women's rights are not shenanigans!"

"In the hands of Elsie Blessings, it is!" he retorted.

"Now, Jackson," Hatfield said. "Miss Blessings and her friends have a right to voice their opinion."

"Not when they pull respectable ladies into the most absurd —"

"I am not one of those ladies, Jack." Adele leaned her parasol against the desk. It slipped and fell to the floor with a crash.

The door opened slowly and Edison, an assistant deputy sheriff, poked his head in. He bowed to Adele and headed for the sink to make a pot of coffee which he would be needing for his nightly duty

"My ma always says a good dinner solves many problems," said Hatfield. "Now that Edison is here, I think we can leave for the day. Edison!" He yelled out the young man's name, a habit he picked up in the days when he was the captain of a fishing boat. "You're late, lad."

"I'm sorry, sir. The storm."

"Speak in complete sentences in front of the lady, Edison," said Hatfield as he put on his usual hummer and scarf.

"Yes, sir."

"Perhaps the dust did settle on my mind," Jackson admitted when they were outside. "I didn't mean to speak sharply, Del, but I don't want Elsie and her friends to pull you into something that might get you into trouble." He put his arm around her shoulders.

"I'm sure your sister has enough sense to keep her head," said Hatfield.

"You always say the kindest things to me, Sheriff," she said.

He would not take her arm as they walked home in a slow pace because of the pushing wind. Soon they were talking about the new section of roses in his mother's garden. The enthusiasm in his voice pulled Adele out of her gloom.

"They're called American Beauties," he said. "Ma is determined to make them stand upright. She insists she's going to win the flower show this year."

"And oust Mrs. Faderman's buttercups out of the running?" Adele smiled.

"Lady Augusta is about the only person who could triumph over Mrs. Faderman in any capacity," Jackson said.

"I must go tomorrow to get the seeds she ordered from the catalogue," said Hatfield. "They mustn't sit in Mr. Duncan's mailbag for too long."

"A shame you didn't tell me," Adele said. "I would have picked them up myself today."

"You had troubles of your own," Hatfield said.

"It appears I'm not the only one," she remarked as they passed by the dark leaves of the avocado trees that marked the beginning of Caliber Lane. "Miss Millie Gibb almost had a fit at the post office this evening."

"Indeed?" Jackson glanced at her. "The imbalances of spinsterhood, no doubt."

Adele gave her brother a look. "That had nothing to do with it. She was anxious for a letter from Sacramento."

"Perhaps she's waiting for word from a sick family member herself," the sheriff suggested.

"I don't think so." Adele raised the veil from her face in an absent-minded way. "It seemed more personal than that."

"What could be more personal than a letter from a sick relative?" Jackson asked as he moved a rock out of their path with his stick.

"I mean more desperate. Selfish, even."

"That hardly makes sense, Del," said her brother.

"I must agree with Adele," said Hatfield. "When one has lived alone for many years, one gets into the habit of thinking of oneself." In a more even tone, he added, "I was that way before Ma came to live with me."

"Miss Gibb was behaving in a rather peculiar way," said Adele.

"Peculiar how?" The sheriff looked at her. He was as interested in human behavior as the scientists they were reading about who toyed with the monkeys to see what they would do.

"The girls told me she's exacting as a teacher," said Adele. "But she was very agitated with Mr. Duncan. Almost demanding."

"When a teacher is out of her element, she can be headstrong," said Jackson. "I remember meeting one of my teachers at The Olympic Club once. Rather jollier there than he ever was scratching on the blackboard."

"But this was so unusual," said Adele.

"I take it she didn't get her letter," her brother remarked.

"No, but she did get a parcel and a magazine," his sister replied. "She treated that parcel as if it were an incantation of a higher being. She even called it magical."

"Your friend ought to know about that," said Jackson. "Perhaps they could go flying around in the air together." He had made no secret of his rather dubious opinions of Nin's gifts.

"It wasn't like that, Jack," she said. "She looked almost —

possessed. In a frightening way." She was feeling disturbed again and would have passed by the gate of their house if her brother hadn't had a firm grip on her arm.

"The storm makes sensitive people behave in mysterious ways." Hatfield put his large hand on top of his hat to keep the wind from taking it off into the wild weeds growing between the Gossling house and the now abandoned Blackstone house.

"That's what Nin said."

"Well, perhaps her instincts were a little earthier this time," said Jackson with a smile as he opened the gate. The Cordobas, who kept the house for them, were standing in their usual place at the front door. Tomas had his hen-like gaze with his hands squeezed to his chin, and his wife Ruth smiled in her strong, soothing way.

Hatfield bowed and sauntered away back toward the direction of Bridge Street.

CHAPTER 3

That Sunday, Adele found herself at breakfast with Jackson on the back porch, feeling the soft breeze the previous week's wind storm had left behind billow through the puffed lace of her blouse. The back screen threw open and Hatfield stepped out. He took off his hat immediately.

"Good morning, sir," said Jackson without looking up from his paper.

"Tomas just brought a fresh pot of coffee," said Adele. "And your favorite corn muffins."

The man was silent for a moment as he looked down at the golden cakes lying in the basket. Then he said, "You'll need to put that paper down, Deputy."

Both Adele and her brother sat up. She realized the sheriff was not dressed in his Sunday best. He wore what he called his clue suit, a slightly shabby but useful ensemble he insisted had brought him luck when he accompanied the stagecoaches with the largest shipments of gold for Wells Fargo. His sheriff's badge was prominently pinned to his lapel.

"It's a crime, isn't it?" Jackson was already reaching for the jacket he had hung on the empty chair next to him.

"Very," Hatfield answered, eyeing Adele. "It looks as if you were right about Miss Millie Gibb."

Adele stared at him. "You mean Miss Gibb is dead?"

He nodded, looking at her with a few lines on his face standing out in the hot sun.

~

*A*dele did not have to persuade the sheriff to allow her to come with them. In fact, he suggested it. "You were one of the last in town to see Miss Gibb," Hatfield said as they hurried toward Bridge Street. "That might prove useful."

Adele felt as if her feet had turned to lead. "To think she was alive only a few days ago!"

"Mrs. Taylor found her this morning." Hatfield held out his arm to her.

"Shouldn't Nin come with us?" asked Adele as she took it. "She saw Miss Gibb too."

"Let's leave her in peace for now," said the sheriff. "Too many of us strolling down Bridge Street is liable to kick up a lot of fuss. We don't know what really happened yet."

"You think it was murder." Jackson crushed the edge of his stick into the red dust.

"She was found dead in her room," said Hatfield. "Mrs. Taylor said it came as a great shock to everyone in the house."

Indeed, Adele felt like a lightning bolt had inserted electricity into everything at Mrs. Taylor's house, from the door knobs to the furniture. The maid, whom Adele sometimes saw bubbling through the streets doing the shopping was now limp like a drowned flower, her thick cotton handkerchief held to her face. As she led them upstairs, her hand trembled as it grasped the bannister with each step.

"Don't be afraid, Lilly," she whispered to her.

"Oh, miss, it's *awful*!" she burst out.

"Yes, well, we're here now," Jackson said in a brisk tone. Hatfield gave him a warning glance. Her brother had a vigorous way about him that worked very well with some of the male suspects but he didn't have much sensitivity for the emotional reactions of the women.

They reached the second floor where Mrs. Taylor housed all her women boarders. Mrs. Taylor herself stood in the hallway. She was a middling woman in every respect — average height, average hair and eyes, average skin, mid-pitched voice, and clothes that had seen better days but at the same time were well taken care of so as not to look shabby. She was intolerant of shabbiness and discord which made her acceptable even to women like Mrs. Faderman. In fact, her sense of decorum was so acute that when she saw Adele, she practically threw herself in the doorway of Miss Gibb's room.

"Miss Gossling, it's hardly proper for you to be here!"

"I may have been one of the last to see Miss Gibb, ma'am," Adele said.

"I forbid you to —" she began but then, as if recalling the correctness of her position in regards to the police, she lowered her voice. "It's not a pretty sight, Sheriff."

"Mrs. Taylor," said Adele, "remember I found a dead girl in my backyard only last year, and I wasn't a bit squeamish about it."

"Perhaps not, Miss Gossling," she said. "I just don't think it fitting for a young woman to see such a thing."

"Maybe it's best if you let us go in first, Del," Jackson suggested.

His sister glared at him, tightening her hand around the ribbon of her magnifying glass. "I daresay you're more squeamish than I am!"

"I prefer you come in with us," said Hatfield. "You might pick up things Jackson and I miss, being unfamiliar with ladies' rooms."

Mrs. Taylor growled but moved aside. "In *my* time —" They were past the doorway before she could finish the sentence.

The room looked fairly typical compared to the boarding houses Adele had visited many times in her settlement house work — small, poorly lit, and plainly furnished. It was perhaps a little softer in color than most she had seen. What struck Adele right away was its disorderliness. A small night table was out of its place near the bed. The curtain looked as if someone had grabbed it, half pulling it from the rod. Next to the bureau, where nothing looked particularly disturbed, a washbasin stood as stout as ever but the pitcher was thrown on the floor, cracked near the spout.

"Odd," she murmured. Hatfield gave her a questioning look. "The girls told me Miss Gibb always had a bee up her bonnet about tidiness. She checked every girl in her class every morning to make sure her appearance was ladylike."

"This room is hardly ladylike." Her brother glanced around.

Hatfield had already moved to the crumbling figure sitting at the desk in the corner. Miss Gibb wore a light gray nightgown and her feet were bare. Adele had worked with a number of school teachers in the city, and she knew their salaries were by no means extravagant and their tastes were usually as bare as their wardrobe. She could not have imagined, staring at the nails on the wall that held a gingham dress, a light green frock, and the white dress she had worn to the post office that the woman had more than this.

She gasped when she saw a large, heart-shaped patch cover Miss Gibb's entire back through the nightgown. Some parts of the patch sank under her arms and Adele knew if she would look at the front of the dress it, too, would have a large patch of dark gray.

Almost immediately, she asked, "Does it get very hot in these rooms at night, Mrs. Taylor?"

The woman was a little outside the door, her arms crossed

against her middling bosom. "I expect it's as hot as the rest of town," she sniffed. "I try to keep things well-aired, but with the dust storms, we have to keep the windows shut. Makes it much easier on Lilly."

"She must have been perspiring terribly all night long." A sharp sound from Mrs. Taylor's throat made the sheriff correct himself. "I mean glowing. Wouldn't you say, Jackson?"

"No doubt about it."

"I've already sent Edison to fetch Dr. Rhodes or Martin," said Hatfield as he gently lifted one of Miss Gibb's arms and then the other, turning them over.

"Let's hope it's the latter." Jackson gave his sister a look. It was no secret Dr. Rhodes had breakfast late on Sunday mornings, and he was less than appeasing when he was called away on duty during mealtimes.

"Scrapes." Hatfield held out a flimsy hand. "Cuts."

"Bumps, more like it," said Jackson. When Adele tried to take a few steps nearer, he stood in the way of the body. "She was walking around and not too steadily."

"Was Miss Gibb fond of wine at dinner, Mrs. Taylor?" Adele asked in a clear high voice, a way of showing her dissatisfaction with her brother's too protective manner.

"None of my guests drink, Miss Gossling," Mrs. Taylor insisted.

"Of course not," Adele said with a lavish smile. "I would never suggest such a thing with the quality of people here." The woman smiled. "But you know sometimes when things grow difficult, wine makes the nerves wary, and if we're not careful, we're apt to overdo, especially if we're not used to it."

"Millie was never that sort," said the woman.

"There are other reasons why one might walk unsteadily, Del," her brother pointed out.

"Fatigue, perhaps," she suggested.

There was a tap on the wooden stairs and Lilly appeared with her half-buried face in the cotton handkerchief followed by Martin Sanders, Dr. Rhodes' assistant. "Good Sunday." The young man bowed. "For some of us, that is." He glanced through the doorway.

Hatfield cleared his throat. "I'd like you to wait outside, Adele."

"Oh, really, Sheriff!" Adele growled.

"This is no place for a woman," Jackson declared.

"Or a yellow-bellied former Anspach detective," she retorted.

"When have I ever been yellow-bellied?" Her brother was more amused than annoyed.

Adele looked at the sheriff. "You of all people."

"I think it's best." There was finality in his quiet voice, and Adele knew better than to try and persuade him when his tone was so determined.

She joined Mrs. Taylor in the hall.

"I warned you it wasn't a pretty sight," said the woman.

"When did you find her, Mrs. Taylor?"

"Just a little while ago," said the woman. "She didn't come down to church or breakfast either. Not like her."

"You knew her habits well?" asked Adele. "I mean in a friendly way, not in the way of a landlady only."

The woman shrugged. "We had a talk or two now and again. Her grandmother used to take in boarders. She knew all about the hard work."

"She wasn't friendly with the other boarders," Adele guessed.

"Now what makes you say that?" The woman looked at her with her clear eyes.

"I saw her in the post office on Wednesday and she seemed — well, the kind to keep to herself."

"Well, most of my boarders are young folks," said Mrs. Taylor. "Not flighty ones, mind you."

"I know you'd never stand for that." Adele patted the woman's shoulder. She was rewarded with a wan smile.

"Millie, was — I don't know what you'd call it. More experienced."

"More worldly?" Adele suggested.

"Not exactly," said Mrs. Taylor. "She's seen something of life, I gathered, but not in the worldly sense. I don't quite know how to explain it."

"You've done very well," said Adele with a smile.

"I hope there isn't a fuss," Mrs. Taylor sighed.

"You mean a scandal?" Adele asked.

It was the wrong word to use, as the woman's entire body tightened. "There have never been any scandals about my house, Miss Gossling."

"Certainly not," said Adele. "I'm sure the police will be discreet."

"We mustn't judge her because she chose a sinful death." Mrs. Taylor whispered the last.

Adele realized what she meant. "You really think that's how she died?"

"Of course." The woman pulled her shawl around her shoulders. Adele saw it had quite a few holes in it.

"She's lived in Arrojo less time than I have, I believe," said Adele.

"Only a little," said Mrs. Taylor. "A year and a half or thereabouts."

"Do you believe she was so unhappy for a year and a half that she would choose a sinful route to death at this particular time?"

"Can we really judge whether anyone is happy or unhappy, Miss Gossling?" The woman peered at her. "In my day, people knew about their neighbors. Now no one knows about anyone. And women are so silent as it is."

"Only when they're forced to be," Adele reminded her.

"Silence is golden." Mrs. Taylor raised an eye at her. "I know young women these days believe in shouting down the streets and having careers and shunning marriage." The last she said with a visible shudder. "But Millie wasn't like that. She was a quiet girl, and she knew her duty. She worked out of necessity, not choice."

"And yet," said Adele in a small voice, "she might have made enemies in her industrious lifetime."

"We all have our enemies, don't we, Miss Gossling?" Martin appeared at the doorway with his doctor's bag held to his chest. "Even a stray dog always has to fight another stray dog for his bone."

"I should hope we're more civilized than dogs." Mrs. Taylor sniffed.

"What did you find?" Adele asked with anxious eyes. "And don't say my brother told you to keep it from me." She could hear Mrs. Taylor "humphing" beside her in a low voice.

Martin laughed. "I wouldn't even if he had, Miss Gossling. You're far too inquisitive to resist."

"And you're far too dedicated to your work not to want to share it," said Adele with a smile.

"I'm as dedicated to justice as you and your brother, that's all," he insisted.

"Mrs. Taylor believes Miss Gibb chose a sinful route to death." Adele glanced at the woman who was speaking to the maid.

"A sinful route?" Martin looked at her.

"What Mrs. Taylor meant," Hatfield said slowly, "is she believes Miss Gibb took her own life."

The young man shrugged. "I've never heard it put quite that way."

"I believe Mrs. Taylor was trying to be discreet," said Adele.

"In my profession, Miss Gossling, discretion is a waste of time," Martin said. "We call it for what it is — suicide."

"And do you believe it was suicide?"

"It's possible," he admitted. "There are no outward signs of violence."

"What about the scrapes on her hands?" Adele remembered the sheriff's words.

"She made those herself," said Martin. "Not deliberately, of course. Must have lost her balance and fell."

"When did she die?" asked Adele.

"I put it at six to eight hours ago."

Adele closed her eyes for a moment as she did when she made calculations in her shop. "That would make it early morning, then."

"Fairly early." Martin suppressed a yawn. "The sheriff puts it at two to four a.m."

"Mrs. Taylor." Adele turned to the woman who was holding her hand up in a scolding way at Lilly. "Was Miss Gibb apt to stay up into the early hours of the morning?"

The boarding house proprietress pivoted her head around, which raised the entire left side of her face. Adele thought she looked almost interesting that way.

"I don't go around creeping in hallways listening at the doorway of my boarders to see if they're asleep, Miss Gossling," she said in a chilly voice.

Adele recalled what Miss Gibb had said at the post office. "If she were excited about something — say, a new book or magazine she received in the mail — could she stay up all night to read it?"

"She was always very punctual and very sensitive to her duties as a teacher," Mrs. Taylor said. Without looking at Lilly, she waved her hand at her, signaling her lecture with her was over. Lilly toddled off but not before she gave Adele a grateful glance.

"What has that to do with Miss Gossling's question?" Martin asked in a sharp voice.

"I believe," said Adele, "Mrs. Taylor is trying to say Miss Gibb would never have risked her good standing with the school by doing anything that might have interfered with her duties. When one stays up all night to read, one might not do their work the following morning in the best way."

Mrs. Taylor gave her a broad smile. Adele felt she had been redeemed at least a little in her eyes, despite the woman's earlier harsh critique of her progressive ways.

"If there was no evidence of violence of any kind," said Adele, "how did she die, do you think?"

"Poison. She died of poison." This was supplied by Hatfield as he slipped out the door of Miss Gibb's room.

"A woman's weapon," Adele murmured.

"Against herself," Martin added.

*I*f Hatfield had disappointed her when he sent her out of the room, he was now fair and gracious. He held out his arm and escorted her back in. Miss Gibb's body was no longer at the desk, having been moved to the bed with the thick blanket rolled over it.

"So glad you decided to make the room presentable to a lady, Sheriff," she said in a wry tone,

"You're lucky you're here at all, Del," snapped her brother from his position behind the desk. "We've gotten more than one complaint about the deputy sheriff's sister sticking her nose into police business."

Hatfield didn't seem the least bit rattled. "It had nothing to do with you, Adele. I wouldn't have subjected Edison to the sight."

"Edison," she said tartly, "gets ill at the sight of a dead cat."

The sheriff couldn't hold back a smile as he joined his deputy at the desk.

It was a large one, larger than any Adele had seen in San Francisco boarding houses, though just as shabby with peeling paint and sharp corners. On the desk lay an open book and paper knife, a lamp and a magazine.

She fingered the cover of the last. The black print and title *American Language Origins* were as bare as the chill that ran through her. She put on her gloves and carefully flipped through it, examining the pages. They were equally uninviting. Their edges were ragged, as if someone had been anxious to get the pages separated so they could read it.

"She tore through this magazine," Adele remarked. "Look at the pages." She ran her finger along the edges of it. "And the book is the same."

"Perhaps you were right, then," said her brother. "She was reading all night, and that's why she was up at two in the morning."

"If that's so," said Hatfield, "the lamp would be turned on, wouldn't it?"

Both the Gosslings stared at the student lamp with its skirt-glass light and misshapen bowl.

"Good Lord, you're right!" Jackson said. "She could hardly read at that hour without light."

"So you think she wasn't reading at two o'clock in the morning?" Adele eyed him.

"Question marks, question marks," murmured Hatfield, rubbing his chin. It was his usual lament when he was perplexed about something during a case, and Adele had learned these were questions he made sure were answered by the time the case was closed.

Jackson turned to Mrs. Taylor. "Was Miss Gibb a spiritual person?"

The woman looked alarmed. "She had no crazy notions about ghosts and such, if that's what you mean. I was just telling Miss Gossling how Millie wasn't like the younger girls these days."

"Yes," Adele said. "A quiet lady who knew her duty." She bit her tongue to keep her own ideas about such women to herself.

"I didn't mean ghosts, ma'am," Jackson said with all the charm of his good breeding. "I meant, did she believe in the healing power of herbs and spices?"

The woman blinked. "I should think your sister's friend would know the answer to that question, since as she has the only place in town where one can get such things."

Jackson turned to his sister. "Perhaps Miss Branch would know."

"The only thing I ever heard her say about Miss Gibb was that she was a nudging nuisance."

Hatfield burst out in his deep laughter, in spite of the fact he usually kept grave in the presence of a dead body.

"And what, pray, did she mean by that?" Jackson eyed her.

"Miss Gibb had a habit of entering shops, asking a lot of questions, and then leaving without buying a thing," Adele said. "She was not a favorite of the business people."

"Miss Branch isn't in the habit of holding back her rather acidic opinion of people, is she?" Jackson asked with a stiff lip.

"Millie had to be frugal," Mrs. Taylor insisted.

"Perhaps you'd better tell us what prompted your strange question, Jack," said his sister.

He opened his hand, also gloved, and revealed a few large pieces of a cinnamon stick.

"Oh, that would have been from her hot toddy," Mrs. Taylor said.

"Hot toddy?"

"Yes, she was quite fond of a hot toddy before bed," said Mrs. Taylor. "She said it helped her sleep."

"At two o'clock in the morning, she would need something to help her sleep," Jackson remarked.

"What else did the hot toddy contain, other than cinnamon?" Hatfield asked, turning his eyes at Jackson, who already had his pad and pencil out.

The woman sniffed. "I wouldn't know, Sheriff. I haven't the

time to putter about the kitchen watching over the cook. I have many other duties."

"Which you fulfill admirably, I'm sure." Hatfield bowed.

The woman gave him a gummy smile and added, "You might ask Mrs. Clogg. She would know about the hot toddy."

Hatfield waited until Mrs. Taylor stepped back into the hallway out of sight. "Jackson, do you notice anything missing from this room?"

"I don't know what you mean, sir," said his deputy.

"If there was a hot toddy here, as it seems there was, or you wouldn't have found the cinnamon stick, it had to come in a glass, didn't it?"

Adele's eyes fell on the desk. There was a lace doily sitting at the other corner as far away from the magazine and book as possible. "She would have put it here," she said, pointing to it. "To make sure it was out of the way of her reading and wouldn't stain the desk."

"I was thinking the same thing," said Hatfield.

"Perhaps she threw it in the fire." Jackson bent down to the grate.

"That wouldn't make much sense," said Adele.

"It would if she did something to it and didn't want people to know." He took one of the pokers, black with coal dust, from the stand and began gently prodding around.

"Did something to it." Adele felt her chest grow cold. "You mean poisoned it."

"It's not uncommon, Del," her brother said. "A lonely, unmarried woman not in her prime, teaching school children, with books her only solace —"

"Too bad she wasn't locked up in an attic like Bertha Rochester," Adele snapped. "Then she would have been not only out of sight but also out of mind."

"Not all women are as dynamic as you are, Adele," said

Hatfield. She detected a tone of admiration she had heard in his voice now and again at the strangest opportunities.

"Sheriff!"

Hatfield joined Jackson at the grate just as two young men in white coats and overlong mustaches peered through the doorway. They indicated they had been sent by Martin to "pick up the body," as they bluntly put it. Adele directed them toward the bed since Hatfield was engrossed in Jackson's discoveries.

After the men left, both her brother and the sheriff rose, brushing coal dust from their clothes. Adele was amused at the thought of Hatfield's unwieldy figure crouched halfway inside the tiny fireplace as he shook out his Sunday handkerchief.

"No glass, I take it," she guessed.

"Something much more interesting," said her brother. "Something in your line of work, Del."

He showed her what looked like a fragment of a note or letter. The edges were crisp and charred. She could see small, dark print but could barely make out the words before he placed it carefully inside a smaller handkerchief he always carried in his coat pocket.

"That explains why there was a fire burning last night even though it's been mild weather," he remarked.

"A disparaging lover, you think?" Hatfield asked.

"It wouldn't be uncommon," said Jackson. "Though perhaps a little surprising."

Adele guessed his meaning. "Miss Gibb might not have been a beauty, Jack, but many men appreciate an intelligent and well-read woman more than giggles and curls."

She was rewarded by Hatfield's deep chuckle.

"Love doesn't usually go with money, though, does it?" Jackson remarked. "Whatever this letter contained, it had to do with a lot of money."

Mrs. Taylor appeared. "Begging your pardon, sir. You understand I don't get into the business of my guests unless —"

"Unless?" Hatfield head bobbed up.

"It's necessary, of course," was her resolute answer.

"You know something about this letter, I take it?" he asked.

"Well, no, sir, not this one in particular," said Mrs. Taylor. "But more than once Millie asked for a few days' extension on her rent payment. She told me she had a cousin she was close to who was rather in a bad way financially." Once she had said it, she seemed embarrassed. "I don't like to go around giving out my guests' private business, but —"

"That's all right, ma'am," said Jackson. "That's very helpful to us."

"Well, now that everything's all right —"

Adele could see she still hesitated and understood the woman's concern. Her sense of decorum had gotten a jolt over a room she only rented out to women boarders being trampled over by male footsteps.

"I'll make sure everything's all right, Mrs. Taylor," she assured her in a low voice.

Mrs. Taylor rewarded her with one of her gummy smiles and departed.

"Could be this cousin was asking for money," Jackson said.

"Why throw it in the fire, then?" asked Hatfield. "I've had more than one of Ma's uncles write for a few coins, and even when I refused, I never threw the letter out."

"It does seem a little excessive," Adele agreed.

"Unless this wasn't the first time," her brother pointed out. "Mrs. Taylor mentioned Miss Gibb had to ask her for an extension several times."

The maid was at the doorway. "Mrs. Taylor, sir." Her voice was still thick with tears. "She wants to know how long before she can get breakfast on the table. She knows you want to speak to everyone, sir, so she waited."

"This late?" Jackson glanced at his watch.

"The guests always dine late on Sundays, sir," said Lilly in a soft voice.

"By all means, tell her to serve breakfast," said Hatfield. "We'll conduct interviews afterward in the parlor. And tell Assistant Deputy Edison I'd like him to send up one of the lads to guard this room so nobody goes in." The young woman curtsied and scurried away.

Jackson insisted on going over the contents of the desk drawers even though Hatfield was of the opinion there was certainly very little in them, as boarding house desks tended to be skeletal versions of what they ought.

"Well, well," she heard Jackson murmur.

He held in his hand a small revolver. She was startled at the little thing as it lay so innocently with its gold plate and shiny pearl handle. The ball of the trigger was perfectly round, and the barrel had figure eights engraved along the muzzle. Despite her abhorrence for such things, she couldn't help but murmur, "So pretty."

"That makes it all the more lethal." The sheriff examined it. "A fine piece of work for a woman's handgun."

"Martin told me there was no violence," Adele said.

"He was quite right," said Hatfield.

"If there are any bullet wounds on Miss Gibb," said Jackson, "we certainly couldn't find them. And there would have been some kind of noise, tiny as the thing is, if there had been a shot at two o'clock in the morning."

Hatfield flicked the cylinder open, and the click made Adele jump.

"Not loaded," Jackson observed. "Not much use for a gun if it isn't loaded."

"For a woman, an unloaded gun might be very useful." Hatfield glanced at him. "As a threat, if nothing else."

"It's not very clean either." Adele peered at it.

"How would you know, Del?" Jackson shot her a look.

She glared at him. "I remember watching Papa clean his shot-gun. I know what a clean gun looks like."

"You're right, Adele," said the sheriff. "It hasn't been cleaned for a while. It isn't very new either. I would say around thirty years old." He wrapped it in cloth and put it in his pocket. "I wouldn't be surprised if it was a gift from Miss Gibb's parents, but she never fired it in her life. Never even purchased the bullets for it, probably."

"She likely would have reached for it if an intruder had come into the room," Adele pointed out.

"How exactly would an intruder have gotten in?" Jackson glanced at the only window in the place, small and narrow. He drew back the curtains and examined it. "Locked."

"I think we can rule that out," said Hatfield.

"Then what are you ruling in?" Adele eyed him.

He only blinked and murmured, "Question marks, question marks."

CHAPTER 5

$\mathcal{A}$dele had only been in Mrs. Taylor's home a few times, so she surveyed the downstairs with curiosity. However small the rooms were, Mrs. Taylor knew the value of first impressions and had given the shared rooms a pleasant and agreeable air. The parlor was longer and wider than most Adele had seen in boarding houses. It was clearly well dusted, and she had no doubt the furniture covers were regularly renewed so as to give a more polished appearance. The drapes were drawn, and the windows partly open. Across the parlor was the dining room with its double doors closed.

A young woman barely out of girlhood hobbled toward them and in a shy voice told the sheriff everyone was still at breakfast.

"We'll help the lads poke around outside," said Hatfield in a brisk voice.

"You think someone might have left something there?" Adele asked.

"We can't rule it out, Del," Jackson said. "Right now, we're looking at suicide or foul play."

"Oh, sir!" The girl's eyes widened as she glanced at Adele.

"Don't worry, dear," Adele said in the soothing voice she used for frightened people. "What's your name?"

"Sally, miss," she said.

"And you work here, Sally?"

"I'm the scullery maid, miss." She blushed.

"Thank you for telling us, Sally." The sheriff smiled. "Don't mention anything about what my deputy just said to the others. We don't want to frighten anyone."

"Oh, no, sir — I mean, Sheriff!" She blushed again.

The small front lawn was filled with young men. As Adele descended the stairs, Edison's lean, bouncing figure nearly bumped into hers. "Sheriff!"

"Don't flit about like a wasp," Hatfield said. "Tell me slowly and calmly what's on your mind."

"Evidence, sir," said the young man. "It looks like evidence, that is."

"'Looks like' is not being." The sheriff descended the steps into the small circle of assistant deputies always recruited for searches. "Well, lads, what's this evidence you've found?"

Edison held up a cigar stub. It was an inch long and had a broken gold seal. The word BLACKJACK was engraved at the bottom of the seal where the edge of the cigar was burned down.

"Fine quality, though not local," said Jackson as he examined it. Adele gave a wry smile. It was rare her brother's taste for fine things helped with an investigation.

"Which one of you found this?" Hatfield held up the stub.

There was a murmur among them. A redhead with a mustache too full and pretentious for his youth stepped forward. He cleared his voice several times before he said, "I did, sir."

"And you are?" The sheriff could hardly contain his grin behind his serious countenance.

"Archibald Dulland, Dooland, sir." He cleared his throat several more times.

"And where did you find it, Assistant Deputy Dooland?"

Even Jackson, who had less faith in the young men's skill than their eagerness to get their names in the *Arrojo Courier*, had his fist over his mouth in an attempt to cover up his smile.

"Over there, sir." The young man pointed in a general direction.

"Over *where*, lad?" Hatfield put his hand on the boy's shoulder. "We must have the precise location."

"I told him that, sir," Edison snarled.

"Show me, then," said the sheriff.

The young man led them to the farthest corner of the house near the back where the fence bordered the sidewalk.

"How was it positioned, Dooland?" asked the sheriff.

"Sir?" The young man squinted.

"Was it put down carefully, tossed in the mud, half-buried, what?"

"Tossed, sir. And quickly, like whoever lit it was in a hurry."

Jackson spoke up, "Smoked a lot of cigars, have you, Assistant Deputy?"

The young man stiffened. "My father smokes quite a bit at home, sir, and always has to throw them into the field because my ma don't like the smell."

"That's very observant, Assistant Deputy," Adele said. "Don't mind my brother. He just likes to tease people." She shot Jackson a look.

Hatfield patted the boy's cheek. "Good work, Dooland. This might be very important."

The young man grinned and followed his comrades as they dispersed once more around the yard.

"What do you think, sir?" Edison asked in an anxious tone.

"It might be a clue," Hatfield lamented. "And then again, it might not."

"We don't even know yet if there are clues to look for," Jackson pointed out.

"True, true," said the sheriff. "There are several young men lodging with Mrs. Taylor. Any one of them could have come out here for a smoke last night after dinner."

"Yes, sir." Edison, clearly defeated, joined the others.

Adele had been eyeing him for a while. "Whether it's a clue or not, you're interested in it."

Hatfield shrugged. "It's not the cigar itself but the way it was half-smoked, as Dooland pointed out, and thrown." He glanced over his shoulder in the parallel line from the fence to the house, then advanced slowly. "One question mark answered." He bent down.

Adele saw what he meant. The shrubs along that side of the house were thick and coarse. The leaves were dusty on the top in the way of an unkept garden, but further down, the leaves were clean. "Someone was hiding here."

"Now you're going to tell us it was the man who murdered Miss Gibb," Jackson groaned. "We can't discard the possibility, Jackson, if the cigar doesn't belong to anyone in the house," Hatfield argued.

"Found all the way over there?" Jackson peered at the fence.

"Dooland knew what he was talking about," said the sheriff. "That cigar was tossed from the distance and in a hurry."

"But why here?" asked Jackson. "Why hide here?"

The door to a slightly sunk-in entrance behind them burst open. Sally lurched forward, knocking over a potted plant. Her shiny face appeared with the same startled eyes and open mouth.

"No need to be frightened, Sally." Hatfield straightened to his full height. "I told you we were poking around."

"Yes, sir." She wrung her hands. "Mrs. Taylor says it's alright to go in now.""Breakfast over?" he asked.

"Yes, sir. Everyone's having their coffee in the dining room. You — you said you wanted the parlor, sir? For questioning?"

"Thank you, my girl." The sheriff tipped his hat and she bowed. She glanced at Adele and smiled as she hastily scooped the dirt that had fallen out of the plant, turned it upright, and closed the door.

"Well, you've charmed the scullery maid at least," Jackson remarked.

"Don't scoff, Jack," she said. "It's the maids and butlers and cooks who fill in the gaps."

"Very well said, Adele," agreed the sheriff.

~

Mrs. Taylor was clearly put out when Sheriff Hatfield informed her he wanted to speak with her first. "I already answered your questions," she said as she went for the winged chair with two pillows, the most comfortable piece of furniture in the whole room.

"Not quite, Mrs. Taylor," Hatfield said. "First, do any of your boarders smoke?"

"Mr. Lyman has a collection of pipes, a very nice collection," she said.

"He would," murmured Jackson. Adele hid her smile.

"And cigars?" asked Hatfield. "Does Mr. Lyman or any of the men smoke cigars?"

"Or the women, for that matter?" Adele chimed in. Her brother gave her a horrified glance. She shrugged and played with the tassel on her skirt.

"I don't allow cigar smoking on the premises," said the woman. "They have the most nauseating scent."

"Does Mr. Lyman go outside to smoke his pipes?" asked Jackson.

"Deputy Gossling, I said he had a collection of pipes," said the woman. "I didn't say he actually *smoked* them. Not that I've seen anyway."

"And you would never allow it," said the sheriff dryly. "Inside or outside the house."

She raised her chin. "Has someone told you they smelled cigar smoke coming from my house?"

"Everybody knows what an immaculate house you keep, Mrs. Taylor," Adele jumped in, seeing the warning glance Hatfield gave Jackson.

The woman relaxed. "I like to think of my house as a sanctuary, a place where my guests can retreat from the harshness of life, since my boarders are as hard-working as I am."

"Does that idea extend to a no-guns rule in the house?" asked Hatfield.

She sniffed. "I don't approve of firearms."

Both Hatfield and Jackson pulled their jackets forward as if to hide their holsters.

"So you had no idea Miss Gibb had a revolver in her desk?" Jackson asked.

The woman turned pale. "Certainly not!"

"It wasn't loaded, Mrs. Taylor," Adele assured her. "No bullets were found anywhere in the room."

"I'm glad of that." She relaxed.

Adele leaned forward. "Mrs. Taylor, you told me Miss Gibb was an upright sort of woman who knew her duty. Sometimes our duty becomes too much."

The woman blinked. "I can't think what you mean, Miss Gossling."

"Was she different lately? Flighty? Nervous or agitated?"

Mrs. Taylor pulled her shawl around her. "She did seem a little — ill-humored."

"When she was home?" asked Hatfield. "Here, I mean."

"Well, yes," said the woman. "We always sit here after dinner and have a jolly time, but lately, she didn't seem very amused."

"Can you describe this jolly time?" asked Jackson.

"Nothing like the sort of entertainment I'm sure you're used to in the city, Deputy Gossling," Mrs. Taylor gave him a sour smile. "But we do have our little talents. Iona and Emily play duets quite well, and Candy has a fine voice when he's in the mood."

"Oh, I see," said Jackson. "You mean parlor amusements."

"I said it wasn't the follies," Mrs. Taylor growled.

"I'm sure you do very well, Mrs. Taylor," Adele said. "Did Miss Gibb have a talent? Did she sing, dance, play?"

"She read," declared the woman. "She read poetry beautifully."

"But she stopped reading lately," Adele guessed.

"We all wanted her to. Last week, there was a poem in one of the magazines Emily gets from the city. A lovely poem about violets in the spring. We begged Millie to read it to us."

"But she was too out of humor to read," Hatfield guessed.

"She threw the magazine on the floor and stomped out," said Mrs. Taylor. "We were all in shock, of course. She was usually so well-mannered."

"And why do you think she behaved that way, Mrs. Taylor?" asked Hatfield. "It was more than just the poem, wasn't it?"

"Perhaps her students annoyed her that day," the woman threw out.

"They are high-spirited," Adele offered.

"But it must have been more than just that to you." Hatfield folded his hands in his lap. "Or you wouldn't have mentioned it."

"I think she was frustrated. There, Sheriff, that is the absolute truth. She was frustrated." Her voice held a sense of finality.

"Frustrated about what?" asked Adele. She felt a creeping sensation at the back of her neck. It was the word she would have used to describe Miss Gibb herself when she saw her that day at the post office.

Mrs. Taylor looked her straight in the eye. "I'm sure you know women like *that*, Miss Gossling."

"I don't think I do," Adele answered.

"In the unmarried way, I mean." Mrs. Taylor's voice was pointing like a finger. "In the unattached way."

"If you're suggesting my sister —" Jackson sat up. Hatfield's hand shot out to quiet him.

"You mean she was frustrated because she wasn't married?" asked the sheriff.

"She was frustrated because she was a spinster and a school teacher." Mrs. Taylor nodded.

"May I ask how you know this?" Adele asked.

"I went after her to see if she was all right," the woman said. "She just kept saying, 'It's all so unfair!' I've known women like that, even if you haven't."

Adele could feel her pulse rising. "I don't suppose you would care to tell us about women like *that*."

"I shall be delighted," the woman challenged, "as a warning to *you*, if nothing else."

Adele settled into the uncomfortable couch.

"I grant you," the woman began, "Millie wasn't as pretty as many girls — as some girls." Here, she cast an eye in Adele's direction. "But she did confide in me she'd had her flirtations when she was younger. Had them and did nothing about them."

"Maybe she wanted to be a teacher instead," Adele insisted. "Maybe she wanted to help educate young women so they could find their place in the world."

"She did not want to be a teacher," Mrs. Taylor declared.

Adele's fingers dug into the hard surface of the couch. "Because no woman would choose anything but marriage if she had a choice?"

"Del, calm down," Jackson hissed.

"How did you know she didn't want to be a teacher, Mrs. Taylor?" Hatfield inquired.

"She mentioned someone had gotten her the position," said the woman. "I've had many people pass through my rooms, Sheriff. Those who enjoy their work talk about it. Millie rarely talked about hers."

"A keen observation," Hatfield said, and she smiled her satisfied smile.

"Mrs. Taylor, do you think Miss Gibb may have taken her own life?" Jackson asked.

"It's what she's been hinting at all along!" Adele's voice rose across the room.

A sob broke through, and Mrs. Taylor produced a handkerchief from her pocket. "Oh, you don't understand!"

"We didn't mean to upset you, ma'am," Hatfield said softly.

"It isn't that," the woman said between tears. "Millie was a nice girl, but she was just like any other boarder. She would have left me sooner or later. I've learned not to take them into my heart."

"Perfectly understandable," the sheriff said in a gentle voice.

"She reminded me of a woman I once knew." Mrs. Taylor calmed herself, dabbing her eyes. "In Santa Barbara, where I grew up. She was like Millie — studious, dutiful, hard-working. We thought she was content even though she wasn't married. And then one day, they found she had jumped from the roof. It was horrible!"

"Yes, yes, we understand," Jackson said.

"She wrote a letter, a very fine letter, about how terrible it was to be years and years alone without any memories of — well — 'dear affection,' she called it. That's why I'm so thankful I had Mr. Taylor for the short while I did."

"You have memories of dear affection," Adele said in a soft voice.

The woman's head shot up. "And don't you deny yourself those memories, Miss Gossling. Progressive or not, don't deny yourself that!"

Adele pressed her hand but inside she was seething to say something snappy about Mrs. Taylor's ideas of what constituted "dear affections."

On a more benign note, the questions moved on to details

about the house routine. These were given with the businesslike briskness of a woman who had been keeping boarders for a good number of years. It was clear she kept a very strict household with strict mealtime hours as well as activities after and in between mealtimes when all were in the house.

"Until when is your after-dinner jolly time?" asked Adele. "Nine o'clock, ten?"

"Well before ten," Mrs. Taylor said. "Why, everyone is up in their rooms by ten, though I can't say for sure whether they actually go to sleep or not."

"And bedtime?" Hatfield asked as Jackson scribbled away. "I assume you have a curfew for your guests?"

"Certainly," she said. "I can't have young people coming in at all hours. It would look indecent." She tied the ends of her shawl together. "I have a strict policy that the doors are locked by eleven p.m. I've had no one come in after that time ever."

"Which doors?" asked the sheriff.

"The front door and the back door to the kitchen, of course."

"And who does that?" Jackson asked.

"Lilly, my maid," said Mrs. Taylor. "Very reliable, very good girl. Her mother worked with me for years. She's in the old folks home now, poor dear." She sighed.

"So if someone had been lurking outside, waiting to get in," Adele said, "Lilly would have seen or heard something."

"You shall have to ask her that." Mrs. Taylor rose. "I assume you want to speak with her as well? And Mrs. Clogg?"

"And Sally," said Hatfield.

"Sally?" She almost spat out the word. "She wouldn't know a grumble from a goose."

"Nevertheless, she is part of the household." Hatfield was firm. "In a case like this, no one can be left out. But we'd like to begin with the guests first, so if you would kindly send in —" he consulted the list Edison had gathered, "— Mr. Lyman, please."

Mrs. Taylor lingered for a moment. "I know you must do your duty, Sheriff —"

"But?" Hatfield prompted.

"I would appreciate it if you wouldn't upset my guests more than necessary."

"We must find out what happened, Mrs. Taylor," said Jackson. "The only way we can is to piece together what happened last night from those who are still alive."

The woman shuddered.

CHAPTER 6

After she was gone, Jackson pounced on his sister. "You're really too much, Del."

"What do you mean?"

"This isn't the time or place for your suffragist lectures!"

"I agree," said Hatfield in a calm voice as he examined a magazine lying on the coffee table.

"This isn't about politics but about a woman who's being judged because of her position in life," Adele insisted. "I was trying to point that out."

"The fact remains," said her brother, "we have three possibilities for Miss Gibb's death — accident, suicide, or murder. We must consider all three equally."

At that point, Edward Lyman appeared at the doorway, lingering with a deep bow as if waiting to be relieved of his duty.

"Yes, come in." Hatfield waved him toward the chair Mrs. Taylor had vacated but the young man frowned at the sheepskin-covered pillows and took one of the wooden rocking chairs instead.

Adele knew the young man from a case the year before where he had been questioned after an argument he had had in her shop with a stranger passing through town. He looked rather uncomfortable and she guessed he was afraid Mr. Abbott, his employer, would frown upon any hint of his employee involved in a murder investigation.

To ease his nervousness, she said kindly, "I'll be getting in the new Waterman Ideals next week, Mr. Lyman, if you'd care to have me put one aside for you." She remembered how particular he was about his writing habits, eager to give the impression of the dignified executive in spite of his junior position at the Arrojo Finance Company.

"That would be grand, Miss Gossling." He relaxed a bit.

"We've only a few questions to ask you, Mr. Lyman," Jackson said.

"We're asking all the boarders these questions," Hatfield added.

"I understand you must do your duty, Sheriff." Mr. Lyman nodded.

"How well did you know Miss Gibb?"

"Hardly at all," he said. "I prefer to associate with people who can help me with my business aspirations. A schoolteacher is hardly in a position to do that."

"I think you underestimate teachers, Mr. Lyman." Adele raised her head. "They know everyone in town and sometimes have good relationships with prominent people through the children they teach. Miss Gibb lived in San Francisco and Sacramento, I believe. She might very well have helped you."

"She wouldn't talk to me, Miss Gossling," the young man said. "Wouldn't talk much to any of the men here. Thought herself too high for us, I suppose." He stiffened.

"And why do you think that?" Hatfield could not hide his amusement.

"Well, she was educated, of course. Bragged about how she had gone to college. College!" He sniffed. "Teacher's seminary more likely. Not a *proper* college."

"So I gather you didn't think much of her," said the sheriff.

"It's difficult to think much of someone who clearly doesn't think much of you." Mr. Lyman slid a tan handkerchief from his coat pocket and dabbed at his chin.

"Mrs. Taylor told us Miss Gibb had been agitated lately," continued Hatfield. "Ill-humored is how she put it."

"Oh, certainly!" the young man burst out. "Tore my head off as to look at me during breakfast. But Miss Gibb was never at her best at breakfast." The last was said with a rather nasty smirk.

"Few of us are, Mr. Lyman," Adele said. This silenced the young man.

"There was a scene, we were told, where Miss Gibb actually became violent," the sheriff said.

"You mean the poem she wouldn't read to us," said the young man. "Yes, well, I was rather glad of that. I'm not much interested in poetry. So many things you can't see, you know."

"Were there any other incidents with Miss Gibb that you can recall?" asked Jackson.

The young man was thoughtful. "Well, there was something about daisies she never liked. A pity since Mrs. Taylor seems to adore them but that might be because the Misses Powletts give her what they have left every evening and Mrs. Taylor is wonderful about preserving flowers. She's wonderfully economical."

"I'm sure," remarked Hatfield. His eyes flew automatically to the gas light hanging above them which Adele knew, upon closer inspection, probably had cobwebs strung between the lamps. "What about the daisies?"

"Well, one morning I was the first one down for breakfast — other than Miss Gibb, who had a habit of being in the dining room at mealtimes when you came in — and when I entered, she was holding the bouquet Mrs. Taylor had set out in the middle of the table. Like this." And he showed them what was clearly a choke hold.

"A rather violent reaction to something as innocuous as posies," Jackson remarked.

"It wasn't only that, sir," said Mr. Lyman. "I could have overlooked *that*. But she was talking to herself too."

"What was she saying?" Adele asked.

"I wasn't really listening," Mr. Lyman admitted. "But I thought I heard some sharp words. Like *rascal* and *grave*."

"What did she do when you came in?" asked Jackson. "Did she stop? Did she let go of the flowers?"

"Well, that's the odd thing," said the young man. "I tried to give her warning. That is, I backed out of the room and came in rather noisily. She heard me all right. I said 'Good morning, Miss Gibb' and she said good morning without looking at me. She threw the daisies on the floor and left the room."

"Just like she did the magazine with the poem," Adele said.

"Yes, miss," he said. "I remember that too."

"Was that before or after the poem incident?" asked Hatfield.

"Oh, a little after. I'd say a day or two."

"And how long ago was that?"

"A week or so." Mr. Lyman sounded almost apologetic. "If I would have known this would happen, I would have made sure to note the dates, Sheriff. I'm usually very good with numbers."

"I'm sure with your work you do quite well with them," Hatfield said. "Mr. Lyman, I'm going to be very honest with you. As of now, we're trying to determine whether Miss Gibb's death was due to accident, suicide, or — foul play. We would appreciate your thoughts on the matter."

Adele glanced at him. It was usually not the sheriff's way to bring forth theories still untested even in the minds of the police and certainly not to someone who clearly would have only prejudice to go on because he didn't know the victim very well.

As if Mr. Lyman himself realized this, he spoke with extreme caution. "I would hate to give a wrong opinion, Sheriff. As I said,

I hardly knew her, like most of us in the house. She wasn't very friendly, you see."

"I understand, sir," said Hatfield. "Nevertheless —"

At this point, even Jackson looked dubious.

"Well." The young man took some time to stuff his handkerchief back in his breast pocket. "If I had to take a guess — and it's a wild guess, mind you — I would say it was probably suicide. Barring evidence of all else, of course."

"And why do you say that, Mr. Lyman?" Adele asked before the sheriff had a chance to speak.

He looked embarrassed. "I don't want to offend you, Miss Gossling."

"My sister has a very strong constitution, sir," Jackson said in a firm voice.

Mr. Lyman acknowledged this with a bow. "Well, Miss Gibb didn't have many prospects, did she?"

"Prospects?" Adele pursued this. "She had an excellent position as a teacher at the Wrigley School. Mrs. Wrigley told me once she had high hopes for Miss Gibb's future there."

"I didn't mean that, miss," the young man continued. "I didn't mean in her profession, although no one more than I know how fulfilling that can be."

The way he let the words fall didn't fool Adele for a moment. She said in a rather arch tone, "You forgot something, Mr. Lyman."

"Did I?" He sat up with a questionable look at her.

"You forgot to add 'fulfilling *for a man*.'"

"Del," Jackson warned.

But Mr. Lyman was already speaking. "Well, to be honest, Miss Gossling, Millie *was* something of a dried-up old maid."

"Indeed?" Her face was arch, and even Jackson visibly shrank back. "Please continue, Mr. Lyman. I'm intrigued by your theories." She leaned forward with her hand on her chin.

"Well." He was clearly flattered by her attention even as he fidgeted with his handkerchief. "Teaching at a girls' school — that isn't really a profession, is it? There is only so far you can go and so much money you can make."

"You're not making your point, sir." Hatfield had clearly had enough of Mr. Lyman's pomp or maybe he was trying to show compassion for the tongue-lashing he knew Adele was dying to give him.

"A woman like that with a job that leads nowhere and no husband likely coming — what is there really left for her in her old age?"

Jackson jumped at this. "But Miss Gibb wasn't old, sir. She was forty-one, forty-two at the most."

Adele felt her face grow cold and tired. "You believe she took her own life because she had nothing to live for? I suspect you're not the only one."

"My deepest apologies if I offended you, Miss Gossling, I have the deepest respect for you," the young man's voice shook. "We didn't have a decent place to buy our stationery until you came here and opened your shop —"

"That will do, Mr. Lyman," Hatfield said. "Thank you for your help. We won't take up any more of your time but if you would send in Mr. Stoker, we would be obliged."

In the interval, Adele could feel Hatfield looking at her, his face closed but sympathetic. He rested his hand on the arm of her chair. "You don't have to stay if it upsets you."

"She shouldn't really be here anyway," Jackson growled. "This is official business."

"I like her thoughts and questions, Jackson," said Hatfield in a firm voice. "We need another perspective."

"I have a duty to stay," she insisted. "I'll try to keep my less relevant thoughts to myself."

The interview with Herbert Stoker was short and to the point. He had come to Mrs. Taylor's at about the same time as Mr. Lyman and, as an accountant for a small firm in Rosa Gris, their situations were similar. But Mr. Stoker was clearly uninterested in anything but his work. His worn appearance made him look five years older than he was, and his speech had the distracted manner of someone with other things on his mind. He left the boarding house early every morning and came back late every night, going to bed right after dinner. He couldn't even recall Miss Gibb was a teacher at the Wrigley School. When asked to give his opinion of the cause of her death, he only shrugged. It soon became clear if Miss Gibb had fallen down dead at his feet, he would hardly have noticed.

The last of the male guests was, however, quite helpful in his own way. Hal "Candy" Walsh, named so because he was the head candymaker at Hyde's Confectionary, had the joviality of someone caught inside the world of children from an early age who had never got out of it, either by choice or fate or both. He took the sheep-skinned chair and almost bounced around in it the entire time. Adele guessed this was more due to his excitable disposition than the nervousness she observed in many people when they were being interviewed by the police.

"You seem like a rather friendly fellow, Mr. Walsh," Hatfield remarked.

"Call me Candy, Sheriff," he said. "You all call me Candy. Don't go for formalities."

"I've observed you like to talk to everyone, Candy," the sheriff continued.

"Oh, you've seen me saying 'good morning' and 'good afternoon' to people," Candy said with a laugh. "It doesn't ever hurt to spread cheer about, does it, Sheriff?"

"No, it certainly doesn't," Hatfield agreed. "It must have been a challenge with Miss Gibb, though. We were told she wasn't always the most amiable creature."

"No, indeed!" Candy said. "She rather put on airs, you know. Never could get her to laugh at my jokes."

"How surprising," said Jackson in a dry voice. Adele knew he had little regard for Candy's sense of humor which somehow always had a tone of indecency. He didn't approve of Candy telling such jokes to ladies.

"I always find your jokes amusing," she said kindly. She didn't tell him what Nin thought about his jokes or of him. If she was visiting Adele in her shop and saw Candy crossing the street, she retreated into the stockroom until she was sure he would not come in.

"Much obliged, miss," he said as he dipped his rather thick figure at her. "Some women don't appreciate a turn on the funny bone, if you know what I mean."

"Miss Gibb didn't appreciate it," Jackson guessed.

"No, sir, not in the least," said Candy. "She was always prune-faced." And he puckered up his entire face to prove his point. They all smiled politely although Adele felt like grinding the edge of her parasol into his soft leather shoe.

"She was serious about her work," Hatfield said.

"About everything, really," said Candy. "Why, I never saw her take a guffaw, not one. Least, not until that shifty-eyed person visited us"

The sheriff shot Jackson a look. "Shifty-eyed person?" the deputy asked.

"Mrs. Taylor, she's a generous one," Candy continued. "She's got a room she doesn't give to regular boarders but she'll rent it for a song to anyone passing by for a day or so if they can't afford a room at the hotel."

"Tell us everything you remember about this person," Hatfield said.

Not only was Candy's face and voice serious but his mind was fertile with memory. He proved, despite his jesting and perhaps sometimes questionable appropriateness, that he was a quick observer. He recalled the man's name was Owen something. He was a traveling salesman, and always carried a display case with books. He had come three weeks ago and suddenly left one early morning.

"To go where?" inquired Jackson.

"That I can't say, Deputy. But I did see him waiting on the platform for a train a little ways past the ticket window."

"Trains to the north," Jackson said to Hatfield. "Sacramento or Eureka, maybe. Crescent City, even."

"What did this man look like?" asked the sheriff.

"Odd sort of a bird," said Candy. "Thin, light on his feet. Red hair and beard like cotton candy. And eyeglasses, real thick. Guess it comes from all that reading." He chuckled. "Wore queer clothes too. Flannel checkered suits and things, all the same pattern but different colors."

"Flannel in this weather?" Jackson remarked.

"Well, Deputy, it wasn't so hot then," said Candy.

"And you say he and Miss Gibb were friendly?" Adele asked.

"Well, miss, don't know I would say they were friendly exactly. But they talked a great deal at mealtimes. Sat one next to the other and just pretended like the rest of us weren't there."

"And after meals?"

"Oh, they were in here with the rest of us but they took that couch you're sitting on and wouldn't even look at us the whole evening. And Millie took sherry!" He said this last as if it were a triumph.

"But she wasn't a member of the Temperance League," said Adele. "We know she drank hot toddy."

"Well, I don't know about that, miss," he said. "But she always refused the sherry when Mrs. Taylor brought it around after dinner. Not with Mr. Owen, though. She took a glass every night he was here."

Hatfield nodded. "We're asking all the guests this question, and we'd like to get your opinion."

The man sat up. "I'll be happy to do what I can."

"How do you think Miss Gibb died?"

Candy was clearly taken aback, fidgeting with the tails of his coat. "Well, I don't like to think of those things, Sheriff."

"I understand." Sheriff Hatfield nodded in sympathy. "But it helps us, nonetheless."

"Well, surely it's clear," said the young man. "Miss Gibb took her own life."

"Why is that clear, Candy?" Adele asked.

"Oh, well, heavens, miss, she hardly had much of a life," he became confidential. "Woman's got to have some appeal to men to get herself in a secure situation and Miss Gibb just didn't have that."

"Naturally, male appeal would be the most important thing," Adele said in a dry tone.

"Oh, I'm not implying — "

"Thank you, Candy," Hatfield rose and stuck out his hand, "you've been very helpful."

Candy turned to Adele, looking genuinely humbled. "I'm sorry if I annoyed you, Miss Gossling."

"You're not the first, Candy," Adele said. "But consider many men don't appeal to women either."

The man laughed, tipping his hat. "There's no denying that, miss. Why, I know men who're no better than a horse!"

Jackson rose, giving Hatfield a look as he followed Candy out of the room.

CHAPTER 7

*A*dele was left alone with the sheriff. Crossing her ankles, she asked "Do you think this Mr. Owen Something is going to be important to the investigation?"

"I would be happy to hear your thoughts on the subject, Adele," he said. "You have better instincts about these things than I do."

"There's no telling how personal their relationship was," she said. "Candy says they spoke but if this Owen is a book seller, wouldn't it be logical he would speak with a teacher?"

"Coveted conversations in the corner of the parlor aren't always about business," he said with a rueful smile.

"Neither can they be very intimate when there is, as Mrs. Taylor implied, the clattering of voices at the piano or a game of charades in the same room," she answered with equal ruefulness.

He bowed his head to concede.

"Nevertheless," she added, "everyone we've interviewed so far agrees Miss Gibb put on airs. She behaved toward Nin and me in the same way."

"And so?" Hatfield prompted.

"When a woman shies away from conversation, intimate or

not, with those she's known for months but covets herself in the parlor with a stranger —"

"That is cause for concern," he finished.

"It's cause for curiosity," Adele corrected.

The sheriff nodded as Jackson strolled back into the room.

"Owen Burke." He tapped his notepad. "He comes from Sacramento."

"Mrs. Taylor remembered?" Hatfield spoke in a lower tone as a young lady lingered at the parlor doorway.

"She would probably remember any guest who stayed with her when she first started her boarding house." Jackson took his chair. "She seems quite proud of them."

Hatfield cleared his throat and rose. He escorted the young woman at the doorway, who gave her name as Emma Craig, one of the female guests in the house, to the sheepskin-cushioned chair.

"Sorry to keep you waiting, Miss Craig." He gave her a gallant bow.

"Your work is so important, isn't it, Sheriff?" With her jewel-like green eyes and dark thick hair, Adele knew right away she was not one for passing up an opportunity to flirt with any man, old or young, whose looks passed muster in her eyes.

"I like to think so, miss." Even though his manner was easy, Adele could see he was uncomfortable. "We're asking everyone in the house their occupation."

"Not much respectable work a young lady can do these days to earn her living, what with no money of her own. Is there?" Her eyes slid in Adele's direction.

"Is there?" Adele echoed as Jackson shot her a warning look. "I should think she could find plenty to interest her if she has gumption and intelligence."

"And connections." The girl's flitting ways did not extend to women, as she spoke in a harsh voice. "Don't forget connections, Miss Gossling."

"I'm sure you have a fine job, Miss Craig," Jackson said with his easy smile.

"Thank you, sir, thank you." She cast her eyes downward, her long lashes showing.

"You travel all the way to work by train every day?"

"Oh, no," she said. "That would be very costly. My means are very modest, Sheriff Hatfield." Again, her slippery eyes cast toward Adele. "Dean — that is, Mr. Skidd — he lives just around the corner, and he's a floor supervisor. He has a lovely little coupe, goes twenty-five miles an hour. All new and spruced." She shot out at Adele, "You really ought to look into them, Miss Gossling. The new models are ever so much cozier and Dean — Mr. Skidd — says they're just right for women drivers."

"So I've heard," Adele said in a dry voice. "I much prefer to give women my business."

"I don't follow." The girl gave a condescending smile.

"My car is custom-made by Cecily and Mary Beaton."

Miss Caulfield's face reddened. "A car made by women?"

"And a very sturdy car." Adele couldn't hide her smile.

"Well, I never!"

"I'm sure you haven't."

Jackson gave his sister a look. "Mr. Skidd drives you, then?"

"Yes, Deputy Gossling."

"You must be very tired at the end of the day," said the sheriff. "Go right to sleep like a good girl?"

She giggled again. "Oh, there are times when I'm just too excited to go to sleep right away. I'm a very excitable girl, Sheriff Hatfield."

Adele let her parasol fall to the floor. It made a crashing sound on the wood that made Mrs. Taylor's head pop into the doorway with a look of disapproval. "Pardon me," she said as she picked it up and laid it across her lap.

"Do you take sleeping powders to help you sleep on nights like that?" asked Hatfield.

"Why, yes, how did you know?" She blinked at him.

"Did you take sleeping powders last night?" asked Jackson.

"Well, yes, I did." Here, Miss Craig's demure eyes filled with tears and she sought her handkerchief. "I feel so responsible, Sheriff Hatfield. Millie's room is right next to mine, and I might have heard something. I might have been able to do something. And yet, I slept like a log. An absolute log."

"That is unfortunate," said Hatfield.

"Miss Craig," Adele cleared her throat, "what exactly do you think you could have done?"

"Why, saved her, of course."

"Saved her? From herself, you mean."

"If you want to put it that way, Miss Gossling," said the girl.

"So you believe Miss Gibb took her own life." Adele took the magnifying glass in her hand, scrutinizing the coquette in front of her.

Miss Craig flinched. "Well, didn't she?"

"We don't yet know what happened, Miss Craig," said Jackson.

"Oh, it was suicide, all right. Had to be," she said.

"Why did it have to be?" Adele shot out.

Miss Craig looked at her with a face set in stone, creating hard lines where there had been soft crevices earlier. "When a woman can't even get a cheap traveling salesman to give her a tip of his hat —"

"But we were told they were on friendly terms," Jackson interrupted. "They even had private conversations in the parlor."

"Oh, *that* proves nothing," Miss Craig said with a sniff. "It's easy to get a man talking. It's what happens when he stops talking that's important. And that man couldn't get out of here fast enough when his business was finished."

"I take it you don't think much of women who don't have a beau," Adele remarked.

"I never said that, Miss Gossling," said the girl. "But women who don't have beaus often draw that conclusion about women who do, don't they?"

Jackson leaned back, throwing her a grin. She could make out what was in his mind: *Take that, my dear sister.*

More to surprise him than for any other reason, Adele said in her most complacent tone, "I concede and apologize, Miss Craig."

This seemed to satisfy the young woman.

When she was gone, her brother burst out laughing. "You concede like that donkey Tomas rides into town concedes to his grip."

Hatfield roared. "I think the point your sister was trying to make was Miss Craig might not be the most reliable witness, Jackson."

"She did confirm what Candy told us," his deputy pointed out. "Mr. Burke had quite a few *tete-a-tete*s with Miss Gibb."

"And she killed herself because he wouldn't move beyond words?" Adele raised an eye. "Really, Jack."

"I never said that!"

"When we find Mr. Burke," Hatfield said, "we'll be sure and ask him exactly why he didn't go beyond words. As discreetly as we can, of course."

A small voice came from behind, "Sheriff, you wanted to see me?"

They turned and a slight young woman with fair coloring stood with her arms pressed into her sides. Adele recognized her as Iona Hoddle, one of the salesgirls at Raleigh's General Store. She and Nin always made sure to seek her out when they went shopping there because Miss Hoddle was always hospitable and never gave Adele a dirty look like most of the other salesgirls at Raleigh's because ever since she had opened her shop, the stationery in his store had suffered losses.

She immediately saw the girl was not well. Her face had a gray pallor and she took careful steps as if she were afraid she would faint if she didn't.

Adele put her arm around the girl. "Jack, ask Mrs. Taylor for a cup of tea."

"Oh, you needn't do that, Miss Gossling," said Miss Hoddle, but her voice was weak.

Hatfield helped the girl into the comfortable chair. "This is all very trying, I know, Miss Hoddle. We won't keep you more than necessary."

"I want to help." Her voice was ragged. "I liked Millie. I know what the others say about her. But I liked her."

"We don't want to pry, but may we ask why?" Hatfield's voice was gentle.

"She was like a mother to me," said the girl. "I think she had a lot of pain in her life, and she didn't want me to have that pain too."

Adele pressed her shoulders. "Did she tell you that?"

"No, Miss Gossling," said Miss Hoddle. "She never said much about herself. It was just a feeling."

Adele was moved by the fact that, of all the people in the house, even Mrs. Taylor, Miss Hoddle seemed the only one genuinely grieving Miss Gibb's death. "I'm sorry your friend died."

Jackson came back with the tea and it seemed to calm the girl. She let out a sigh and sat back. "I know I'm being childish. I don't want to be childish."

Hatfield gave Adele the quiet sign between them. People who were shy or afraid warmed to her and she had a comforting way of questioning them that was far better than the more officious inquiries of the police.

"You're not being the least bit childish," Adele reassured her. "You cared about Miss Gibb, and it's very natural you would mourn her passing."

"She gave me books." Miss Hoddle took up her handkerchief. "My father — he was a farmer — didn't like the idea of his children knowing more than he did. Especially the girls."

Adele bit back her opinion of this. "She told me about her passion for words."

"Yes, she was going to be a great etymologist someday!" The girl let out a sob.

"She told me," Adele said softly. At the clearing of the sheriff's throat, she knew she had to get on with it. "Where is your room in this house, Miss Hoddle?"

"Just at the end near the stairs on the third floor," she said.

"So you would have heard if anyone came up the stairs last night."

"Oh, yes," said the girl. "And if anyone had been in the hallway." Her eyes were bright with anxiety. "Do you think someone came in and tried to rob her?"

"Nothing was taken, Miss Hoddle, at least as far as we know," Adele assured her.

"Not even her revolver. Oh!" She almost dropped the empty teacup.

"You knew she had a revolver," Adele said.

The startled eyes glossed over. "She said it didn't have any bullets!" She peered at Adele. "How did you know she had one?"

"The police found it in her drawer," said Adele.

"Her father gave it to her," said Miss Hoddle. "I told her my brothers taught me to shoot ducks — when Pa wasn't around, of course — and she said her father taught her boy things too."

"Boy things?"

"Silly things," she said with a little smile. "How to tie a knot, that sort of thing."

"Teaching someone how to shoot a gun is hardly silly, Miss Hoddle," Jackson ventured.

"I didn't mean that." Her face turned red. "He gave it to her on her twenty-first birthday so her mother wouldn't know. And he took her out to the Presidio and taught her how to shoot it. But she said she didn't do very well."

"He gave it to her for protection," Adele suggested.

"I think he was trying to scare her," said Mrs. Hoddle. "That's why she never kept it loaded."

"Did she seem disturbed enough to have used the gun lately?" asked Jackson.

For a moment the gray pallor became dangerously white. Hatfield glared at Jackson, who rose and fetched a glass of water. Adele put it to Miss Hobble's lips, and she drank it like a good child drank her hot milk before bed.

"My brother didn't mean to hurt you." Adele pressed her hand. "The police must explore every avenue. It's the only way they can find out what really happened."

"But she wasn't disturbed!" her soft voice rang out like a shot. "She was happy!"

"Please calm yourself, Miss Hoddle," the sheriff said. "We could call Mrs. Taylor."

"No, don't!" She grabbed Adele's forearm, looking at her with frightened eyes. "It's the truth, Miss Gossling. Millie was walking on air the last few days. Truly."

"Because of Mr. Burke?" asked Adele.

"Mr. Burke?"

"The traveling salesman who was passing through a few weeks ago," Adele said. "We were told they were quite compatible."

"Oh, Millie didn't care a fig about him!" Miss Hoddle's hand was shaking against Adele's arm. "He sold books. That's why she was so attentive toward him."

Adele glanced at the sheriff with a sign that it was time for him to take over.

He pulled his chair closer to Miss Hoddle. "Why do you believe Miss Gibb was happy, Miss Hoddle?"

"She wouldn't tell me," said the girl. "She only said she would soon be leaving Mrs. Taylor's, the school, the whole grubby thing, she said. Those were her words. But she promised she would write me." Her face turned iron. "Oh, God. Do you think — I though she was going away but not like that!" She had grabbed on to Adele's hand. "But it can't be, can it? She wouldn't have said she would write me if that were true, would she?"

"No, she wouldn't," Adele said in a gentle voice.

"I knew I should have gone in!" The cry came into the room with the squeak of a mouse.

"Gone in?" Adele looked at her.

"Last night," she said. "I woke up to — you know — and I passed by her door. I thought I saw a light but then it was gone. She's just going to bed, I said to myself. I can't disturb her, not now. I wish I had! I wish I had!" The last came out as a wail and she bent her small face into her handkerchief.

They all waited until she had calmed down and Hatfield asked in a sedate voice, "Do you remember what time this was, Miss Hoddle?"

"Very late," she said. "That is very early."

"In the morning?" Adele asked. "After midnight?"

"Oh, certainly after midnight. Not long before dawn, I would even say. That's why I didn't want to disturb her. I wanted —" She sighed. "I thought she could get at least a few hours' sleep before we all went to church."

"You did what any compassionate, thoughtful human being would have done." Adele embraced the tiny young woman. "You have nothing to reproach yourself for. You couldn't have done anything."

This seemed like a strange, if slight, comfort to the salesgirl and she smiled at Adele through her tears and gray face.

CHAPTER 8

After Miss Hoddle left, Hatfield offered to call Edison to see Adele home, but she insisted on sitting through the interviews with the servants.

"You ought to be resting on your day of rest," Jackson reminded her. "You work long hours all week."

"You're not exactly with your feet on the fender all day yourself, Jack," she said with a wry smile. "I ought to be here when you interview Sally. No one seems to regard her as more than a part of the furniture and she needs a little encouragement."

"Mrs. Clogg as well," Hatfield admitted. "I hear she's a tough old sole."

The sheriff's assessment proved accurate. Mrs. Clogg sat at the small table where the servants had their meals perfectly upright with her hands folded and her elbows aligned as if she were a bad pupil expecting punishment. Her face crumpled in the sour way of a woman who had been doing her work exactly as she had been told for more years than they were worth.

"You make an excellent tea, Mrs. Clogg," Hatfield began as he sat down. He looked almost like a schoolboy himself.

"That," she said dryly, "was Sally's doing. Got to learn some time, though the girl is hardly worth more than a wooden nickel."

"Did Sally make Miss Gibb's hot toddy?" asked Hatfield. "Mrs. Taylor told us Miss Gibb was rather fussy about it."

"Not fussy, sir," said the woman. "Orderly. She had her habits just like the rest of us, and she lived by them."

"Just like the rest of us," Adele added.

Mrs. Clogg gave her a look. "If you say so, miss."

"If she was orderly, she would have had the most experienced person in the kitchen make it for her, or she would have made it herself," Hatfield guessed.

"Yes, sir."

"That would be you, then." He pointed a large finger at her.

"Yes, sir."

"Mrs. Clogg." The sheriff leaned forward, placing his hands on the table. "I feel it's my duty to let you know the coroner's assistant determined Miss Gibb died of some kind of poison."

Adele had no idea what effect Hatfield hoped these words would have upon the woman but Mrs. Clogg didn't bat an eye.

"I'm sorry to hear that, sir," she said.

"I don't think you quite understand what the sheriff is trying to tell you, ma'am," Jackson said. "We believe Miss Gibb poisoned herself or was poisoned."

This created more of an impression, as the sour face ease. "I fully understand, sir. You want to examine the remains of the dinner we had last night."

"Not exactly," Hatfield said. "The poison most likely wasn't from anything at dinner, as no one else had any ill effects. You *do* understand, Mrs. Clogg, we're not implying you or Sally had anything to do with the poisoning. We're trying to be cautious for the sake of everyone in the house."

"I see, sir," she said.

"Going back to my original question, then." He wiped his

brow with his handkerchief. "Who made Miss Gibb's hot toddy every night?"

"Evening, sir," corrected Mrs. Clogg. "I made it in the evening and Miss Gibb herself made one at night, when she had it."

It was as if a light had gone on in the darkened kitchen with its heavy scent of garlic and onions. Jackson, who was standing against the pantry door because there were not enough chairs, straightened.

"Miss Gibb had two hot toddies every night?" he asked.

"Not every night, sir," Mrs. Clogg said. "Every other Saturday night, I'd say."

"Your exactness does you credit, Mrs. Clogg," said Hatfield. "So she would make it herself?"

"When she stayed up late to read." The tone in her voice clearly marked her disapproval. "Ruin her eyes, I don't wonder, all that reading by gaslight. Couldn't get to sleep, I heard her say, unless she had her hot toddy before bed on those nights."

"So when bed was very late, she would make herself a hot toddy," the sheriff concluded. "Do you recall if she made it herself last night?"

"I can't say for sure, sir," she said. "I only know she didn't ask me to make it for her."

"And she wouldn't have asked anyone else?" Adele inquired. "Sally, for instance?"

The woman's crumpled face almost broke into a snide smile. "Sally don't even know what's in it."

"What *is* in it, Mrs. Clogg?" asked Jackson. "This is important, you understand."

She ticked off the ingredients in the old-fashioned way on her thick wrinkled fingers. "Hot water, or hot cider if Mr. Poland brings it around. Mrs. Taylor is fond of a bit of hot cider in the evening."

"Yes, go on," said Jackson.

She seemed annoyed at his rushing her, as her tone deliberately slowed down. "Sugar. Lemon juice. Just a bit of whiskey, but only a bit, mind you. She had good sense about the devil drink."

"And orderliness," Adele remarked.

The woman glanced at her but didn't seem to comprehend.

"Is that all, Mrs. Clogg?" inquired the sheriff.

"All but the trimmings."

"Trimmings?" Jackson raised an eye.

"Have you never had a hot toddy, Deputy Gossling?" She glanced over her shoulder. "You look like one who knows about such things, if you'll pardon my saying so."

Adele expected her brother to show his staunch side, as he prided himself on his clean and measured appearance. But to her surprise, he turned away from her.

"There are many different ways to make a hot toddy, Mrs. Clogg," Hatfield said. "I'm sure your recipe is above all others."

But the woman wasn't taken in. "Ain't mine, sir. It was Miss Gibb's. Sort of threw me when she first come. But, well —" And here she stopped with a hesitation clearly not typical of her.

"But?" Hatfield probed lightly.

"I had a feeling a gentleman taught it to her," said Mrs. Clogg. "Least it seemed like a gentleman's hand wrote the recipe she gave me."

"The trimmings, Mrs. Clogg," Jackson reminded her.

"A cinnamon stick," she ticked off. "Never went for the powder. She always insisted on the stick."

Jackson's head shot up, and Adele could almost see the remains of the stick he found on the floor of Miss Gibb's room.

"Is that all?" asked the sheriff.

"Well, there's the lemon slices, of course," said Mrs. Clogg. Here, her crumpled face returned in all its glory.

"Lemon slices? You mean like on the side of the glass as a decoration?" Adele inquired.

"Well, no, miss. Miss Gibb had a love of lemons. You might say a passion even."

"What sort of passion?"

"She'd had it since she was a little girl. That's all I know." Her gaze lifted and Adele guessed she was looking at the clock on the wall. Her guess proved right when next the woman half rose. "If you don't mind, sir, I should start getting lunch ready. Will you be staying?"

"Thank you for the invitation, but no," said Hatfield.

Adele and Jackson exchanged a smile. It was rare that the sheriff refused an open invitation to a meal, as he loved sampling all kinds of cooking.

"One more point, Mrs. Clogg," he went on. "You keep all sorts of household necessities in the pantry?"

"I imagine so," she said but she sounded vague. It was clear to Adele she had no idea what the sheriff meant.

"I mean baking soda and that sort of thing."

"Oh, that kind of necessities," she said. "Yes, sir."

"And among such household necessities, you keep arsenic or some other poison to rid yourself of rodents that might try to sample your good cooking," the sheriff continued.

"Arsenic? Dear me!" said the woman.

"I believe the sheriff is referring to rat poison," Jackson supplied. "It's a common household item in pantries. We have a box in ours."

"Well, yes, of course," said Mrs. Clogg. "Not that we have many rodents, mind you. I keep a very clean kitchen."

"I'm sure you do." Hatfield smiled. "The rat poison is in the pantry along with the baking soda and the sugar?"

"Yes, sir, in a manner of speaking." She gave a crooked smile. "Not on the same shelf, of course. Ain't proper to put such a thing on the same shelf with the food stuff."

"You keep an excellent kitchen, Mrs. Clogg," he said. "Do you think it's possible Miss Gibb might have reached for the rat poison on the wrong shelf and mistaken it for sugar? Early morning hours, you know, we're usually only half awake."

"If she had been reading, her eyesight might have been a little blurred," Jackson added. "Roaming around in a dark kitchen, it's possible she made a mistake."

The woman came to life, shedding the lascivious manner in which she had been answering questions. Her crumpled face became cold and alert. "No, sir. It isn't possible!"

"You seem very sure of that, Mrs. Clogg," said Jackson.

"Miss Gibb was an intelligent woman, sir. The best in the house." Here, the woman's voice showed an undertone of emotion. "She knew her way around a kitchen. Used to do all the housework for her parents when they got ill."

"So she would know what to stay away from in the pantry," Adele said.

"Yes, miss," the woman said. "Ain't no chance of her taking rat poison instead of sugar. She — well, she just wouldn't do that."

"Still," Hatfield persisted, "they look very similar."

"They do not!" The woman was emphatic. "The one's very fine, and the other is like sand, sir." She added in an almost rueful tone, "When you spend your days in a kitchen, sir, you get to knowing the difference between them all. Powder ain't just powder to you."

Hatfield conceded with a bow. "May we see the pantry, Mrs. Clogg? We won't disturb anything."

"If you're looking for the rat poison, sir, you won't find none." Both men looked at her. "Sally had an accident with the larder a few days ago. Spilled it all over the shelf. She's a clumsy one."

"Yes, we know," said Jackson.

"Spilled a mess of things that day," the woman lamented.

"Such as?" Hatfield asked.

Here she ticked on her fingers again. "Salt, flour, and the spices I had in the bowl for a cake I was making." This clearly agitated her more than anything else. "Among the things were soap flakes and Rough On Rats."

"The rat poison," Adele said. "I've seen it on Mr. Raleigh's shelves."

"Yes, miss."

"Soap flakes and salt?" Jackson inquired. "You said you don't keep food stuff on the same shelf as the non-food stuff."

"Sally don't confine her accidents to one shelf, sir," said Mrs. Clogg with a tight smile.

"And what happened with this accident?" asked the sheriff.

"Well, what always happens with accidents, sir." The woman's crooked smile returned. "Waste."

"I think, Sheriff," Adele put in. "What Mrs. Clogg is trying to tell us is there is no Rough on Rats in the house because of Sally's accident."

"When did Sally have this accident?"

"Two days ago, to be exact," said the woman.

This made both the men lean back with serious contemplation.

"Do you still have the box, Mrs. Clogg?" Hatfield was the first to speak. "I mean, in the refuse?"

The question took her aback. "Well, I suppose so, sir. Sally probably hasn't gotten around to burning it yet. She don't seem to get around to much."

Jackson closed his pad. "We'd like to see the refuse, if you don't mind."

"Do what you must, sir." The woman rose.

"You've been most helpful, Mrs. Clogg," Adele said with a gracious smile.

The sheriff quickly held up his hand. "I'm afraid we'll need one more thing from you, Mrs. Clogg. Or rather, your kitchen."

The woman was clearly displeased with the demands on her terrain. Her face crumpled again. "Anything you wish, sir."

"It's imperative we take every ingredient used to make Miss Gibb's hot toddy."

This she clearly did not expect. "All of it, sir?" She gasped.

"As I said before, Mrs. Clogg," said Hatfield, "we don't believe you or Sally had anything to do with Miss Gibb's death. However, since poison is the cause of her death, we must explore the possibility this poison went into her hot toddy. Now if that's so, you wouldn't want to make cinnamon rolls, say, with cinnamon sticks that might contain —"

"Oh, no, sir!" The idea made all of the lines on her face disappear. "You mean someone might have come in while I wasn't looking and —" She looked so dazed Adele patted the woman's arm reassuringly.

"Has anyone had any of the hot toddy ingredients since last night?" Jackson moved toward the back door.

"Hardly, sir," said Mrs. Clogg. "Not much breakfasting with lemons and whiskey."

"Good." Hatfield rose. "We'll get what we need and then we'd like to talk to Sally after we've spoken with Lilly."

"Lilly ain't my responsibility, sir," said the woman in a brisk voice. "I'll just go out and see if Mrs. Taylor needs anything, if you don't mind."

Adele glanced after her as Jackson talked to some of the lads still waiting in the courtyard. "She certainly keeps to her place, doesn't she, Sheriff?"

"She's the kind who doesn't approve of meddling," Hatfield agreed. "A shame, as the busybody is the most helpful person for a police investigation."

The young men gathered things in the kitchen according to the list Jackson had given Edison. She followed the sheriff and her brother to the back of the house where the refuse was placed. It had the usual unsavory scent and Adele kept back near the rose bush, which, despite the dust, was throwing out strong scents, while Hatfield and Jackson went through it with sticks. Jackson lifted a round smashed box with the red Rough on Rats label.

"Not much good in it now," Hatfield remarked. "I think we can finally rule out accident, Jackson."

"Unless Miss Gibb bought her own from Raleigh's," Jackson pointed out, "or induced Mr. Brent to provide her with another kind of poison."

"If she meant to do away with herself, she wouldn't have bought the poison here in town," the sheriff said. "Not where people know her and would gossip about it."

"Still might be worth checking at Brent's Drugstore, sir," Jackson said.

Adele glanced at the roses to steady her annoyance. They were pink roses and reminded her of Lucy Blackstone's flower garden in the first case she had helped the police. But these weren't nearly as brilliant or as soothing.

CHAPTER 9

They went back inside and found Lilly sitting at the servants' table. She had calmed down but her face was still stained with leftover tears. Her hands flew to her head and she tried to slide the pins over the fallen strands of hair. "Pardon me," she apologized. "With all that's happened, I don't got my wits about me. I look a mess!"

"The death of a guest in the house would fluster even the most experienced maid," the sheriff said kindly.

"Yes, sir," she said in a meek voice. Adele was afraid she was going to begin weeping again but her face remained pale.

She took the chair next to Lilly and, using her soothing voice, said, "You liked Miss Gibb?"

"She wasn't no better or worse than the others, miss," said the girl in an even voice.

"Mrs. Taylor doesn't approve of favorites, does she?" Adele remarked with a little smile.

The girl blinked at her. "She's always fair and square to everyone."

"But if you had favorites," Adele said, "Miss Gibb would be on the list?"

"Well, not so much favorites, miss. But she wasn't fussy, asking me to fetch this or that or wash the dust off her shoes like some people."

Adele smiled. She didn't have to guess that Mr. Lyman was at the top of her "fussy" list. "But there were other reasons why you liked Miss Gibb, weren't there? Women generally don't like other women for just one reason."

The girl smiled. "You see things, miss. That's what I've heard."

"Thank you for the compliment." Adele swept her parasol from one side to the other in a pointed way so the men would not miss the remark. "We found Miss Gibb's room admiringly undisturbed when we came up. Was that your doing?"

"Yes, miss," she said with pride. "Mrs. Taylor wanted me to clean things up but I told her the police wouldn't want that."

"That was very smart," Jackson said. Hatfield glanced at him with a little smile.

"I read lots of detective stories, sir," she said in a fluttery voice. "They always say, never touch nothing until the police arrive."

"Indeed," Hatfield said in a dry voice. Adele knew he held a low opinion of the detectives in the magazines.

"Were you with Mrs. Taylor when she found Miss Gibb?"

"You mean dead?" Lilly's lower lip quivered. "No, praise God, miss." Here, she crossed herself.

"Did you have a look at the room before the police came?"

"Well, I had to, miss. Mrs. Taylor insisted because of the cleaning. I saw all the things out of place, and that's when I told her we ought not to touch anything until the police get there." Again, there was a shade of pride on her face.

"Very sensible," Jackson said with a nod, making the young woman blush again.

"Did you happen to notice the lemon peel?"

"Lemon peel, miss?"

"Yes," said Adele, "from Miss Gibb's hot toddy."

"Oh, there weren't no hot toddy," Lilly said. "At least, I didn't see the glass."

"We know that, Lilly," said Adele. "But there were pieces of cinnamon stick found on the floor and no lemon peel. We understand Miss Gibb liked lemons."

"Yes, miss," said the girl. "Ate them like you would oranges. Oddest thing!" Here, as if she had realized her impropriety, she pressed her lips together.

"Yes, it was strange," Adele agreed. "We all have our strange habits, don't we?"

"I suppose so, miss," she said. "Like I wake up in the middle of the night and feel my legs all jumpy and I have to walk around or I can't go back to bed. Now there's a strange habit if ever there was one!" She smiled sheepishly.

"Did you wake up last night in the middle of the night?" Hatfield asked

"Yes, Sheriff," said the girl. "I do almost every night when it's hot like this."

"Did you hear anything?" asked Adele. "I know the servants' rooms must be far away from the guests —"

"Not very far away, miss," said Lilly. "Right underneath, in fact. This ain't a very big house."

"Underneath where?" asked Adele.

"Why, the ladies' floor," said the girl. "We're on the first floor, ladies on the second, gentlemen on the third. Mrs. Taylor wanted it that way though I don't see what difference it makes." She shrugged.

"Who is 'we,' Lilly?" I asked.

"Miss?"

"You said 'we're on the first floor,' and I'm asking who 'we' is," Adele repeated.

"Me and Sally and Mrs. Clogg," said the girl. "And the temporary guest, if we've got one."

"Oh, the temporary guest stays on the first floor?"

"Yes, miss," said Lilly. "Mrs. Taylor says if they ain't going to make their permanent home here, they may as well sleep with us. In a manner of speaking." Her eyes darted toward the men.

"So Mr. Burke stayed on the first floor when he was here?" Jackson asked.

"Beg pardon, sir? Mr. Burke?" Her brow rose.

"Yes," said Jackson. "He was a guest here a few weeks ago."

"Oh, yes!" The girl nodded. "Strange bird, he was. Bushy red hair all around and glasses that looked, well, not cared for, if you know what I mean."

"Was Mr. Burke's room underneath Miss Gibb's?" asked Adele as she glanced at Hatfield.

"Oh, no, miss, it's at the other end," she said. "Near the kitchen."

"I see," Adele said. "Whose room is underneath hers, then?"

"Well, I suppose mine is but it ain't exactly underneath," said Lilly. "Close to it, though."

"Close enough to have heard something last night?" Jackson leaned forward.

"Yes, sir," said Lilly. "I *did* hear something last night, as a matter of fact."

"At about what time?" the sheriff asked

She shrank back, and her voice was just audible as she answered, "About one-thirty in the morning, sir. I told you I wake up in the middle of the night."

"And what did you hear, Lilly?" Jackson asked. "This could be very important. You're a good girl, and you want to help us, don't you?"

"Certainly, sir," she said with a furious blush. "But I'm afraid I can't really say what I heard. It was sort of like — like moving around."

"You mean reeling?" asked Adele. "Like a drunkard?"

"I don't know what a drunkard looks like." Lilly was arch for a moment.

"Of course you don't," Jackson said with a kind smile.

"I mean, did it sound as if someone — Miss Gibb or someone else — was swaying or walking as if about to fall?" Adele was anxious now.

"Well, I suppose you could say that, miss." Lilly sat back, her blue eyes distant. "Yes, I guess that would be a good way of putting it."

"And did you hear anything else in the night?" she asked.

Lilly rubbed her hands together. The kitchen had grown a little chilly. "I thought — but I don't know."

"Every small detail is important," Jackson reminded her.

"Yes, sir," she said. "I thought I heard bouncing on the ceiling. Like someone was flitting about."

"Someone," Adele said. "But not Miss Gibb?"

"The steps were lighter than hers, miss," said the girl. "Miss Gibb had a heavy step, sort of dragging. Miss Hoddle, now, she's like a goose, beg your pardon." Again, the red spots appeared on her cheeks.

"But these footsteps didn't belong to Miss Hoddle," Jackson guessed.

"No, sir." Lilly wrinkled her nose. "At least, they didn't sound like hers."

"At what time of night was this?"

"I can't say, sir," she said. "I look at the clock once when I wake up but, you know, it don't do to keep watching the clock. Then I wake up ever so many more times."

"Can you at least give us an idea of how long it was after the reeling sounds you heard?" Adele could tell by her brother's tone he was beginning to lose patience.

"A few hours at least," said Lilly.

"Thank you, dear, that's very helpful to us," Adele said and the girl gave her a gracious smile.

There was silence for a moment as everyone seemed to catch their breath except for Jackson flipping through the pages of his pad. "Lilly, when you were in Miss Gibb's room early this morning, before the police arrived, did you notice the fireplace?"

"Notice it, sir?"

"The ashes," said Jackson. "Someone lit a fire last night."

"Oh!"

This came with the deep strike of a bird, as if a cuckoo clock were suddenly going off somewhere. Adele remembered she had seen a big grandfather clock with a tomb-like appearance in the hall. "We're keeping you from your work," she said in a kind voice.

"It's all right, miss," said Lilly. "I want to help, just as the deputy said." She blushed.

"You're surprised to hear there was a fire in the room," Hatfield put in.

She shrank back again. "It's been so warm at night, Sheriff. It hardly seems likely anyone would light a fire."

"So you didn't light it?" asked Jackson.

"Oh, no, sir!"

"Do you think Miss Gibb did?" asked Adele.

"She never did before," Lilly remarked. "Didn't think she even knew how."

"She used to take care of her parents when she was living in San Francisco," Adele said in a soft voice. "I'm sure she knew how to do a lot of things."

Lilly looked agitated. "I didn't mean no disrespect."

"Of course not, dear." Adele patted her hand.

"I suppose she might have lit it," said the girl. "She came from San Francisco, and they're used to cold nights there, aren't they? I come from the country, miss, and a little frost is nothing but an ill wind to me." She grinned.

Adele glanced at Jackson with an amused look. Neither of them had ever lit a fire when they were living with their father in the city.

"One more thing, Lilly," Jackson said. "Mrs. Taylor is rather strict about the curfew in the house, isn't she?"

"Yes, sir," said Lilly. "She don't like people roaming about too late at night."

"That's understandable," he said. "She told us everyone is in bed by ten."

"Well, in their room, sir." The girl gave a quick smile. "Whether they go to bed or not is something else."

"Quite," he agreed. "We were also told you lock the doors at eleven?"

The girl's countenance changed. She was flushing again but not from the kind of shyness that came when a young woman faced a handsome and successful man. This redness came more from embarrassment.

"I lock the doors at night, sir, that's right," she said.

"But not always at eleven?" Adele leaned forward. "We won't tell Mrs. Taylor, Lilly, but we do need to know."

She broke out, "I don't mean anything by it, miss!"

"Of course you don't," Adele soothed.

She glanced at the sheriff. "A gentleman passes by every night at about that time and, you see, he likes to stop and chat a bit and seeing as Mrs. Taylor's always trying to get the word out about her place and he knows so many people —"

"Who," Hatfield asked in a careful voice, "is this gentleman?"

"Do I have to give the name, sir?" Her face was so tight she looked almost like Mrs. Clogg. "I don't want to get him into trouble."

"No one's going to get in trouble, Lilly," Jackson assured her.

"Well, sir. It's Assistant Deputy Edison."

Adele bit her lip as she thought of the moony young man whose gawky politeness and rubber limbs could hardly classify him as a gentleman.

"And where," Hatfield asked in an even voice, "do you and my assistant deputy have this chat?"

"Right outside the front door, sir," she said. "He doesn't stay more than ten or fifteen minutes, I swear, sir!"

The sheriff laid a hand on the back of Adele's chair. "Did he stop and chat with you last night, Lilly?"

"Well, yes, sir, he did."

"At his usual time?"

"Yes, sir." She pressed her hands on the table. "You're not mad at him, sir, are you?"

"Lads will chat up pretty girls," Hatfield remarked. "I can't fault him for that."

This made Lilly smile, and Adele appreciated his delicacy.

"So you locked the doors at around eleven-fifteen," Adele concluded.

"Yes, miss, about that," she said.

With a nod from Hatfield, she said, "Thank you, Lilly. You've been a great help to us and I'm sure you're anxious to get back to your work."

The girl let out a big sigh, as if she had been holding in her breath throughout the entire interview. She scurried out but not without one last admiring glance at Jackson.

The moment she left Hatfield broke out in his deep laughter. "Our Edison is getting to be quite a devil with the ladies, Jackson," he remarked, taking out his handkerchief and wiping his hands with it.

Her brother was less amused. "He ought to have mentioned it," he said in a severe voice. "He knows very well how important the little details are to our investigation."

"A detail like the weight of footsteps," Adele said. "Lilly was quite certain they didn't belong to Miss Gibb or any of the other young ladies on the floor. So there *was* someone in her room last night."

"We can't be sure of that, Del," said her brother. "It's easy to mistake light footfalls for heavier ones."

"Well, we shall see what Sally has to say," Hatfield said. "Her room is on the same floor, after all."

Try as they might, they could not get Mrs. Clogg to allow Sally to stop her work for the interview.

"She's slow as well as clumsy," said the cook. "And what with the goings-on this morning, she hasn't even finished the breakfast dishes yet."

"Mrs. Clogg," said Adele in a pointed tone, "we need Sally to answer the sheriff's questions. How can she concentrate when she's washing dishes?"

The woman glanced at her as if she were looking at a fly. "Sally's used to doing several things at once, miss. If you'll pardon me, them that know only one kind of work don't always realize the head can do one thing while the hands are doing something else."

Adele felt her temper rise but she knew it wasn't her place to argue. She was there as a courtesy because she had helped the police a number of times and because her brother was the deputy. She knew many in Arrojo thought the interference of a woman in a crime was nothing short of blasphemous and it would be useless to argue with a woman like Mrs. Clogg who had her mind set one way.

Hatfield, apparently, felt the same way, or perhaps he respected Mrs. Clogg's position as the head of the kitchen staff and did not wish to tread on her authority. He accepted her insistence that Sally continue her work while she was interviewed and all three herded to the tight room in the kitchen reserved for the sink and dirty dishes.

Sally looked haggard in her uneven apron and her hair floating away from her in the airy way of someone who had been working since dawn. Adele's heart went out to her as the girl bent over the sink clearly too low for her, made even lower by a stool on which she stood.

"Here, dear, you don't need that." Adele moved her aside as

she took the stool away. And indeed, the girl's shoulders were more relaxed when she reached into the sink.

"Thank you ever so much, miss," she said in a tweeting voice.

"You're rather tall for a scullery, aren't you, Sally?" Hatfield asked.

His paternal manner did not seem to frighten Sally as it had Lilly. She gave him a large grin that showed an uneven set of teeth. "My whole family's tall, sir. God bless us with the same divine reach to the heavens, sir."

"Yes." Hatfield cleared his throat. "We won't disturb you in your work for long, Sally."

"I don't mind, sir," she said in an almost robust tone, but then looked embarrassingly at Adele. "I mean, it's horrible what happened to Miss Gibb."

"It is, Sally," Adele agreed. "Lilly heard something late last night from her room, like someone walking around on the second floor. We want to know if you heard anything."

"I don't hear nothing what goes above me except a message from the Lord once in a while." Sally leaned toward her, her hands dripping soapy water all over the floor. "I ain't one of those odd girls, see, but sometimes I hear Him whisper. He knows when I'm a bad girl, see."

Adele saw Jackson's eyes roll at Hatfield but hers remained on Sally. She learned long ago to listen when people confided such things in her because they wanted to be taken seriously. And perhaps they confided in her because she *did* take them seriously. Such was the case with Sally. She almost had tears in her eyes when she bent down and wiped the wet floor with her apron.

"So you didn't hear anything last night?" Adele asked.

The girl shook out her apron and went back to the dishes, cranking the water pump with strong arms. "I didn't exactly say that, miss."

"Then you did hear something?" Jackson prompted.

"Yes, sir, but not from above. From across."

"Sally," Jackson sighed. "It's been a very long day. Please be clear."

"Clear, sir?"

"What do you mean by across?" asked Adele.

"Well, miss, my room's right across from the kitchen."

"Oh," Adele said. "You heard something in the kitchen."

"Yes, miss."

"Can you tell us when, Sally?" asked the sheriff. "Times are important, you know."

"I don't have a watch, sir," she said. "But the old grandpa in the hall sounded like he always does in the middle of the night."

"The clock in the hall chimes at midnight?" Adele asked.

"I expect so, miss," said Sally but she looked confused.

"Very well," said the sheriff. Adele could sense he was losing his patience too. "And what was it you heard in the kitchen?"

"A door, sir," she said. Just then a plate slipped from her hands and Adele caught it before it fell to the floor.

"Lord, miss, you saved me!" Sally screeched. "I break things all the time, and Mrs. Taylor said if one more thing get broken, she'll take it out of me wages." Her eyes grew damp. "Me ma needs those wages, miss."

"You're very good to send her money." Adele was touched. "I don't know if I would have done the same."

"You would've, miss, you would've. Can't let folks starve, can you?" She sighed and went back to the pump.

"Was the door opening or closing?"

"One or the other, miss," she said. "I heard two times."

"Twice?" Hatfield asked.

"Yes, sir. Two open or two close."

"Or a door opening and then closing," Jackson corrected.

Sally's eyes opened wide. "Why, you're right, sir! A door can't open without closing, can it?"

"Not likely," he said in a dry tone.

"You heard nothing else?" Hatfield asked. "No bumping around, no footsteps on the ceiling?"

"Bumping around? Footsteps on the ceiling?" The girl was clearly alarmed. "You mean like Lucifer dancing in the night?"

"Not quite, dear," said Adele. "But someone might have come into the house and gone upstairs."

"And killed Miss Gibb?" The plate jumped out of her hand and this time fell to the floor, breaking into several pieces. She screeched and dropped to her knees.

Adele put her hands on her shoulders. "It's all right, Sally, don't cry. I'll tell Mrs. Taylor I broke it."

She looked up, her face stained with tears. "Thank you, miss."

"We don't know Miss Gibb was killed," Adele said. "So don't be frightened."

"I'm not frightened, miss." She straightened up, almost determined. "The Lord takes care of those who need it."

"Yes," Adele said, smiling. "Yes, the Lord will provide."

Before they left the kitchen, Adele slipped a few gold coins in the pocket of Sally's apron.

CHAPTER 10

lthough it was nearly dinnertime when they let themselves out of the yellow gate of Mrs. Taylor's house, Hatfield wanted to go to the police station and Jackson insisted on accompanying him. Adele didn't want to go home alone, agitated as she was, so she joined them.

The Arrojo Police Station was not very big and its windows were poorly sealed. So it was no surprise when Hatfield swung open the door, it was as if someone had spilled flour all over the floor. Adele immediately set about sweeping the place with the mangy broom thrown in the corner.

"Let's take a look at that letter," Hatfield said, fishing it out of the box.

Adele held out her hand. "Perhaps you should let the expert see it, gentlemen." They looked at her. "You forget I know something of letters."

"That's more a hobby than anything else."

"It's my business, Jack," she insisted.

"Perhaps you'd like to take it to Dr. Blessings for examination," Jackson said with a glint in his eye.

83

"Why not?" Adele shot out. "Oh, for heaven's sake, let me at least *look* at it."

Hatfield slid the letter fragment toward Adele. "Have a go, Adele."

Jackson stared at him. "It's evidence, sir."

"It wouldn't hurt to hear what she has to say, Jackson," he said.

Edison came flying through the doorway, followed by the recruited deputies.

"Edison!"

The young man halted in his tracks. "Got everything down to the lab, sir. Mr. Sanders said he'd keep it locked up safe. Said Dr. Rhodes probably wouldn't get to it till tomorrow morning. He's at home with his Sunday roast."

"He would be," Hatfield grumbled. "And by the way," his face grew severe, "what's this I hear about you keeping young Lilly Brownhill from her duties?"

"Sir?"

Jackson threw his sister a look of amusement.

"She has strict orders to lock the doors at eleven but she's been interrupted every night by a certain young man who just can't seem to stop his tongue from wagging." Hatfield leaned forward. "She identified that young man as you."

"Oh, sir, I was just — well, you know how some girls like to talk —"

"I have no objection to young men chatting with young girls," said the sheriff. "But do you realize if Mrs. Taylor came down and caught her chatting with you past eleven, she would lose her job?"

"I never realized, sir —"

"That's the trouble with you, Edison," Jackson said. "You never use one brain in your head."

"Don't be hard on him, Jack," Adele said. "He's only being friendly."

"Well, in future, lad, be friendly when there's still some

sunshine outside," Hatfield said. He could no longer keep the smile from his face. "While we're on the subject, did you hear or see anything unusual last night when you were on your nightly prattle with Lilly?"

"I can't recall, sir," The young man as he sat down at his desk, looking as if he wanted to hide under it.

"Well, think!" Hatfield growled. "We'll wait for you."

The office was now empty of young men. Adele guessed as soon as they saw the ogre look on the sheriff's face, they had fled like rabbits.

"Well, sir." Edison cocked his head. "I remember after I went out the gate, I thought I heard a rustling sound."

"Rustling?" Jackson asked.

"In the shrubs, sir. But way in the back of the house, not near the street."

"You bumbling fool!" Jackson's voice struck like lightning. "Why didn't you investigate?"

"Well, sir, I thought it was a mouse or a raccoon." Edison stood his ground. "We've been seeing a lot of critters lately at our house, and it's not so far away from Mrs. Taylor's."

"Do you realize you could have apprehended —"

"Oh, but it isn't as if Miss Gibb died *that* way, sir, is it?" Edison looked lost.

Hatfield sighed. "Go home and have your Sunday ham, lad."

The young man didn't need to be told twice. He ran out of the building.

"Edison isn't only ill from that dead cat but he's afraid of it too," Jackson snarled. "Just as you said, Del."

She looked at the sheriff with intent eyes. "You can't still believe it could have been suicide, Sheriff."

The man did not answer right away. He tapped the edge of the evidence box.

"It's still a possibility, sir," said Jackson.

"We know she was poisoned," Hatfield said. "I think Mrs.

Clogg, for all her prudishness, knows enough about the guests' habits and manners that we can assume Miss Gibb didn't mistake the rat poison for something else."

Jackson leaned against the desk. "We have only her word the box was thrown out before last night."

"Nevertheless," Adele said. "Even if it had been in the cupboard, Miss Gibb was far too bright put it in her hot toddy."

"Perhaps she bought her own box," Jackson said.

"She would have hidden it in her room," Adele pointed out. "We would have found it."

"Another poison, then?" Hatfield suggested.

"She would have needed to convince Mr. Brent to give it to her," Jackson said. "I highly doubt he would have found reason to give poison to a schoolteacher." He added thoughtfully, "It can't be very intellectual work teaching little girls their letters."

Adele looked at him with stormy eyes. "Perhaps Miss Gibb preferred it over the stimulating work of slinking around with the revolver always at your side like you did with the Anspaches."

His eyes were equally stormy. He didn't like to be reminded of his years with the detective agency which, like the Pinkertons, had their own idea of justice.

Hatfield cleared his throat. "Mr. Brent is always saying how eager he is to help the police. I'm sure he wouldn't object to having his Sunday dinner interrupted for a few questions."

Jackson rose. "I'll go, sir."

When he was gone, the air in the small office cleared but Adele felt the sharp sting of resistance as she always did when she and her brother had an argument.

Hatfield tapped at the letter fragment. "You can help us here, Adele. I trust your instincts about such things." Here, he gave one of his shy smiles.

She put on her gloves and carefully handled the fragment. It was not very big and the charred edges made it difficult to read even with her magnifying glass._The fragment was torn from three lines with the following words:

Line 1: *of $200*

Line 2: *pride and j*

Line 3: *of his birth*

"It looks as if it came from the lower half, if there was indeed a lower half," she began.

"Why 'if'?" asked the sheriff.

"The white spaces," she said. "The left margin is entirely blank. You don't leave the margin blank unless you haven't much to say."

He nodded. "Go on."

She bent down with her magnifying glass. "Do you notice anything striking about the writing, Sheriff?"

"It's difficult to tell if it's a man or a woman's," he said.

"Yes, but I didn't mean just that." Adele laid the fragment down. "It's printed. What do you make of that?"

"What do *you* make of that?"

"A very impersonal relationship."

He leaned back in the leather chair. "I don't quite follow you."

She cocked her head. "Do you handwrite letters in print, Sheriff?"

"No, of course not. Unless —" He sat up.

"Unless you don't know the person you're writing to very well," she finished. "Or you know them but don't like them."

"I see," he said slowly.

"That rather rules out the possibility of the letter being written by a cousin begging for money, doesn't it?" she asked. "A relative in need of funds would be a fool not to write with the warmest possible regards."

Jackson stepped into the station. "Mr. Brent didn't even have to look in his record book. Miss Gibb never purchased anything remotely poisonous from him."

"Well, it was a chance," Hatfield said. "We must consider she might have purchased something from an out-of-town druggist."

"He's fairly certain she wouldn't have gone elsewhere," said Jackson.

Hatfield eyed him. "Why is that?"

"Miss Gibb and Mrs. Brent were apparently on good terms," he said. "Miss Gibb thought she reminded her of her mother."

Hatfield sat up. "Perhaps we ought to interview Mrs. Brent, then."

"I did, sir," Jackson said with a small smile. "She confirms what you said, Del."

"What did I say?" she asked.

"Miss Gibb was not herself for at least a week before her death," he said. "Anxious and, what do you call it? Fluttery. Mrs. Brent was quite worried about her. In fact, she tried to persuade Miss Gibb to allow her husband to give her a mild sedative."

"And she refused?"

"Miss Gibb said she didn't believe in pills and powders." Jackson eyed her. "Never took them. She told Mrs. Brent she'd rather die than fill herself with noxious things."

"Odd," murmured Adele.

"Many people choose not to take medicines, Del," said Jackson. "They don't trust them."

She looked at Hatfield peering into the evidence box. "So you've ruled out accident, Sheriff?"

"I believe we can," he confirmed.

"But suicide?" she asked. "You won't rule that out?"

"The letter might tell us something." Jackson leaned forward. "Did you examine it, Del?" She nodded. "And what did you find? Without your circle talk, if you please."

She wrinkled her nose at him. "It wasn't a suicide note, if that's what you're implying."

"It hardly would be," the sheriff said. "People don't usually burn suicide notes."

"Any other conclusions?" Jackson asked.

"It's a short letter not written by a cousin."

"And how do you deduce that?"

"White spaces," she said, "and print instead of cursive."

Jackson glanced at Hatfield. "Circle talk."

"I think she has something there, Jackson," the sheriff insisted.

"No one prints a letter to a relative," Adele pointed out. "And people usually don't write a short letter to a relative either. A telegram, certainly. A postcard, even. But not a letter."

"Perhaps it was a letter from the cousin's creditors or his lawyer," Jackson suggested. "That would be short and business-like, wouldn't it?"

Hatfield bent over the fragment and Adele could see he was straining to read the words. She handed him her magnifying glass without a word and he rewarded her with a warm smile.

"The two hundred dollars I can understand," he remarked. "Even if the amount is a bit high even for a relative. But *pride*? And *birth*? If only we had the rest of it!"

Jackson peered through the magnifying glass. "I do believe it was *pride and joy*. See the 'j' cut off?"

"Perhaps it was a letter asking for a loan because of a new addition to the family," Hatfield said. "Though two hundred dollars still seems like a large sum for one baby."

"And what would Miss Gibb have to do with new addition to the family?"

"Much she was involved in the sort of work you do, Del," Jackson said, "if Vanya or one of your suffragist friends wrote asking for your help with some of those poor wretches at the settlement houses, you would wire money, wouldn't you?"

"Poor wretches don't ask for two hundred dollars!" Adele insisted.

"It could have been for many pride and joys, not just one," her brother argued.

Hatfield sighed. "I'm beginning to think this letter had nothing to do with Miss Gibb's death."

"That puts us back where we started." Adele hooked the magnifying glass on the chain.

"Which is where?" Jackson inquired.

"Death by suicide or murder," she announced.

CHAPTER 11

It was no surprise to Adele when she left Jackson at the police station and crossed Bridge Street to open her shop, she saw the women in town gathered in the middle of the street. When something happened in Arrojo, they congregated where everyone could see them, their tongues wagging with the latest gossip. It usually amused her to see them flocking like geese around Mrs. Faderman, but this morning Adele was anything but amused.

She saw Nin standing with a cup of tea in her hand made of energetic herbs. As she drank it, she observed Mr. Duncan had joined the ladies, his mail bag over his shoulder. She realized they had papers in their hands with the familiar gray tint of the early morning edition of the *Arrojo Courier*.

"*She* was there!" Mr. Duncan pointed at Adele. "Frightening thing, wasn't it, Miss Gossling?"

"Why, what do you mean, Mr. Duncan?" Adele finished her tea.

"I was just telling them about Miss Gibb."

"Terrible thing, terrible thing," Mrs. Lynn lamented, her small hands grasping the newspaper.

"At least we needn't suffer as much of a blot this time," Mrs. Faderman said, her voice as tight as her coiled hair.

"A blot, ma'am?" asked Mr. Duncan.

"On our town's good name," she said as if he should have known. "Miss Gibb was, after all, almost a stranger."

Adele glared at the woman. She had discovered early on Mrs. Faderman had an inflated sense of civic pride because her ancestors had stumbled upon this speck of red dust land and had built a town on it. "She lived here for a year, Mrs. Faderman. Not a life-long citizen like yourself, perhaps, but someone whom we can feel was one of our own."

"Even if she didn't like anybody in town," Nin added.

Mrs. Faderman regarded her through her tortoiseshell pince-nez with a spider's gaze. "Which is precisely the reason she was *not* one of our own."

"She was in a strange mood that day, wouldn't you say, Miss Gossling?" Mr. Duncan peered at her.

"I didn't know her well enough to know her moods, sir." She put her parasol up to the wind. "And, I suspect, neither did you."

He turned to the other ladies. "Almost bit my head off when I told her she didn't have any letters."

"Anxious to hear from her city relations, no doubt," sniffed Mrs. Cricket. "Always boasting about her city connections. I could boast about my husband's family being connected to the Duke of Wellington, but —"

"I knew she was about to go, I just knew it," Mr. Duncan leaned back a little, brushing his hands as if he were ridding himself of the whole mess.

Adele gave him a direct look. "If you knew, Mr. Duncan, why didn't you do something about it?"

"Eh?" He looked at her startled.

"You work for the government," Adele continued. "You're a public servant, as it were. It's your duty to keep an eye on the public. If you thought Miss Gibb was about to go, as you put it, why didn't you tell the police or Mrs. Taylor?"

"Well." The man seemed genuinely perplexed. "Well."

All the ladies looked at him like foxes at a hen. Mrs. Faderman had a nasty glint in her eye.

"You didn't do your duty, Mr. Duncan," Nin slipped in.

"Well, it isn't my business, is it?" he insisted. "It wasn't my business."

"Ours is not that kind of town, Mr. Duncan." Mrs. Faderman's shrill voice swept through the street. "We look out for our citizens."

"You just said she wasn't one of our own," Nin pointed out.

"She was *temporarily* one of our own, Miss Branch," said the woman sharply.

Mr. Duncan mumbled something about delivering his mail and slunk down the street.

"It says here she left San Francisco on account of —" Mrs. Fourier squinted at the black print in the newspaper. "Oh, it doesn't say. Well, if it doesn't say, you know it's something of a questionable nature."

"Then she oughtn't to have been boasting about knowing congressmen and the like," Mrs. Cricket pronounced.

"May I?" Adele held out her hand.

Mrs. Faderman thrust the paper at her. "I suppose you trust your friend Miss Grace to state the facts? Not that I approve of her rather sensationalistic story."

"You never approved of her anyway," Nin remarked.

The woman shot her a look.

"Miss Grace has to earn her living, dear." Mrs. Jessel's voice always rose in defense of women-owned businesses. "And, anyway, I gather most of it comes straight from the mouth of Mrs. Taylor's boarders."

"And if that isn't better than the police, who is?" Mrs. Lynn said with a shrill laugh. "Mrs. Taylor is being hush-hush about the whole thing, and they lived in the same house with the dead girl."

Adele's heart sank as she read the story. It was only a few paragraphs but Missy's account of Miss Gibb's life was nothing short of a story taken from one of the cheap magazines. Her tone was almost melodramatic as she told of the schoolteacher coming into middle age, bored with her position in a small town, and hinting at unrequited love for the town candymaker (Adele felt a wave of anger when she realized where this idea had come from) and a passing salesman. Unable to stand it any longer, she had at last, with a heart heavy as stone, taken her own life in the company of the only companions she had ever known: her books.

"What nonsense!" She thrust the paper back into Mrs. Faderman's hands.

"At least we won't have the grubby police asking a lot of questions and taking the men's boots like the last time," Mrs. Faderman said in a snide voice. She had never forgiven the sheriff for collecting her husband and son's boots last year after they attended a party the night Lucy Blackstone was killed.

"I'll thank you to remember my brother is one of those grubby policemen, Mrs. Faderman," Adele said in a tight voice.

"The police aren't grubby anyway," Nin said. "They have a dirty job and they must do it. The grub isn't their fault."

"Mrs. Faderman didn't mean that, dear," Mrs. Lynn's said, her voice shaking.

Mrs. Faderman's lips were pressed together as if she were fighting with herself to apologize. But, then, in one of her usual turns of good sense, she said in an even tone, "Mrs. Lynn is right, Miss Gossling. I wasn't speaking literally. As Miss Branch pointed out, the police have a job to do and they must do it. *We all know that.*"

"But it's horrible just the same," Vanessa Faderman said. "Miss Gibb wasn't so very old."This brought Mrs. Faderman back to life. "Naturally, it's horrible. I never thought for a moment it wasn't." She folded the paper and put it under her arm. "Come along, Vanessa. We're late."

The rest of the ladies took their cue and dispersed to go about their usual business. Adele's feet stamped into the dust, making small whirls of smoke as she went into her shop. "Those cold, chattering fish!"

Nin was watching her. "You don't believe Missy's story, do you?"

"Do you?"

"I'd sooner believe the words of a crow."

Adele gave her a mournful smile.

Even though she wasn't hungry at noon, Nin persuaded her to come into her small flat for lunch. Her shop of herbs and curios was too dim and shadowy for Adele's taste, but her flat was a delight. Nin had removed all the doors so one room opened into the other, making the place light and airy, showing off the brilliant colors of the scant but quality furnishings Nin had chosen.

Her friend sliced a loaf of brown bread with savagery that made Adele flinch. "You look like I feel," she remarked.

"You shouldn't let those ladies upset you."

"They didn't upset me," Adele said. "That ridiculous story about Miss Gibb did."

Nin nodded. "I expected Missy to be more sympathetic."

"Since the Blackstone case, her readers outside of Arrojo have grown," Adele said with a shrug. "I suppose she thinks they expect gruesome details about our town."

"One needn't stoop to such tactics to sell papers," her friend sniffed.

The stew Nin served her was hot and spicy and felt like a ring of warmth inside Adele's stomach. "Perhaps it's not a lie. Millie *was* alone and had no marriage proposals and she might have taken her own life because of it."

Her friend's spoon dropped in her plate. "We saw her ourselves. She was only interested in words."

"We don't know that for sure."

"Did you ever see her so much as look at any of the men in town?" Nin looked at her carefully. "She paid as little attention to them as they did to her."

Adele pressed her friend's hand. "You're right, of course."

There were three knocks on the door and then a pause before one more, as if it were a code.

"Your brother needn't treat me as if I were part of some secret society," Nin grumbled. "No one comes up here but you and he and you're already here."

Jackson looked very business-like in the dark brown suit. He kept his hat on his head. "I didn't mean to interrupt." He glanced down at the table. "I saw both shop doors locked and deduced where you were."

"Perhaps more intuition on your part would serve you well, Mr. Gossling," said Nin.

"Call it what you like, then." Jackson leaned forward with his hands on the table. "The sheriff wants to interview Mrs. Wrigley at the school. He thought it might be a good idea if you would come along since you have connections with her."

"With those silly girls, you mean," Nin said.

"Those silly girls have done a lot of good work for us," Adele reminded her.

"We'd like to speak to the girls too, if she'll let us," he said. "You could be a great help there as well."

"We'll do what we can." She took the last of the bread as she rose.

"We?" her friend asked.

Adele grabbed her hand. "They think you're fascinating."

"Haunting is more the word," Jackson murmured. Nin stiffened. "I'm sorry. That was rude of me."

"Yes, it was Jack," Adele snapped. "Rude and untrue." She took his arm. "I know how unhinged you are during a case, and I'm sure Nin is generous enough to forgive you."

"Forgive, yes," her friend said and then added in a soft voice, "but not forget."

CHAPTER 12

*H*atfield leaned against the streetlight. Though his election as sheriff had been almost incidental, he had proven himself an honest, sober man and, even now, people passing on the street greeting him with a cordiality Adele had rarely seen toward the policemen who roamed the streets of San Francisco.

"Sheriff, what is it you hope to gain from questioning Mrs. Wrigley and the girls?" she inquired.

"Some insights into Miss Gibb's character," he said, tipping his hat to them. "I'm glad you and Miss Branch decided to join us. I've a feeling trying to get information from Mrs. Wrigley is going to be like pulling teeth, and she might be more amenable if you both are there."

"Adele doesn't believe it was suicide," said Nin in her blunt way.

"I'm well aware of it, Miss Branch," he said. "But for right now, it's the only thing we have to go on."

"We must follow the path to the end," Jackson said with a sigh. "The nature of detective work, wouldn't you say, sir?"

"To our folly, perhaps," said the older man in a wry tone.

The school was deadly quiet when they arrived. They were told the girls had finished lunch and were having their afternoon rest in their rooms. They found Mrs. Wrigley in her office sitting at a small table in the corner. The small dishes in front of her attested to her bird-like manner and grace and her black dress looked like a curtain around her small figure.

"Good afternoon." Her eyes were on Adele, specifically on the net blouse Adele wore which, Adele knew, looked a little transparent in the eyes of someone as conservative as Mrs. Wrigley. Adele wished she had worn a brooch or a scarf with it.

The sheriff took off his hat. "We apologize for the disturbance, ma'am."

"Not at all," she said. "Though I did read once an uninterrupted digestion makes for higher spirits." She wiped her immaculate hands with a napkin. "Perhaps you'd like to sit down."

The men declined but Adele found a small stool and sat down even as Mrs. Wrigley protested, "That's no place for a lady, Miss Gossling. My place will do." She gestured toward the comfortable office chair.

"I don't mind, really." She smiled.

"Miss Branch, if you care to —" Before she could finish, Nin had flopped down on the floor with her legs folded next to her friend. The quiver of horror around her eyes was unmistaken. "Really, I don't —"

"It's all right," Nin said in a merry voice. "I'm no lady."

"Indeed," the woman murmured but then remembered herself and looked toward the men.

"Let us say first, ma'am, we're sorry for your loss," Hatfield began.

"Loss?"

"Your teacher, Miss Gibb."

"Oh." The look on her face made Adele doubt Mrs. Wrigley had thought of it in that way. "Yes, a great loss to the school and certainly to the girls."

"I understood they weren't very fond of her," Adele remarked.

"Miss Gossling, you don't understand the changeable nature of children." Mrs. Wrigley's chin rose. "Especially girls and especially at their age. One day is sunshine, the next thunderstorms."

"They were quite definite about it," Adele said in a dry voice.

"Damned definite," Nin added.

"Miss Branch." The woman's pleasant voice became stoic. "I ask that you maintain some sense of grace in my presence. I know you have the upbringing."

Adele expected her friend to give Mrs. Wrigley a taste of her cat-like gaze. Instead, she bowed her head and said, "I apologize, ma'am." It was the first time Adele had heard her friend address anyone as "ma'am."

"That's better." Mrs. Wrigley nodded in a condescending way.

"Regardless of what the girls thought of her, Mrs. Wrigley, you obviously appreciated her," Jackson guessed.

"I wouldn't have hired her otherwise."

"I meant beyond her skills as a teacher," he said.

"She was strict, I grant you." She threw Adele a look. "But she'd had many years of experience and a fine ear for the English language. I know the girls benefited from it. Even now, I hear them using richer expressions when they speak." Her eyes wandered to the half-eaten plate in front of her.

"We don't want to disturb your lunch, Mrs. Wrigley," Adele said with a gracious smile.Mrs. Wrigley picked up her fork and knife. But Adele knew she wouldn't touch a morsel until they had gone.

"She did her job well?" Hatfield continued.

"Oh, very fine, very fine. She loved words so."

"Yes, she told us," said Nin.

The woman ignored this. "She was fussy about grammar in the way an English teacher ought to be. Children can't learn to speak well if they aren't constantly corrected."

"You were lucky to get her," said the sheriff. "How *did* you get her?"

Two spots appeared on the woman's cheeks, the red contrasting her pale features. "Through a mutual friend, Sheriff."

"Can you give us the name of this friend?" Jackson asked. "We need to talk to everyone who knew Miss Gibb."

"Professor McCabe," she said. "He teaches at the college in Rosa Gris."

"First name?" Jackson held his pencil poised.

Her voice was barely audible. "Elias."

"I beg your pardon?"

"Elias."

Adele realized why she was embarrassed. Widowed since she was a young woman and still donning touches of black crepe in favor of the Queen Victoria method of mourning, to Mrs. Wrigley, the idea of having a male friend was nothing short of scandalous or, at the very least, imprudent.

"A colleague with whom you consult about school business," she guessed.

"Yes, a colleague." Mrs. Wrigley was relieved. "He'll be at the funeral tomorrow morning, of course. You'll come?" She turned to Adele. "I don't think Millie has any family left and it would be terrible if the girls got wind of an empty service."

"Of course we'll come," she reassured.

"Mr. McCabe must have known Miss Gibb for some time to attend her funeral," said the sheriff.

"I couldn't say," she said. "You'll have to ask him." Her hands folded in her lap. "Millie was an asset to the school, a great asset. We're sorry to lose her, the girls and I."

"Did you notice any change in her behavior lately?" asked Hatfield. "Anything that seemed out of place?"

Mrs. Wrigley seemed to fumble with an idea but said at last, "No, I don't think so. She was always rather sharp, I'll admit. Not that sharpness isn't sometimes necessary with young girls." She eyed Jackson, not forgetting for a moment the stirring hearts he had caused in her girls during the Blackstone case.

"There's sharp and there's sharp," Nin pointed out.

"It wasn't the kind of sharpness you're used to in teachers, was it, Mrs. Wrigley?" Adele asked in a gentle voice.

"Ma'am," Hatfield said in a firm but kind tone, "in these matters, even the smallest gesture can shed light."

"I wasn't trying to hold anything back," said Mrs. Wrigley. "I simply didn't know quite how to put it. I don't have Millie's ease with words." She gave a little laugh.

"Was she angry, impatient, even violent with the girls?" Jackson prompted.

"I would never permit any kind of violence in my school, Mr. Gossling, neither in word nor deed." She stiffened.

"Of course not, ma'am," he said in a polite voice.

"She *was* sharp," said Mrs. Wrigley. "But wary too. I know that's a contradiction but, well, she had her burdens, just like the rest of us."

"We get tired of the world sometimes," Nin agreed.

"That's a very astute observation, Miss Branch." Mrs. Wrigley leaned back. "Perhaps you missed your calling as a philosophy teacher."

Nin snorted, unable to hide her annoyance.

Adele put her hand on Mrs. Wrigley's arm. "You felt Miss Gibb was tired of the world?"

"Well, tired of something," the woman said. "Perhaps not the world exactly."

"But of her job," Hatfield finished. "I know what that feels like, ma'am. I wouldn't have become a law officer if I hadn't been tired of going out to sea."

"Yes, I do believe she was tired of her job," Mrs. Wrigley admitted, then added quickly, "not that it affected her work in the least. But, well, teaching can be very trying on the nerves."

"Do you think her fatigue came from her work here or her profession?" asked Adele.

Immediately after the words came out, she could have kicked herself. Mrs. Wrigley's shoulders became even more strained. Adele thought she would float up to the ceiling.

"She was on the most excellent terms here, Miss Gossling," said the woman. "Perhaps you listen too much to the girls' complaints. No girl ever really appreciates the education she is fortunate to receive from generous parents until well after it's gone."

"My sister received a similar education, Mrs. Wrigley," Jackson said. "She's done some fine work helping others in the city."

"I realize that," said Mrs. Wrigley.

"Are you saying Miss Gibb was happy at the school but unhappy with her position as a teacher?" Hatfield suggested.

"Yes, Sheriff, that's exactly what I'm saying." Mrs. Wrigley's eyes wandered at the plates again, and Adele knew she was thinking of the piece of cold apple pie.

"Did Miss Gibb tell you?" he inquired.

"We did have some discussion of it when she first came here," Mrs. Wrigley admitted. "She was very honest with me."

"Honest about what?" asked Adele.

"She was at a crossroad, you might say," said the woman. "With her job, that is. She felt she hadn't progressed in her teaching as much as she would have liked."

"She came to the Wrigley School to remedy that?"

"In a way, yes." Mrs. Wrigley nodded. "I've been taking on more pupils as the years pass, and my school's fine reputation is growing. You recall I *did* tell you that, Miss Gossling?" A sly look appeared on her beaming face, as Adele had first met her on a pretense of wanting to enroll a fictitious niece.

Adele rewarded her with her defiant smile. "I know how much the girls enjoy it here, and I'm glad to hear there will be more coming in the future." She could feel Nin looking at her with an ironic smile

"I'm glad you see it that way, Miss Gossling," said Mrs. Wrigley.

"Naturally, you'll be needing more staff on the administrative side," Adele guessed.

"Yes, that's it," said the woman.

"Did you tell Miss Gibb?" Jackson asked.

A blush appeared on Mrs. Wrigley's face. "Not exactly."

"You hinted at it."

"Yes. Yes, I did," said the woman. "I suppose I did say something about how much I had to cope with in the way of paperwork and meetings with people eager to help improve the minds and manners of young girls."

"Because you saw she was amenable to this?" Hatfield guessed.

Her voice dropped a little. "Sheriff, if you had a child, you would know it's nearly impossible to find a good teacher who knows the finer points of English grammar, especially in California. In the East, it would have been easier, but here — well, people simply do not speak the same language."

The sheriff held up his hand. "Say no more, ma'am. I was once acquainted with a country schoolhouse teacher."

Nin let out a soft giggle, and Adele looked at him with interest.

"Good education is a well-neglected area," he continued. "You have to beg, steal, or borrow sometimes to get the best."

"Or tell them what they want to hear," Jackson remarked. Despite his cultivated charm and refinement, he had a way of bringing out the edges of an inquiry Hatfield tried to smooth down.

"It was nothing like that, Deputy, I assure you," Mrs. Wrigley insisted. "I saw from the start she had the discipline needed to help young ladies, and I thought she could convince parents of that." She blinked. "I had every intention of moving her to the first floor here with me. Eventually."

"And Miss Gibb thought eventually should be sooner than you did," Adele guessed.

The woman put the linen napkin back in her lap. It looked as if she were going to eat that piece of pie she had been eyeing. But she looked down at it as if she had suddenly lost her appetite. "I had every intention for it to be sooner rather than later."

Hatfield studied her. "Something changed your mind."

"Millie changed my mind," said Mrs. Wrigley.

"She wasn't as good a teacher as you thought," Jackson said softly.

"On the contrary." She looked at him. "She was an excellent teacher."

Adele suddenly understood what the woman was trying to say. "An excellent teacher," she said gently, "but nothing more."

"Yes."

"She wanted the brass ring, and you wouldn't give it to her," Nin said.

Adele pressed her wrist. Nin's bald honesty could come out sounding too tart and insensitive at times.

But Mrs. Wrigley seemed relieved the cards were on the table. "I thought she would be on the first floor before the year was out. I really did."

"What was wrong with her?" asked Jackson.

"Nothing was wrong with her, Deputy. But it takes a certain —" she spread her hands on the table, "— finesse to be in the front office. A certain serenity. And jumping at cues."

"And Miss Gibb wasn't good at jumping at cues." Hatfield was almost amused.

"She was very orderly, very neat," said Mrs. Wrigley. "Never a paper out of place. Her lessons were always complete from beginning to end."

"But it takes more than order to convince reluctant parents to leave their child with strangers," Adele remarked.

"Yes, that's it exactly," said the woman.

Hatfield leaned his elbows on his knees, looking like a curious schoolboy. "This is an important question, ma'am. Did Miss Gibb know you felt this way?"

There was silence for a moment except for a few flies hovering over the lingering lunch. Mrs. Wrigley said in a slow voice, "She knew everything."

"You told her?" Jackson asked.

"Of course I told her," the woman said in a thin voice. "I never mislead my teachers, Deputy, nor my students."

"No," he murmured. "You just avoid."

The flies flew out the window. Adele thought Mrs. Wrigley was going to respond in a shrill voice as she usually did when she was defending the school's integrity. But she answered Jackson in an almost complacent tone. "I don't like to disappoint anyone, but sometimes it's unavoidable."

"And Miss Gibb's confronting you about it made it unavoidable," Hatfield concluded.

"Well, she came into my office a few months ago with demands."

"What sort of demands?" asked Adele.

"She wanted to know when she would be moving to the first floor," said the woman "That was just how she said it: 'I want to know when I'll be moving to the first floor.'" She looked almost like a bird frozen to death, sitting up with its eyes open and shining.

"You told her the truth," said Nin.

"I believe in forthrightness in all things, Miss Branch," said Mrs. Wrigley. "I teach that to my girls."

"Practicing what you preach." Adele nodded. "That's one of the reasons your reputation is growing, Mrs. Wrigley."

The woman could not hide her pride underneath the seemly

demure smile.

"What *did* you say to her, Mrs. Wrigley?" asked the sheriff. "This could be important too."

"I told her I needed her right now as an English teacher." she said, "It was a perfectly forthright answer. I really do need an English teacher, now more than ever." But she looked uncomfortable even in the plush chair.

"You didn't tell her you thought she wasn't right for administrative duties," said Jackson.

"Well, it was too soon to tell, Deputy," said the woman in a sharp voice. "She had been here barely a year when she came to me."

"A year is enough to know someone's frame of mind," Adele said in a soft voice.

"Still, Miss Gossling," Her hands pulled down the edges of her jacket, "I couldn't employ someone because she expected it."

"We appreciate you must think of the reputation of your school," Hatfield said. "What did Miss Gibb say when you told her this?"

Again, Mrs. Wrigley looked uncomfortable. As if she could no longer stand it, Nin sprang to her feet and grabbed a silk pillow lying on the small chaise lounge chair in the corner of the room. She inserted it behind her back, smoothly and delicately. Nin had odd moments of compassion for people, even those she, for the most part, disliked.

"Thank you," murmured Mrs. Wrigley.

"Was she angry or unhappy?" Adele prompted. "She must have said *something*."

"Millie never got angry," said Mrs. Wrigley. "She didn't say much either, but she was deflated, I suppose you could call it. As if the life went out of her. Then she asked me when I thought we might discuss it again. I told her in another six months or so and that seemed to satisfy her."

"Seemed to?" Hatfield asked.

"Well, I suppose you ought to know the whole story," she sighed. "As I was going to my classroom later that day, I heard crying from the girls' washrooms."

"Crying or sobbing?" Adele asked.

It took a moment for Mrs. Wrigley to answer. "Sobbing, I suppose. That's why I thought it was one of the girls at first. Ladies don't sob, you know."

"But it wasn't?"

"I peeked in to see what I could do and saw Millie's shoes and the hem of her skirt. I didn't open the door all the way. I thought it better to let her be."

"You're very considerate, ma'am," said the sheriff.

"I ought to have gone to her." There was genuine distress on her face. "I raised her salary, so I didn't think it would matter to her to wait another six months."

"We can't know what's in someone's mind or what they're feeling," said the sheriff. "We can't know what they might do as a result of what we say."

Mrs. Wrigley's face tightened. "What are you implying, Sheriff?"

"Do you think Miss Gibb might have been disheartened about the incident to — take measures?"

"Measures?" The woman sat up. "You mean look for another job?"

"No, ma'am." Hatfield's voice grew even milder. "I mean to end her misery in a more permanent way."

To say Mrs. Wrigley was shocked was an understatement. Adele had never seen her so aghast, and she knew the kind of tricks the girls sometimes played to rattle her unyielding sense of decorum. Her skin grew greenish in the clouded light coming through the window, and her eyes looked ready to pounce out of her thin face.

"Oh, no!" The words came out with a gasping breath. "Oh, no!"

The sheriff gave Jackson a sign, but Nin rushed to the pitcher of water sitting on the desk. She poured some into the glass, disturbing a brass paperweight as she did so, and put it in front of Mrs. Wrigley, watching over her like a tidy nurse as she drank it.

"Thank you, Miss Branch," the woman said in a rusty voice. "Most kind."

Nin took her hand, her beautiful face stretched up in the appealing way of a begging child.

"I'm all right, really," Mrs. Wrigley regained her composure. "I assumed Millie died of an accident and now you're telling me —"

"We weren't telling you anything, ma'am," Hatfield said. "We're exploring all possibilities. Had we known it would upset you —"

"I'm not upset." Her voice held its usual brisk tone. "I feel foolish, really. I should have read the paper this morning. I thought it best to avoid it, what with Miss Grace's connections." Her eyes swept toward Adele, who had befriended Missy as another sister of progress of which Mrs. Wrigley disapproved. "Oh, this is going to cause a scandal, I know it!" She covered her mouth.

"It's not your fault," Nin assured her. "No one will blame you."

"Blame *me?*" The woman stared at her.

"Sometimes Miss Branch says things she doesn't mean." Jackson glared at her. Nin rose and sat next to Adele on the floor. Adele reached down and quietly took her friend's hand.

Mrs. Wrigley looked down at her for a moment. "Perhaps you're right, Miss Branch. Perhaps I am to blame."

"If Miss Gibb took her own life, it was *not* because of one person, ma'am," Hatfield said in a firm voice. "I can assure you of that."

"You did your job just as you ought," Jackson put in. "What happened after that has nothing to do with you."

"Thank you, gentlemen," said Mrs. Wrigley.

"We know from Mrs. Taylor that Miss Gibb kept to herself at

the boarding house," the sheriff said. "What about here at the school? Was there anyone she was close to, any of the teachers, a pet student, anyone?"

"No, Millie wasn't that sort," said the woman. "She was professional at all times."

"But even professionals make friends," Jackson pointed out.

"There was Dr. McCabe, as I mentioned earlier," she said.

"What does he teach?" asked Jackson.

"Literature and language." She smiled a little. "He's a linguist and etymologist, one of the few in the West."

Adele looked up sharply at the word *etymologist*.

Mrs. Wrigley rose, the school mistress in command of her environment. "I'm afraid lunch is almost over, and I must get back to my girls, gentlemen."

Jackson glanced at his superior, who gave him a cautious look. "We'd like to speak to the girls who were in Miss Gibb's class, if we may."

"You may *not*," the woman snapped. "It's entirely improper. I'm surprised you of all people would ask such a thing, Deputy. Considering your upbringing."

"We won't ask anything that might upset them," he assured her.

"Nevertheless, it's entirely improper," she repeated.

"They could give us a good deal of good information, Mrs. Wrigley," Hatfield said in a gentle voice. "You're welcome to come with us to ensure everything is properly done."

"Impossible," said the woman.

"Mrs. Wrigley," Adele appealed to her. "The sheriff wouldn't ask if it weren't important."

"There is nothing my girls could tell you," she insisted. "I'm sorry, but that is my final decision."

They lingered a few minutes longer trying to persuade her, but Mrs. Wrigley would not be moved. It was clear they had infringed on her ideas of propriety far too much.

CHAPTER 13

The sun had come out from behind the clouds but so had the afternoon breeze and they had to hold down their hats so they wouldn't fly off their heads. All except Nin, who rarely wore a hat or gloves and never carried a parasol. She roamed around town like a wild child with her hair unpinned and her head uncovered, her dresses flowing with no corsets underneath and there were even times in the summer when she went without shoes entirely.

Adele had already made up her mind and stopped them not far from the school. "Sheriff, let Nin and I speak to the girls this evening." She appealed to him without feminine wiles or honey charms. She appreciated the sheriff was less susceptible to these artificial qualities than other men, even her brother.

"You?" He stared at her.

"You recall Nin and I have a different relationship with them."

"We don't have badges," Nin added.

"Exactly." Adele took her friend's arm. "There's no harm in our chatting with them, and by-the-by, Miss Gibb's name comes up in conversation."

Jackson shook his head. "I'll never understand this strange

idea of yours, Del. Taking schoolgirls into your confidence, scattering them all about town to hunt up information. It's as bad as a den of thieves sending boys to pick pockets for them."

"Your sister is hardly a Fagin, Jackson," Hatfield remarked.

"We're speaking here about helping the police," Adele reminded him.

"But schoolgirls!"

A wry smile appeared on Hatfield's face. "Who better to shed light on a teacher than schoolgirls?"

"If Mrs. Wrigley finds out you're asking questions —"

"My dear brother," Adele said, "Mrs. Wrigley has no idea the girls work for me."

"We don't poke and prod," Nin said. "And we give them money for sweets."

"If you insist on chatting up the girls on your way home this evening," the sheriff said, "I certainly can't stop you."

Adele smiled as a look of understanding passed between them.

She and the girls had arranged a series of signs for when she needed to talk to them. She and Nin reached the school from the parallel street less exposed to Mrs. Wrigley and the excellent if draconian staff of teachers. They entered the alley where a wooden shack stood encrusted in weeds. Adele threw stones against the second-floor window of the girls' study. Usually, one of the girls appeared at the window holding up a sign: "yes," if they were alone on the floor, "no," if they were not, and an arrow pointing up if the girls were to be found in the shack.

That evening, Adele's signal was answered with the arrow. She and Nin made their way through a loose panel in the gate shielding the trees and stepped between small holes in the mud where ground animals burrowed. They reached the shack and found Beatrice and Rachel with some of the younger girls. When Adele had first met the two, they had been plucky and eager girls of eleven and twelve, a little prone to romanticizing but sharp and willing. Their pluckiness had been somewhat tamed but their sense of adventure and romanticizing remained.

Beatrice ran to them first. Her strawberry blond hair filled out so it was sometimes difficult for her to keep the smaller hats on her head. She gave Adele and Nin a kiss on the cheek, something that always seemed to fluster the latter.

"It's been ages, Adele." Rachel was more reserved in her greeting. She introduced the three younger girls — Madge, Leonie, and Helen. Adele only knew them slightly, as they had arrived at the school at the beginning of that year and the older girls always delegated duties to the younger girls.

"You're here about Miss Gibb, aren't you?" Beatrice started in right away with her foxy dark eyes.

"She killed herself!" Leonie looked frightened.

"Don't be such a goose." The girl tapped her on the head. "Ask us any question you like." She pushed a few crates forward.

"I can't," said Adele.

"Oh, the dragon woman!" Beatrice snorted.

"It doesn't become you to call her such names, Bea," Rachel said. "She's been very kind to us."

"She's ridiculous," Beatrice said. "She tried to hide the paper from us this morning. You ought to have seen her grab the paper boy by the shoulders. I thought she would tear his coat right off."

"And then she hid it from us," Madge added.

"But you got it anyway," Nin said.

"Naturally," Rachel said with pride. "You can't hide anything from Bea."

Adele leaned on her parasol. "We're only here for a friendly chat, mind you."

"We ought to be studying for the etiquette exam, Bea," Rachel ventured.

"Oh, bother etiquette!" Beatrice said. "You only need to be polite when you're in formal company."

Adele laughed. "Did Miss Gibb teach you that?"

Rachel gave her a lopsided look. "Why would Miss Gibb have anything to do with it?"

"Etiquette is about words, isn't it?" asked Adele. "Miss Gibb loved words. She told us so herself."

"She used lots of 'em," Helen piped up. "She always corrected us right in the middle of a sentence. Even in the washroom!" She looked away.

"Not last week," said Madge. "Last week I said 'ain't' three times, and she looked at me like I was talking Greek."

"She never let you slip by with an 'ain't' before?" Adele asked.

"Not hardly." Madge giggled.

"She was a real stickler, Miss Adele." Helen looked at her with bulging eyes. Adele had the feeling she was trying to impress her as someone who could be relied upon to tell every little detail, and she wondered what tales these girls had overheard from the older ones about scavenging for her.

"You're to call her Miss Gossling," Beatrice said in a tight voice as she whipped out a handkerchief, a pretty lace thing in faded blue with her initials on it embroidered in white. "You haven't the privilege of calling her Adele yet."

Adele smiled. "They can call me Miss Adele if they like. And this is Miss Branch." She touched her friend's arm. "You must be respectful toward her, no matter what people in town say." Nin's face became a little despondent. "Mrs. Wrigley seems to think she was an excellent teacher," Adele continued.

"Oh, I suppose she was alright," said Beatrice.

"People have been giving me compliments about the high-toned way I speak lately," Rachel added. "Mama says I owe that to Miss Gibb."

"I can't imagine you would need to be corrected very much when it comes to high-toned speaking," Nin said with one of her sugary smiles.

Rachel was almost fluttering with gratitude but both Adele and Beatrice saw the slap behind the complement. Adele pretended not to notice. Beatrice was not so considerate and laughed outright.

Adele turned to the younger girls. "When did she start letting go of your grammar?"

"Ages ago," Madge said.

"That ain't right. She wants a real time," said Helen waving her away like a bird. "When we all came back to school after the holidays, Miss Adele."

"No, it was after that!" Madge insisted.

Adele peered at Leonie who was looking down at her lap. She touched the girl's knee and gave her a comforting smile. "Leonie, that's your name, isn't it?"

"Yes, Miss Adele."

"Oh, she don't talk," said Helen. "*She* wouldn't know."

"I know more than *you!*" the girl shot out. "Especially about Miss Gibb."

Adele bent down to the girl. "We want to know everything we can so we can find out about Miss Gibb."

"Nothing to find out if she killed herself," Beatrice said in a final tone.

"Bea!" Rachel's hand flew into the pocket of her pinafore. Adele imagined she was reaching for the rosary she always carried with her. "You mustn't say such things in front of the children."

"Yes, the children," Nin said in a dry voice. "*All* of them." Her wide eyes took in the two older girls.

"Oh, stop being so prissy, Rachel," Beatrice said with a snort. "They know everything already."

Leonie looked at Adele above her long lashes. She was really a very pretty girl with her dark hair and very red lips. "Then she didn't kill herself?"

Adele took a liking to the girl. She felt sorry for her shyness, mirroring her own at that age. The silence clearly hid a more observing eye and an astute awareness.

"Don't be a fool," said Beatrice.

"It's not your business if she did or didn't," Rachel said with airs. "That's for the police to decide."

"We're trying to help the police," Adele said. "What is it you know, Leonie?"

"Well, Miss Adele," said the girl, clearly feeling more comfortable. "I have lessons with her every Thursday afternoon."

"How can you have lessons with her if she's dead?" Marge demanded.

The girl blushed.

"Go on, dear," Adele said.

"It's not my grammar, Miss Adele. I don't say 'ain't' and all like *some* people." Her eyes slid toward the other two. "But I don't spell so good. So Miss Gibb makes — made — oh, she isn't here!" The girl's eyes filled with tears.

"It's alright, Leonie." Beatrice put her arm around the girl. "Tell Adele what you know."

"Well, I *had* lessons with her every day," the girl corrected. "She would make me write the words I got wrong over and over again."

"Where were these lessons?" asked Adele.

"In the schoolroom, Miss Adele," said the girl. "She'd let me sit at the big desk."

"Hers is the big desk," Rachel supplied.

"It's nice to see the room from there." Leonie smiled in spite of her tears. "It looks so much bigger."

"And where was Miss Gibb while you were at the big desk?" asked Adele.

"She was up and about. That is, she used to be up and about," Leonie sighed. "She'd walk around the room, at least, for a time. Then she stopped."

"Stopped?" Adele asked.

"Yes, miss," the girl said. "She would just stand at the window looking out and mumbling."

"Mumbling?"

"That's what it sounded like to me," said Leonie.

"Grown-ups don't mumble," Helen insisted.

"Grown-ups do all the things children do," Rachel said. "Be polite, dear."

"Well, Miss Gibb was mumbling," said Leonie.

"Mumbling what?" asked Beatrice.

"Oh, strange things," said Leonie. "Mishmash, my papa calls it."

"Do you remember some of that mishmash?" asked Adele.

The girl shut her eyes here and leaned back, putting her index fingers on her temples, clearly imitating someone she had seen. Nin raised her eyebrow.

"*She'll come through. Just deserts. Just deserts.*" Here, Leonie's eyes flew open. "Miss Adele, what's just deserts?"

"It means one gets what one deserves," Adele said. The phrase struck her like one of Hatfield's question marks.

CHAPTER 14

Adele was able to see Hatfield at the station the next morning, bringing Nin with her. Jackson had been dispatched on the early morning train to Sacramento to see if the police there had discovered anything about Owen Burke. The sheriff was finishing his shave over the sink in the corner and they listened to him humming a tune. Then he started singing of an ancient mariner with such nostalgia that Adele wondered if he suddenly missed his years as the sea captain of a whaling ship on the San Francisco Bay.

"Depressing song, isn't it, miss?" Edison whispered. "Storm blasts and dead albatrosses and all that."

"Albatross," Adele couldn't resist correcting him. "It's a sea bird."

"A bad sea bird," the young man said. "I seem to remember —"

"Only if you kill it," said Nin as she sat on the floor in front of the sheriff's desk. "Any living thing is bad luck if you kill it."

Edison shrugged. "I suppose if you got a reason for killing it, miss, it's more bad luck if it stays."

"Only animals, Mr. Edison?" Adele raised her eyebrows. "Or do you mean people too?"

He blushed. "No, indeed, miss! People are a whole different story."

"Why?" Nin looked at him with her cat eyes. "Because we pretend we're more civilized than they are?"

"Why, miss, I don't mean that at all!" His face was almost purple with embarrassment. "I reckon killing's a savage deed, whether it's a man or a beast."

"We know you didn't mean what you said, Assistant Deputy." Adele laid her parasol on the sheriff's desk. "One can't work for the law and believe killing, man or beast, is justified."

"Oh, that's not to say there aren't many a badman in this world," the young man continued with an air of importance. "Why, I hear the sheriff say —"

"The sheriff would never say such a thing," Adele said in a sharp voice. "He's not the kind."

"No, miss. I meant the old sheriff, Sheriff Nealy," said Edison. "He used to say God leads the bullet where the heart is full of black blood."

"He would," Nin snorted.

"I hadn't realized you worked under him," said Adele. "I thought he left well before you and the others came on the scene with Sheriff Hatfield."

"The others ain't — aren't regulars," Edison said, his nose getting more to the air every moment. "I tell them what to do and they do it. Why, if I weren't there to —"

"Edison!"

The familiar growl made the young man's nose dive back to shuffle papers. Hatfield emerged completely dressed and shaven as if he were going to a party.

"What twaddle are you giving these young women?" he asked in an accusing voice.

"We were talking about albatrosses, Sheriff." Adele winked at the young man, making him color again. "Weren't we, Nin?" Her friend, though having little sympathy for the foolish Edison, nodded.

The sheriff offered Adele his chair which was the most comfortable in the office. "I'm beginning to think this Gibb case will be one of mine."

"Nonsense," Adele said. "You never failed to close a case yet."

"And always with dignity and honesty," Nin added.

The sheriff gave them both his shy smile. "I assume you have news for me from those girls yesterday."

"Not much." Adele peeled off her gloves. "Most of it is rather one-sided."

"Always the way with school children," Hatfield nodded. "Were these the younger or the older girls?"

"Both," said Adele. "They all agree — Miss Gibb was strict with their P's and Q's until about three or four months ago."

"What occurred three or four months ago? Edison! To your work!" The young man's hands had stopped on the new typewriter the office had bought for reports, which, since no one else in the station liked it, had been pushed to Edison. The young man flinched and his fingers began pounding the keys again.

"Take that thing into the file room," Hatfield ordered.

Edison toddled off to the dusty back room and shut the door.

"What happened three or four months ago?" he repeated

"Miss Gibb's meeting with her employer, for a start," Nin said.

"Very good memory, Miss Branch," said the sheriff.

"That was about the time she met with Mrs. Wrigley," Adele said with a nod.

"And about the time she was told she wouldn't be seeing a promotion for a while," said the sheriff. "That kind of news might deflate any teacher's motivation to do her job well."

"Not a *good* teacher," Adele said. "Miss Gibb was a good teacher. Even the girls admitted this. The older ones, that is."

"What did the younger ones have to say?" asked Hatfield. "Little ones say things much more boldly."

"One of them certainly did," Nin remarked. "A little pie-faced thing."

"She was a lovely girl," Adele objected. "Leonie was her name. Shy but observant."

"I see her on your list of nimble spies in the future." Hatfield grinned.

"I did rather like her, yes," said Adele. "She had private lessons with Miss Gibb after school and thought the woman acted in a peculiar way."

"Peculiar?" The sheriff sat up.

"She was talking mishmash," Nin said.

"She was mumbling to herself," Adele supplied. "Leonie called it mishmash but I think it's a clue." She took out the tiny pad she carried in her purse and showed him the words she had written.

"Just deserts," he said in a quiet voice.

"Intriguing, isn't it?" Adele's eyes sparkled. "Whose, I'd like to know."

"If she was distracted by her own frustration," Hatfield said, "it might very well have been mishmash, as your Leonie puts it. Still, I agree it likely had some kind of meaning for Miss Gibb." He folded the piece of paper and put it in the box marked MILLIE GIBB CASE on his desk.

"I wonder whom 'she' refers to," said Adele. "'She'll come through.' Come through with what?"

"And did she come through before Millie died?" Nin added.

"Question marks, question marks," Hatfield mused. "And now we've mishmash to add to it."

"Whose mishmash?" a loud voice grumbled. It belonged to a man whose hair was already beginning to silver even though he was about ten years younger than Hatfield. The man was Dr. Anvil Rhodes, the county medical examiner. Martin followed sheepishly at his heels, his glasses in hand.

"This is a rare honor, Doctor," Hatfield muttered. Dr. Rhodes was a man of timetables and interruptions because of what he considered meager details, such as a crime scene examination, which always made the sheriff testy.

"I was on my way home." He glanced at the chairs in the room as if he were surveying which one was more worthy of him. "I thought I would drop in and get this over with."

"By 'this,' you mean Miss Gibb's autopsy report?" Hatfield was full attention.

"The little school marm, yes."

Adele stiffened. "She was a person, Dr. Rhodes. A school teacher isn't any less important than the mayor's wife."

The man gave her a sniveling look, then turned to the sheriff. "Mrs. Taylor asked me to come especially, even though I told her I would send over my written report this evening. She's anxious to make funeral arrangements."

"And as you were on your way home, you thought you'd stop by and get it over with," Hatfield repeated. "That was kind of you."

"Exceedingly kind," Nin muttered. "And very uncharacteristic."

Adele caught sight of Martin's shaking shoulders though his face remained impassive.

"I'm sure a *private* conversation would be more prudent." Dr. Rhodes gave Nin the same sniveling look he had given Adele.

"You're always admiringly prudent and speedy with your reports, Doctor," Hatfield said. "There's no need for privacy. Miss Gossling was present when we inspected the crime scene, and Miss Branch is as knowledgeable about the case as we are. You remember how helpful they both were with the Blackstone murder investigation."

"Helpful is a relative term, Sheriff," said Dr. Rhodes. "In my experience, women meddle more than help." As if trying to temper the instant annoyance that appeared on both women's faces, he added, "Though I do admit sometimes there is a morsel of good in their meddling."

"How generous of you to admit it." Adele exchanged an arch look with her friend.

"Well, this shouldn't take long anyway." The man threw one leg over the other. "Millicent Gibb died of poisoning."

Hatfield leaned on the desk with his hands cupped. "I need more detail than that."

"Arsenic poisoning," the doctor snapped.

"Most likely," Martin chimed in. "It's of course impossible to be one hundred percent sure."

"There's nothing one hundred percent sure in this world but death," Dr. Rhodes said. "Everything else is estimations."

"I thought arsenic poisoning took a long time," Adele said.

"It depends how much, Miss Gossling," the doctor said. "The powder is odorless and tasteless. One could easily consume enough to kill ten men without even knowing it."

"Why do you think it was arsenic?" asked Adele. "I know Martin told us a little, but —"

"The final word is mine, *not* Mr. Sanders," the man said. "Certain outward signs on the body led Mr. Sanders to make that diagnosis."

"Which, according to your estimation, happens to be correct," Hatfield said in his quiet voice. "Did you perform an autopsy?"

"As much as I was able with the limited tools I have," Dr. Rhodes snapped. "I intend to bring that up at the town council meeting next month."

"Then how can you be so sure it was arsenic?" Adele asked.

"The signs, naturally," he said. "Just as I said."

Hatfield was losing patience, as his face which was beginning to show some of its coarser features. "Dr. Rhodes," he said in a measured voice, "perhaps I didn't make myself clear. I need answers to these questions. You know how this game works."

"I find it interesting you use the word *game*, Sheriff," said the man. "We all have our little games, don't we? The game of search and spend, for example?"

The silence made Adele curious. She had known for some time there was a point of contention between the medical examiner and the sheriff. But even Jackson had no idea what it was.

"I only ask for the details I need." The sheriff cleared his throat. "What signs led you to diagnose arsenic poisoning and not another poison, for example?"

"Now you're being more precise." The doctor leaned back. "I believe Mr. Sanders told me you already observed she had been perspiring — glowing —" he threw his head back at Adele as he corrected himself, "— through her clothes. Her lips were swelled and her skin was yellow and cracked. All signs of arsenic poisoning."

Hatfield remarked, "I imagine one poison works similar to another."

The man sat up. "If you're not satisfied, Sheriff, I could send for a Marsh test in San Francisco. Of course," he added with deliberate slyness, "that would be very costly and, in my view, unnecessary. Both, I suspect, wouldn't speak very well in your favor."

Again, Adele felt some hidden meaning behind his words, and Hatfield's face showed he understood the insinuation.

"It seems odd nothing else was swollen but her lips," she said to divert attention away from Hatfield's growing anger.

"Not in the least, Miss Gossling." The doctor cradled his hands on the back of his head. "The poison probably touched her lips in some way, and that's what caused the swelling."

"It must have been an enormous amount," Nin said.

"For once, Miss Branch, you are correct," said Dr. Rhodes. "It's heartening to see your mesmeric methods haven't replaced your common sense."

Adele anticipated her friend's reaction and calmed her with soothing words, even as she glared at the doctor. "Do you mean an enormous amount of arsenic was given to achieve such a reaction on the lips?" she asked.

"'Enormous' is perhaps not the right word," said Dr. Rhodes. He let go of his previous viper tactics and fell into his matter-of-fact tone. "Direct contact is what I meant."

"You mean the arsenic was administered *directly* on the lips and not indirectly through, say, food or drink?" Hatfield's eyes looked almost like a cat's. "Why didn't you say so before?"

"I don't see it matters," said the doctor. "Arsenic poisoning is arsenic poisoning."

Adele leaned sideways so she could catch the doctor's eye. "So if arsenic was placed only in Miss Gibb's hot toddy, it would have killed her but the effect on the lips wouldn't have been so severe."

"Correct, Miss Gossling," said the doctor, only slightly impressed.

"We analyzed the contents of the cinnamon stick," Martin piped up. "No arsenic was found."

"I thought he said you don't have the proper lab," Nin said.

"A body is different from a cinnamon stick, Miss Branch," the doctor said.

"There was no arsenic found on it?" Sheriff Hatfield eyed him.

"None at all, Sheriff," Martin replied.

"That's not quite true," Dr. Rhodes snapped. "I was just coming to that."

"Yes, sir." Martin shrank back.

"We found no traces of arsenic on the cinnamon sticks we took from the kitchen," said the doctor. "We did find evidence of arsenic on the remains of the stick you found in Miss Gibb's room."

"Was it enough to kill her?" asked the sheriff.

The doctor shook his head. "We found no traces of arsenic in the whiskey, the cider, or the sugar."

"And the lemon slices?" Adele asked.

Dr. Rhodes glanced at her with a stony look, and she realized he was staring at her hands clutching the lace layer on her skirt.

"You have reason to be nervous, Miss Gossling," he said in his scratchy voice. "They were saturated in arsenic."

"Saturated!" Hatfield sat back, his chair rocking back and forth.

A door behind them flew open and Edison trotted out, carrying the unwieldy typewriter with both hands. A stern look from his employer made him turn around and scurry back to the room, shutting the door behind him.

"You mean they were covered with poison?" Nin sat up very straight, her arms pressed to her sides. Her usual intense countenance was even more deeply disturbed.

"Not merely coated," Dr. Rhodes said in an almost bored voice. "Like you would flour a chicken thigh before frying it." He rose. "That reminds me. I'm late for an appointment."

"You believe the poison came from the lemon slices?" Hatfield asked.

"I neither believe nor disbelieve," said the doctor. "I simply report my findings. You make the connections, Sheriff." He was halfway to the door when he stopped and leaned against a desk. "Are you going to rule this a suicide?"

"As you say, sir," Hatfield's voice was sharp, "you report your findings and I make the connections. And may I commend you for having done so in your usual speedy way."

"Speed is key, Sheriff." There was something a little too self-satisfying in his tone. "The citizens of this town appreciate speed."

Adele was sure now there had been some kind of argument or even confrontation between the doctor and Hatfield about the sheriff's job. A feeling of sympathy filled her as she glanced at Hatfield, who was fiddling with some papers on his desk but, from the staunch look on his face, he was determined not to lose his temper.

"Yes, speed is key," Hatfield mumbled. "But not to the detriment of a thorough job."

The doctor's face turned red. "Are you insinuating I'm not doing a thorough job?"

Hatfield bowed his head. "I was speaking in generalities, Doctor."

Dr. Rhodes saluted him but it was clearly more for mockery than respect. At the door, he threw out, "There are ways of doing a thorough job without wasting precious resources like time and money. Perhaps you ought to think about *that*, Sheriff."

As he stepped outside, Adele called, "Wait!"

The doctor jerked his head back. "What is it, Miss Gossling?"

"Are there any more signs of arsenic poisoning?"

"I've explained —"

"I mean *before* the others. When the poison begins to take effect."

She thought he was going to give her another of his wary gazes but he considered this with full medical attention. "Dizziness, confusion. The person doesn't know what's going on around him, trying to find his bearings. How much depends on the amount of arsenic the person has consumed."

"Thank you, Dr. Rhodes," she said. "That was very helpful."

He eyed the sheriff. "I can tell Mrs. Taylor she's welcome to the body?"

"You might put it more delicately," Nin snapped.

"Since as Miss Branch rightly points out, delicacy is needed in a situation like this," the sheriff said, "I think it's best if I tell her."

The doctor sniffed and strolled out, Martin following close behind.

Adele looked fully at Hatfield. "What does that man have against you, Sheriff?"

He sighed. "There are some things better left unexplained, Adele."

"Because ladies wouldn't understand them?" She rolled her eyes.

"Because they involve dirt, and I wouldn't want such a fine person as yourself soiled by them," he said.

"I'm no cooing dove, Sheriff," she reminded him. "I've seen many soiled doves and worse in my settlement work."

"But you didn't come to Arrojo for that," he pointed out. "You came for peace and small pleasures, as I recall."

She couldn't help but smile. "He ought to treat you with more respect."

"Respect where respect is due," Nin agreed.

"Quite right," said Hatfield. "But I can't vouch for my own respect toward him. So you see, we're on the same plane."

Adele was about to answer when the squeak of the file room door sounded again and Edison emerged with trepidation, carrying the typewriter like a crying infant.

"It's all right, lad," said Hatfield. "Suppose you give up that infernal pounding and call the Sacramento police department to see if Deputy Gossling arrived?" When the young man retired into the furthest corner of the room where they kept the station house phone, he turned back to Adele. "Now, what was all that about first signs of poisoning?"

"I thought you were trying to get at something," Nin said with a lazy eye on her friend.

"The room, Sheriff," she said. "Remember how disordered it was with the pitcher on the floor, and the water spilled all over the bureau? She must have risen when she began to feel the effects of the poison and tried to wash her face in the washstand."

"The poor thing," Nin said with a genuine sadness in her voice.

"That would account for the reeling we suspected," the sheriff agreed. "It seems Miss Gibb's habit of eating lemon did not serve her well in this instance."

"You saw that too," Adele said. "One of your question marks answered, Sheriff. We now know how she died."

"It seems so odd," said Nin. "Putting arsenic on the lemon

peels so she could eat them and die? I don't think I would have had the courage."

"We don't know she wanted to die," Adele reminded her.

"Perhaps it was a trick." Hatfield folded his hands across his chest.

"On whom?" Adele stared.

"On herself, naturally," he answered. "Like the desperate man who plays Russian roulette. He knows one of those barrels must contain the bullet, but he plays a game to trick his mind into thinking it will never come."

"If Miss Gibb had really wanted to kill herself," said Adele, "do you think she would need a trick to do it? I always thought suicides were quite resolved in their purpose. Elated, even, to be ending their misery in this life in anticipation of more peace in the next."

The sheriff glanced down at Nin. "*Is* the life in the next world more peaceful than this one?"

Nin stiffened. "I do not communicate with the dead, Sheriff. I have never had a chat with ghosts or tea with the spirits."

The man bowed with conceding humbleness at his error.

"Sheriff," Adele rose, dusting her skirt from sawdust, "as long as we're speaking of respect, you know my respect for you is most sincere."

"As is my respect for *you*, Adele," he said, not a little bashful.

"I honor that," she said with her eyes cast down. "That's why I know you wouldn't shrug me off if I asked a favor of you. Professionally, that is."

"You have a right to ask whatever you wish," he said. "I am, as the old gentlemen used to say, your humble servant, ma'am."

"I hope you keep an open mind, in spite of what the doctor says."

"I've always been told my mind is a little too open," Hatfield said in a rueful voice. "According to Mrs. Faderman and her brood."

"You know what I mean, Sheriff," she said as she picked up her parasol. "All the fingers can point, but that doesn't mean they point in the right direction."

"I'm not sure I follow you, Adele."

"She means," said Nin, rising, "don't let everyone else tell you Miss Gibb was one thing or another."

Sheriff Hatfield gave them a little smile as he glanced out the window just above the place where Edison was sitting, still hunched over the phone.

CHAPTER 15

*L*ater that same day, Missy Grace put a notice in the evening edition of the *Arrojo Courier* that Miss Gibb's funeral would be tomorrow morning at ten. Already as the sun came up, there was a smattering of rainfall. Adele woke up to a pattering like children's feet on her window. She parted the lace curtains to watch the little teardrops make dashes against the shiny glass. The sound of the light rain gave her a feeling of comfort.

Neither she nor her brother ate much, enduring the cluck-clucking of Tomas' tongue as he stood in the corner of the dining room with his hands behind his back, determined always to act like a footman or a butler even though they made it clear to the Cordobas they were not servants.

"You're looking a little hazy, Del." Jackson folded the *San Francisco Chronicle* in fours. It was still a mystery to her how he got the city papers so early every morning.

"I was thinking of Miss Gibb," she said. "May we refer to her as Millie among ourselves now?"

"I suppose so," Jackson said. "We know her intimately enough by now to be on a first-name basis."

"Death is an intimate thing," she mused. "Remember when Papa died, and we went through all his things? So much we never knew about him, like that immigrant woman he helped get out of the country."

"And his handkerchief fetish," Jackson said with a rueful glance at his watch.

"And the locket with Mama's hair." Adele's face felt cool despite the heavy warmth of the morning air.

"I never would have thought him so sentimental," her brother murmured.

"Why shouldn't he be?"

He shrugged, his gaze distant and bothered.

"I never knew she had red hair," Adele said.

"Mustn't be late," Jackson mumbled. She knew speaking of their mother always made him melancholy and they were already about to attend a sad occasion.

The Arrojo Cemetery looked almost picturesque in the rain with its ivy-crawled stone walls and redwoods watching over the dead. Millie's city roots did not make her privy to a choice spot. Her grave was in one of the more remote corners where the trees gathered almost into one dark eye. Her tombstone, too, was plain gray rather than the more polished granite like Lucy Blackstone's, who had been the daughter of one of the founder families. Even the engraving contained only her name, year of birth, and the current year.

"Mr. Collie certainly has established his priorities," Adele snapped as she stood with her arm through Nin's. "Millie's relations wouldn't be able to find her grave with a compass."

"Well, she may not have been much of a stranger to you or me, Miss Gossling, but she was a stranger in town," Mrs. Taylor pointed out. The woman had hardly changed out of her widow's garb with the guests of the house beside her, all looking rather put out by a rushed breakfast that morning.

"She may not have had roots here in Arrojo but she had roots *somewhere,*" Adele insisted.

"Yes, she had roots," said Mrs. Brent in a quiet voice. She had taken on the role of a grieving mother in her heavy black crepe and veil, her handkerchief already damp from earlier that morning. Mr. Brent stood in a dark suit casting anxious looks toward her as if he expected her to swoon at any moment.

Nin's eyes drooped almost as much. "Is this all?" She was referring to the attendance of only the Bents, Mrs. Taylor, the boarding house guests, and themselves.

Mrs. Brent pressed her handkerchief to her face. Adele approached her, Nin following. "We'll do right by Millie," she promised.

"I only hope I have," the woman whispered.

The parson arrived with Hatfield. To Adele's surprise, the sheriff came down the path with his mother Lady Augusta, who was dressed in dark clothes for the occasion.

"She insisted," he whispered to Adele as if anticipating her next words.

"But you never even met the woman," Adele pointed out.

"Must one meet an unfortunate lady to feel compassion?" Lady Augusta asked in her usual attention-drawing voice.

Adele pressed the elderly woman's hand. "You're so good, Lady Augusta."

"Ma puts humanity first," said Hatfield with pride.

"As do you, Horatio," she said warmly. "It is perhaps your greatest strength as a detective."

"And my greatest weakness," he mumbled.

Adele looked around for her brother and found Jackson standing behind the tombstone talking to a man she had never seen. The man seemed a little out of place in his brown suit and large hat. His bespectacled face gave a feeling of someone alarmed by social occasions. His eyes met hers. The man tweaked the tip of his hat at her in greeting.

"Who is that, Sheriff?" she asked.

"Dr. McCabe from Rosa Gris," Hatfield answered. "He came last night."

"He's not quite dressed for the occasion, is he?" Lady Augusta squinted at him.

"He's one of those dusty professors, Ma," said her son. "Doesn't get out much."

The somber service began and Adele couldn't help but feel annoyed at Parson Masters' monotone as he read from the Bible. What angered her more was his words made it clear he had taken his cue from the town gossips as to the cause of Millie's death. He lamented the "unfortunate and unhappy soul" of a woman who had been "a morsel of a stranger" in their midst, how this "hapless creature" had "no one to whom she could turn in troubled times" and her "sin in the eyes of God" might be forgiven because of her "womanly frailties." At this, Adele turned toward the cluster of redwoods to keep from barking at the man.

She saw a figure standing a little behind the fold of a redwood trunk. She leaned toward her friend. "That queer man!"

"What man?" Nin asked.

"There near the trees," she said.

"I don't see any man," her friend sniffed.

"He certainly is trying to keep himself hidden," Adele remarked. She saw a flash of thin lips. "Nin! I think he's laughing."

"Yes, there's a cruel mirth in the air," Nin said vaguely.

"He's laughing like a clown in the circus," she murmured.

"I've never been to a circus," Nin remarked.

"The clowns paint their smiles on," Adele said. "This man's smile spells drunken joy." She felt ill. "I saw a clown like that once when I was a child. It made me feel so ashamed I ran out of the circus tent and hid behind it. Papa had to coax me out." Her voice became misty. "It's like belittling the dead. Oh, I can't stand it!" She turned away, meeting Hatfield's alarmed gaze.

The sermon was over and people shuffled out of the graveyard. As she and Nin followed the procession, she glanced at the redwoods again but the dark figure had disappeared.

The parson bowed at them. "Miss Gossling. Miss Branch. Kind of you to come."

"Thank you for the sermon," Adele mumbled.

"When one is called to duty —" He sighed.

"And when one is handsomely paid for it," Nin said with a grimace.

He glared at her. "I understand you're not a Christian, but you might have respect for those who were. Mrs. Taylor told me Miss Gibb was a Christian." He marched to the head of the procession.

"My mother called him a backscratcher," Nin said in a low voice. "Always eager to do things for whoever will do things for him."

"He would have fared well in the city," said Adele. "The political machines would have made his work very easy."

"It's easy enough here," Nin snorted.

Hatfield was waiting for them at the gate with his mother resting in her moveable chair. Jackson had gone on ahead with Mrs. Taylor's boarders.

"A rather dull piece of work, that man," Lady Augusta remarked as they watched the parson walking along the road a little apart from everyone else.

"And not altogether happy about his duty today," Hatfield said. "What was it Mr. Tanner said at Miss Blackstone's funeral about the social divide in small towns being even more prominent than in the big cities?"

"Not that we didn't have our share of skeptics when we first came," his mother reminded him. "But you saw to it they warmed quickly to us."

"That's different, Ma," he said. "They can't very well shun the sheriff, can they?"

As they reached the fork in the road, Adele asked, "Did you see the man in the trees?"

This made Lady Augusta laugh. "Horatio always faces away from redwoods. Their size offends him. When he was a boy, he used to shout at them how one day he would be bigger than they were." Her eyes arched in his direction. "Damn near succeeded too."

This made the sheriff turn away, his face hot and red.

"Did you see him, Lady Augusta?" asked Adele.

"I saw *something*," she admitted. "But an old woman's eyes are apt to be rather blurred."

"He was laughing." Adele shuddered.

"Maybe it was the elusive Mr. Owen Burke," Nin suggested.

"Mr. Owen Burke is hardly elusive," said the sheriff. "We discovered his place of employment easily enough, though it's odd no one seemed to know his address."

"A man needn't be hard to find to be elusive," Adele pointed out.

"How true, my dear, how true," Lady Augusta echoed.

They arrived at Mrs. Taylor's house which had a black wreath hanging on the door.

"Raleigh's special order, I see," observed the sheriff as they entered.

"The flowers are special order from the Misses Powletts." Lady Augusta's nose wrinkled as her son wheeled her into the parlor. "Lilies are an awful choice."

"Not to mention a rather romantic one." Adele nodded. "I wouldn't have thought they suited Millie."

"Mrs. Taylor's taste," said Nin. "Widows forget not every mourning is for a beloved husband."

In spite of the solemnness, the occasion felt more like an afternoon tea than a wake. The only ones who seemed to be mourning were Iona Hoddle and Mrs. Brent. Mrs. Taylor looked almost delighted to see her parlor filled with more than just her usual guests. Miss Hoddle crushed herself into a corner with her handkerchief over her face until Miss Craig coaxed her to take a glass of sherry. Mrs. Brent sat in a hard chair watching everyone with careful eyes. Her husband had less scruples and sat with Mr. Lyman discussing business and politics, but he occasionally shot worried glances in her direction.

Adele felt a wave of sympathy for the woman who had truly cared for the deceased. "Would you like a glass of sherry, Mrs. Brent?"

"No, I —" She remained silent for a moment, then spit out, "I made a mistake!"

"I beg your pardon?" Adele pulled a chair out from a corner and sat down. Nin bent down beside her.

"I shouldn't have brought so much food," she lamented.

"I'm sure Mrs. Taylor appreciated it," said Adele. "It's not easy to arrange things, and Millie was only a boarder, not a relative."

"No, you see, I was the one who volunteered to make the arrangements." She turned to her. "I wanted Millie to have a proper burial. And now look!" She sobbed inside a handkerchief.

Mr. Brent stepped toward her, but when he saw Adele put her arm around his wife's shoulders and Nin lean closer to pat her hand, he returned to his conversation with Mr. Lyman.

"Millie wouldn't have wanted everyone to be melancholy, would she?" She had no idea if this was true.

Mrs. Brent latched on to this. "No, she certainly wouldn't. She never had much joy in her life, Miss Gossling. I know you didn't know her very well, and I'm sure you thought her harsh and severe like everyone, but she didn't have an easy life."

"No woman has an easy life, in spite of what people think," Nin said.

"You're right, of course, Miss Branch," the woman said.

"Tell us about Millie — Miss Gibb," Adele said.

The woman smiled. "It's nice you call her Millie. Like a friend." She took a breath, now only too eager to talk. "She was born in San Francisco, I'm sure you know. She never spoke much about her life there, except —" she glanced down at the rather frayed parlor rug, "she wasn't a pretty girl. Homely, I think you'd call it."

"But she had other gifts," Adele put in. "I know from the girls at Mrs. Wrigley's school she was a very good English teacher."

"Then why aren't they here now?" the woman countered.

Adele knew the answer or could guess it. Mrs. Wrigley, in her rigid way of thinking about feminine manners, had decided it was best not to attend the funeral so the girls wouldn't start asking questions about their teacher's death.

"I'm sure Mrs. Wrigley would have brought them if she could," Nin offered.

"She never took the trouble to find out who Millie really was," Mrs. Brent said with a sniff. "Millie suffered, oh, indeed, she suffered!"

"It's a sad fact that girls who aren't pretty suffer in San Francisco," Adele said in a soft voice. "Especially when they have ambitions that go beyond beauty."

"Millie didn't have ambitions. Not then," said Mrs. Brent. "She said her father told her once it was better she wasn't pretty so she would never be tempted to go away and leave them." She sighed. "She was her parents' caretaker, you know."

"What a selfish man," Nin growled.

"I thought that too when Millie told me," said Mrs. Brent. "I think it was more laziness than cruelty on their part."

"And yet, she did leave them and became a teacher," Adele said. "Is that the ambition you were referring to?"

"That happened after they died," said Mrs. Brent. "She was twenty, still homely, and there were circumstances. She had no choice but to take a job as a teacher."

"What circumstances?" Curiosity got the better of Adele.

"She never told me," said Mrs. Brent. "I saw Millie didn't want to talk about it, and I didn't want to ask."

"That's very considerate of you," Nin said.

"I gathered there was some trouble, but I can't say what it

was," the woman said. "Someone got her the job as a teacher, but I don't know who."

"A friend of her parents, perhaps," Adele suggested.

"This was in Sacramento," said Mrs. Brent. "I can't think her parents would have friends there. She told me they were very isolated, rarely venturing beyond their neighborhood."

Adele pressed her hand. "Do you think Millie was happy here in Arrojo?"

"Oh, she had her moments of dissatisfaction," said Mrs. Brent. "My goodness, who doesn't?"

"But not inordinately."

"No, certainly not," said the woman. "I think she found a certain peace here."

"Yes, one comes to the country to find peace," Adele murmured, remembering her own situation. "So you don't think she was so unhappy she would have ended her life?"

The woman shot her a look. "No, Miss Gossling. I do not. I don't believe what the newspaper said."

"But she was dissatisfied?" she persevered.

"Lately, perhaps, she was a little frustrated with her job at the Wrigley School," said Mrs. Brent. "But I believe she was trying to look for another, and she must have succeeded."

"Oh?" Adele sat up. "Why do you say that?"

"I can't put my finger on it exactly." The woman's shoes slid back and forth against the rose-patterned rug, making Mrs. Taylor turn sharp eyes on her. "But she was elated about something. She came into the drugstore one day, and it was as if she were about to jump out of her own skin."

"Did she say explain why?" Adele leaned forward.

"I see it's true what they say about you being the extra eyes and ears of the law, Miss Gossling," the woman mused.

"Adele is never nosy for the sake of being nosy," Nin defended. "She wants to help." The young woman's dark eyes peered at Mrs.

Brent. "Don't you want us to find out what really happened to Miss Gibb?"

The woman was quiet for a moment. "She said she liked it here, but it wouldn't do for her, not for much longer anyway. She wasn't mean about it. She was quite calm, in fact."

"What made her come to Arrojo in the first place?" asked Adele.

"She didn't come to Arrojo at first," said Mrs. Brent. "She came to Rosa Gris to see Dr. McCabe. That's the man over there." They glanced toward the settee where Jackson was still chatting away with the professor. "Millie saw him as a father figure, the kind she would have liked, anyway. She wanted to do some work for him, but he had nothing for her. He got her the job with Mrs. Wrigley."

"Odd, a university professor knowing about an opening at a private girls' school," Nin remarked.

"I believe Mr. Wrigley and Dr. McCabe grew up in the same town," said the woman. "He and Mrs. Wrigley have been friends for years."

"He seems like a nice man." Adele glanced at him as he bent forward with Jackson, intently explaining something to him.

"Millie thought the world of him," said Mrs. Brent. "She said he's a world-renowned etmologist."

"Do you mean etymologist?" Adele asked, her ears perking.

"Yes, that's it." Mrs. Brent said. "Do you know what that is? I was too embarrassed to ask Millie."

"A word expert," said Adele. "That's what the sheriff told me."

"She did love words," Mrs. Brent said with a sigh.

"And correct grammar," Nin added.

Mr. Brent came up to them, his impassive face determined. "Eleanor, my dear, we must be getting along. The lunch rush at the drug store, you understand." He sounded almost apologetic as he glanced at the two women who had been comforting his wife.

Mrs. Brent grasped both Adele and Nin's hands. "Thank you

for listening. I was feeling as if I were the only one interested in Millie. I don't feel so alone now."

"You're not the only one, Mrs. Brent," Adele assured her. "We're very interested in Millie." She threw another look toward the settee at her brother and Dr. McCabe.

fter the Bents left, Adele expected others to make their excuses. But only the parson left, bowing to those around him without paying any particular attention to anyone. Adele and Nin watched him go with some relief, and they were not the only ones. It seemed almost as if the room relaxed after Lilly shut the door after him.

She was drawn to the little group of Mrs. Taylor's boarders near the piano, though no one dared to play any music. The two lady boarders were seated at the piano bench. Miss Hoddle seemed more composed and Miss Craig sipped daintily from her sherry glass. Mr. Walsh and Mr. Lyman stood against the piano facing them. Mr. Stoker, due to his early morning hours, was not there.

"I think it's a disgrace!" Miss Hoddle declared.

"What is?" Nin asked.

Miss Craig threw her a wary look. "Mrs. Wrigley isn't here."

"She has the school reputation to think of," Mr. Walsh pointed out. "You can't expect her to leave everything and attend a funeral."

"I agree with Iona," said Miss Craig. "This is the funeral of one of her teachers. I think it only proper she ought to have attended."

"It would be proper," Mr. Lyman sniffed into his glass of brandy, "if Millie had died a natural death."

"Natural?" Miss Hobble peered up at him.

"Yes, *that's* the thing," Mr. Walsh inserted. "An unnatural death is quite scandalous for an establishment like hers, wouldn't you say, Lyman?" He glanced at the young man, who nodded.

"I don't see why," said Miss Craig. She had her hands on the piano as if she were dying to play a waltz or a ragtime. "Millie didn't like her life, so she decided to end it. It's not as if she were *murdered*."

"The police are still trying to decide as to that, as far as I can tell," said Mr. Walsh. "Can't think why. It's open and shut, as they say in the detective stories." He gave her one of his salacious grins.

"But it isn't!"

Adele thought at first she was the only one who had heard these words coming from Miss Hoddle, as she spoke in a mumble. But she turned a little and caught Dr. McCabe's eye. He quickly averted his eyes and nodded at Jackson but Adele knew he hadn't been listening to her brother.

"What do you mean, Miss Hoddle?" she asked.

"Oh!" She looked disturbed. "Why, I didn't say anything, Miss Gossling."

"But you did," Adele said in a gentle voice. "And you're quite right saying it. It's easy for people to jump to conclusions when something like this happens, especially when they don't know the person involved very well. But *you* knew her. More than any of us here."

She gave a meaningful glance around the piano at the young faces. Some flinched while some stuck out their chin in resistance.

The rather creased but lively face of Lady Augusta appeared

next to Miss Craig. The woman looked satisfied, nodding with approval. "Go ahead, dear," she said to Miss Hoddle. "We must have all sides to the story."

This flattered the young woman. "Why, you and Miss Gossling ought to know what the police are thinking better than anyone, Lady Augusta."

"They think suicide, just like you all think," Nin spoke up.

For once, Adele was glad of the blunt slap her friend's words often delivered, which never failed to create a wave of discomfort or shock. Dr. McCabe had his eyes averted to the window. The sunlight streaked across his face, slashing it with hard, troubled lines.

"But you think differently, don't you, Miss Hoddle?" Adele tried to sound as gentle as possible. "You don't believe Millie killed herself."

"Do you?" the young woman shot out.

She was taken aback for a moment. "No. But I didn't know her."

"I'm surprised at you, Miss Gossling," Mr. Lyman said. "Miss Branch just said the police think it's suicide. I should think you would agree with them, seeing as how one of them is your brother."

"Jackson and I don't always agree, Mr. Lyman," she said. "We respect one another's opinion when we don't."

"But it's the police who decide, isn't it?" asked Mr. Walsh. "And if they think it's suicide, that means they'll close the case, and Millie's room will be available for let." He turned to his fellow boarders with a jovial look. "I know a most pleasant young woman who's looking for a place just now."

"Is that all you can think about?" Miss Hoddle slipped a handkerchief out of her pocket. "Who will occupy Millie's room?"

"Don't be sad, dear." Miss Craig put her hand on her shoulder. "She wanted to die, after all."

"I don't believe it." The girl heaved a sob. "Millie wasn't that kind of person. After all she went through in her life, she wouldn't just give up!"

"All she went through?" Lady Augusta asked. "What do you mean, child?"

"Her parents dying and leaving her without a penny and having to go to work," she said. "It isn't easy. I know."

Lady Augusta laid a jeweled hand over the young woman's. "Yes. I expect you do, dear."

Miss Hoddle rewarded the elderly woman with a grateful smile. She turned to Adele, her eyes pleading. "Miss Gossling, find out the truth, whatever it is."

"She's not the police," Mr. Lyman insisted. "You ought to be asking her brother."

"Find out the truth." The young woman's eyes captured Adele's like two bright stones.

There was something almost frightening about the way Miss Hoddle looked at her, commanding and begging at the same time. It made Adele like the young woman. She had the spark of one who was determined to see justice done for her only friend.

Adele laid her hand across the top of the piano. Even though it didn't touch Miss Hoddle's, she felt an understanding exchanged in their gaze of one another.

A touch on her elbow made her jump. Jackson was looking at her. "The sheriff wants to see you, Del. You too, Miss Branch." He held up his arm to Nin but, as usual, she ignored it.

Hatfield was settled in the comfortable chair they had used for interviews only the day before. "This is Dr. McCabe, Miss Gossling." He tapped the man's shoulder in his usual polite if pointed way.

"I've been most anxious to meet you, Miss Gossling," said the man. "Most anxious."

"It's a pleasure." She let him take her hand. "My friend, Miss Branch."

Nin gave a quick curtsy but kept both hands hidden. She despised men kissing her hand.

"Dr. McCabe has kindly consented to an interview," Hatfield continued, "but he has to be back at Rosa Gris this afternoon, so we must leave immediately. It would be most helpful to me if you and Miss Branch would take my mother home."

"We'd be delighted," said Adele, turning toward the piano.

"I was most interested in what you had to say, Miss Gossling," Dr. McCabe said. "It's a pity you won't be there so we could chat about it."

"Yes, a pity." She felt a twinge of regret but looked at the sheriff's face and saw the anxiousness in his eyes as he glanced toward his mother. "I'm sure we'll have a chance to talk some other time."

They said their farewells and parted ways, the men going toward the police station on Bridge Street while she and Nin went with Lady Augusta in the other direction to the Hatfield home.

"Poor child!" Lady Augusta sighed as she tilted her hat against the sun.

"Miss Hoddle, you mean?" Nin asked. She insisted on pushing the elderly woman and did so with the utmost delicacy and expertise.

"I hope Horatio won't be too pigheaded," said his mother.

"I'm sure he'll be fair and impartial as always," Adele assured her.

"He has his stubborn moments, dear," she said. "When he was a boy, he could take a notion to something and hold on to it for dear life." A leaf from an oak tree fell into her lap as they passed and she examined it before letting it flutter to the ground.

"And you, Lady Augusta?" asked Adele. "What do *you* believe?"

"I reserve my judgment for the time being," the woman said.

Adele smiled. "I would hardly think you don't have some view on the matter."

The woman was silent for a moment. The creak of her chair made the only sound in the pleasant, sunny day. Then, she said, "Did I ever tell you the story of the young lady Rowena knew in her youth?"

"Somehow, I can't imagine Rowena having had a youth." Adele and her friend smiled.

"My dear, she wasn't always our housekeeper," Lady Augusta chuckled. "She grew up in a very indelicate place, as a matter of fact. St. Louis or thereabouts. One of those places where families live eight or ten people to two rooms."

"You mean tenements," Adele said in a soft voice. She remembered those she had seen in San Francisco and flinched.

"In the cellar of this rat trap, as she called it," she continued, "a woman about her age lived with her aunt. Just the two of them. Quite the envy of everyone in the building, of course."

"I can imagine," Nin said dryly.

"The aunt eventually died, and the woman discovered she'd had a fortune tucked away somewhere in the gold mines of Africa."

"Indeed?" Adele raised her eyebrows.

"The niece went rather mad," Lady Augusta said. "Sold the mine, moved into some absurdly gigantic mansion where Rowena says you couldn't even hear your own voice from one end to the other. She gave elaborate parties every evening. Well, you can imagine what sort of people came to those."

"Hangers-on and parasites," Nin growled.

"Precisely." The woman nodded. "Rowena tried to reason with her, of course. But when one has spent one's youth tending someone else —" She sighed.

"What happened to her?" Adele asked.

"The hangers-on came one day for their usual hullabaloo and found the girl's body laid out very peacefully on the bed. She had turned on the gas."

"Horrible!" Nin cringed.

Lady Augusta held up her gloved hand. "Suicide can be a very mysterious thing. It may come without a moment's hesitation or a moment's anticipation."

"So you think Millie did take her own life," Nin said.

Lady Augusta's hand raked inside her handbag as she searched for the key to the gate even though Rowena was already coming down the walkway to open it for them. "In the absence of the obvious, one can only guess." She snapped her purse closed as the gate swung open before her with a squeak. "And so I reserve judgment until the police have done their duty." She shooed Nin away, now mistress of her territory, wheeling herself down the platform walkway. She spun around. "And you, my dears, must do yours."

Rowena cleared her throat. "I'll order the tea, ma'am."

"You will do no such thing," Lady Augusta snapped. "You will help me to the parlor where I shall engage in my usual nap before lunch, and these two young ladies will turn their heels around and go straight to the police station. And make haste before Horatio's chat with this doctor is over." She shooed them away.

~

The interview was still going on when they reached the station. Dr. McCabe sat across from Hatfield in the room used for interviews, an ashen look on his face and a handkerchief in his hand.

All three men's heads jerked up when she and Nin entered. Dr. McCabe was just speaking but stopped with a startled look on his face. Hatfield's lopsided smile told her he had been expecting them. Jackson looked annoyed.

"We're here at Lady Augusta's insistence," Nin said.

"If there is no objection," Adele added.

"My sister has a gnawing curiosity, Dr. McCabe, but she's

harmless enough," Jackson said. "More to the point, she and Miss Branch are discreet."

"I've no objection," the professor said.

"Dr. McCabe was just telling me he's known Miss Gibb for quite some time," Hatfield said.

"That's right," said the man. "We met through a mutual friend."

"May we have the name of this friend?" Jackson asked.

Adele did not miss the shift in the man's countenance. "The man's been dead for several years, and the family never had any contact with Millie. They could be of no use to you."

"Perhaps it's best you let us be the judge of that, sir," Jackson began but Hatfield shot him a severe look. He obeyed the silent command.

"I assume you and Miss Gibb met in some professional capacity through this friend," the sheriff said.

Dr. McCabe smiled. "I had nothing more than fatherly interest in Millie, I assure you, Sheriff."

"I wasn't suggesting you had, sir," Hatfield insisted.

"If you were, you wouldn't be the first." Dr. McCabe seemed not the least bit ruffled. "Millie never told me much about her background but I had the feeling she stopped getting along with her father at some point, and she and her mother were always at odds."

"Fathers are most important to a young woman," Adele said in a gentle voice. "Sometimes more than mothers even."

She heard Nin, whose father had left when she was barely old enough to crawl, growl. Jackson's affectionate look showed he understood what she meant.

"We had mutual professional interests, of course," said the professor. "That was chiefly why we were friends."

"What is it exactly you teach, Professor?" asked Hatfield.

"I'm not really a teacher, Sheriff. Not anymore, that is." He smiled. "I'm a linguist."

"I'm not familiar with that term," said Hatfield.

"I'm not familiar with it either," Jackson admitted.

"I would have been surprised if you had been," said Dr. McCabe. "It's a rather new idea. A linguist is a scientist of language. That's the best way I can put it."

"You mean the study of how people speak and write?" Adele asked.

"Something like that, Miss Gossling," he said. "I've always been fascinated with the origins of words. Individual words, you know, they're what really count." He sat back with pride.

"So you're an etymologist as well," she said.

He seemed delighted. "How did you know about that?"

"Millie," she said. "She told us she was going to be an etymologist someday. I gather she got the idea from you."

Dr. McCabe seemed flattered by this, as he leaned all the way into the back of the chair.

"How did Miss Gibb strike you, sir?" Hatfield asked.

"Strike me?"

"Her person, that is," he said. "When you first met her."

"Oh, she was a very serious young woman," said the professor. "Anxious to be a good teacher, of course, but more than that."

"How so?" Jackson asked.

"Soon after she started teaching at her first school, she showed me a list of improvements she thought might help students learn better," he said. "She even wrote down how much the improvements would cost and had ideas on where to get the money so the school wouldn't need to pay a penny."

"That's very unusual, isn't it?" Hatfield eyed him.

"Most unusual," said Dr. McCabe. "I wasn't very surprised, though. I knew she had managed the accounts for her family for a long time."

"It was the desire to do so that surprised you," Adele guessed. "The ambition."

"Exactly, Miss Gossling." the man admitted. "I began my

career working with the Sacramento schools. I had known many teachers and most — well, they were so overwrought, they only wished to get through the day and come home with their wits about them, never mind anything else."

"I gather she didn't get very far with her ideas," Hatfield said. "Otherwise, she wouldn't have left to come work at the Wrigley School."

Dr. McCabe gave a little smile. "You're very astute, Sheriff. I suppose someone in your position must be."

Adele liked how Hatfield always turned a slight shade of scarlet when people complimented him. Jackson had told her often enough about the arrogance of the men he had worked with when he was an Anspach who seemed to change overnight from hat-tipping gentlemen to swaggering idiots once they had a gun in their holsters. But the sheriff always stayed a gentleman in spite of his authority.

"She presented the school boards with several ideas throughout her years of teaching in Sacramento," Dr. McCabe said. "She got nowhere with them."

"So she left to take the job at the Wrigley School," Jackson said.

The man shifted in his chair. "It was more complicated than that, Deputy."

"She had plans other than teaching," Adele guessed.

"Plans with words," Nin added.

The professor smiled. "We spoke about it, yes."

"That puts you in a unique position to know much more about her than anyone else we've spoken to so far, sir." Hatfield leaned forward.

"What did you speak about, Dr. McCabe?" asked Adele.

"She wanted to study with me."

Silence filled the room, punctuated by Edison's coughing fit outside the room.

"She wanted to be an etymologist?" Jackson inquired.

"Follow in your footsteps, so to speak," said the sheriff.

The man couldn't hide a smile. "I'm the only one in California at the moment."

"Millie would have made two," Nin said.

"Yes," said the professor. "She would have." He clutched his handkerchief.

"That would have cost money," said Hatfield. "Is that why she left Sacramento for Mrs. Wrigley? Because she was offered a higher salary."

"Primarily, yes," said Dr. McCabe. "And she wanted to be nearer to me. I can't say an old man isn't flattered by that."

"I don't blame her," said Adele. "If I were in her position, I would have left too."

"She couldn't have saved very much in only a year," said Jackson. "We can check with the bank, of course."

"Oh, but everything was settled," said Dr. McCabe. "At least partially. That's what we spoke about the last time we met, Sheriff."

"When was this?"

"A week or so ago," said the professor in a sad voice. "She was so happy she was finally going to come study under me, It's what she had wanted for years."

Hatfield rubbed his chin. "She actually told you this?"

"Not in so many words," the professor admitted.

"But that was your impression?" Jackson asked. "She was going to leave the Wrigley School and join you at the university. You're sure of this?"

Dr. McCabe was thoughtful for a moment. "It was almost as if —"

"As if what?" Adele felt a flutter in her chest.

"As if she were finally going to get what she deserved," the man finished.

Adele looked at the floor, which was meticulously dust-free.

Its gray blocks shone glossy in the light. "Or someone else was going to get their just deserts."

"I beg your pardon, miss?" the man asked.

She looked up. "What did she actually say, Dr. McCabe?"

"She didn't *say* anything really," said the man. "She asked a lot of questions."

"Oh?" Jackson steadied his pencil.

"She wanted to know if she were to move to Rosa Gris, would she need to rent a room or could she stay with me," he said. "It seemed an odd question. So calculating."

"Calculating?" Jackson asked.

"Yes. I could see her mind working," said the professor with a smile. "Millie had a precise nature. That would have served her well as a scientist," he added in a sad tone.

"What was she calculating? Money?" asked Nin.

Both Jackson and Hatfield glanced at her, but the professor seemed very interested.

"Well, yes," he said. "I told her that, naturally, I couldn't accommodate her in my bachelor quarters, but I knew a boarding house for ladies not far from the university. She asked the price, and when I told her, she said, 'Two hundred more. That should do it. Two hundred more.'"

"Dollars?"

"I don't know, sir." Dr. McCabe shrugged. "I didn't think it was my place to ask."

"Did she say anything else?" asked the sheriff.

"She promised she would see me very soon." The man looked somber. "I didn't think it would be like this!"

"And all this was a week ago?" Adele asked.

"A week, maybe a little more," said the man.

"And her mood?" Adele bent forward, feeling her skirt crumpling against the table, not caring that Ruth would later reprimand her for being careless with her dress. "Would you say she was happy?"

"Yes," Dr. McCabe said in a firm voice. He turned to the sheriff. "You must see now how the thought of Millie committing suicide is absurd."

"A lot can happen in a week, sir," Jackson pointed out. "A woman's whole life can change in a week."

"And the sky could fall in a week," Nin snapped. "A hurricane could sweep us all into the arms of fate in an hour."

"There are no hurricanes in California, Miss Branch," Jackson said in a wry voice.

"An earthquake, then," Nin said. "You don't deny California's swallowing ground, do you, Mr. Gossling?"

"We won't debate the caprices of Mother Nature." Hatfield's voice rang through the room with such sharpness that even Edison with his typewriter outside the door jerked his head up, his fingers frozen over the machine with alarm.

"I apologize," Jackson said, though it was clear his apology was more directed toward his employer than Nin.

"We thank you for taking the time to speak with us." The sheriff rose and the others followed. "We know how difficult this has been for you."

"I'm a scientist, sir." Dr. McCabe gathered his hat and gloves. "As a scientist, I don't like loose ends. I feel those people today were making some foul assumptions about Millie. If I can help dispel those assumptions —"

"We'll see, Dr. McCabe," Hatfield said.

Though it wasn't the first time the sheriff was evasive, it was the first time Adele felt uncomfortable about it.

CHAPTER 17

There wasn't much left of the day by the time they emerged from the station. There were few horses and wagons on Bridge Street and one automobile — Mr. Duncan's — parked in an alley near the post office.

Nin stared at it, her eyes glassy. She stopped and grabbed Adele's arm with such force that Adele drew in her breath. "She was elated!"

"You mean Millie?" Adele asked.

"She was dancing in her room with her arms flying out."

Adele put her arm around the woman's shoulders. "You've had a feeling?"

"A fleeting one," said Nin. "It's been trying to come through all morning, ever since we left the cemetery. I felt it but I wasn't sure —"

"And it's telling you Millie was elated?" Adele inquired.

"She was almost in a state of hysteria." The woman shivered.

Adele had never seen her friend this way. She was shaking and her hands were cold. Adele steered her toward her shop and set her down on a chair. She gave her a glass of water and the shaking stopped.

Nin clasped her hands. "I didn't mean to frighten you."

"I was more concerned than frightened," said Adele with a smile.

The woman threw her arms around her, then drew back and let out a little laugh. "I used to scare even Mama sometimes."

"I think you ought to keep your place closed today," said Adele. "Go and rest."

Nin rose, slow but steady on her feet. "I need air. I need the woods."

Adele understood. There was a place not far away with redwoods and brush Nin had shown her not long after they became acquainted. Her mother had gone there to collect most of her herbs, and it was where Nin felt her mother's spirit the strongest.

Adele had a steady flow of people for the rest of the day, though she knew they came more to ask questions about Millie's funeral. They were especially inquisitive about whether the schoolteacher's family and friends had attended and when Adele admitted none had, they looked almost satisfied. She was no longer angry at their insensitivity. Sadness clung to every part of her, making her feel heavy and tired.

No one was keener to her moods than Jackson. She felt his eyes on her that evening as they retired to the parlor after dinner. She had hardly eaten anything, even under Tomas' gentle prodding. Everything sat in her stomach like lead with the same dragging sensation she had been feeling all day.

She sat with her lacework, something she had begun from her first days in Arrojo because she had some vague idea she had to show at least a little domestic aptitude. She had barely gotten past a few rows since she started. Now she made one row of heart-shaped loops in the pattern and started poking the needle through it.

"You're going to ruin that before it gets finished," Jackson said quietly.

"Bother!" She tossed it aside, and the needle slid out of the thread and hit the wooden floor with a clank.

"Are you going to have a temper tantrum now?" He regarded her with amusement, pipe and San Francisco paper in hand.

"Maybe I should," she growled. "It would at least be doing *something!*"

"You'd scare the Cordovas out of their wits." He grinned. "Tomas would think we were having a devil of a row."

"Then I'll go down to Bridge Street and have my tantrum in the middle of the road," Adele declared.

Jackson laughed. "So you're upset at a street, not a person?" He lit his pipe.

"Correction," she said, "many people. All they wanted to know was whether anyone who knew Millie had come to the funeral and they looked so smug when I told them no."

"You didn't have to tell them anything, Del."

"I'm not a liar, Jack," she snapped.

"I suppose if Millie were a man, you would you have been more tolerant of their insensitivity." He eyed her.

"If Millie had been a man, they wouldn't have asked!"

He toyed with the edge of the newspaper. "I shouldn't have thought you would be so sympathetic, Del."

"A woman's life was stolen from her," Adele said. "A woman whom we now know had ambitions."

"Perhaps she stole her own life," Jackson pointed out.

"Don't start that again." She glared at him.

"Millie's life ended too soon and that is upsetting," he agreed. "It's upsetting when anyone, woman or man, has their flame snuffed out before its time. We can only do them justice in this life. They're responsible for justice in the next."

"And *will* you and Hatfield do Millie justice?" She picked at the afghan on the back of the couch.

"We intend to."

Adele found the lace half slid under the coffee table and took it up again. "Nin had a feeling this afternoon."

"Indeed?"

"This one was quite serious."

"And what was her feeling this time?"

"She said Dr. McCabe was right."

"Right about what? That Millie didn't commit suicide?" He cocked his head. "You've been telling us that from the beginning. Perhaps she was just tuning into your sentiments."

Adele looked to the window. "This is was quite sudden and a little alarming."

"I prefer to believe it was an echo." He chewed on the edge of his pipe.

"You must admit, Jack, Nin's readings have been accurate," Adele pointed out. "A little vague at times, but they never steered you in the wrong direction. Even Hatfield has respect for them."

"Hatfield is more open-minded than I am," he said. "I never denied that. Maybe it's his age and experience that make him so. I believe in following more logical routes. Many lawmen have had a great success that way."

He watched while she tried to untangle the lace thread that had wound itself through one of the loops. "Hatfield is sending me to Sacramento tomorrow."

"You're going to see Mr. Burke?" She sat up.

"I'm going to try," he said. "We're hoping Mr. Burke will be cooperative." He was quiet for a moment. "I thought it would be nice to have some company."

It took her a moment to realize what he was saying. She leapt from the chair and threw her arms around his shoulders. "How early does the train leave?"

He laughed. "I thought that would cheer you up."

"Provided Hatfield agrees, of course," she said with caution.

"I asked him this afternoon," said Jackson. "He thought it was a good idea."

"You're a treasure, Jack." She playfully pinched his cheek. "And so is Hatfield."

"Don't let him know that!"

Tomas was hovering near the entrance to the parlor in his usual discreet way, holding the hand of Ana, the youngest of the Cordova children, who was somewhat infatuated with Jackson. Adele caught the five-year-old's sulky little face, knowing she was envious of her brother's affection toward his sister. But when she held out her arms to the girl, the sulk broke into a smile.

~

They left on the seven o'clock train. Tomas insisted they have coffee and toast even though they told him they would breakfast on the train. He made clear he did not approve of empty stomachs on a long and dusty train ride.

She sat back in the red velvet Pullman, content to look out the window at the passing scenery while Jackson, having snatched up all the Sacramento papers he could find, read. They were the only ones in the car and the quiet rumble made Adele feel calm and contemplative.

At nine o'clock, they entered the dining car for breakfast, laughing and joking back and forth with one another.

"Perhaps we oughtn't to tell Tomas the coffee is much stronger than Ruth's," Jackson said as he signaled the waiter for a fresh pot. "He's so terribly sensitive about his wife's cooking, we don't want to upset him."

"They're good people," Adele said with a sigh. "You're always complaining I'm too friendly but you don't seem to have any trouble with my friendliness toward *them*."

"That's different, Del," he said. "We must be fair and kind to those who work for us. Strangers are an entirely different thing."

"I recall times when you brought strangers home for breakfast after one of your nightly sojourns," she pointed out. "And some looked a little shifty."

This brought an immediate shadow to his face against the light from the dining car window. "I was a foolish young man then."

"I don't know," she said. "Some of them were quite interesting. I think even Papa lingered on beyond his usual time because he was so enthralled by what they had to say."

"It was a fool's gesture," he insisted. "I wish you wouldn't remind me of it."

"'Folly brings an open window to one's soul,'" she quoted.

He stared at her. "Where did you hear that?"

"I read it," she said. "You might be surprised where."

He put his hand under his chin. "I like surprises when they're pleasant ones."

"Millie's work," she said. "When I was looking over one of the girls' papers, I saw she had written it at the bottom of the page. I thought it odd at the time." Her face wrinkled.

"Perhaps she was referring to something the class had read," Jackson suggested.

"It was a paper on a poem about Helen of Troy," she said. "It was written as if a thought had suddenly struck Millie, and she had to write it down. I don't know it was even intended for the girl."

"You're telling me you think it has something to do with her death, I suppose?" He eyed her sharply. "Really, Del, you have no sense of method. You don't look for random pieces when you're investigating someone's death. You look for connections between them."

"Why, then, are you going to speak to a man who saw Millie a few weeks ago and knew her only slightly?"

Her brother rolled the small spoon that lay in the saucer back and forth like a boat. He said in a rather sheepish voice, "Because we're desperate. In most cases, there are friends or family, people who knew something about the victim's life. Millie's parents are long gone."

"And this cousin who bled her for money?"

"Hatfield had a conversation with him," said Jackson. "He had no idea Millie was even working at a private girls' school."

"And no other relatives?"

"None that we could find." Adele sighed as he went on. "She had no friends, save Mrs. Brent and Miss Hoddle, both of whom knew only bits and pieces of her life."

Adele nodded. "I shouldn't think a woman like Millie would have been very forthcoming with details from her past."

"She didn't even have a relationship with the other teachers at the school," Jackson reminded her.

"What of Dr. McCabe?"

"He saw her infrequently, Del. They're not exactly in the same class."

Adele pushed her cup and saucer away from the edge of the table and rested her elbows on it, a gesture that always annoyed her brother. "Millie seems to have isolated herself from the world deliberately."

"Perhaps she simply wasn't very social," said her brother.

"You forget, Jack, it's expected of ladies to be social, even unmarried ones," she said gently.

"But some ladies have more opportunities to develop their social skills than others," he said. "You, for example, have always had a lively disposition. I've been told by several young men, including your intended —"

"John Bellows is *not* my intended," Adele insisted.

"I've been told," Jackson continued with an amused smile, "you have prettiness and grace enough for any man to enjoy your company."

"I would rather they say I have intelligence and wit," Adele said dryly.

"Oddly, they never mentioned either of those."

Adele rewarded him with a kick under the table. "Are you implying Millie was missing qualities that would have allowed her to develop her social skills?"

"She didn't have your opportunities," he pointed out. "From what we know, she was rather put upon by her mother and father. She took care of them for most of her adult life. That would leave little time for socializing, whatever society might have offered her."

"But afterward," said Adele. "After they died, I mean. She might have blossomed."

"She had to work, Del," he said in a gentle voice.

She looked down at the table. The black marble reflected back her face like a mirror. "Yes, that's true," she said in a soft voice. "A woman who must earn her living in earnest has little time to see people." She looked up. "But we mustn't misjudge Millie's death by her life."

"As others have?" He raised an eye.

"As others might," she answered.

The train arrived late in Sacramento. They found a cab and the horse clumped through the streets to the more industrial side of town. The crowds of people thinned out, replaced by workmen hauling packages, sliding as they walked. Adele did not see one woman on the street.

The Bain Publishing Company was an anomaly among the industrial companies that surrounded it. It was a small place caught between the bolder Sacramento Trade Company and Fowler and Sons Shipping. But the slim two-story building with the scroll-like pillars at the front entrance held its own against the two giants twice as tall and wide.

Here, at least, Adele saw women, or, rather, one woman. As they entered, an operator sat at the switchboard. She looked already frazzled even though the office could not have been open for more than a few hours. She wore the kind of sensible clothes Adele had seen on office girls from the settlement houses. Her shirtwaist blouse and skirt showed signs of withering from the heat in the small room. Already a few curls escaped her pinned hair. She seemed to have the hands of an octopus, one ready to connect the caller she was speaking to while the other was already picking up a new plug to put inside the peg lit up with another call.

Jackson smiled at her and held up his hand to show they could wait. She smiled back and Adele did not miss the spark in her eye as the woman continued to look at Jackson sideways.

The large mahogany doors opposite the switchboard opened and a man came out. He immediately radiated authority despite his young age, as his blond hair had a natural shine even under the dull lights, and his suit was impeccable. He had blue eyes the same color as the suit, narrowed a little like a hound always on the lookout for a fox.

"Good morning," he said in a cordial voice. "May I help you?"

"We wish to see Mr. Owen Burke," said her brother.

The man blinked as if he were trying to recall the name. Adele heard a breath behind her. On an impulse, she dropped her handkerchief on the floor. She turned and caught a glimpse of the woman at the switchboard. There was no mistaking her confused expression.

The man snatched up her handkerchief, blocking the view of the switchboard. He held it out to her.

"Thank you," she murmured.

"May I ask your business with Mr. Burke?"

"May I ask who *you* are, sir?" Jackson returned in an even tone.

"Perhaps we should talk in my office," said the man. "I don't want to disturb Miss Taper in her work."

Adele glanced at the young woman who was wiping her hands with a piece of cloth in her lap as discreetly as she could. Adele found herself saying, "A switchboard and front office are a lot for one woman to handle."

The young man gave her an odd look, but, to her surprise, he nodded. "You're quite right, Miss —"

"Gossling, Miss Adele Gossling," she said.

"I'm Huey Bain Jr." He held his hand out to Jackson, then

kissed Adele's, which she thought too decorative. He leaned one elbow against the high desk. "You see that space over there?" He motioned toward the opposite side of the small room which did indeed contain a generous space. "Next week, we're having a desk put in. I've just hired a girl to take over the reception so Miss Taper can be left to the telephones, as she's rather good with callers." He threw an admiring glance at the young woman who had just taken a call. "I'm looking for a seasoned secretary for my own office." His eyes sparkled. "You don't happen to know of anyone, do you?"

Adele was taken aback. She held one hand on the handle of her purse, the other on handle of her parasol.

Jackson looked impressed that someone caused his sister to be speechless for once. "We don't live in Sacramento, sir. We're from Arrojo."

"I see," said the young man. "My office?" He ushered them through the large wooden doors.

The office was clearly meant to impress. Adele gathered an architect had been hired during the last century who had lavished it with the latest styles but the decor had not been renewed since. The carpet made a scratching sound under her heels and when she looked down at its foliage pattern, she felt as if she were stepping around an unkept garden. Although the space was ample, it seemed almost as if every part of the room was crowded with furnishings, most of which matched the mahogany doors. She imagined twenty years ago when the office would have been at the height of fashion, a woman with a bustle would have been challenged to move around. Two walls held only bookcases with books encased in glass. There were no pictures on the walls save a rather solemn portrait of an older man with thinning white hair and the same straight glare and blue foxhound eyes as the young man.

"I've never been to Arrojo," Mr. Bain said, "but, of course, our salesmen have. It's in our territory."

"I'm from the police." Jackson took out his deputy badge and held it up for the man to see. "I gather you're the owner of this company?"

The young man moved some papers around on the desk. "Only recently. My father died two years ago."

"I'm sorry to hear that, sir," said Jackson.

"Thank you, Deputy," said Mr. Bain. "Since Miss Taper is so busy, may I offer you coffee or tea?"

"Very kind of you, no," Adele said.

"A glass of water, then? It's very hot today, isn't it?" He glanced around the room.

"Perhaps if you opened a window," she suggested.

Mr. Bain chuckled. "I'm afraid, Miss Gossling, opening a window in this part of town lets in more smoke than air."

"My sister and I won't take up much of your time," Jackson said in a decisive manner.

"I don't think I've ever heard of a deputy bringing his sister to an interview." He glanced past Adele's shoulder, and she realized he was looking at the painting on the wall behind her.

"My sister is no ordinary woman," said Jackson. "I assure you, we have the cooperation of the Sacramento police, if you care to contact them."

"I wasn't questioning it, Deputy, merely commenting on the unusual circumstance." Mr. Bain pushed the papers aside and folded his hands on the desk. "Of course, I'm happy to answer any questions."

"You must be quite a bookworm, Mr. Bain," Adele commented as she glanced at the glass-encased books.

"We *are* a publishing company, Miss Gossling," he said. "My father liked to have a copy of all our books where he could see them."

"*All* of them?" She laid the parasol against the side of the couch.

"Well, a good many of them," he said.

"What sort of books do you publish?" Jackson removed his pad and pencil from his jacket pocket.

"If you'd like to use my desk, Deputy —"

"I'm perfectly fine here, sir," said Jackson.

Mr. Bain sat down again. "We deal mostly in educational material," said the young man. "Schoolbooks, instructional guides, scholarly magazines, that sort of thing."

"I can see why Mr. Burke and Miss Gibb had much in common," Adele remarked.

He leaned forward. "Mr. Burke and who?"

"Miss Millie Gibb," said Jackson. "She's the reason we're here. She was found dead a few days ago."

"Oh!" The young man's alarm was fleeting. He picked up a lighter sitting on a mahogany box and began rolling it between his palms. "I thought you were here about Mr. Burke."

"We're here to talk to Mr. Burke in connection with Miss Gibb," Jackson corrected.

"As his employer, I believe I have a right to ask why," said Mr. Bain. "It might reflect on the company, you see."

"I understand your concern, sir," said Jackson. "Mr. Burke was in Arrojo staying at a Mrs. Taylor's boarding house for a week while on business, and we've been told he and Miss Gibb became quite friendly."

Mr. Bain held the lighter in both hands now, peering at it as if looking at a small bird. "I would hardly think so, Deputy."

"Why is that, Mr. Bain?" Adele asked.

"He was there on business, Miss Gossling." He snapped the lighter open and then snapped it shut again. "Mr. Burke was a salesman and salesmen — well, chatting up potential clients is part of their forte."

"Your knowledge of that aspect of your company is admirable," said Jackson. "I've known young men who had a business fall into their hands who hadn't even the first knowledge of how many employees worked for them."

"I haven't always sat behind this desk," Mr. Bain said with a faint smile. "My father hired me as a salesman on salary when I was eighteen." He leaned forward, addressing Adele. "So you see, I know it's not easy selling educational materials, not like soap or jewelry. Sometimes a salesman has to be more amiable than he might wish to get anywhere. It's the nature of the beast, as they say." He turned to Jackson. "I'm sure you sometimes have to use more convincing methods than you'd like to get information. It's not always a pleasant task but it is a necessary one."

"My brother and the sheriff never use violence, sir," Adele said in a sharp voice.

"I would never suggest that, Miss Gossling," he assured her.

"I believe I understood Mr. Bain's meaning, Del," Jackson said. "However, everyone in Mrs. Taylor's house knew Miss Gibb, and they say she showed a special interest in Mr. Burke. They all agree the feeling seemed mutual."

Mr. Bain laid down the lighter on the leather blotter. "I don't wish to be indiscreet in front of a lady, but Mr. Burke *is* a single man, Deputy. And if this Miss Gibb was pretty —"

"She was neither pretty nor young, at least most men wouldn't think so, sir," Adele said.

Mr. Bain chuckled. "Miss Gossling, Mr. Burke is neither handsome nor young himself. That might explain a lot of things."

"We'd like to see that for ourselves." Jackson cocked his head.

Mr. Bain leaned forward. "I'm afraid you've come at an inopportune time. We just sent Mr. Burke to the Arizona territory. We're trying to establish an office there."

"He must be quite a salesman," Jackson remarked.

"One of our best," said the young man. "My father put his trust in him and so do I. That's why I sent him."

"And when will he return?" asked Jackson.

"Not for some time. I could call him back, of course, if it's urgent."

Adele had been watching the young man. He seemed inordinately preoccupied with the lighter, placing it in one hand and then transferring it to the other as if he were trying to guess its weight.

"That's a very attractive little thing, Mr. Bain," she remarked.

He gave her a faint smile. "It was a gift from my father just before he died."

She held out her hand. "May I see it?"

It was clear the young man was not pleased but Adele relied on his obvious breeding not to refuse her.

He deposited the lighter in her gloved hand. The pattern on the silver was carved into ostrich feathers shaped like a fan, and the bar at the top was smooth. When Adele pressed down on it with her thumb, it made a pleasant sound as the flame rose up.

"Pretty little thing," she murmured as she handed it back to him.

"I'm glad you think my father had good taste." Mr. Bain put it on top of the cigar box. "*Do* you want me to call Mr. Burke back, Deputy? If so, I'll send a telegram this very afternoon."

"That might be wise," said Jackson. "I'll need his address as well."

Adele could see a visible flush in Mr. Bain's cheeks.

"You do have employee addresses, don't you, sir?" Jackson asked in a careful voice.

"We do, sir." Mr. Bain stiffened. "But they're confidential."

"Even to the police?" Adele eyed him.

"I'm afraid so, Miss Gossling. My father absolutely insisted on that, and I won't go against his wishes." He straightened the blotter on his desk. "If you would like to speak to the man, as I said before, I'll be glad to contact him."

Jackson was clearly annoyed. "Don't you think it's rather more important than that, sir?"

"If it were," said the young man, "you would have brought a warrant with you." He rose. "Is there anything else I can help you with?"

"One more question, sir." Jackson remained firmly in his chair. "We need to check whether Mr. Burke sold anything to Miss Gibb. We found a few things in her room that look as if they could have come from your company."

"We're hardly the only press that publishes such things," said Mr. Bain. "If Miss Gibb worked as a teacher, she would have had many such books from many companies."

Something pricked Adele's eyes, and she realized Mr. Bain had parted the curtains. The sun was glaring through the slit. "How did you know she was a teacher, Mr. Bain?"

The young man looked startled, blinking at the ray of light hitting the shiny desk. "Most of our clients are teachers, Miss Gossling. You see, I know my business." He snapped the curtains closed. "I'll be happy to check Mr. Burke's sales slips. If he sold anything to Miss Gibb, the receipts will be there."

"Didn't your father insist on confidentiality with those too?" Adele asked in an arch tone.

"Only from our competitors, Miss Gossling." The young man bowed. "If you'll pardon me for a moment. Are you sure I can't get you anything while I'm out? That cup of coffee, perhaps?" He blinked at her.

Adele shook her head. He bowed again and left the room, closing the doors after him.

She let out a breath the moment he was gone. The office felt less oppressive now that she and her brother were left alone. "Not a very cheerful room, is it?" Her eyes fell to the portrait on the wall. "A rather intimidating man, I would say."

"He was generous to his son." Jackson crossed his legs. "A father doesn't hand over a business to a man that young unless he's confident he can run it."

"I have no doubt he can run it." Adele rose. "Like a well-oiled machine."

"I can see I don't have to ask you what you think of Mr. Bain," her brother grinned.

She wandered to the bookshelves. She couldn't read the titles through the glass which was less polished than she had first thought. The tip of her parasol crushed against the rug as she tried to find a way to open the glass doors, fussing with the handle. But they would neither slide nor pull back. Annoyed, she swung around and caught sight of the large desk and plopped herself right inside the chair Mr. Bain had vacated.

"Del!" Her brother's voice made his discomfort clear.

"I'm not the police, dear brother," she reminded him. "I don't need a warrant."

"Nevertheless, it's not very dignified to nose around a man's things," he said.

"I'm merely interested in a young businessman's office."

"You ought to know," he said dryly. "You help young businessmen decorate them."

"I would hardly call this one decorative," she sniffed.

There was nothing of real interest on Mr. Bain's desk. It looked like any other with papers, an ink-streaked blotter, a steel paperweight that looked as if it had been given as a gift and used for the sake of economy, and a holder with pens and various small equipment. Everything was in its place with the perfect symmetry of one who checked it every morning to make sure nothing had been moved.

"Mr. Bain must be terribly fussy," she remarked.

"A tidy desk doesn't necessarily translate to fussiness," said her brother.

"It's not the tidiness, Jack," she said. "It's the suspiciousness."

He gave her a quick look.

"Would you notice if Edison went to your desk to borrow a pen and moved the rubber stamp in the middle instead of the corner?" She gave him a meaningful look. "I'm sure Mr. Bain would."

"Well, some men are like that," he said.

She turned to more interesting items. There were two silver

framed pictures, one of a woman with a boy sitting in her lap and another with the same woman but much older. She was an attractive lady, though it was clear even in her youth she had looked middle-aged. The boy, she imagined, was Mr. Bain as a child. He too already had the look of a man in his boyish face underneath the smooth features.

She could examine the cigar box from up close. It had the same feathered pattern as the lighter. Adele ran her finger over the embossed cover. "He ought to have at least offered you a cigar," she said in an even voice.

"You know I only smoke a pipe," he said, a little amused.

"That doesn't mean he shouldn't have offered you one."

She opened the box. It was filled three-quarters of the way with cigars that had black skins and were pointed like long bullets. Sitting in its own encased corner was the silver lighter.

"I wonder when Mr. Bain had a chance to slip it back in," she mused. "I didn't see him do it. Did you?"

"I think it best if you come away from there, Del," said Jackson. "He's bound to come any moment."

But as was usually the case, when she had her eye on something, she was loath to let it go. She took out the lighter and examined it more closely than she had before.

"Not a very big one, is it?" she remarked. "And very lightweight."

"Del, put that down." She knew by the tone in her brother's voice he had come to the end of his tolerance.

"He didn't object before when I asked to see it," she insisted.

"But he didn't like it," said her brother. "And I can't say I blame him. A man's lighter is a very personal thing."

"Apparently," she said with a wry smile. She had already seen the engraving on the bottom of it. It was more of a heavy scratch really, as if done more with passion than elegance: *M, with love, H.* "An admirer, no doubt," she remarked as she held it out to him.

There was a flash and her hand gave way. She thought for a

moment her brother was now as interested in the lighter as she was and wanted to examine it himself. But she realized Mr. Bain was gripping her wrist. His previous cordiality vanished and his face was contorted with rage like a wax figure melting in a fire.

"How dare you!"

She heard her brother's quiet but dangerous voice. "I suggest you take your hands off my sister."

The young man dropped her hand and collapsed into the nearest chair. "Forgive me, Miss Gossling. I don't know what came over me."

She gently laid the lighter down on top of the cigar case. "It was my fault, Mr. Bain. My brother warned me a man's lighter is a very personal thing."

Jackson gave her a stern look. "Your curiosity will get the better of you one day, Del."

"Like the cat," she remarked as she took her position on the couch again. For once, she was glad of an overstuffed cushion to comfort her. "Maybe like the cat, I too have nine lives. If so, I'm sure I've used up at least two and a half of them."

This made Mr. Bain's rage disappear. "The lighter was my father's, you see."

"Yes," Jackson said. "You've already explained that."

"Your father's name was Huey as well?" Adele asked.

He blinked at her. "How did you know?"

"The 'H' carved on the bottom," she said. She wanted to ask who "M" was but knew she had dared enough for one day.

"Did you find what you were looking for, Mr. Bain?" Jackson changed the subject. "You were rather a long time."

"Yes, I'm sorry about that." The young man laid a large book he had been carrying on the arm of the couch. "Mr. Burke sold a subscription of *American Language Origins* and a book titled *Fundamentals of English In Our Times* to a Miss Millicent Gibb on January twentieth."

Jackson consulted his notes. "That fits our information about when Mr. Burke was in Arrojo."

"I'll assume you need nothing more from me." Mr. Bain closed the book with a resolute slap, one Adele felt was filled more with relief than finality.

"Not at the present moment, sir." Jackson picked up the stick he always carried as well as the gloves he had set aside on the arm of the couch. "I hope, of course, you'll be available if we have further questions."

"Naturally." The young man already had his hand on the doorknob.

The switchboard quiet, Miss Taper was putting on her hat and gloves while a scraggly-looking woman sat in her place.

Mr. Bain leaned against the counter. "Going to lunch, Miss Taper?"

"Yes, sir," mumbled the young woman.

"The Blue Goat, no doubt?" He raised a knowing eye at Jackson as if the two shared a manly secret.

"What a funny name," Adele remarked.

"It's a funny place, miss," said the young woman. "I mean, it's a nice place with lots of good people going there."

"I'm sure it has," she said with a smile.

"Now, Miss Taper, you just make sure you're sitting with good people," said Mr. Bain. "Lots of older men looking for young pretty girls like yourself to make their lunch hour more interesting."

Adele's annoyance with the man grew as she saw the young woman blush. "Have you ever been there, Mr. Bain?"

"Why, no."

"Then it's hardly fair for you to judge it, is it?"

He bowed. "You're right, of course, Miss Gossling. I don't know the place. But I have an imagination." He turned to Miss Taper. "I don't mean to insinuate you're that kind of girl, Miss Taper. But, well, it's the men I'm thinking about. You know how it is in the city — a young, unmarried woman lunching with an older man, even if they're simply sitting next to one another, causes talk."

One of Miss Taper's eyes appeared sharper than the other. "Thank you for the advice, Mr. Bain. I'll be very careful." She nodded at the Gosslings and headed for the door.

"Have a good lunch, Miss Taper," Adele called after her.

The young woman glanced back and gave her a pleasant smile.

When she was gone, Mr. Bain looked at her. "I suppose you think I was rather severe."

"Actually, I think you were rather too personal," Adele said.

The man considered this. "My mother does charity work with such girls, and most of the young women working here come from her. I suppose I think of them as my responsibility."

Jackson glanced at the watch on his chain. "Del, we don't want to miss the train." He took a card from his coat pocket. "You'll let me know when Mr. Burke is back in town?"

The young man nodded as he bid them both good day and disappeared behind the mahogany doors.

They had just time to catch the afternoon train and settle in for the ride back to Arrojo.

"All right, Del," said her brother in an amused voice. "Let's have it."

Ever since they were children, Jackson had a sense for her moods. It was a quality she had come to appreciate since they had been in Arrojo.

"Oh, the arrogance! The ghastly nerve of the man!" She pushed her parasol on top of the seat beside her so hard, it fell to the floor with a clatter.

"You must admit, Del, you had no right to touch his things," said Jackson. "I don't know that I blame him for reacting so violently."

"Violent is right," she said. "I still feel his grip on my wrist."

Her brother eyed her. "I have a feeling it's less about his grip and more about his lecture to that telephone operator."

"An employer has no right to dig into an office worker's personal life," she said with a sniff. "I should have been quick to reproach him if it had been me."

"I have no doubt," mumbled her brother.

"I noticed you didn't seem surprised either," she said with a wary smile.

"Not that I condone it," he assured her.

"Do you believe what he said about Mr. Burke, Jack?" Adele adjusted the blanket the porter had given her. "About being away and all that?"

"Apparently, you didn't." He folded his gloves in his lap.

"It's rather convenient, isn't it?" she asked. "This Mr. Burke being away just when Millie's death is making the papers."

"What are you suggesting, Del?"

His sister looked out the window, folding her hands in her lap. "I don't know that I'm suggesting anything," she admitted. "Except I feel there is something to suggest."

He chuckled. "Circle talk, Del." But he knew better than to try and dissuade her.

CHAPTER 19

They reached Arrojo in the early evening. Adele swung her head back to look at the sky as they walked home. The violet and blue shadows behind the clouds always filled her with the peace she had sought after her father died three years ago.

"Hatfield wanted a report of our trip the moment we arrived," Jackson said.

"Do you mind if I come along?" Adele asked.

Jackson shrugged. "I'm sure Lady Augusta will be happy to see you."

Adele was happy to receive the warm smile from the woman, who sat with her son in the parlor. Rowena, Lady Augusta's companion and housekeeper, was nowhere to be found.

"She's gone to help Mrs. Taylor serve dinner to her guests," said Lady Augusta. "It seems one of the servants there —"

"Lilly?" Adele asked.

"No, no, the other one, the one who looks like a mangy dog," said the woman, waving her hand.

"Sally," she said with a smile.

"She went in a swoon this afternoon," the elderly woman

continued. "She was washing dishes, or doing some such drudgery, when she saw Miss Gibb's ghost floating out of the pantry. It looked straight at her, or so she says. And just to add color to the story, the ghost had the face of Miss Gibb in death, not in life."

"Scullery maids have wild imaginations," Jackson said.

"It's not entirely imagination," said Sheriff Hatfield. "It seems she caught a glimpse of Miss Gibb's face when the men took the body to the morgue."

"The poor girl," Adele said.

"Horatio! You should never have allowed it. That was most careless." Lady Augusta hit him in the leg with her cane.

"I've already reprimanded Edison about that, Ma," Hatfield assured her. "I also had a chat with Dr. Rhodes." The last he said with a grim smile.

"I hope you weren't too hard on him," said Adele. "Edison, I mean."

"As hard as the law requires," said Lady Augusta with her eye on her son. "I believe sometimes Horatio forgets he's no longer the captain of his own ship."

Hatfield looked away.

Adele rose. "If Rowena is out, you've no one to make tea. I'll be glad to do it."

"Nonsense. Horatio!" The blast came out in the scratchy command. "Make tea for our guests."

"I'd be happy to, Ma." He slid his chair back.

"I'll go," Adele insisted.

"I don't mean to interfere," said Jackson in a light voice, "but Del makes a fine cup of tea, sir."

"Better than mine, I'm sure," Hatfield said with a lopsided grin.

Adele made the tea as quickly as she could, as she knew her brother was already telling Hatfield of their trip in Sacramento, and she wanted to hear what he would say about Mr. Bain.

As she came in with the tea tray, she heard Hatfield ask, "So he struck you as the usual sort of businessman?"

"The usual sort of a certain *type* of businessman," Jackson corrected.

"We didn't see Mr. Burke." Adele accepted Lady Augusta shooing her away so she could play hostess and pour the tea. "Mr. Bain told us he was away."

"But he offered to send a wire to call him back and arrange a meeting so we can speak with him," Jackson put in.

Hatfield was watching Adele. "You don't believe Mr. Burke is out of town?"

"Del isn't likely to believe much of what Mr. Bain said." Jackson gave the sheriff a knowing look. "You ought to know by now how she gets when she takes a disliking to a person."

"I didn't take a disliking to him," Adele insisted as she sat down on the couch near Lady Augusta. "I simply didn't like his manners."

Jackson couldn't hold back a grin. "I believe the words you used to describe him on the train were 'arrogant' and 'ghastly.'"

Hatfield tilted his head back and roared with laughter. "I gather he impressed you unfavorably."

"Men, especially young men, can be brutes in the flash of an eye," said Lady Augusta. "Mark my words."

"I always do, Ma," said her son with affection. He turned to his deputy. "Was he a brute, Jackson?"

"I think Del is exaggerating," her brother answered.

"Am I?" She glared at him. "And what would you call a man who grabs a woman's wrist as if it were a turkey leg?"

"Perhaps you ought to tell the sheriff the whole story." Her brother was starting to grow impatient as he had during many of their arguments as children. "He went to check some records and found Del pawing —"

"I was not pawing!"

"Handling a lighter his father gave him before his death," Jackson finished. "He naturally got upset about it."

"I was satisfying a curiosity," Adele said.

"Well, I hope you satisfied it." Hatfield poured himself more tea. "So if you didn't think he was a brute, what did you think of him, Jackson?"

"He was like most young men who inherit their father's business too young," the deputy said. "Showy, a little condescending, and puts on an air of authority that doesn't yet belong to him. But very serious about his business."

"And serious about his switchboard operator's business," Adele snorted.

Hatfield leaned forward. The teacup and saucer looked like toys in his large hands. "What exactly did he say about Mr. Burke?"

"He sent the man to the Arizona territory on business, and he would call him back," said Jackson. "I found him very cooperative." He fingered a sugar cookie. They were his favorites.

"But you didn't." Hatfield glanced at Adele.

"He refused to give Jack Mr. Burke's address," she said. "I would hardly call that cooperative."

"He didn't completely refuse," Jackson argued. "He said it was confidential and his father insisted upon it. That's his right."

"I never deny anyone his or her rights," Hatfield said in a rueful voice.

"Maybe you ought to question it, Horatio," his mother said.

"What exactly should I be questioning, Ma?"

"Mr. Bain sounds quite calculating to me." Lady Augusta folded her lace handkerchief with the violet LAH in her lap. "'An uneager beaver is a calculating one,' the lord used to say. He wasn't much for words, but those he did use were memorable."

"He probably said it on one of his hunting trips about a real beaver," Hatfield snorted. Adele looked at him with surprise. She had never heard the sheriff speak of his father in such a disparaging way.

"Mr. Bain is being protective of his employee, certainly, but why wouldn't he be?" Jackson asked. "No company wants a police inquiry on its doorstep."

"I think you ought to get that warrant and force Mr. Bain to give you Mr. Burke's address," Adele said.

"I agree." Lady Augusta put down her teacup.

Hatfield began walking around the room, his hands behind his back. Adele realized each step was deliberate, as if shaken by agitation. Then, he leaned his hands on the back of the sofa in the empty place next to where Adele sat.

"You *do* want to speak with him, don't you, Sheriff?" Adele peered at him.

He looked away. "I'm not sure it's really necessary now."

"Why?" Jackson looked genuinely perplexed.

There was a small flurry coming from the direction of the kitchen and Rowena emerged, lending her all-too-sensible presence to the sudden tense moment. She stopped when she saw the Gosslings, bowing in her half-serving, half-friendly way.

"We were just discussing this Mr. Burke," Lady Augusta said.

"Shifty character, if you ask me," Rowena said.

"Oh? Why do you think that?" Adele set her cup down.

"Chatted Miss Gibb up just to sell her something," said the woman. "That's as shifty as they come in my book."

"Mr. Bain confirmed that Mr. Burke sold Millie a subscription to the magazine we found on her desk and the book she was reading when she died," said Jackson. "So we know he was there at Mrs. Taylor's like the guests said."

"I never doubted their word." Hatfield sat down in the large chair.

Jackson watched him for a moment. "Sir, what do you *really* think? About Mr. Burke, that is?"

"What do *I* think?" Hatfield asked. "I would like to know what Mr. Burke thinks of Miss Gibb's state of mind at the time."

"According to Mr. Bain, he wouldn't have thought anything of it," Jackson remarked.

"I hardly think Mr. Burke would be entirely oblivious as to what's happened with Miss Gibb," Adele said. "Missy told me it's been carried into all the local papers."

"He may not have made the connection between the woman he met at Mrs. Taylor's and Miss Gibb," Jackson argued. "And if he did, he may not have attached much importance to a stranger he knew for only a week. So you see, sir," he rose, "your question mark has several answers."

Hatfield glanced at him with a grimace. "Your experience with the Anspaches has taught you to be reductive, Jackson."

"No, sir," he said in a stiff voice. "Only logical."

"If you decide Miss Gibb's death wasn't suicide, he'll have to be called back from Arizona," Adele said. "He was really the only suspicious character in her life."

"*If* I decide it wasn't suicide," Hatfield said.

Adele didn't like the uneven tone in his voice.

~

The next morning the Gosslings were having breakfast on the veranda overlooking the back yard when Tomas announced Hatfield, looking up at the large man with his usual fearful eyes even though the sheriff had been nothing but kind to him and his family. Hatfield came out with his hat in both hands, his stride swift and determined.

"I wanted to catch you before you went into the station," he said, declining the chair Jackson pushed toward him.

"Oh?" The deputy put his cup down.

The sheriff looked out to the gazebo, his eyes squinting a little. "I've decided Miss Gibb's death was suicide."

Jackson let the paper drop in his lap. Adele stared up at him.

"You can't deny the pieces fit, Jackson," Hatfield insisted.

"No, I can't deny it," he said with a sigh. "I wish you would let us talk to Mr. Burke first, though."

The sheriff stooped a little to look at him. "If the man is conducting important business out of the state, I don't wish to have him called back unnecessarily. I don't think he could add much anyway."

"You believed it enough to send Jack all the way to Sacramento to speak with him," Adele said. She was trying to keep her voice steady.

"That was procedure," he said. "I doubt Mr. Burke can tell us anything we don't already know."

"Why not have him called back from the Arizona territory and find out?" Adele's voice grew a little shrill.

"Del, keep quiet," Jackson said. "The sheriff knows what he's doing."

"I would never imply he didn't," Adele said. "But why do I get the feeling there's more to it than that?"

He glanced up at her. "You're too astute, Adele."

"My misfortune," Jackson growled.

"I received a visit yesterday after you left," he said, "from members of the town council. I'm sure you can guess which ones."

"Dr. Rhodes spoke to them," Adele guessed.

The sheriff looked at her sharply, then went on. "They believe we've lingered far too long on this case. They demand it be closed by the end of the day Friday."

"That's two days from now!" Adele said

Jackson leaned back, rubbing his chin but it was clear from his forehead that this annoyed him.

"We know her death wasn't an accident," Hatfield said. "We've found nothing to make us suspect it was anything but suicide. I see no reason to prolong the investigation."

"What about Mr. Burke?" Adele asked, laying down her fork and knife.

"Your brother brought up some excellent points."

"Such as?"

"Mr. Burke only knew Miss Gibb for a very short time and his purpose was to sell her some of his merchandise. He achieved that goal. There's no more to it than that."

"Mrs. Taylor's guests said they were quite taken with one another —" Adele began.

"Speculation," said the sheriff. "I've lived in boarding houses myself. One of the favorite pastimes is to create gossip about the inhabitants."

Adele threw down her napkin. It slid to the floor, and Tomas, with his usual diligence, retrieved it.

"At this point, Adele," he said in his soft but plaintive voice, "what I believe or don't believe doesn't stand up to the facts. You don't solve cases based on belief but on fact."

Adele began to walk the border of the veranda. Her heels scratched the thin layer of red dust that always seemed to coat the floor no matter how much Ruth and her daughters swept. The grating sound echoed like a saw in the quiet morning air and she could see Hatfield's hands tighten on the rim of his hat.

"I never question your decisions. You know that, Sheriff," she said.

"Del," her brother started but Hatfield waved him silent.

"But are you really being honest?" she continued. "Honest with yourself, I mean. With your own feeling of the case."

"The sheriff's right, Del. You don't solve cases on belief," Jackson snapped.

"Belief and feeling are two very different things, dear brother," she said. "I think Sheriff Hatfield knows what I mean."

"Yes, I believe I do," he said in his quiet way. "But it doesn't alter the fact that I agree with the council."

"What?" Adele leaned over a chair.

"Perhaps I got a little too sentimental about Miss Gibb." The sheriff shrugged. "A woman still in her prime, solitary, perhaps looking toward a brighter future. But apparently it wasn't bright enough." He rose. "You may tell Mr. Bain he needn't call Mr. Burke back from his work. I don't want to waste anybody's time any longer, not ours or anyone else's."

"As you say, sir," Jackson said.

The sheriff stood for a moment as if unsure what to do as a pair of birds landed on the veranda, looking at them, then flew away. His hand reached and gave Jackson's back a quick pat. He then put his hat on, bowed, and left without another glance at Adele.

CHAPTER 20

That morning brought additional business for Adele's shop. Mrs. Lynn's cousin Mrs. Nitt was visiting her from the Midwest. Since her visit the year before, Mrs. Nitt decided Adele was the authority on city living and all that was fashionable about it. Her social standing in Red Gulch where she lived was rising, and she came into the shop to buy a supply of calling cards. Adele was visibly distracted as she kept thinking about what the sheriff had told her that morning.

Mrs. Lynn's pale blue eyes watched her as she went through the motions of helping Mrs. Nitt choose patterns for the cards. As they were paying for their purchases, she finally spoke in her usual light timid voice. "This dreadful business with Miss Gibb is still heavy on your heart, isn't it, dear?"

Adele scribbled in her account book. "You've no idea, Mrs. Lynn."

"Yes, I heard about that poor girl," said Mrs. Nitt with a deep sigh. "Teachers are simply so unappreciated. Even in Red Gulch, we have a Miss Bath who taught all of my children and she's a whirl of a — I mean, she's a very informed person. But some think her rather common."

"Miss Gibb was far from common," said Mrs. Lynn.

Adele looked up from the cash register. "How do you know that, Mrs. Lynn?"

"Oh, well, I don't *really* know it." She looked like a confused bird that had chosen the wrong nest. "I know she was a good girl. Did her due diligence, as they say."

"School teachers are always thorough," Mrs. Nitt said with a nod.

"No, I didn't mean that." Mrs. Lynn adjusted her spectacles. "I mean she did a lot of charity work."

"Charity work?" Adele asked.

"For the Sacramento Children's Home." Mrs. Lynn sighed. "My, but she asked a lot of questions."

"What questions?"

"Oh, she wanted to know about some of the families in the city that might be willing to contribute," said the woman.

"Why would she ask you, I wonder?" Adele asked.

"Well, dear, some of the Lynns and Granvilles — that was my maiden name — lived among Sacramento's best families."

"They were all very nice people," Mrs. Nitt remarked.

"Yes, they were." Mrs. Lynn smiled. "The Strouds, the Insworths, the Eccelstons —"

"Sound Episcopalian," Mrs. Nitt remarked but her cousin paid no attention to her.

"The Slopers, the Bains —"

Adele's finger pressed hard on the cash register keys. Its harsh ring made Mrs. Nitt jump.

"Careful, dear," said the woman with a nervous laugh. "Young businesswomen are so eager nowadays."

"The Bains own a publishing company, don't they?" Adele asked.

"You know them?" Mrs. Lynn asked. "I suppose they associated with some of the best families in San Francisco, and I must confess, Miss Gossling, I do sometimes forget you're — well, you weren't always a shopkeeper."

"It's all right, dear, we know many people fell on harder times during the panic of '93," said Mrs. Nitt in a tone that tried but failed to show sympathy in its harsh prairie twang.

"I work because I choose to, Mrs. Nitt," Adele said with a smile. "I don't like to be idle and keeping a shop is as good a way to occupy my time as any."

"Very sensible of you," the woman murmured.

"And you say Miss Gibb wanted to know about families who might donate to charity?" Adele asked.

"She was helping to organize a bazaar and thought they might have something for her," said Mrs. Lynn.

"We do have a responsibility to educate those poor children." Mrs. Nitt clucked her tongue. "Mr. Nitt says without education, they'll simply be litter in the street."

"Of course I told her she oughtn't to bother with the Fells and the Bains," Mrs. Lynn said.

"Oh? Why is that?" Adele asked.

"The Fells were in Europe at the time and the Bains —" she heaved a sigh. "Well, Huey Bain, poor man, passed away and the family is still in mourning."

"How terrible." Adele's eyebrows shot up.

"She was most persistent, though." Mrs. Lynn leafed through a box of writing paper. "She still wanted the addresses, as she intended to contact the Fells when they returned."

"And the Bains?"

"She thought she could persuade Mrs. Bain when she was out of mourning."

"It's as I said, Caroline," her cousin declared with some triumph, "school teachers are very thorough. Miss Bath —"

"I'm sorry I've been so slow, Mrs. Nitt." Adele's hands fluttered over the box ribbons. "I'd like to give you a box of pencils to take to the school children in Red Gulch with my compliments."

This last delighted the woman to no end, and she shifted her chatter to Red Gulch.

When the ladies left, she hung her *Out to Lunch* sign on the door and proceeded to the police station where, in his usual courteous way, Hatfield sent his deputies away while he remained alone to guard the place.

"Sheriff, I just found out something about Millie!" she sputtered.

"I'm sorry, Adele," he said. "You won't change my mind."

"Will you at least come to lunch with me so I can explain?"

"I can't leave the station. You know that."

"Then I shall bring lunch to you," she said stubbornly.

By the time she returned with sandwiches, she was surprised to see he had laid out the table used for interrogations with a cloth, a bottle of wine, and a few glasses. His face was a glossy red as he said, "Ma taught me to be a good host."

"I'm anxious to know how you keep such fineries away from the lads," she said, smiling.

"I've told them the file cabinet near the sink is for confidential files only and not to be touched." He laughed. "I can't say they were too disappointed to hear that."

They sat down across from one another and as he unwrapped a sandwich, he asked, "All right, what is this new information?"

Adele told him everything Mrs. Lynn had said. He listened with expressionless eyes.

"I'm as surprised as you that Miss Gibb would be so civic-minded, but Mrs. Wrigley did tell us she was diligent in her work," he said.

Adele leaned forward. "But now we know there's a connection between Millie and the Bains."

He shrugged. "Plenty of teachers come into contact with wealthy people doing charity work."

"But of all the people in Sacramento?" Adele said. "Surely, you can't ignore it!"

"I'm not ignoring anything, Adele," he said. "I'm only putting it in context."

"In other words?" Her voice was arch.

"In other words," he said slowly, "there's nothing unusual about Miss Gibb putting the Bains on her list for a donation if they're one of Sacramento's prominent families."

"But they weren't just a name on her list," Adele insisted. "Mrs. Lynn said she insisted on contacting them, even though she knew Mr. Bain had died and the family was in mourning."

"I assume you have a theory?" The sheriff poured himself another glass of wine.

"I think she knew or wanted to know the Bains, and her excuse was the charity."

He leaned his head to one side. "Why would she want to do that?"

"I don't know," Adele admitted. "But I'm sure with some discreet inquiries, you could find out."

"And maybe some not-so-discreet inquiries?" he asked with amusement. "Even if I did make inquiries, I'm afraid it wouldn't do any good."

"But this is new information!"

"New or not," he said, his voice resolute, "it's too late."

They were silent for a moment.

"I suppose I should clarify," he said.

"I suppose you should," she echoed.

"I'm going to the county courthouse to file the final papers to close Miss Gibb's case once the lads return from lunch."

Adele folded the linen napkin into quarters. "My, but you're in rather a hurry, aren't you?"

He swatted at a fly hovering over his glass. "I know you're disappointed, but there are things you don't know that make it necessary."

"I know!" she snapped. "I couldn't work with the poor and needy without knowing about the political machine spitting out its little cogs, giving no thought to how many other cogs it breaks."

"Your metaphor is a little off," he said with a prickly smile. "But apt, I'll admit."

She sighed and sat back. "I suppose that's that."

The light immediately fell as if a wind had extinguished it. The room became as dark and dingy as a cellar.

"You can be quite relentless, Adele," he said in a quiet voice.

"What do you mean?" She stared at him.

"You weren't very kind this morning.

"I never meant to offend you, Sheriff," she said. "I only wanted to be heard."

He threw the sandwich down as if sick at the sight of it. "You refused to believe from the beginning that Miss Gibb may have committed suicide. Why?"

"I know about women like Millie," she said. "Unmarried, approaching middle-age, a profession she's grown to loathe. People want to believe she had nothing to live for."

"May I remind you none of us knew Miss Gibb intimately?" He peered at her.

"Perhaps not." She leaned her elbows on the table. "But those who did tell a different story."

"Dr. McCabe?" he asked in a wry voice.

"And Iona Hoddle and Mrs. Brent," she pointed out. "They all describe a completely different woman."

"Not completely," he insisted. "Only a different version of the same woman."

She looked away. "I don't consider a fluttery, nervous bird a different version of a suicidal woman!"

"It's the other side of the same coin," he insisted. "You're not giving me any conclusive evidence, Adele."

"I see." She lifted her chin. "The police always want something concrete, something tangible. What about the gun?"

He glanced at her. "What gun?"

"Millie's gun," she said. "Her pretty little ladies' gun, as you would call it."

"There is nothing pretty about a weapon like that." He sniffed.

"Miss Hoddle told us Millie knew how to shoot it." She leaned forward. "So why didn't she?"

"That's not very concrete or tangible," he remarked. "That's merely a guess."

"A woman has a gun and knows how to use it but decides to poison herself?" She eyed him. "And with one of the most horrifying and painful poisons?"

"And one of the most widely available," he reminded her.

"It makes no sense," she insisted.

"Now I'll tell you something you're forgetting." He wiped his mouth. "Guns make noise. Even a ladies' gun makes a very loud noise. Boarding houses walls are thin, and many people don't sleep well. The sound of a gun would have awakened Mrs. Taylor's household and perhaps the neighbors as well."

"You're saying Millie didn't want to attract attention?" Adele asked.

"You saw the funeral," he said. "She didn't attract much attention in life. It's not a stretch to assume she would want to attract even less in death."

Adele rose and walked to the window. She heard the chair scrape and felt Hatfield's looming figure behind her. "Given the evidence we had, I had no choice but to go ahead with the paperwork," he said.

"No," she said softly. "I suppose you didn't."

"Bring me more evidence," he said. "Bring me reasonable doubt, even."

She turned, catching the tight expression on his usually serene face.

CHAPTER 21

The next day, Adele deliberately stayed away from the police station, her mind buzzing as if a nest of bees had taken root. She filled the emptiness of the day with catalogues of new stock she had put aside for some time. She left the door of her shop half-open so the bell would ring if someone should come in.

In the midst of the quiet morning, she heard the clang of the bell. She smoothed down her skirt, disregarding crumbs of paper on her blouse and went to the front of the shop, her sleeves pushed up to her elbows. Nin was leaning against the counter, a newspaper in her hands.

"Millie's case is closed?"

Her friend nodded.

She glanced out the window. "I see Mrs. Faderman and the ladies didn't waste any time."

The finer ladies in town were parading up and down the street. Nin called it a moveable tea party, always organized by Mrs. Faderman. Maids trailed after them with the teapot and tiered platters of cake with anxious eyes.

"They couldn't wait." Nin held out the newspaper.

Adele's eyes caught a grainy photo of Millie, stiffly posed, the light capturing the sharp angles of her face. Beside it the headline read LOCAL SCHOOLTEACHER'S DEATH RULED SUICIDE.

She read the short article with a sinking heart:

An inquest was held today at the Arrojo county courthouse about the shocking death of Miss Millicent Gibb, English teacher at the Wrigley School for Girls. Sheriff Horatio Hatfield, also Arrojo's coroner, ruled Miss Gibb had taken her own life. Though there was no evidence of foul play, Sheriff Hatfield and Deputy Jackson Gossling were, as usual, thorough in their investigation, interviewing members of Mrs. Abigail Taylor's boarding house where Miss Gibb was residing as well as her employer, Mrs. Clara Wrigley, and Dr. Elias McCabe of Rosa Gris who knew the young woman in her early days as a teacher in the Sacramento school system. They could account for Miss Gibb's state of mind and disposition which pointed toward a solitary and melancholic existence. The police also attempted to locate a Mr. Owen Burke, traveling salesman of the Bain Publishing Company, who was staying at Mrs. Taylor's and struck up a friendship with Miss Gibb but Mr. Burke has been out of the state on business and the police felt he could add nothing to their investigation.

Adele could feel her friend watching her carefully. Her green eyes arched with cat-like grace.

She folded the paper and laid it on the counter.

"You're not angry?" Nin asked.

"At who? Missy?" Adele shrugged. "She has her job to do just as you and I have ours. She didn't say anything she shouldn't have nor did she insinuate anything improper."

Mrs. Faderman came into view across the street and waved her handkerchief, as if she wanted to make sure she had gotten Adele's attention.

"Lord have mercy," Nin mumbled.

"There are times, dear, when one needs more patience than mercy," Adele said.

"Miss Gossling!" the older woman screeched as she made her way across the red dust road. "I must speak with you!"

"And this is certainly one of those times." Adele glanced at Nin.

The usual clump of followers trailed behind her. Missy Grace, editor and sole proprietor of the *Arrojo Courier*, the only newspaper in town, took her place next to Adele with her usual frayed look.

"You've seen the paper, I take it?" Mrs. Faderman began, her pince-nez perched on her lumpy nose.

"I thought Missy related the facts well." Her warm smile seemed to ease the young woman's anxiety. She and Missy were friends, and she knew the editor was worried about what she might say regarding her reports of police business.

"But are they *all* the facts?" The woman's face puckered like a frog's when she was agitated.

"I don't think Miss Grace left anything out," said Adele. "Anything that should have been left out, that is." One of the ladies pushed a teacup into her hands as well as a plate of cake, though she hardly had the appetite for either.

"That's what I want to know," said Mrs. Faderman. "You've been in on the case from the beginning, as you always are."

"Much to your chagrin," Nin murmured.

"Am I to understand, Mrs. Faderman," Adele said, feeling the edge of her lip stiffen, "that you're perfectly willing to needle me for details when it suits you even though you've made no secret of your disapproval for what you once called my filthy criminal interests?" She heard her friend giggle behind her.

"Oh, but this isn't a crime," Mrs. Faderman insisted. "The poor woman killed herself."

"Then there's no reason for you to be concerned, is there?" Adele asked sharply.

"You New Women don't understand community responsibility," Mrs. Faderman snapped. "You only think about yourselves."

"We have a responsibility to ourselves just as everyone has," Adele said. "It's not a selfish act, Mrs. Faderman."

"I'm not interested in arguing the philosophies of self-preservation at the moment, Miss Gossling," she said. "I want to know what you know."

"What I know?" She blinked.

"About Miss Gibb's life."

"But she's dead," Nin declared.

"We're all well aware of that, Miss Branch," said Mrs. Cricket in her razor voice.

"Miss Gossling." Mrs. Faderman took a breath. "You understand it's not enough for a death to have been respectable —"

"I'm glad you think suicide is respectable," Adele interrupted. "I was afraid you might label it a disgrace."

"The poor girl." Mrs. Lynn heaved a sigh, her small face sagging in all its sagging places. "Poor girl."

"She was hardly a girl, Caroline," Mrs. Cricket said. "My goodness, she was nearly forty!"

"An ancient relic," Nin snorted.

"As I was saying." Mrs. Faderman's voice rose, "one's death may be respectable, but it's one's life that counts."

"I don't think Miss Gibb had anything to leave behind in life in the way you mean," said Adele. "Although according to Mrs. Lynn, she did set about doing some charity work."

"That's true, Irene," said the woman.

"I was referring to her reputation." Mrs. Faderman's voice dropped on the last word.

"She means, was Miss Gibb a good girl?" Mrs. Cricket thundered. "I wish you wouldn't be so wishy-washy, Irene."

Adele exchanged a look of amusement with her friend. She could almost see Mrs. Faderman sitting at the head of the town council meeting, making promises to "inquire" regarding Millie's conduct so they could close the book on one more citizen in Arrojo who had the misfortunate to end up dead in their midst.

"Perhaps you wouldn't think so, Mrs. Faderman," she said in a mild voice. "She cared more about her career than she did about finding a husband. I know how high that rates on the scale of acceptable behavior for women in your book."

Missy let out a low chuckle.

"I never in my life said such a thing, Miss Gossling," said the woman, her pince-nez dropping from her nose. "An unmarried woman is, under certain circumstances, acceptable. Even preferred."

"As in Miss Gibb's case?" she asked with a wry smile.

"She was devoted to children," Mrs. Lynn said eagerly. "Mrs. Brent told me herself, and she knew her well."

"Apparently not so well," Adele remarked.

"Millie called them spoiled, insolent girls," Nin added.

Mrs. Lynn's eyes became like coins. "Oh, she couldn't have said that!"

"Please, Caroline." Mrs. Faderman cleared of her throat. "Was there — is there anything we need be concerned about?"

"I can't think why you would be concerned, Mrs. Faderman." Adele leaned against the doorframe. "I should think you hardly knew the woman, unless she was a secret guest at your tea parties."

"I meant *we*." Her arms swept around. "The town. Any smear on one member of the community is a smear on all. Surely you know *that*, Miss Gossling."

Adele felt herself begin to rattle inside, the sure signs of her temper getting the better of her. "The only oddity about Miss Gibb was her death, and if it should come as a smear, it would be from people like you." She retreated inside her shop but the woman caught her arm.

"Explain yourself, Miss Gossling!" The high demand in her voice didn't hide her genuine terror.

Adele realized the anger that had burst forward was not because of Mrs. Faderman's selfish fears, which she was used to.

It was disappointment and dissatisfaction from her conversation with Hatfield.

She was about to apologize, which always placated Mrs. Faderman to a degree, but Nin's propensity for bald outbursts overrode her.

"We think she was murdered."

The only sound was sheets of wind pressing against the display windows. Then Adele heard a cry and crushing footsteps like someone running away from the crowd. Mrs. Faderman seemed to catch her breath and spoke in a calm, authoritative manner, "I'm sure you're exaggerating, Miss Branch."

"Nin may be bold, Mrs. Faderman," Adele said in a quiet voice, "but she never exaggerates."

"It's *your* opinion Miss Gibb was murdered," the woman ventured. "Yours alone and no one else's."

Adele recalled the conversation with Sheriff Hatfield. "Mine alone."

"May I inquire why you believe Miss Gibb's death was — unnatural?" Mrs. Cricket's voice was thick and fearful.

"I don't think that need concern us, Belinda," Mrs. Faderman said briskly. "Miss Gossling's involvement with the law hasn't always been entirely disinterested."

Adele's annoyance fell with this surprisingly accurate remark. "You may be right, Mrs. Faderman," she said. "Everybody believes Miss Gibb was a rather pathetic creature whose dedication to her work replaced husband and home. I object to that, as you know. I've worked enough with women from all walks of life to know their lives are much more complex than others would have it be known. Even the lives of schoolteachers." She said the last with a small wry smile.

"It's clear the sheriff doesn't share your views," Mrs. Cricket sneered.

"That's true enough, isn't it, Miss Grace?" Mrs. Faderman turned but the young woman was no longer with them.

Adele felt a cold piercing in her throat. Without even looking at the stunned ladies, she picked up the edge of her skirt and ran to the newspaper office.

She found Missy bent over her desk, scribbling furiously on an ink-stained page. The typewriter was spewed on the floor as if it had been pushed aside. Adele guessed she had made an attempt to use it but had some trouble and her determination to get down her story forced her to use pencil and paper.

Adele grabbed the pencil from her hand. "Missy, you can't!"

"Can't what?" The young woman looked up, tendrils of hair falling across her forehead.

"You're going to print what I just said, aren't you?" Adele perched herself on the edge of the desk. "About Millie's death not being suicide?"

"I have a duty to print the news as I find it," Missy said in a determined voice. But the way she leaned back against the leather cushion of the chair made it clear to Adele she felt some guilt over swiping the news she righteously professed to be duty-bound to print from street gossip.

"But this is an opinion, not news," Adele insisted.

"Then I'll print it as an opinion piece," Missy insisted.

"I tell you, you can't do it!"

"Why not?" The young woman stared. "You've always been willing to give me your opinion before."

"I've never completely disagreed with the sheriff's judgment before," said Adele. "And, well, people might think him a fool if you imply his decision may not have been conclusive."

"There are plenty of people in this town who think him a fool and not just a bit," Missy said in a low voice. "You know that, don't you?"

"They can think what they like!" Adele snapped. "But thinking in silence and having something they can point to as justification for their thinking are two different things." She put her hand on Missy's wrist. "Please, I'm asking you. Don't print it."

The newspaperwoman's eyes clouded for a moment, staring into some distant space. Adele realized her gaze had fallen on the rather musty painting hung on the wall of a man with the last century's sideburns and severe expression that could not hide the kindness of his eyes. She knew it to be a painting of Missy's father who had started the newspaper as one of the first generations of settlers in Arrojo. She also knew of the man's reputation for high-mindedness and integrity in what he print.

Adele wandered to the painting "You ought to get it cleaned."

"I will one of these days." Missy crumpled the paper she had been writing. The pencil went back into the desk drawer.

"Thank you." Adele pressed the young woman's hand.

"I'll hold off for now," Missy said. "Perhaps you'll tell me — not for print — what you intend to do."

"Do?" Adele asked.

A gust of wind flew into the office and a sweep of dust blasted in their faces. Both she and Missy grabbed for their handkerchiefs. When Adele's eyes cleared, she saw Iona Hoddle standing just beyond the doorway.

The young woman was without her hat and gloves, and the pocket of her salesgirl frock gaped open with a folded newspaper. Her blond hair looked amiss and her dress had a few light smears of ink.

Her blue eyes, watery and almost white, appealed to Missy. "Is it true?"

Missy approached the young woman and set her down into a chair, glancing at Adele. Adele quickly poured a glass of water from the pitcher on the sideboard and put it in Miss Hoddle's shaking hands.

"Is what true?" Missy asked.

"The newspaper, of course!" The young woman's voice came out in the same croak Adele remembered from the funeral.

"You mean about the inquest?" Adele said gently. "Yes, it's true."

"The police decided it was suicide?" The last word brought a fresh breakdown of tears. The sobs were deep and loud.

Adele put her arm around the young woman's shoulders. "That was the sheriff's ruling, yes."

"But does he really think it was suicide?" Miss Hoddle's head shot up as her voice pierced with a wail.

In a quiet voice, Adele said, "He says he does."

"Why? Why?" The voice swiveled like a siren.

Missy looked at Adele with sad eyes.

Adele felt her tongue stumbling on the words. "He says the evidence points to it."

The young woman grabbed both her arms as if she were standing on a ledge and trying to keep from falling over. "*He* says, but what do you say?"

"I'm not a lawman, dear," Adele said in a gentle voice.

"But you don't believe it!" Miss Hoddle looked at her with ragged eyes. "I know you don't. That day of the funeral, you said —"

"I'm not a lawman," Adele repeated.

Miss Hoddle's eyes were so wild Adele feared she was going to faint. She grabbed her purse, searching for the velvet box of dry peppermint Nin had given her in lieu of smelling salts.

But the young woman regained her composure and fury replaced the wild look. She jumped out of the chair. "You promised!" she screeched.

Missy looked at Adele with alarm. Adele rose carefully and leaned against the desk, feeling her own head begin to grow dizzy.

"You promised!"

"Dear, calm yourself," Missy said in a soft voice. To Adele, she mumbled, "Perhaps we ought to send for Dr. Barnes."

"I'll be all right," Miss Hoddle said. And she did indeed seem calmer as she sank back into the chair like a rag.

"What promise?" asked Missy in a soft voice.

"She said she would find out the truth." Miss Hoddle wiped both her eyes. "That's what you said, isn't it? And don't tell me again you're not a lawman!"

Adele's chest grew tight. The scene in Miss Taylor's parlor with the people sitting around the piano, Miss Hoddle's folded figure, the others' indifference to their recently deceased fellow boarder. She remembered the deepened look in the girl's eyes that had found comfort when Adele had indeed made the promise.

She heard Missy's voice. "Didn't you once tell me something about fighting for the dead as well as the living?"

She looked at the newswoman with her straightened figure and pinned shoulders. "How can I fight now when the sheriff has given his ruling?"

"Rulings can be reversed," Missy insisted. "Find new evidence. If you do, I'll print it so he can't ignore it."

"Yes, yes!" Miss Hoddle grabbed her hand. "Millie doesn't deserve to be pitied over and forgotten. She deserves more than that."

"You know she's right," Missy said quietly.

Adele looked from one to the other. "You're both right."

Miss Hoddle pressed her hands against Adele's. "You'll keep your promise? You'll find out what happened to Millie?"

"I'll keep my promise, dear." Adele was touched by the childish appeal in the girl's face. "I'll do what I can."

The young woman threw her arms around her in a tight embrace. "Thank you, Miss Gossling. I knew you wouldn't refuse."

The room filled with calm air as the gust that had brought in the dust and leaves hailed the sun and the blue sky.

$\mathcal{A}$dele walked back to her shop, her feet dragging along the red road, dust getting between the laces of her boots.

As she entered her shop, her friend eyed her, fanning the edge of the yellow sales book. "Are you'll right, Adele?"

She stood against the doorway. "I was reminded of a promise I made."

"To Iona Hoddle?" Nin asked. "I saw her go into the newspaper office. She had no right to say such a thing."

"She had every right," Adele said. "I made a promise, and I must keep it."

"You mean find out if Millie's death was really suicide?"

"Or murder," Adele added. "I don't know where to start."

"Perhaps we ought to start where the police start," Nin mused. "At the scene of the crime."

Adele glanced at the sales book, distracted. Then, she smiled. "Get your hat, dear. We're paying a call."

"Bother the hat," Nin said.

Adele persuaded her they had important business and as such, formalities were in order. So Nin chose the hat with the least wear, a heavily veiled thing. Adele wondered if she had last worn it at her mother's funeral.

The late morning had now folded into the afternoon and people filtered onto Bridge Street for the lunch hour. Most headed toward the tea shop or Pringle's, and a few salespeople who had less to spend on their midday meal slunk past the train station to Quarry Lane which offered more affordable restaurants.

"I'm hungry," Nin declared.

"Perhaps Mrs. Taylor will offer us a meal," Adele said as she held her friend's arm.

"Mrs. Taylor?"

Adele smiled. "You see now why you needed the hat."

"The scene of the crime?" Nin smiled.

"Not officially," Adele said. "Although Mrs. Taylor need not know that."

"We might get ourselves in trouble." But as Nin said it, a devilish grin formed on her lips.

Mrs. Taylor was delighted to see them. The house rang with emptiness, as the boarders had all gone about their business. "I so hate to be alone here," the woman admitted.

"You're not alone," Nin said. "You have servants."

"Oh, my dear, but they have their work to do," the woman said.

"I can imagine it's much more cheerful with people about," Adele said with sympathy. "Especially young company."

"Yes," said Mrs. Taylor. "Yes, of course." It was clear this had not been on her mind when she made her assertion.

"The unpleasantness of death leaves its mark, doesn't it?" Nin added.

Adele pinched her friend's waist. "Miss Branch doesn't mean any harm, ma'am."

Mrs. Taylor, unlike many others in Arrojo, seemed not to be disturbed by Nin's forthrightness. She answered in wary tone,

"There does seem to be some kind of — I don't know — aura Millie left behind. Not a ghost, though I'm used to ghosts. Mr. Taylor, you know."

Adele said quickly, "You'll be glad to occupy Miss Gibb's room again, I'm sure."

"When the sheriff allows it," said the woman with a sigh. "Though I don't know what I'm to do about keeping the tragedy connected to that room hushed up."

"You didn't read, then —"

Adele pinched Nin again. "The assistant deputy isn't too intrusive, I hope?"

"He's a nice boy," Mrs. Taylor said. "I asked him to lunch with me, but he seemed intent on meeting some of his friends. A prearranged appointment, he said." Her voice was a little arch. "I almost feel as if he's avoiding the cook's chicken salad."

Adele tried not to smile. She had heard rumors that the fare at Mrs. Taylor's was not the most flavorful. "I wonder, Mrs. Taylor, if you would let Nin and me take one more look in Miss Gibb's room. There are things — of a feminine nature — the police often miss that might be important."

Mrs. Taylor patted her arm. "I was thinking the very same thing when they were here! But of course, I wouldn't dream of interfering with police business."

"We always do," Nin said. Mrs. Taylor looked slightly disturbed.

"We help the police when we can," Adele said. "I like to think of myself as an unofficial deputy, given my brother's position."

"I'm sure he's taught you quite a bit about his work," Mrs. Taylor said with a smile, sweeping them up the stairs.

She and Nin found the room and shut the door. "We have half an hour before the assistant deputy comes back," Adele said. "He'll probably return with the paper and that will be that."

"What are we looking for?"

"Just what I said." Adele gave her a knowing look. "Things of a feminine nature."

Nin snorted but walked around the peripheral of the room. Adele concentrated more on the center. The room had not been touched since the police had been through it. Everything remained as it was, from the overturned wash basin to the magazine on the table. Adele sat at the desk where Millie's body had been found.

Nin shivered. "I don't see how you can bear it."

Adele eyed her. "I never knew you to be squeamish."

"My senses are more acute than yours," her friend said. "I feel things differently."

Adele touched the pages of the book still open in front of her. She imagined Millie having drunk the hot toddy, feeling the burn of the cinnamon, the sweetness of the sugar, and the buzz of the whiskey. And then — what happened? She remembered Dr. Rhodes' words at the police station the day before: *Dizziness. Confusion. Trying to gather her bearings.*

She rose, surveying the room behind her. "The path," she murmured. "Follow the path, follow the path…"

Nin looked at her with hollow eyes.

"Dizziness." Adele began walking across the room slowly, her steps tracing the empty spaces between the furniture still in disarray. "Confusion." She reached the fireplace and the night table lying on its side. She headed toward the washbasin. "Trying to find her bearings." She reached the broken pitcher. "Yes, I see now."

"Horrible." Nin shivered again.

"But effective." Adele's voice was soft. "Someone knew what they were doing. Whether it was Millie herself or —"

"Adele!"

Her friend's face had suddenly turned pale, and she stumbled as she grabbed the edge of the bed.

Adele put her arm around her shoulders. "I'm sorry, dear. Jack always accuses me of being gruesome."

"Well, stop, stop!" Her friend breathed heavily. "I'm all right. A glass of water —"

Adele went down the hall and found a glass in the bathroom. Filling it with water, she brought it to Nin. A few moments and her friend was almost herself again.

"This room," she said. "There's something —" But she could not finish.

Adele thought it best to leave her alone, and she completed her walk around the room at the fireplace. She let her toe play with the remaining black dust from the grate. She bit back a smile as she thought of what Tomas would say if he saw it. What words he would have, in English and Spanish, for Mrs. Taylor's maid!

She absently took up a brush and bent down to fling the dust back into the dead fireplace. She saw the pile of coal sitting in the corner. Coal chips were spread all over the side of the fireplace, carelessly flung about, the bricks smeared with black. For a moment, she was taken by the shining edge of the chips. The sun was coming through the small window and gave them a crystal-like shine.

"Pretty," she murmured. "I never knew anything so common could be pretty."

Among the pretty black chips was one misshapen with spots of glaring yellow. She adjusted her magnifying glass.

"Good Lord!" She snapped up one of her gloves from her purse and retrieved the object. "Millie's lemon!"

It came out a scratchy breath. She knew it had to have been Millie's because its folds of fruit were scrunched and eaten. "She tried to throw it in the fire, and it didn't quite make it. Or whoever killed her tried to throw it to get rid of the evidence. Saturated with arsenic." Dr. Rhodes' words. *Saturated.*

She heard a scream and saw her friend was reeling again.

Adele had never seen her friend in this kind of distress. Nin's breath was coming out in shallow puffs, and her face was very pale.

Adele rushed to her friend, speaking in a soothing voice, "What is it?"

"I feel it," said her friend. "The pressing air." She grabbed Adele's arm with both hands to steady herself. Her breath was coming back to normal.

"Pressing air," Adele repeated.

"Like a whirlpool," said Nin. "Something trying to draw me out."

"Whirlpools draw people in," Adele said gently.

"This one is drawing out," Nin insisted. "Trying to draw out my blood." She shivered and threw her arms around Adele's neck.

Adele was touched by the sudden change in her friend. She looked soft and vulnerable like a child.

"It's all right, dear," she said. "Whatever it is, it won't hurt you."

Her friend dropped her arms. It was the first time Adele could remember her being more enraged than peevish. "It wasn't trying to hurt me. It was trying to draw me out."

Adele led her friend into the hall to a bench near the stairwell. The cool air made Nin lose her angry countenance. "The whirlpool wasn't evil. It was vibrant, alive with energy." Her large eyes surveyed Adele. "I've never been good at explaining these things. It's damned inconvenient!"

Adele could not help smiling. She gave her a quick embrace. "I don't think you and I have a problem understanding one another." She went to the bathroom and brought her another glass of water. "Just rest now. I want to look at one more thing and then we'll go."

Adele returned to Millie's room. Something about the fireplace beckoned to her, as if it had something else to show her. She dropped to her hands and knees in spite of the smear of ashes still prevalent on the brick. All she saw was black and ashes.

She went over every inch of the fireplace. Near the far right corner, a bit of white appeared and she snatched it up, blind to the gray and black powder gathering on her sleeve.

She bounded out of the room, her steps crunching the wooden floor. "Another clue, Nin!"

Fully recovered, her friend jumped from the bench, almost upsetting it. They both inspected it, their fingers blackening with the burned edges of the paper.

"Another part of the letter the police found?" Nin asked.

"I don't think so." Adele scrutinized it. "The writing looks the same. But the paper is different." She looked at her friend. "Letters come in envelopes, don't they?"

"Millie received a disturbing letter and tried to burn it," Nin guessed. "The police already know that."

Adele took her magnifying glass and inspected the writing:

04 Mulli

rcamen

"It doesn't make much sense." Her friend peered over her shoulder.

"Fragments rarely do," she said. "It's important nonetheless."

"Are you're giving it to the police?"

Adele did not answer. She folded the fragment in her handkerchief.

Mrs. Taylor and Lilly appeared on the stairway.

"I just came to see how you both were getting on — why, Miss Gossling, your hands!" The woman stared. "Oh, your pretty blouse!"

"And yours too, miss," Lilly said to Nin.

Adele remembered the ash powder. "Oh, it's nothing, ma'am. Just a little soap and water will wash it right out."

"Indeed," said Mrs. Taylor. "You shall have it right away. Lilly, take the young ladies down to the kitchen and get Sally to stop whatever she's doing and help them clean their clothes. Will you stay for lunch?" The last was asked in a hopeful tone.

"We'd be delighted," Adele said even as she heard a groan from Nin, whose love of social visits was about as high as her love of walking into a lion's den.

CHAPTER 23

As they headed down the stairs, Nin grabbed Adele's wrist. "You *are* going to show Hatfield what you found, aren't you?"

Adele again did not answer. She put her hand on Lilly's shoulder, who was trudging down the stairs, her skirt flouncing behind her. Adele imagined she was used to such quick step with her many errands around the house. "You needn't hurry for us, Lilly."

"Oh, but, miss, that ash will set if you don't get it off," the girl insisted. "It isn't seemingly to let pretty blouses keep their stains for too long." There was a wistfulness in her voice.

"You like pretty things, don't you?" Adele smiled.

"What woman doesn't, miss?" She stopped. "I mean, it ain't hardly womanly not to like pretty things." Her eyes slid for a moment to Nin, whose clothes were always haphazardly fitted to her. "I don't think I've ever seen you with a hat, miss, if you'll pardon my saying so."

Nin threw the veil back and plucked it off her head, letting her loosely pinned hair fall to her shoulders. A rare self-conscious look appeared on her face.

"I'd be glad to pin your hair back up for you, miss," said the young woman in an eager voice.

"You'd like to be a lady's maid, wouldn't you?" Adele asked.

The girl stiffened. "I once was, miss, to a fine lady in Sacramento, until —"

"Until?" Adele leaned against the bannister.

Her voice lowered. "The woman had a son, you see —"

"The beast!" This came from Nin in such a vicious tone that Lilly's eyes flew up, as if afraid Mrs. Taylor would hear.

"I'm sorry for that, Lilly." Adele took the girl's arm. "Perhaps it's better you're here where your virtue is safe."

"Oh, yes, miss," said the girl. "Mrs. Taylor has been very kind." As if remembering her duty, she adjusted her apron and began descending the stairs, at a slower pace this time.

"Tell me, Lilly," said Adele. "You said before you didn't light the fire in Millie's room on the night of her death."

"No, indeed, miss," the girl said. "I suppose Miss Gibb lit it."

"She might have," said Adele. "But not because she was cold."

"Indeed, miss?" The girl peered at her.

"She was trying to burn something," said Adele. "Or someone was."

"You mean — oh, Lord, miss!" The girl looked white as she stumbled down the last few steps.

Adele caught her arm. "Where would the coal for the fire have come from?"

"Oh, we got that out back, miss," she said. "Shed's always open. I been telling Mrs. Taylor about that stuck door, but she doesn't seem to have time to attend to it." She looked a little pale. "I ought to ask Mr. Lyman or Mr. Stoker to attend to it." Her voice was firm, as if reprimanding herself. "Awful stupid of me not to have done that. Even Mr. Walsh knows how to fix a door, and seeing how he's always talking me up —" The girl blushed. "Oh, I'm sorry, miss. I go off sometimes, with so many things to do, it slips my mind!"

Adele said kindly, "I understand. Tell me, is the shed well hidden?"

"Miss?" They were now at the kitchen doorway where Adele could see Sally bent over the washbasin and hear the clattering of dishes.

"I don't remember seeing the shed when I went with the sheriff and my brother around the house," said Adele. "I was just wondering if it was well hidden."

"Well, miss, it's really more like a hole in the ground than a shed, if you know what I mean," said the girl. "It's got a hatch and shrubs all around it. Would you like me to show you?"

"No, that's all right, Lilly." She hooked her parasol to the back of a chair.

"My, but you are an inquisitive one, miss." The girl shook her head. "I heard about town, of course, but I never realized —"

"Nor do you realize you're being impertinent," Nin snapped. She sat down on the floor, earning a gasp from Sally.

"The floor ain't clean, miss!" the girl screeched.

"What does that matter?" Nin gave her a sly look.

"Mrs. Taylor says you're to stop whatever you're doing and tend to these ladies' blouses, Sally." Lilly spoke with an authority too elevated for her position. "Sally, did you hear me?"

The girl was staring at the cupboard door, her mouth gaping open.

"Sally, did you hear me?" the maid repeated.

The girl jumped. The plate slipped in her hands but didn't fall. "Yes, miss. Stop my work and clean the blouses."

"We can do it ourselves," Adele began.

"Heavens, no, miss," Lilly said with a laugh. "Sally, don't dawdle about!" She turned on her heels and left the kitchen.

"How d'you do, miss?" The girl curtsied, smiling to show her rather bent teeth.

"This is hardly a time for 'how do you do,'" Nin remarked.

Adele gave her a silencing glance. The girl's thin face drew down and her eyes widened. She reminded Adele of a ghost.

"We don't want to disturb your work, Sally," she said. "If you have some soap and water and a clean rag, we're perfectly capable of doing it ourselves."

"Capable?" The girl stared.

"We can take care of ourselves," Nin said, rising. "We don't need anybody spilling water all over us."

"Oh, yes, miss." The girl curtsied and soon the soap and bucket of water were on the table, in addition to a rag that looked as if it could have been scrubbed a bit more. Adele watched as the girl's hands moved carefully. Her jerky walk with her hard shoes made the floor squeak.

"Would you kindly move a little less like a wooden soldier?" Nin snapped. Adele realized her friend was still nervous from the incident upstairs.

"I'm sorry miss, I don't know what's wrong with me." The girl sounded weepy.

"Perhaps it's the ghost you saw," Adele ventured.

The girl had taken up the dishes again and this time she did drop one. But it was in the basin and it didn't break. "Oh, miss, it ain't good to talk of them! You don't know as they're lurking about." Her eyes truly looked as if they would pop out of her face.

Adele regretted having mentioned it. She carefully led the girl to a chair. "Now, I'm going to make you a cup of tea." The girl's mouth gaped open. "You'd like that, wouldn't you, Sally?"

"Why, miss, nobody's made me a cup of tea since — well, since I was at home." The last was said in a sad voice.

"When was that?" Adele asked as she put the kettle on the stove.

"Three years ago, miss."

Nin, who had been scrubbing her blouse with the rough rag, looked up in alarm. "You mean you haven't seen your family in three years?"

"No, indeed, miss."

"Are they good enough to be seen?" the woman questioned.

"Miss?"

"Some families are better left for dead." Her voice was harsh, and Adele knew she was thinking of her mother's family.

"Not mine, miss." For the first time, the fear left her face, and Sally looked in command of her own person. "We had hard times and still do, but we always got along just fine."

"You're lucky, then." Nin's voice was soft. "Very lucky."

Adele made the tea and sat down beside Sally. "Is that why you've been so troubled, Sally?"

"Miss?"

"It hasn't been easy with Miss Gibb's death," she said kindly. "One needs one's family during troubling times."

"I'm used to trouble, miss," she said. "I been troubled, yes, indeed. You — you know things, they say." She seemed proud of using the word.

"It's not hard to know when a woman is troubled," Adele said. "I met many troubled women and it shows, even when they try to hide it."

"Ain't it the truth, miss?" The girl sighed. "Troubles are like wild mushrooms. They come up even when you're trying to keep them out."

Nin finished with the rag and handed it to Adele. She sat down on the other side of Sally and her tone ceased to be guarded. "Ghosts aren't always evil, Sally. I know."

"Yes, miss, I expect you do," she said. "Miss Gibb, hers weren't an evil ghost. She was always kind to me."

"And yet, you've been frightened." Adele rubbed at the stain on her blouse.

"Oh, not so much that, miss." Suddenly, the girl burst into tears, burying her face in her sopping apron.

Nin bent toward the girl, her face genuinely sympathetic. "If I bring around some nettles against the ghost, will you stop crying?"

"No, miss, I told you, it wasn't that!" the girl's shrill voice rose from under the apron. She raised her head. "It's that I sinned! I sinned!"

"How did you sin, Sally?" Adele took her hand.

"I told a lie!"

Adele gave Nin a quick glance. They both realized from the first Sally took her religion quite seriously. "We all do wrong from time to time," she said gently. "God forgives us if we're good on the whole."

"I didn't mean to sin," the girl sniffed. "I didn't mean to lie. I don't know clocks too well is all, miss."

"What have clocks to do with it?" Nin asked.

Sally turned to Adele. "If I tell you, will you absolve me?"

Adele tried not to smile. "I'm not a priest, Sally."

"I know, miss," she said. "But if I confess to you, Reverend McNeal won't be so hard on me when I go to confession. It's as good as penance."

"I see," Adele said. "Yes, do tell me about it."

"Well, miss, it was the night of — Miss Gibb doing herself in. They said in the paper she done herself in, didn't they?"

Adele glanced at Nin. "Yes, they said that."

"Well, it was that night."

"You said you heard the door to the kitchen open and close," Adele remembered.

"You lied about that?" Nin asked.

The girl once again lost her timidity. "No, indeed, miss! I didn't lie in that way. I heard what I heard, and I got good ears."

"Of course you do, Sally," said Adele. "You mentioned clocks. Does that mean you weren't truthful about the time you told us you heard the door open and close?"

"Well miss, yes."

"You told us you heard footsteps when the grandfather clock in the hall chimed midnight," Adele prompted.

The girl let out a sob. "That's just it, miss. My mind's all mixed up. I heard the footsteps lots before the clock."

Adele leaned back, giving her friend a look. It would seem Sally's notion of sin extended far beyond most people's.

"You heard someone in the kitchen before midnight, Sally?" she asked gently.

"Yes, miss. Lots before."

"What do you mean by lots?" Nin again lost her patience. "Be specific!"

The girl began to sob. "That's what the sheriff said and I got all confused!"

"It's all right, Sally." Adele patted her hand. "Please try to remember."

The girl peered from under her apron. "It's that important, miss?"

"It might be," said Adele. "I know you said you didn't have a clock, so you can't say when you heard the footsteps. Now you say you heard them a long time before the clock chimed midnight. Was it light outside when you heard them?"

"No, miss."

"Had it just turned dark when you heard them or had it been dark for some time?"

"Some time, I'd say." The girl began to calm down.

"Your window was open, Sally?" The girl nodded. "You can hear from outside if people are talking, can't you?"

The girl blinked. "I suppose, miss. That is, if they're on the street."

"Did you hear a young man talking, maybe laughing, that night?"

"Well, there's the boys that walk Miss Craig home from the factory," she said.

"But it would have been light outside then," Adele said. "I imagine they come home at around six or seven."

"Yes, miss." The girl's eyes were now dry and her manner more serene. "I see what you mean now. I did hear them young men and Mr. Walsh calling out to his friend. He walks partways with him after work."

"And later?" Nin asked.

The girl narrowed her eyes. "Wait, now. Yes, there was Lilly's young man. Oh, miss!"

"What is it, Sally?" Adele leaned forward.

"Why, my mind ain't mixed up anymore!"

"Yes?"

"I remember now. It was just after Lilly said goodnight to the young man who always talks with her on his beat. The young deputy."

Nin gave Adele a questioning look as Adele continued, "You mean Assistant Deputy Edison."

"Yes, miss," she said. "Lilly said 'goodnight, you young fox' or some such thing —" Adele bit her lip to keep from smiling but Nin laughed outright at the idea of Edison being a young fox, "— and then I heard the click of the lock."

"So you heard Lilly locking the door?" Adele asked.

"Yes, and then, the footsteps weren't long after. Maybe five or ten minutes."

"I thought you couldn't remember times," Nin said.

"I know what five and ten minutes are, miss," said the girl in a stoic voice. "Miss Taylor's always giving me five or ten minutes to do this or that. And she looks at her watch!"

Adele pressed Sally's hand. "You must have heard the footsteps at around eleven o'clock, not midnight. Thank you for telling us, Sally."

"You won't tell Mrs. Taylor?" The girl looked at her with hanging eyes. "Or Mrs. Clogg? Mrs. Clogg can get mighty fierce, and if she thought I was sinning to the police —"

"You weren't, Sally," Adele soothed. "It's hard to remember exact times when you aren't conscious of it."

"Conscious?"

"When you're not paying attention on purpose," Nin supplied.

Mrs. Clogg appeared at the door. "Sally! What are you gibbering about to these young ladies?"

"Sally was only helping us with these stains, Mrs. Clogg," Adele said. "She's been most kind."

"Sakes alive!" The woman studied the blouses. "Well, why didn't you use the kerosine, girl?" she scolded Sally as the scullery maid puttered to the pantry. "And me with the cake to finish before lunch —"

"Don't fret, Mrs. Clogg," said Adele. "We're nearly done here."

"Yes, and you're staying for lunch, you and Miss Branch," said Mrs. Clogg. "Happy to have you." She sounded anything but pleased, nor was her face less sour as she left the kitchen.

Adele trailed Sally to the pantry, a wide one with shelves neatly arranged in rows. Every bottle and jar was labeled.

"A place for everything and everything in its place," she murmured.

"What was that, miss?" Sally whirled around.

"I was merely admiring the way Mrs. Clogg arranges the pantry," she said. "I've a woman at home who does my cooking, and she's a wonder, but she doesn't come near Mrs. Clogg when it comes to organization."

"Yes, miss, she's ever so fussy." The girl ducked her head.

"I can see why she was so insistent that Millie couldn't have mistaken Rough on Rats for sugar."

The girl turned pale. "No, indeed, miss! Mrs. Clogg is ever so particular about things one oughtn't to take into one's belly, if you know what I mean."

"I know just what you mean," said Adele. "I'm sure she has the ice box organized in much the same way." Before the girl could object, she opened the door of the ice box.

"Just as I thought." Adele smiled. "A place for everything and everything in its place here too."

Nin peered into the ice box. There was wonderment on her face though Adele knew she had no use for such modern gadgets. "I'm sure no boarder would think of taking so much as a glass of milk with the way she has it marked."

Though Sally had been generous with her criticism at her employer's expense, she was clearly offended. "Mrs. Clogg ain't that kind, and neither is Mrs. Taylor. Many's a time I've seen Mr. Lyman or Mr. Walsh tiptoe down while I was at the washbasin and steal an orange or a slice of cake after dinner and when I told Mrs. Clogg, she said, 'Ain't no use trying to keep men away from the food. They're worse than mice.'"

"They are," Adele agreed with a grin, thinking of how many times she caught Jackson sneaking into the pantry after midnight. "But ladies don't do that, do they?"

"No, miss," said the girl. "They always ask polite if they want something. Most of them don't, though."

"Except Millie," said Adele. "She used to ask for her hot toddy, didn't she?"

"Yes, miss." A sadness swept over her face. "She would come down late, while I was lighting the fire for the morning some-times. Even then, she would ask nice-like, 'Sally, I'm not disturbing you?' She had respect for a girl and her work, she did."

"Yes, she did," Adele said softly, for she had never met a working woman who didn't have respect for other women who had to earn their bread. "Is that why she always made the hot toddy herself?"

"Yes, miss," she said. "She didn't want nobody waiting on her, she said. I think — if you'll pardon my saying so, miss — I think she had to wait on people herself, so she knew what it felt like."

"You're right, Sally, she did," Adele said. "It's very sensitive of you to see that."

The girl gave a broad grin. "She knew I never minded when she took an extra lemon slice or two."

"Oh?"

"I don't mean she stole them, miss," she said. "She was welcome to them. Mrs. Clogg's not stingy, as I said. But she ate them right there and then. Down to the rind, she did!" The girl shivered.

"Down to the rind?"

"Yes, miss," said Sally. "Like my brother Jim. Only his is oranges. Every Christmas my pa used to bring each of us an orange and Jim would eat the fruit like the rest of us, but then he'd go about eating the white part too."

"The pith?" Nin asked. She had managed to make her blouse spotless with the kerosine.

"Oh, miss, you look ever so pretty with your clean blouse," said the girl, her eyes wide. Nin blushed.

"Miss Branch means the white part of an orange and lemon is called the pith," Adele explained. "So Millie ate the pith too?"

"Bitter it was." Sally wrinkled her nose. "I tried it once and had to spit it out."

"Sally." Adele gripped her wrist. "Did Miss Gibb also eat the pith of the lemons she put in her hot toddy?"

"Oh, yes, miss," said the girl. "She used to say it was the best part. Always found them like that, the skins, that is, in the morning when I washed out the glass."

"How interesting," Adele murmured.

Heavy footsteps sounded in the hallway and Mrs. Clogg appeared, the white box carefully balanced in her thick hands. "Sakes, you're still chattering your head off with these nice young ladies, Sally?"

"We've had a good talk, Mrs. Clogg."

"Indeed?" The woman looked suspicious. "About what?"

Adele flashed Sally a smile. "Oranges at Christmas."

~

*S*he and Nin had an amiable cold lunch with Mrs. Taylor, as it seemed the woman didn't make much of meals she ate by herself when her boarders were away. She was at ease and eager to chat with them about her life before she had to take in boarders. Mrs. Taylor, though apt to amplify the experiences of a train conductor's widow, nonetheless had more substance to her character than Adele first thought.

Mrs. Taylor left them in the hallway to gather their hats and gloves with Lilly in attendance while she ambled upstairs, anxious to rest before her guests arrived home in the evening.

As Lilly opened the front door for them, a young man appeared. Adele recognized him as Dooland, the assistant deputy whom Hatfield had praised for his astuteness in finding the cigar stub during their first examination after Millie's death.

The young man stumbled against a loose floorboard and fell, sprawled in the hallway. He looked at her, dumbfounded.

"Good afternoon, Assistant Deputy," she said in a dignified voice. "I'm sure you wouldn't like me to tell your superior officer you do your work from the ground."

The young man scrambled to his feet, hastening a greeting with the tip of his hat. "I didn't know you were coming, miss."

"Yes, yes." Adele took Nin's arm. "We were just leaving. Good afternoon, and be careful!" She swung out the door, catching a glance at the young man's bewildered face as Lilly shut it.

"That ape will tell the sheriff we've been here," Nin snarled.

"He probably will, though quite innocently," said Adele. "I don't imagine he has a devious enough mind to realize we weren't supposed to be here."

"Speaking of deviousness," Nin glanced at her, "what was all that about lemon pith? And why so interested in where the shed is?"

Adele led her around the house to the back. There was more

overgrowth from the last time she had been there with Jackson and the sheriff, as if Millie's passing had suddenly brought in a late spring. She noticed for the first time how Mrs. Taylor cultivated a fine garden of flowers, and in addition to the roses she had seen the last time, there were violets, hyacinths, and geraniums. There were also many spruce-like shrubs and the scent of citrus filled the garden.

Adele tapped the bark of a tree with her parasol. "Now I see where the lemons come from." She stared at the bobbing yellow fruit.

"The ones Millie ate down to the rind," Nin added. "No wonder she was so bitter."

Adele stepped carefully between the shrubs, looking out for small holes she guessed were from gophers or rabbits. She came to the corner where the shrubs grew especially heavy and saw the cave-like entrance with a heavy wooden hatch.

"Lilly was right," she said. "The shed is well hidden."

"I suppose they don't want boys stealing wood and coal," Nin observed. "Easier to steal from a neighbor's shed than chop or gather your own."

"Nin, dear, if you're not careful, you'll begin to think like a detective." Adele smiled at her.

The woman snorted.

"It makes me wonder." Adele sighed.

"Wonder what?"

"We know Lilly didn't light the fire in Millie's room that night," she said. "And Millie herself didn't light the fire either."

"We don't know that," her friend reminded her.

"All right, we don't know that," Adele conceded. "But let us be hypothetical like the police."

"I hardly relish being like the police," her friend said.

"But let's suppose." Adele fingered the ridges of the lemon tree. "Let's suppose Millie didn't light the fire. Let's suppose her killer lit it. He — or she — wanted to burn that letter and enve-lope so desperately, they lit a fire on a hot and muggy night."

Her friend crossed her arms. "So we're supposing this reptile lit a fire."

"He or she would have known where the coal was stored," Adele said. "Since it was a hot day and no one would expect a fire, it's unlikely Lilly or Sally would have brought up the coal in the morning or evening."

Her friend's face began to clear. "I see what you're getting at."

"And if they knew where the shed was, so nicely hidden away, he or she would have been here before, either as a visitor or a boarder."

"That chuckling clown looks like a good culprit," Nin shot out. "The candymaker."

Adele burst out laughing. "I imagine we can rule out Mr. Walsh or any of the young men in the house. They wouldn't have much of a reason to kill Millie, much less the gumption."

"Except possibly Owen Burke," Nin pointed out.

"Yes," Adele said. "Mr. Owen Burke. The elusive, invisible Mr. Owen Burke." She tapped on the ground with her parasol.

CHAPTER 24

The next morning, Adele put together a basket with some of Ruth's boiled eggs, corn muffins, and home-made jam and left the house before Jackson woke up.

She went to Nin's flat. Her friend had been up with the sun and already finished her morning rituals which involved the scent of sage. Adele never asked questions about Nin's strange habits, nor had she ever asked about the shrine in the corner of the living room with candles and brass goblets, though she caught a glimpse once of a daguerreotype of a young woman not unlike Nin in her exotic beauty.

"I've brought you breakfast." Adele smiled. "A reward for accompanying me yesterday. I never dreamed it would cause you trouble."

"It caused me no trouble," Nin assured her. "The Generous Ones are powerful but not dangerous."

"You once told me we can never fully understand them," Adele ventured.

Nin did not answer. Adele knew when it came to her gift, she was reluctant to speak of it, even to her.

Her friend stared at the basket in her hands. "That looks rather refined."

"Why not?" Adele asked. "We're both refined ladies, aren't we?"

"I should hope not!" Nin slipped on a shawl. "Refined ladies are no better than statues."

"Refined ladies rather fallen from their pedestal, then," Adele corrected.

Her friend laughed.

Nin made a pot of strong coffee, and Adele consented to sit on the floor with a blanket so they could feel as if they were having a picnic.

"I've been thinking all night about that room," Adele began.

Nin shuddered. "That horrid place!"

"I fancy Mrs. Taylor knows the verdict on Millie's death by now. I imagine Lilly was ordered to clean and refresh it for a new boarder. It will be nothing more than another room by the end of the day."

"A place for everything and everything in its place," Nin echoed Adele's words.

Adele put her chin in her hand. "The chaos in that room will be only a memory."

"There was certainly chaos," Nin remarked.

"I'm convinced Millie was murdered and the murderer wanted her to suffer," Adele said. "There are other poisons that are easy to get hold of, if one knows how, and that don't leave such a trace as arsenic."

"Perhaps he or she didn't know how," Nin said.

"Perhaps," Adele said vaguely. "Perhaps not. This was a very intimate death."

Nin put down the egg. "I felt that too."

"The murderer knew Millie's habits down to the letter," Adele said. "He or she knew she would sit up all night reading." Adele toyed with the coffee spoon. "I think that was the whirlpool you felt. Millie's hysterical passion for that book she was reading."

"Her death dirge," Nin agreed.

Adele poured her another cup of coffee. "He knew it was safe to put the arsenic on the lemon because no one else would eat it. He knew Millie would, and when, and how."

"You've switched pronouns," Nin pointed out. "You're going under the assumption that it was a *he* now?"

"Not necessarily," her friend insisted. "They say poison is a woman's weapon, you know."

"And yet, there's a man involved," Nin murmured.

Adele sat up. "Was he in your whirlpool?"

"I can't say," said her friend. "I only know there was the heavy breath of a man in the room. A beastly breath."

"Murder is beastly," Adele said.

"And the fire," her friend reminded her. "That was intimate too. I often think there is nothing so intimate as a cozy fire, even on a hot night."

"And he knew where to get the coal," Adele said. "Then there's the letter and envelope. He had to burn them, but why, why?" She sighed.

"The uncle, perhaps?" Nin suggested. "If he wrote the letter —"

"He didn't write the letter," Adele said. "And even if he did, it would have been very unlikely he would have come down here. The man lives in South Carolina and travel is nearly impossible for him. He was wounded in the Civil War."

Nin stared. "Was he?"

"Jack did some checking with his friends in the South," she said. "He told me last night. He admitted he did write asking Millie for money several times. But that was before he entered a home for wounded soldiers. He's now quite happy. He told the police he hadn't written to Millie in months."

"And your brother believes him?"

"He believes his friends," Adele said. "They're Anspach people."

"Not a very honorable lot," Nin reminded her.

Adele couldn't help but smile. "They are to their own."

"If this uncle didn't write the letter, then who did?" Nin asked.

"That's what I want to know." Adele drank the last of her coffee and rose. "I'm going to take a look at that letter again."

"What for?"

"If I can decipher the letter goes with the envelope, and they're not just words of a passing acquaintance," Adele said, "it might convince the sheriff Millie's death wasn't suicide, and he'll open the case again."

"That won't be easy," said her friend. "He's probably had the evidence put in those dusty files of his already. Case closed."

"Then I shall get at the dusty files," Adele said with a smile. "You know I know just how to do it."

~

She waited until lunchtime before she went to the station. Jackson told her the night before he and Hatfield would be gone all afternoon to Rosa Gris, and she knew the station would be left in the hands of the amiable but somewhat dimwitted Edison.

Edison was there alone, gnawing at a limp sandwich and looking perplexed over the page in the typewriting machine. He jumped to attention, knocking over the chair.

"I'm sorry to startle you, Assistant Deputy." She used his full title, knowing it always made him feel important.

"No trouble, miss," said the young man, smiling. "The sheriff and Deputy Gossling ain't here."

"Aren't here," she gently corrected, sitting on the edge of the desk. "I thought my brother was teaching you to speak like a gentleman."

"Oh, he tries awfully, miss." The young man sank into the chair behind the sheriff's desk, where he always sat when the station was empty. "I guess I'm just not very bright when it comes to good speaking."

"Nonsense," Adele protested. "You're as intelligent as any young policeman I've seen."

"Thank you for saying so, miss." He bowed his head, and she could see the color creeping in his cheeks. It was no surprise to her, as she had known Edison was a little taken by her ever since she came to town. She met many young men who were in awe of the New Woman, looking upon her as other young men looked upon a woman on the stage.

"Someone else thinks so too," Adele said. "That young maid of Mrs. Taylor's."

"Oh, please don't mention that!" He glanced at the door, as if frightened the sheriff would stroll in any moment. "I got a tongue lashing for that, miss!"

"I don't see why you should have." Adele remembered the sheriff's belly laugh when he found out Edison was chatting up Lilly. "Young men have a right to converse with young ladies, as long as their intentions are honorable."

"Oh, I wouldn't think —" Edison looked genuinely horrified.

"Of course you wouldn't," Adele assured him. "You would just as soon help an old lady across the street as bat eyes where they're not wanted."

"That's a fact miss." He straightened with pride. "My ma always makes sure I'm a gentleman in my manner. She says it will take me far."

"And she's right." Adele laid a small package on the table. "Now put that flimsy egg sandwich aside. I brought you some roast beef."

"Roast beef!" The young man looked down at the box. "You needn't have done that, miss."

Adele peeled off her gloves. "I know how a warm stomach is important to a man in his work."

"Well—" the young man considered. "It wouldn't be gentlemanly to refuse, would it?" He tore through the wax paper and began to eat in a rather ungentlemanly fashion.

"Tell me, Edison." She leaned forward. "Has Sheriff Hatfield put away the evidence from the Millie Gibb case yet?"

"Not that I've seen, miss," said the young man. "Since yesterday, he's been taken up by those horse bandits in Blue Springs."

"Yes, I heard about that." Adele played with a ruffle on her skirt. "Assistant Deputy Edison, what do you think of the case?"

"Eh, miss?"

"I mean, do you think Miss Gibb committed suicide?"

The young man was so startled he dropped the apple in his hand on a pile of papers. "Well, I don't know —"

"You've been working here long enough to form your own opinions about these cases," Adele pointed out.

"Oh, it's my opinion you want." This calmed him. "I don't know as I would say Miss Gibb were one to kill herself."

"Really?" Adele had not expected this response. "You knew her enough to form that opinion?"

"Lord, no!" The idea seemed to terrify him. "It's from what Lilly said. She was always talking about the boarders."

"She seemed to me to have a mind of her own," Adele agreed, remembering the conversation from the day before with the maid.

"Lilly's a good girl. Never talking bad about any of 'em — them," he corrected. "She said Miss Gibb was — well, she was like you, miss. Knew her own mind."

"And women who know their own mind don't commit suicide," said Adele. "I think you're quite right, Edison." He beamed with pride. "I wish the sheriff thought as you did."

"He's the finest man I've ever worked for," Edison declared.

"I agree, Assistant Deputy." She shifted a little. "But I'll tell you a secret. I'm certain Miss Gibb didn't commit suicide, and I think I can prove it."

"Really, miss?" The young man leaned forward with interest.

"It would be quite an achievement if both you and I could bring some new evidence to the sheriff," said Adele. "After all, he wants justice as much as any of us."

"That's the truth, miss," said the young man. "The sheriff will do anything for justice!"

"But I need some information," said Adele, taking a breath. "I need to see that letter fragment we found in Miss Gibb's room."

"Well, I don't know, miss." He slid his feet back and forth against the wooden floor, the sawdust scraping against it. "You know the sheriff don't — doesn't — like it when you take evidence."

"I know what you're thinking," said Adele. "But didn't I help with that letter in the Blackstone case?"

"Well, that's true, miss."

"And would that have happened if you hadn't been generous enough to give it to me so I could take it to Dr. Blessings?"

"Well, no, miss —"

"Then in the name of justice, let me look at the letter fragment," Adele said. "The case is officially closed anyway."

"I never thought of that, miss. I guess it's alright, since the sheriff won't be needing it anymore." The young man jumped up. "The box is in the file room."

Adele rose. "I'll get it myself. You finish your lunch. There's a piece of cake in there, you know."

"If the sheriff knew I was letting you into the file room —"

"I'm practically one of you, Edison." She turned with dignity. "You ought to know that by now."

The young man had little to say against this and sat down again.

The file room was a cramped space in the corner of the station with only a high window and one gas lamp. She found a few candles on a shelf and lit one. The glow made her feel a little less prying. She found the box marked MILLICENT GIBB CASE sitting on the floor waiting to be put away.

She rifled through the bags and tissue paper, wincing when she saw the magazine under Millie's head when they had found her body, the pages crumbling at the edges. She found the letter carefully wrapped at the bottom of the box, no doubt Jackson's doing.

She studied the fragment. "Oh, how odd!"

"Everything all right, miss?" Edison called out.

She folded the fragment back into the tissue and placed it in her bag, brushing the dust from her skirt.

"You've been a great help, Assistant Deputy," she said as she passed his desk.

"Find what you were looking for, miss?" he asked.

"Indeed." She held up the fragment.

He fumbled to his feet. "Why, miss, you're not taking it out of the station?"

"Naturally," she said. "I may want to take it to Dr. Blessings. He's a consultant with us now." She put on her gloves.

"I don't know what the sheriff will say!" the young man declared.

"He won't say a word because we won't tell him," said Adele. "It's old evidence now. I'll bring it back just as I did the letter in the Blackstone case."

"Oh, I'm not worried about that," said Edison. "I know you take care of things, miss."

Adele patted his cheek. "You're sweet, Assistant Deputy. Not many like you."

The deep crimson in his face almost made her wish she hadn't said it. But just as he seemed about to speak, the door to the station flew open and the sheriff and Jackson sauntered in.

"Sheriff!" Edison gave her a frightened *I told you so* look. "We were just —"

"Good afternoon, Sheriff," Adele said. "I wanted to take Jack to lunch, but it seems you got there ahead of me."

"I told you I wouldn't be in until later this afternoon." Jackson gave her a sly look. "You're up to something, Del."

"Is that what you learned at the Anspach Agency?" she asked archly. "To be suspicious even of kin?"

"No," he muttered. "I learned that from our father."

Adele felt the sting. "That's unworthy of you, Jack."

"Now don't start a family quarrel." Hatfield hung up his holster.

"Maybe you ought to put us both under lock and key, Sheriff." Adele smiled.

"Not unless you give me a reason," he said seriously. "I suspect you might one of these days. Edison!" The young man jumped. "Get Miss Gossling some coffee or tea, whatever she would like."

"He already did," Adele said. "Assistant Deputy Edison is always most polite to me, Sheriff."

"And Assistant Deputy Dooland?" Jackson growled. "Is he always polite too?"

She tried not to flinch. "I don't believe I've spoken two words to him."

"Don't play innocent, Del!" her brother snarled.

"Assistant Deputy Dooland is the lad I sent to Mrs. Taylor's house to watch over Miss Gibb's room." Hatfield sat down slowly. "He told us you and Miss Branch were there yesterday."

"Nothing wrong with ladies lunching together," Adele said in a brisk voice.

"Ladies lunching!" Jackson grumbled.

"As a matter of fact, we lunched with Mrs. Taylor," Adele said. "You were always trying to persuade me to accept invitations with ladies in the city." She eyed her brother. "It's a wonder you're not as fussy about the company I keep here in Arrojo."

"Perhaps I ought to be," he said gruffly. "You weren't there to lunch. Dooland said he saw you and Miss Branch slithering around the back of the house."

"Slithering!" She was annoyed. "Does he think we're snakes?"

"Rather more like serpents in the Garden of Eden," Hatfield remarked.

"Despite what the Bible says, Sheriff, I don't believe all women are descendants of Eve!" She flounced out of the station.

CHAPTER 25

*A*dele knew her brother was far from finished with her. He had a habit of brooding over things and then letting them out during quiet moments. So it was no surprise to her after they had both retired to the parlor for coffee that evening, his face showed agitation as he watched her pour the coffee.

"Two lumps this time?" She tried to keep the mood pleasant. "You look as if you could use some sweetening."

"And you could use a good spanking!" he burst out.

She raised her eyebrow. "Even Papa never thought that of me."

"Oh, he found your moments of rebellion very amusing," Jackson said coldly. "Perhaps because they never interfered with his line of work. I rather think they were in tune with it."

"Jack, don't start." She handed him a coffee cup. "Whatever your anger is against me, don't put him down."

He sighed. "I'm sorry, Del. But sometimes I feel you've picked up the worst of his habits."

"Such as?"

"Prying."

"Prying!" She took up the needlework that looked already sloppy. "Whatever do you mean?"

"I mean your little visit to Mrs. Taylor's for a start." He crossed his legs. "You didn't fool anybody this afternoon. Hatfield and I know what that was about."

"Indeed?" She smiled at the thought of Assistant Deputy Dooland, aided by his inflated sense of self-importance when the sheriff had praised him, so eager to spill what he knew.

"Mrs. Taylor told us you and Miss Branch were in Millie's room."

"Well, since you and Hatfield officially closed the case, I didn't see the harm in it," she insisted.

"We haven't officially closed it."

She sat up. "You mean the sheriff is seeing sense at last?"

"I mean the paperwork hasn't gone through yet," Jackson corrected. "It's closed all right, but not officially. Until it is, no one is allowed at the crime scene."

"Then Assistant Deputy Dooland was remiss in his duties," she insisted. "He took a rather long lunch."

"Or he was intimidated by the deputy sheriff's sister taking liberties!" Jackson threw down the newspaper.

"In the most charming way, I assure you, Jack," she said.

"And what did you get out of Edison this afternoon?"

"A cup of tea," she retorted.

"Really, Del," he sighed. "This is me you're talking to. And don't think the sheriff won't get it out of him."

"I'm sure he will," said Adele. "But by then, it won't matter."

Her brother leaned forward. "I wish I could make you understand how interfering with a case —"

"A closed case," she reminded him.

"An unofficially closed case could be construed as breaking the law if the sheriff chose to see it that way."

"The sheriff, my dear brother, has more respect for my efforts than you have," she snapped.

"You mean he has more patience." He leaned back. "I don't know what you intend to prove about this case, Del."

She fiddled with the knitting needles. "If I were able to prove, or at least raise a shadow of doubt, that Millie's death was not suicide, the sheriff would reopen the case, wouldn't he?"

"He might and he might not," said her brother.

She rested a hand on his arm. "Jack, I thought you believe in justice."

"Justice?"

"If Millie didn't kill herself," Adele began, "and you've already ruled out accident, that means there's only one option left."

"She was murdered." Jackson nodded.

"Is it just to let a murderer get away with killing a woman, even if you all seem to think that woman had nothing to look forward to in life but books and words?"

"Murder is murder, Del." He chewed at the end of his pipe. "I just don't want you intruding."

"I do not intrude," she insisted. "I go by my wits, just as you and the sheriff do. I just go about it in my own way." She gave him a look. "You and Sheriff Hatfield had no complaints when I brought you the Lucy Blackstone murderer on a silver platter."

"Silver platter!" He grunted. "You think rather highly of yourself, don't you?"

She threw a pillow at him.

~

She slept half the night, awakening with the vision of Millie's bloated face in her mind. She felt almost as Sally must have when they carried out the body. She tried to construct the woman in her mind as one constructed a house of cards. But every time she thought she had a grasp on it, the house of cards toppled into a heap of darkness.

By the time the sun glowed through the frosty curtains, she knew what her next step would be.

She spent the morning in her shop attending to a few of Arrojo's younger generation elite who came to buy gifts for one of their own coming out into society very soon. When they left, she closed her shop and went into Nin's. The place was filled with the scent of lemongrass, and she found her friend in the back filling packets with the herb.

"Very good for stomachaches," Nin advised.

"I must buy one for Jack," Adele said. "He likes his steaks a little too much." She reached into her purse for coins but her friend shook her head and shoved a few packets in her hands without a word. "You should never give away your wares, dear," Adele said softly.

"I give anything to a friend," said Nin kindly.

"Even if it means incurring the wrath of the friend's ungrateful brother?" Adele asked with a smile. "He and the sheriff know we were at Mrs. Taylor's yesterday."

Nin wiped her hands on her apron. "It does men good to be irked by women once in a while."

Adele laughed and took her hand. "Then we'll be irking Jack even more. I'm off to send a telegram."

"To whom?" Her friend closed the shutters of her shop and locked the door.

"Mr. Owen Burke," Adele announced.

"Owen Burke!"

"Mr. Bain offered to call Mr. Burke back from Arizona territory if Jack wished to speak to him," said Adele as they crossed the street to the post office. "Now Jack wishes to speak to him."

"I thought the case was closed," said Nin.

"It is, unofficially," said Adele. "But I hardly think Mr. Bain would know that."

A slow smile appeared on Nin's face. "In other words, the deputy sheriff doesn't want to speak to Mr. Burke."

"For our purposes, he does," said Adele.

As it was just after lunchtime, the post office was empty. Mr.

Duncan sat behind the counter, gnawing on an apple. He did not bother to put the apple down as they approached.

"Why, Miss Gossling!" He grinned, showing yellow teeth. "I haven't seen you in, oh, since poor Miss Gibb came in that day."

"You could at least take the apple out of your mouth when you speak of the dead," Nin snapped.

The man gave her a severe look. "What can I do for you, Miss Gossling?"

"My brother asked me to send a telegram for him," she said.

"Not like the deputy sheriff to send someone else to do his errands." The man rubbed his chin.

"I'm not someone else," Adele said in a firm voice. "I'm his sister."

The man flinched as he handed her a telegraph form and a pencil. "I wasn't implying, miss."

"I know you weren't, Mr. Duncan." Adele smiled.

"You ought to sit down to lunch," Nin observed.

"Now, how can I sit down when there's work to do, Miss Branch?" He glanced at the pile of envelopes on the table behind him. "Mail needs sorting, and Miss Gossling needs to send a telegram."

"We'll only take up a moment of your time, sir," Adele said.

She wrote out the telegram:

Please arrange meeting with Mr. Owen Burke. Will be in Sacramento day after tomorrow. Send when and where to Adele Stationery Shop. Deputy Sheriff Jackson Gossling, Arrojo Police.

"Well, that's short and sweet, isn't it?" The man glanced down at it.

"Will you please make sure it's sent today?" Adele asked. "It's official police business, you know."

"I always send telegrams right away." Mr. Duncan grumbled "We're all glad your brother took that job, Miss Gossling. Oh, not that there's a thing wrong with the sheriff, but, well, Mr. Gossling is so refined!"

"Yes, he is," Adele said with a small smile. She knew Jackson wouldn't think much of the country bumpkin version of the refined gentleman.

"Mr. Burke might be awfully disappointed when he finds two ladies meeting him instead of the Arrojo police," Nin remarked as she swept the shawl over her shoulders against the wind.

"We?" Adele glanced at her.

"I'm coming with you," said her friend.

"That's kind of you, dear, but I might go by train." She remembered only too well Nin's fear of confined spaces.

The woman braced herself with a determined look on her face. "I'll brave it if you will."

Adele smiled and took her friend's arm. "He might not be disappointed. He might in fact be pleased."

"If his flirtations with Millie were anything to go by —" her friend snorted.

"Exactly," said Adele with a sly eye.

They walked down Bridge Street, men tipping their hats to them.

"What now?" Nin asked as they passed her shop.

"I have one more place I'd like to go," said Adele. "To play a hunch, as Jack would say."

"Where are we going?"

"The Wrigley School," said Adele. "I want to speak to Mrs. Wrigley again. My way."

"Our way," her friend corrected.

They reached the school just as the girls were finishing their afternoon studies. They dodged the flying ribbons and skirts, avoiding the questions from those who knew them by sight, and made their way to Mrs. Wrigley's office.

The woman was glad to see them. "Always a trial with the first few months of the school year," she admitted, brushing her ruffled sleeves over her bony wrists. "But we must do our best to educate young girls properly."

"Miss Gibb believed in women's education as much as you do, didn't she, Mrs. Wrigley?" Adele asked.

The woman flinched. "I really don't know what she believed anymore, Miss Gossling. I always prided myself in knowing my teachers but this entire ordeal has shaken my faith in my own judgment."

"You mustn't think that," Nin said softly.

"You're kind, Miss Branch." The woman smiled. "I don't mean I'm giving up my intentions to educate my young ladies. Let's just say I shall be much more careful next time and hire a teacher whose mind is as stable as her teaching."

"You think Miss Gibb was unstable?" Adele eyed her.

"Isn't it obvious?" Mrs. Wrigley set two small teacups in front of them with a sugar cube at the edge of each.

"From what everyone said, Miss Gibb was the epitome of stability," Adele said.

"But, Miss Gossling, you cannot deny she — did herself in." The last was said with a glance toward the closed door, as if she expected some of her delicate charges to burst in any moment. "I don't believe anyone would consider that balanced."

"You don't entertain the idea it might have been something else?"

Mrs. Wrigley stared at her. "You mean an accident?"

"She means murder," said Nin with a rough voice.

The woman dropped her spoon on the floor. It made a hollow sound against the dusty rug. "Who would want to do such a horrific thing?"

"It's only a theory, Mrs. Wrigley," Adele said mildly. "You needn't fear it will scandalize your school."

"I should hope not!" Mrs. Wrigley stiffened.

"I'm interested in one thing, Mrs. Wrigley, and I thought you could help me."

"Yes?"

"You told us Mis Gibb was — well, dejected was the word you

used, I think — when she discovered she wasn't going to get an administrative position at the school."

"Not yet," the woman corrected. "I still had hopes she would show herself as suitable for the position sometime in the future."

"Of course you did," Adele said. "Do you remember if she said anything?"

"Said anything?" The woman wrinkled her nose.

"When she left your office after your meeting or even later," said Adele. "You see, Miss Gibb took great stock in words, so what she said, even if it seemed like a trifle, might have been important."

"You mean a clue as to why she committed suicide?" Mrs. Wrigley asked.

"A clue to why someone might have killed her," Nin said. Her friend pressed her hand.

"Her family wishes to know," Adele fibbed. "She has an uncle, you see, a war veteran, and he's rather keen on details."

"I completely understand." The woman nodded. "Must be a poor, lonely man, and those type always cling to their women-folk, like Mr. Wrigley." She sighed. "I was all he had, you see."

"And he used you like a sponge," Nin growled.

Mrs. Wrigley glared at her, but her tone was composed as she said, "I really don't recall anything in particular," said the woman. "I do recall her mumbling."

"Mumbling?" Adele asked.

"Oh, there was nothing odd about it," said Mrs. Wrigley. "She was always mumbling to herself."

"Did you happen to catch the words?"

"No, I'm afraid not," said the woman. She leaned back, staring at the wall opposite with a wistful look.

"But later?" Adele prompted.

"Oh, well, later," she said, "now that you ask me, I remember it. We gave a tea for one of our benefactors, the teachers and I, that is. And when we were clearing up, Miss Gibb said to me, 'I've found another avenue.'"

Adele grasped her parasol. "Do you know what she meant?"

"I'm afraid not," said Mrs. Wrigley. "I was alarmed, of course, as it immediately came to my mind she intended to leave us. At the beginning of the school year, it would have been difficult for me to find someone to replace her."

"Now you must replace her anyway," Nin pointed out. The woman winced.

"But she didn't leave," Adele murmured.

"No, indeed," said Mrs. Wrigley. "I thought — well, I thought she might be taking other students outside of school. Private students, you see."

"Why is that?" Adele set down her cup.

"Something was distracting from her teaching," said Mrs. Wrigley. "Private students can distract one. They require so much attention." She sighed.

"Would that have been allowed?" Nin asked.

"Well, strictly speaking, no," said the woman. "I don't allow my teachers to take other work outside of the school." The stoicism came back in her voice. "I make it very clear the higher salary I pay is because I expect them to devote their time exclusively to my girls."

"But you didn't confront her about it?" Adele asked.

"I thought after our meeting, I'd better not," said the woman. "I felt Miss Gibb was — I don't know how to put it — on edge. And I didn't want to push her."

Adele patted her hand. "It's best sometimes to leave people alone."

"I left her alone, and look what happened!" The woman covered her face with her handkerchief. "Oh, forgive me!"

Nin was at her side but Mrs. Wrigley seemed reluctant to surrender to her sympathy. "I'm quite all right, Miss Branch, quite all right. I'm anxious to put this distressing business behind me, for my own sake and the girls." She gathered the tea things. "I think the less said about Miss Gibb from now on, the better, don't you, Miss Gossling?"

Adele rose, taking her friend's arm. "Thank you for being so patient, Mrs. Wrigley. I'm sure you'll find a very good teacher to replace Miss Gibb."

"Oh, I've several candidates already," said the woman in a cheerful voice. "She was not indispensable, after all."

"Not indispensable!" Nin growled as they left the office. "No wonder Millie was so happy she found another avenue."

"Yes, but what avenue?" Adele asked. "And was it worth her life?"

She felt clawing fingers grasp her hand.

"Gracious!" She glanced down at Beatrice's familiar strawberry blond hair. Carolyn took Nin's hand.

"For young ladies, you certainly behave like heathens," Nin snarled.

"You would know," Beatrice snapped back.

"None of that, Bea," Caroline insisted, brushing back the untamed hair. "I think Miss Branch is a very nice person."

"It's unworthy of you to be so cruel, Beatrice." Adele managed to wrench free from the girl's grasp.

"Oh, bum it!" the girl declared.

"You'd better not let Mrs. Wrigley hear you speak in such a manner," Carolyn said. "She said she would give you a tongue lashing the last time."

"That was before Miss Gibb killed herself," the girl said. "Now, all Mrs. Wrigley cares about is our parents don't hear of it." She took Adele's arm. "I've something to show you."

"You'll have to come upstairs," added Carolyn. "It's hidden in one of the classrooms."

"Nin, wait here," Adele whispered. "I won't be a minute."

The girls practically pulled her up the stairs.

"You're not being naughty again, are you, Bea?" she asked.

"You're outgrowing that, you know."

"I know," said the girl. "Mother says she might let me wear my hair up next year."

"Aren't you a little young for that?" Adele asked. "My father didn't allow me to wear mine up until I was fifteen."

"Mother says I'm precocious," said Beatrice. "I suppose that makes me older than my years." And jilting her chin up, picking up the edge of her skirt as she walked, Adele couldn't help but admit she did look older than eleven.

The girls led her to a dark classroom still dusty with chalk from the day's studies. Beatrice flooded the place with light, though the buzz of the electric bulbs hurt Adele's ears. "This was Miss Gibb's classroom," she said in a mysterious voice.

"Indeed?" Adele had been wary, knowing the girls liked to make a fuss over nothing, but now she was interested.

"Every teacher has her own classroom for the term," Carolyn explained. "Everything in it is hers."

"Of course it's not hers!" Beatrice snapped.

"I meant it's hers until the end of the year," her friend insisted.

"She can do what she pleases with it," Beatrice continued. "Mrs. Hastings put flowers all around her room. She says they were painted by children she used to teach back in Iowa. Mrs. Flip's is filled with her own needlework."

"I see Miss Gibb wasn't very keen on decorations," Adele remarked as she looked around the bare room.

"They wouldn't be here if she had," said Carolyn. "They came and took everything away."

"Who did?" Adele stared.

"Oh, some crotchety old lady," said the girl with a yawn. "She said she was a friend of Miss Gibb's uncle or something. Just wanted the goods, if you ask me."

"She didn't ask you, Carolyn," said Beatrice. The girl went to the desk and slid out the top drawer. "The old woman didn't even think to look at the desk." She pulled something from the back of the drawer. "Here's what we found."

"My, but you've been studious, haven't you?" Adele remarked.

Beatrice stiffened. "You said we were astute."

"And, indeed, you are," said Adele as she examined the object. It was a silver fountain pen engraved with scrolls and leaves.

"I think it's ugly," Carolyn prompted.

"Not ugly, but certainly coarse," Beatrice said.

"It's a man's pen." Adele turned it around. She spotted faint engraved letters on the side: *M to H. With love.* "That sounds familiar." But her mind was blank.

"What is it? What did you find?" Beatrice was at her side, her eyes wide. "Did Miss Gibb have a lover?"

"Don't use such words, Beatrice." Her friend shivered. "They're wicked."

"A lover is one who loves," Beatrice argued. "How is that wicked?"

"It might be, and then again, it might not." Adele slipped the pen in her bag. "You've both been very naughty but very useful." She pressed pennies into their hands. "Don't make yourself sick now."

Beatrice's eyes were still wide. "Maybe that's why she killed herself. She wanted to marry him, and he told her to go to the devil!"

"Bea," Adele said, "I really think you ought to stop using such words. On school grounds at least."

"I thought you believed in ladies saying what they meant," Beatrice insisted.

"Only after they say what they don't mean," Adele remarked as they led her out of the room. "While we're on the subject of words, have either of you anything with Miss Gibb's handwriting you could give me? Any graded papers, reports, that sort of thing?"

The girls were only too happy to oblige, and she realized why as she glanced down at them. Miss Gibb had been verbose and not very complimentary with her grading. The tone did indeed confirm Millie's opinion of their being "spoiled, insolent girls."

Nin was outside, her shawl drawn over her head, as the dust floated around in the evening wind. "Schoolgirl nonsense, as usual?" she asked as they began walking toward Bridge Street.

"Not this time." Adele showed her the pen. "I don't think there's much doubt some man had affection for her."

"It must have been a long time ago," Nin said.

"The events of the past often have repercussions on the present," Adele said.

When she reached her store, there was a telegram slipped under her door. It read, *Owen Burke will meet Deputy Sheriff Gossling at The Blue Goat on Wall Street tomorrow at one o'clock.* There was no signature.

CHAPTER 26

Sacramento was cheerful with a deep blue sky and pleasant breeze that was refreshing without being cold. This affected Nin for the better. Her color returned, and her step livened as they made their way out of the station.

Adele took her arm. "Elsie will be glad to see us. She's taken a fancy to you."

"I'm still the country mouse in her eyes," her friend snorted.

"I was hoping to see the Blessings first, but we'll be late." Adele glanced at her watch. "We don't want to keep Mr. Burke waiting."

They caught a hackney cab waiting in the corner, and Adele directed the driver to The Blue Goat.

When they entered, she was reluctant to admit Mr. Bain had not been far off the mark in his warnings about the place. The bar was crowded, and tables squeezed up against the walls. Everything was dark, and dampness in the air gave the restaurant a putrid scent.

"Not a very comforting place," Nin observed.

"Working people hurry through lunch so they never notice." Adele nodded. She caught a glimpse of a young woman with dull blond hair and a shirtwaist sitting in the corner of the bar, giggling at something a barman was telling her. She turned her head and looked straight at Adele without acknowledging her.

Mr. Owen Burke sat at a corner table. He looked as if he had been waiting for some time. Soup and bread sat in front of him untouched. The owlish eyes peered behind thick glasses, and the warm air outside made his hair almost like cotton.

Adele held out her hand. "Good afternoon, Mr. Burke."

The man jumped. "Have we met?"

"Not officially." Adele took the chair opposite him. Nin perched at the edge of her seat, regarding the man with a cat-like stare.

"I'm afraid I don't understand, Miss —"

"Gossling," Adele said.

"Oh, I see." The man seemed to glance over her head. "And Deputy Sheriff Gossling —"

"—is my brother," she finished.

"Don't tell me he sent you in his stead." The man's brows arched.

"Certainly not!" Nin growled.

"I have a confession to make, Mr. Burke." Adele folded her hands. "I'm afraid we've deceived you."

"Oh?"

"I sent you that telegram, not my brother."

"What is the meaning of this?" the man snarled.

"Keep your voice down!" Nin snarled back.

Mr. Burke sank into his chair. "I'm terribly sorry. So ungentlemanly of me. But then, Mr. Bain is always trying to teach me manners."

"It's clear he failed miserably," Nin said.

"I oughtn't to have done it," Adele admitted. "I don't blame you for being angry."

"Angry?" The man grinned. "I should say I'm charmed. Two pretty ladies pretending to be a deputy sheriff just to see me." His eyes slid toward Nin, who regarded him with loathing.

"We know how busy you must be," Adele said, "setting up a branch in the Arizona territory."

"Eh?" The man squinted.

"Mr. Bain told us you were sent there," she said.

"Oh, of course." The man gulped. "Well, as a matter of fact, I was coming home in a day or two anyway."

"Are the as receptive to your educational materials in Arizona as they are here?" Adele inquired.

"I wasn't there to sell, Miss Gossling." The man leaned back, toying with a spoon. "I was there to instruct salesmen."

"I see," said Adele, smiling. "Doing a little educating yourself."

"A charming way of putting it." He glanced down at the basket of rolls on the table. "Oh, how rude of me. Will you take some lunch? A sherry, perhaps?" He signaled the waitress.

"Sherry will do," Adele said. "You like to see women drinking sherry, Mr. Burke?"

"Truth be told, Miss Gossling, I scarcely like to see women drink anything but tea." He laughed. "They do it so neatly that it's a treat to watch."

"We're not puppets for your amusement," Nin grumbled.

"No, naturally not," said the man glancing at her. "Are you the deputy sheriff's sister too?"

"Heaven forbid!" Nin spat this out with such alarming intensity the people at the next table looked up.

"Don't like the fellow, eh?" Mr. Burke asked. "Mr. Bain told me he was a likable man."

"I'm glad you think so," said Adele. The sherry arrived and she studied the tiny glass. "You persuaded Millie Gibb to drink sherry every evening."

"Who?"

"Miss Millie Gibb," Adele said. "A guest at Mrs. Taylor's boarding house in Arrojo."

"Oh, yes, Mr. Bain told me about her," he said. "Recently died or something." The man picked up a roll but did not tear into it. He held it like a baseball.

"Yes, she died," Adele said. "I'm sorry you had to find out while you were away."

"I shouldn't think it was much of a surprise," he said nonchalantly. "I've met many schoolteachers whose lives were, well, lacking excitement."

"You thought Miss Gibb was lacking excitement?" Adele asked. Nin rose and wandered to the corner, staring at the wall.

"My dear woman," the man said. "I knew her only slightly."

Adele drank the sherry. It was vile stuff, bitter on her tongue. "I was told otherwise, Mr. Burke."

"Who told you? Mrs. Taylor?" He barked out a laugh and ripped into the roll. "Shall I tell you something about boarding-house keepers, Miss Gossling?"

"I should be glad to hear it," she said.

He leaned forward. "They're romantics at heart. Their lives are rather boring, ordering about maids and feeding guests. So they dream up little intrigues, most of them taking place among their boarders. No doubt what you heard was just such a story."

"There was some hint of romantic intrigue," Adele admitted.

"Precisely!" The man looked triumphant. "A traveling salesman has, I don't know what you would call it — a sort of allure for some ladies because he's been all over the territory. All over the country, in some cases."

"I'm sure," Adele said dryly.

"I can't tell you how many middle-aged ladies keeping boardinghouses and hotels I've met who hinted this or that lady would certainly be a good match for me," he confessed. "What a bachelor must endure!"

"I have every sympathy, Mr. Burke," Adele said with a fluttering tone. "But I confess, I have even more sympathy for the ladies."

"Oh, they're nice enough old birds, I suppose," he mumbled.

"I wasn't referring to the boardinghouse keepers," she said. "I was referring to the ladies mentioned."

"Eh?" The man squinted again.

"I can only hope a man like you would let them down easy," she continued, seeing the spark of superiority in his eye.

"Oh, indeed," he said. "Why, there's never a tear when I leave."

Nin returned, her shawl wrapped tightly around her shoulders.

"So you don't remember Miss Gibb?" Adele asked.

"I remember what I sold her," he said. "A subscription of *American Language Origins* and our latest edition of *Fundamentals of English In Our Times*." He wiped his mouth with satisfaction.

"You have a remarkable memory, Mr. Burke," Nin said.

"For sales, yes," he said. "I couldn't describe the customers if my life depended on it." He rose. "Well, ladies, it's been charming, but I really must be off on my route." He laid some bills on the table and reached behind him. Adele noticed a large trunk resting against the wall.

"Are these your wares?" Adele asked.

"Indeed," he said.

"I thought salesmen carried suitcases," Nin said.

"They do, dear lady," he said. "But, you see, you never know when you'll run into a potential customer. I like having as many books with me as possible."

"Like your employer likes to have all his books in front of him?" Adele asked.

The man stared. "Oh, you mean Mr. Bain's office? Yes, I suppose we're of the same frame of mind on that score." He stepped aside to let them pass. "Please give my regards to your brother and tell him it was most delightful of him to send two ladies in his stead."

"But he didn't send us in his stead," Nin said. "We invited ourselves."

"Eh? Well, all the same, it was a pleasure." He shook both their hands and trudged down the road, the trunk swinging at his side.

"Do you hold the same opinion about The Blue Goat as your employer, Mr. Burke?" Adele called out after him.

He whirled around "Eh?"

"When I was there with my brother, Mr. Bain warned Miss Taper against becoming too familiar with the place."

"Well, I suppose women will do what they like these days, won't they?" He tipped his hat and continued down the road.

"Whether you men like it or not," Adele mumbled after him. "I see why Mr. Bain praised him. They think alike." She glanced at her friend, who was watching after the now-empty length of street. "Are you all right, dear?"

Nin looked as pale and shaken as she had the day they examined Millie's room. Adele led her across the street to what looked like a respectable tea shop. She ordered them tea and sandwiches and the waitress, taking one glance at Nin, immediately set a pitcher of cold water in front of them.

"That man!" Nin breathed.

"Yes, he was rather horrible," Adele agreed. "I can't think what Millie saw in him, though intelligent and independent women often fall for snakes like that."

"I couldn't take it anymore!"

"I suppose he wasn't any different than most salesmen," Adele said. "A little too sure of himself with the ladies."

"No, it wasn't that," Nin said. "Looking into his eyes was like looking into the eyes of a stranger."

Adele picked at the sandwich. "Well, he was a stranger to us."

"There was venom in every word he said."

"I thought it odd he denied he knew Millie," Adele said. "He wasn't exactly trying to hide his interest in her at Mrs. Taylor's."

"Yes, I suppose that's it," Nin murmured. "Rather stupid of him."

"Mr. Burke didn't strike me as much of an intellectual," Adele said dryly.

Nin returned to herself as she ate. "I wonder what your friend Elsie would think of him."

"Elsie would eat him alive!" Adele declared. Her friend laughed.

CHAPTER 27

They went through the city's main bustling street and into a quieter residential district where buildings stood in three and four stories. Windows were open and people, mostly women, stuck their heads out, glancing at their passing cab with interest. Children playing on the sidewalk trotted alongside it, looking up with open stares at her and Nin. Adele was surprised when her friend opened the window all the way and put out her hand. Many took it, holding as they rushed alongside the cab.

"They're simple and happy," she said with a soft smile.

"My father once said the irony of life is the more prosperous one becomes, the more complicated life gets," Adele remarked. "Even when one has all the luxuries money can buy."

"I hate money!" Nin growled.

"We can afford to hate it," Adele reminded her. "We have enough of it."

"It makes slaves of women." Nin glared at the road.

"That I don't deny," Adele said. "Ladies suffer more than men."

"I didn't say ladies," Nin pointed out. "I said women!"

"So you did." Adele smiled.

255

They were grave and silent as the cab pulled up next to a house that looked a little more scrubbed than the others with a modest garden. The door opened and Elsie came flying out. Jackson always said Elsie reminded him of a colt, her largess dwarfing in the blunter aspects of her sprightly step and warmth.

She embraced Adele with the vigor of a colt as Nin shrank back near a tree.

"Del, dear, at last." She glanced at Nin. "Don't be afraid, Miss Branch. We're bold but we're harmless." She called over her shoulder, "Oda, come out and meet my friends from the country!"

A woman emerged from the house whom Adele could only describe as holding herself like a Russian princess. The stiff gait almost intimidated her.

"One of the warriors for our cause, Oda Kriska," Elsie introduced. "Adele Gossling and her friend, Miss Branch."

The woman spoke in a smooth voice with a soft accent, "I'm very glad to meet you."

"We're just visiting, of course," Adele said. "We don't want to impose."

"Impose?" Elsie put her arm around her shoulders. "On the contrary. You've come at just the right time."

Adele's gut tightened. "I haven't come for politics Elsie."

"Call it opportunity." She led her into the house with Nin trailing behind. "We have it all arranged. The governor is giving some dinner party tomorrow, so we've moved our demonstration then."

"Elsie, I don't think —"

"You and Miss Branch could stay the night and come with us tomorrow. You needn't even raise your voice. It's the numbers that count."

"Why not place cardboard figures of the governor with his throat cut on his lawn?" Nin asked warily.

Elsie glared at her. "That would hardly get our point across, Miss Branch."

"And what do you intend to do to get your point across?" Adele asked. "Burn the house down?"

"Heavens, no, dear, we're not rioters," she insisted. "We might bring a few smoke bombs —"

"Elsie!"

"They're harmless enough," she snapped. "That man and his comrades must know we mean business."

"You do not approve, Miss Gossling?" Oda had been watching silently.

"Del is for more temperate methods," Elsie said, not without a little scorn. "Like that bird Vanya and her ladies."

"I thought you liked Vanya," Adele said.

"We fight for the same things, I'll admit," Elsie said. "But our methods are very different and so are our results."

Adele put her parasol in the stand next to the door. "I told you, we didn't come for politics. We've really come to see your father."

"You found another body in your garden?" Elsie winked at Oda.

"Elsie told me about that," said the woman. "Rather intriguing."

"I don't find a young lady dead before her life really begins very intriguing," Adele said dryly.

"Del takes such things seriously, Oda," said Elsie. "Her father was one of the most influential lawyers in San Francisco, and her brother is now a country deputy sheriff."

"You make us sound like outlaws," Adele grumbled.

Elsie laughed, leading them out the back door. "Papa is enjoying the sun. Such lovely weather here." She lowered her voice. "I don't think we'll be able to stay in the city much longer, Del. His rheumatism and the dampness —"

"The poor man!" Nin burst out.

The man in question sat on a wicker chair with his glasses perched on his nose and a book in his lap, but looked up when he heard the voices.

"Silence!" Elsie hissed.

"Don't fret, Elsie, dear," he said, amused. "A poor old man's ears never burn."

"You're nothing of the kind." Adele greeted him with a kiss on the cheek.

He eyed Nin. "As I recall, Miss Branch has a refreshing forthrightness. I like forthright people."

Nin's face softened and she delivered a kiss on his cheek just as Adele had done.

"Elsie wrote me you were here," said Adele.

"I had a time persuading him to come," Elsie insisted. "He's giving a paper for the Nebraska conference next month and he keeps saying he ought to be writing."

The man tapped his cigar on the page in front of him. "One cannot speak until one has something to speak about."

"Bah!" Elsie snorted. "You could give a million speeches in your sleep."

Dr. Blessings laughed and took her hand. "I wouldn't dare for fear of keeping you awake all night." In a more tentative voice, he said, "I could do with some lemonade, dear, and I think our guests would appreciate some of those spice cookies you made this morning."

"Your wish is my command, sire." She gave him an exaggerated bow and went into the house.

When she was gone, Adele said, "She wrote me all about the rally."

"It's quite trying to have a revolutionary daughter," he sighed. "I believe in everything she stands for, but the thought of those smoke bombs — heavens!"

"There won't be any smoke," Nin said in an authoritative tone.

"You can trust Nin." Adele gave her an affectionate look. "She has insights others don't."

"All the same —" He looked worried.

"I'll get her to promise they won't go too far," Adele assured him.

He pressed her hand. "It's been too long since we've seen you."

"Not since we came about Lucy Blackstone."

Elsie came out with the tray. "I think Del is playing sleuth again, Papa," she said in a sly voice.

"I was hoping you could help us," Adele admitted, slipping the letter fragment and envelope out of her purse. "There's been another death in Arrojo."

"My, but you're becoming the crime capital of the Far West," Elsie remarked.

"Hardly that," said Adele. "In fact, the sheriff and Jack are convinced it wasn't a crime at all."

"Oh?" Dr. Blessings held the glass of lemonade with both hands.

"They think it was suicide," said Adele.

"And you and Miss Branch believe differently."

"I don't care one way or the other." Nin shrugged. "She was a lizard!"

"Such talk about a sister," Elsie reprimanded.

"It's true the woman who died wasn't very well liked," Adele admitted. "But if someone did kill her, which I believe they did, it shouldn't go unpunished."

"The dead women's crusader," Elsie said. "Good for you!" She held up a spoon like a sword.

"What can I do?" Dr. Blessings asked.

"The police found this in the grate." She handed him the letter. "Nin and I discovered this later on." She put the envelope on the table. "The police believe the letter is from Millie's — the dead woman's — uncle asking for money. He's rather a sponger."

"Most men are," Elsie grumbled.

"Not all of us, I hope," Dr. Blessings said in a playful tone. Elsie blushed and turned away.

"I believe the letter and envelope weren't sent," Adele continued. "I think they weren't written by her uncle either."

"Then who did write them?" Elsie asked.

Adele looked at Dr. Blessings. "I want you to help me find that out. I think I have the documents you need."

"Well, let's have it," he said. "You have me curious now."

She took out some folded papers and a gold case. "These are papers Millie graded for some of the girls she taught. She was a teacher at a boarding school." He nodded. "And this is a pen that was found in the back of her desk."

"You think she used the pen to write this letter and address this envelope?" He held it up to the light.

"She might have," Nin ventured.

"That would be rather colossal," Elsie said. "If Papa knew just by the pen and the writing that this woman wrote the letter."

"That's what I'm here to find out," Adele said.

"I cannot commit myself—" the professor began.

"Oh, Papa, who's asking you to commit yourself?" Elsie groaned. "Del is only asking you to look at it."

"Please, sir," Adele laid her hand on his wrist.

He studied her. "Did you know the woman well?"

"Not very," she said.

"And she wasn't very well liked," he continued.

"What does that matter?" Elsie growled.

Adele picked a daisy from the small plot at her feet. "Everyone in town believes she killed herself because she was a spinster with no future prospects," she said. "Perhaps they're right. Perhaps they're wrong. But to disregard a woman's death because she's unmarried and not young —"

"I agree," Elsie declared. "If she was a teacher, she was an important contributor to society. Such a valuable asset ought not to be overlooked, Papa."

Dr. Blessings was silent for a moment. "Elsie, my dear, will you please get me my kit? You know the one. It's in the first drawer of the bureau."

The kit in question was really more like a doctor's bag with odd little things, including several magnifying glasses much more powerful than Adele's. In the methodical way of a scientist, he laid out the letter fragment, envelope, papers from the Wrigley girls, and the pen in a row on the table. He examined them one at a time with various tools.

His work did not take long, though it seemed to Adele the later afternoon passed into early evening by the time he finished. Oda and two young girls came out to gather dead leaves from the trees in a basket but they were discreet and silent.

Dr. Blessings leaned back in the chair and took off his glasses. "Your eye for details does you credit, Adele. I often think you ought to have been a scientist."

"I'm right, then?" Adele pressed her hands together, feeling them dampen.

"I cannot commit myself," he repeated. "But to the best of my ability as an expert, I would say the letter was definitely written by a woman."

"How can you tell?" Adele asked.

"There are ways, my dear," he said, smiling. "I shan't give out my secrets, but let us say it's a prettier hand than the man's."

"Bosh!" Elsie growled. "My hand's as strong as any man's, and so are my words."

"I don't know that I would be so proud of that," Nin murmured.

"But characteristics that make for a woman's hand are in the letter?" Adele asked.

"Enough to make me quite sure." Dr. Blessings nodded.

"So it couldn't have been written by Millie's uncle," Nin said.

"Not unless he has a very feminine penmanship," said Dr.

Blessings. "Which is quite possible. I would need to see a sample to be sure."

"Let us assume the handwriting is a woman's," Adele said. "Do you think it might be the dead woman's?"

Dr. Blessings chewed on the end of his glasses. "That I'm less sure of. There isn't much to go on, you know. A small fragment, an address on an envelope."

"But you've those papers too, Papa," Elsie pointed out. "I've never known a teacher who wasn't verbose."

"And these girls certainly aren't scholars," Nin added. "I'm sure Millie had plenty to tell them."

"But you see, my dears, an expert must have samples to go by," said Dr. Blessings. "Many samples, as many as possible. A few papers and some fragments are rarely enough to make a positive identification."

"But you think it's possible."

"Possible, yes." He put his glasses back on and put one of the graded papers and the letter fragment side by side. "The 'A's' and 'E's' are fairly consistent throughout, even in this small fragment. And the lovely curves through the 'D' in 'Dear' here matches this one in 'Don't' for Beatrice Langley's essay."

"But you won't commit yourself," Adele said dryly.

"Not without further examination," he insisted.

She gathered the fragments. "And the pen? What do you make of that?"

"The ink in the letter might have been from this pen," he said. "I wonder —" He stared at it. "Adele, have you one of your calling cards?" She slipped it out of her bag. "Could you write 'I shall see you Sunday' on the back of it?"

"But her handwriting isn't Millie's," Nin reminded him.

"Nevertheless —"

Adele did as she was told and gave it to him.

"You see here how the backtracking of the pen makes a thick mark?" he inquired. "The nib of the pen is longer than what we see today, so it's less steady in the writing. That lets out more of the ink."

Adele examined it. "I estimated the pen to be about ten or twelve years old. Now I know why."

"I didn't know there was any difference in today's pen over a pen ten years ago," Elsie remarked.

"That's because you're not in the business of selling them, Elsie, dear." Adele smiled. "It would scarcely do me much good to order a Waterman from 1890 for someone like Mr. Lyman, who prides himself on having the latest business fashion."

"Grubby commerce," Elsie snarled.

"But profitable." Adele slipped the pen back in its box. "Thank you, Dr. Blessings. As always, you've been invaluable."

"Does this absolve an innocent man from murder?" His eyes sparkled.

"Not in the least," Adele said as she rose. "But it might point toward a crime as a crime."

CHAPTER 28

*O*da joined them. She had changed into a lighter dress of pale pink with a gold cross hanging from her neck. The two girls in pinafores trailed after her. "Dinner is in a half hour," she said. "You will stay?" She looked at Adele and Nin.

"I'm afraid we can't," Adele said.

"Of course you'll stay," Elsie insisted. "They're staying the night. You promised, remember?"

"We promised no such thing!" Adele snapped. "Elsie, you're too much."

"Stay for moral support," her friend begged. "If you don't want to come with us, you needn't. But we haven't seen you in so long."

"Yes, please do stay," Dr. Blessings said. The look in his eyes made Adele melt and Nin nodded.

Dr. Blessings, however, was incapacitated when the dinner bell rang. "He needs to rest," Elsie said. There was a strain of worry on her brow. "He asked for dinner to be sent to his room."

"It shall be done." Oda dispensed one of the young girls, whom Adele had since found out were her sisters, to the kitchen. "We live very modestly, Miss Gossling. We have no servants so we fend for ourselves."

"My brother and I live a very modest life in the country too," Adele said. "We have a couple who take care of us. They fret over us like hens."

"You're in the country — if you pardon — because of reduced circumstances?" Oda asked. Though her voice was somewhat abrasive, her manner was delicate.

"Not all of us who live in the country are poor," Nin objected. Her cat-like stare matched the woman's regal glare.

"I ask only to help," the woman said. "Americans, they don't like to admit they need help."

"Indeed we don't," Elsie said in a fierce voice.

Adele smiled. "That's very kind of you. No, my father left my brother and me with sufficient means. We came to the country after my father died."

"And you wanted to escape the memories," Oda finished with a smile that softened her angular face. "How well I understand." She looked down at the checkered tablecloth. "My father came to Sacramento for the same reason. He was a landowner in Odessa. Here, he was a streetcar conductor."

"He was happy?" Adele asked gently.

"He was free," she said. "He wanted his children to be born free, not subjects of a monarchy. He was — how do you say it — very democratic."

"And why not?" Elsie asked briskly. "I've heard women are treated like cattle in the monarchies."

"I'm sure Queen Victoria would have been most offended to hear that," Nin said dryly.

Oda laughed and nodded at the two young girls, who had been staring silently with wide eyes. They jumped up and brought in a roast and a platter of potatoes and green beans, handling each plate with both hands, as if afraid they would fall.

"What do you do in your small town?" Oda asked. "You're not bored without society?"

"On the contrary," Adele said. "I'm relieved to be away from it.

I own a shop."

"Oh?"

"A stationery shop."

"A lively one," Nin put in. "Lively for Arrojo, that is."

"I shall order all my writing supplies from you," said the woman, smiling. "I tell Elsie she should be a dressmaker. She has a fine figure for it." Elsie actually blushed.

Adele laughed. "She would have women wearing purple bloomers and carrying torches in their hats."

"It wouldn't be so bad," Oda said seriously. "Your Statue of Liberty carries her torch, does she not?"

"Yes," Adele said. "She carries a torch for liberty." Sadness filled her. "When someone's life is taken, so is their liberty." She felt Nin's hand on hers under the table.

"Del has a mad sense of justice," Elsie said. "She has a woman's way of approaching it, though."

"You mean because I don't throw smoke bombs through windows?" Adele looked at her sharply.

"Because you're sly about it," Elsie said, just as sharply. "Stealing around like a human bloodhound."

"I have heard this before," Oda put her fork down. "What is this human bloodhound?"

"A detective," Nin said. "Except we're not."

"When a crime happens in that country town of hers, Adele is on the scent just like a bloodhound," Elsie explained.

"Nothing of the kind," Adele objected. "My brother Jack is the deputy sheriff, and I help him sometimes."

"I suppose you're going to tell me he sent you here to speak to Papa?" Elsie speared another potato and dropped it in her plate.

"Not exactly," Adele said.

"Does he know you're here?"

"Not exactly." Adele shifted in her chair. "I told him we're here to see you."

"Elsie's eyebrows went up. "And he didn't lock you in your

room just to make sure your fight for women's rights wouldn't meddle with his perfectly ordered life?"

"Jack's not as bad as all that," Adele protested. "He won't be happy we're staying, though."

"You see, Oda, Jackson thinks we're all harpies." Elsie glanced at her friend.

"He thinks you're criminals," Nin corrected.

Oda laughed. "Perhaps we are. Or we shall be in a short time. Perhaps Mrs. Pankhurst and her daughters will pay California a visit one day."

"I hope they do," Elsie said. "They could teach us a thing or two about progress."

Adele crumpled her napkin and threw it on the table. "Elsie Blessings, how can you speak that way when you know you're breaking your father's heart?"

Her friend's cheeks were red. "Papa knows I wouldn't do anything to hurt him."

"Then prove it," Adele said. "Don't go to this demonstration tomorrow night."

"Why don't you and Miss Branch come with us and see that I don't do anything Papa wouldn't want me to do?" she challenged.

"You know you came very close to going to jail the last time," Adele said. "How do you think your father would feel if you actually were arrested?"

"Adele." Oda pushed back her chair. "I may call you Adele?"

"Please do," she said.

"You have my word it will be a peaceful demonstration," the woman promised. "I don't intend that I should be arrested either. I have two little ones to care for." Her long arm swept toward the two girls, who giggled and ducked their heads. "I fight for a better future for them, but I shall not risk my liberty for it. If I am in jail, they have no one to care for them."

Elsie took Adele's hand. "We have no intention of doing anything that might land us in jail."

Adele softened. "I know your word is your bond, Elsie."

Oda smiled. "We shall retire, as you say here, to the parlor for coffee."

Nin sat on the rug by the fire along with the two girls. "It's a shame you and Miss Branch won't stay," Oda said, watching her.

"We really must get back," Adele said.

"If you stay, I will show you something of Sacramento," said the woman. "I know it, how do you say, like the back of my hand. I rode in the street cars without paying money because of my father, you see. When I was a child, I could ride from one end of the line to the other." She laughed. "I suppose it made me feel as if I were traveling very far even though I was only going around the city."

Adele set her coffee down. "If you know the city that well, perhaps you can help us." She took the envelope from her bag. "Could you tell me where this address is?"

The woman examined the faded writing.

"I thought the 'rcament' might be Sacramento," Adele ventured.

"It is Sacramento," the woman confirmed. "But the rest is difficult."

"The envelope was mostly burned," Adele said. "We found it in the fireplace in Millie's room."

"Millie?"

"A woman who was found dead a few weeks ago," Adele said. "We think she was killed."

The woman took out a lorgnette and studied the envelope more closely. "I think the 'Mulli' could be Mulligan Street."

"Mulligan Street," Adele repeated.

"It's rather high society," said the woman. "All the rich people in town live there. Like your Nob Hill."

Adele leaned back. "How very interesting."

"I could show you," Oda offered.

"I think it better if Nin and I went alone," she said. "If you would tell us what streetcar to take.'"

"Then you'll stay tonight?"

"We'll stay, but we must leave tomorrow morning very early," Adele cautioned. She glanced at Nin. "If you've no objection, dear."

"Not if you don't," said her friend.

The woman smiled. "There is the Morris-Mulligan line. Take it to the end."

"Thank you." Adele put the envelope back in her reticule. "You've been so kind. To all of us."

The woman smiled, her sharp features almost pleasing.

Later, when she and Nin prepared for bed in the nightgowns Oda had given them, Adele said, "The pieces begin to fit, Nin."

"What pieces?"

"I believe Millie wrote that letter she — or someone else — tried to burn because she wanted her liberty," she said. "The contents of that letter were the only way she could get it."

"You mean like a woman writing to an estranged husband asking to be let go?" Nin turned out the gaslight.

"Or one woman writing to another asking for money."

The gaslight switched on and her friend stared at her. "You mean blackmail!"

Adele put her hands under her head. "Not necessarily. Perhaps she was asking for compensation for a job she was never paid for."

"Why do you assume she wrote to a woman?" Nin turned the light off again.

"Because of the stationery," Adele said. "A woman writes on the finest paper she has to another woman she wants to impress or a man she's in love with."

"Perhaps it was the latter," her friend pointed out.

"We shall find out tomorrow," Adele said, turning to her side.

～

269

They managed to wrangle away from Elsie and her demanding questions in the morning and took the streetcar. Mulligan Street was, like many wealthy districts, perched on a hill towering above the rest of the city as if it lorded over without an actual monarchy to its name. But unlike Nob Hill, the street was peppered with smaller houses as elegant as the bigger mansions.

"Who are we looking for?" Nin asked, brushing dust from her skirt as the streetcar pulled away.

"The name may have been burned off," Adele said. "But the number wasn't. That's what we want to look for. The number '04.'"

"So we knock on every door with '04?'" Nin's fear of strangers returned.

Adele took her arm. "We're two church ladies looking for donations," she insisted. "No one could resist opening the door to two sweet faces like ours."

Her friend snorted but tried to put on a sweet face.

They rang the bell of 104 and it was promptly opened by an elderly man. "Well, isn't this something!" He pulled his velvet jacket around him. "How do you do?"

"We're collecting for the milk fund, sir, and we wanted to speak to the lady of the house," Adele said quickly. Something about the wet look in the man's eyes grated her nerves.

"Oh? Well, that might be rather difficult, but I assure you, I have every sympathy for the milk fund." His eyes scanned her from head to toe, and then he turned to Nin. "And such charming little milkmaids too."

"If we could see the lady of the house —" Adele repeated in a firmer tone.

"There is no lady of the house, my dear," he said, grasping her arm. "I'm a bachelor, a very lonely bachelor in this big house all on my own. Life can be so unfair, can't it?"

"I wouldn't say so, sir," she said briskly. "Our reverend was speaking only last Sunday about how everyone gets what they deserve." She slipped out from under his grasp and pulled Nin down the street.

"Lecherous old coot!" her friend snarled.

"I shouldn't wonder he's been alone all these years," Adele remarked. "Even the stupidest woman would reject living in a big house with the prospect of something like that greeting her every morning."

"I shouldn't think Millie would have had anything to do with someone like him," Nin agreed. "She thought far too much of herself."

"And there is no woman in the house," Adele added. "So it could hardly serve our purposes." She peered at the gold numbers. "Next is 204."

"Perhaps we oughtn't to go on," Nin ventured. "It's like looking for a needle in a haystack. And we don't even know if Millie wrote to anyone here."

Adele found 204 and stared at the mailbox: *Mr. Huey Bain and Mrs. Carrie Bain.*

"Bain!" Adele clutched her parasol.

"What of it?" Nin asked.

"Bain Publishing Company," Adele said. "Mr. Huey Bain lives here. And so does his wife."

"What a coincidence," Nin murmured.

"Perhaps not such a coincidence," Adele said. "This is the most opulent street in town, and the Bain Publishing Company is quite successful. What is odd is the address on the envelope should match it."

"We don't know that," her friend reminded her. "It could be 304, 404 —"

"It's too much of a coincidence, Nin," Adele insisted. "Jack once told me a crime is like links in the chain. Each link either binds the chain or breaks it."

They approached a massive house with an extravagant garden.

"We'd like to see Mrs. Bain, please," Adele said to the maid who answered their ring.

"I'll see if she's in, miss," said the girl. "Whom shall I say is calling?"

"We're friends of her husband's," Adele said.

The maid looked so startled she grabbed the doorknob. "Friends of Mr. Bain?"

"Yes," Adele answered. "I'm sure she'll see us." She took out one of her cards and handed it to the maid.

"I expect she will," said the maid, more to herself.

They had only to wait a few minutes before they were shown in to the parlor. The room had partially drawn curtains, making it appear darker than it was. Adele noticed the stark furnishings in comparison to the excessive garden. Several paintings of good taste hung on the walls, and daguerreotypes stood on the piano. The photographs were the type one would expect from a small family with a mother, father, and son taken some time ago.

She heard a light but sad voice behind her. "Miss Gossling?"

Adele turned and faced the woman who was clearly the subject of the photographs but whose face was now wrought with wrinkles. Slight but strong, she swished in with a dress of dull blue-gray, elegant in spite of its drab color.

She found her voice. "Mrs. Carrie Bain?"

"Yes, that's my name," said the woman. She motioned toward the couch. "You told Matilda you knew my husband."

"Well, yes, in a way."

"Did you work for his company?"

"No, not quite." Adele fumbled with her gloves. "We worked for the Sacramento Children's Home."

"Oh," she said. "We've had so many nice young women stop by since the funeral. My husband worked with many charities."

"We're both very sorry for your loss," Nin said.

"Yes, it was a loss," sighed the woman.

"A pillar of Sacramento community," Adele guessed.

"And San Francisco as well," Mrs. Bain said. "Well, that was quite a while ago."

"When did he die?" Nin asked with her childlike way.

Adele pressed her hand, but the woman didn't seem to mind. "Almost two years now." She looked down at her sedate dress.

"You needn't explain," Adele said. "I lost my father a few years ago also. It's difficult to forget, isn't it?"

"One must never forget." Mrs. Bain's tone was almost harsh.

"We worked with Miss Millie Gibb on the education fund for the children," Adele said.

Mrs. Bain's face changed. She twisted her handkerchief in her lap. "I don't know the name, Miss Gossling."

"She's lying!" Nin hissed in her ear.

"There's no reason why you should," Adele continued. "She was a schoolteacher, you see."

"Then of course I wouldn't know her." The woman rose. "It was good of you both to come, but if you'll excuse me —"

"You said your husband worked with many young ladies on his charities," Adele ventured.

"I knew very little about my husband's charitable activities," said the woman in a light voice. It was almost too light.

"I find that rather surprising," Adele said. "All the charities I've worked with often involved not only businessmen but their wives. Sometimes the wives were even more involved than their husbands."

"They give the money and you give the time," Nin chimed in. Adele glanced at her, realizing Nin might have gotten this from her mother.

"I did take part in some charitable events," the woman admitted. "I don't recall meeting a Miss Gibb."

"She spoke very highly of you." Adele watched the woman's face.

"Did she?" The placid smile never wavered. "May I ask why she didn't come herself?"

"She died just a few weeks ago."

"I'm sorry to hear it." The woman fiddled with the edge of the pillow lying next to her.

"We think she was murdered," Nin said abruptly.

Adele studied the woman's face. The lines smoothed and there was not a quiver on her lips as she said, "How horrible."

"Yes, it is," Adele said. "She was young enough to have much of her life ahead of her. She meant to do something worthwhile with it before it was cut short."

"Oh? What worthwhile thing?" the woman asked.

"She was rather taken by words," Nin said.

The woman gave her a funny look.

"She was interested in etymology," Adele supplied. "The study of words. Rather goes well with the educational books your husband publishes, doesn't it?"

The woman's figure was stiff. "Miss Gossling, I have already told you, I never knew Miss Gibb. If my husband knew her, I could scarcely ask him now." She reached for the bell cord.

Adele put out her hand and stopped her. "Are you quite sure, Mrs. Bain?"

"Of course I'm sure!" A snarl escaped in her even tone.

"Are you sure she didn't write your son a letter?"

"My son? What would my son have to do with it?"

"You would know that more than I."

"I don't think I like your tone, Miss Gossling," she said icily. "I leave my son to his own affairs."

"Was your son close to his father?" Adele inquired.

The woman stared. "What an impertinent question!"

"Perhaps it is. But I have reasons for asking." Adele put the letter fragment and envelope on the table. "Do you recognize these?"

The woman did not even glance down. "I should hardly

think so."

Again, Nin hissed in her ear, "She's lying!"

"You haven't really looked at them," Adele pointed out. "Would you please, for the sake of our friend?"

"What has this to do with me?"

"Perhaps nothing," Adele said. "Perhaps everything. Look at them, please."

Mrs Bain cast her eyes down on the table. She looked at them for a long time, so long the maid Matilda slipped into the room and closed the shutters on the windows before slipping out again.

"I see you do," Adele said quietly.

"Well — why, yes — how did you get them?"

"We found them," Adele said. "In Miss Gibb's fireplace."

"Oh, I see."

"Then you admit the letter was written to you." Adele leaned back. "And the handwriting belongs to Miss Gibb. We've already ascertained that."

"Yes," said the woman. In a firmer voice, she added, "Yes, Miss Gibb did write me. A condolence letter after my husband's death. I remember now. She worked with my husband on several committees for women's education."

"And you knew her?" Adele asked.

"I can't say I really *knew* her." Mrs. Bain was speaking very carefully, weighing her words. "But she did write me, yes. A very respectful letter telling me how much my husband did for her committees."

There was silence in the room. Nin was digging one hand into the other, a sign she was feeling something was not quite right in the room. Adele didn't have to guess what it was.

"Mrs. Bain," she said, "this is not a condolence letter."

"I beg your pardon?" She stared at her.

"I own a stationery shop in Arrojo," she said. "The only one in town that sells condolence letter paper. If Millie were writing such a letter, she would have bought it in my shop."

"Perhaps she bought it in the city," the woman lamented.

"She didn't buy it in the city and you know it," Nin said.

"What are you implying?" The woman sat straight and sharp like an arrow.

"It seems quite odd the number '200' appears in a condolence letter," Adele remarked.

The woman looked almost relieved. "I can explain that quite easily."

"Indeed?"

"Miss Gibb, as you know, was interested in children's education," she said. "And, quite naturally, since she and my husband had worked together in the past, she wrote to my husband for a contribution."

"So it wasn't a condolence letter?" Adele eyed her.

"No," said Mrs. Bain. "No, it wasn't. But it seemed so sordid to admit she was asking for money from a man who had died. She is — was — your friend, after all."

"She asked for a contribution of two hundred dollars?" Adele inquired.

"Yes, something like that."

"That seems like an awful lot for a contribution," Nin said.

"Not at all, Miss Branch." Mrs. Bain adopted the high tone of her breed. "It's a mere trifle for such a cause."

"You gave it to her?" Adele asked.

"Well, no," she admitted. "The letter arrived while we were in mourning. It was hardly appropriate. I let her know this and invited her to ask me again after our mourning was over."

"Did she write to you again?"

"No." The woman rose. "I'm sorry the woman is dead, but I'm sure I can't help you. I hope you find out who did this terrible thing."

Adele put her hand on Nin's shoulder. "I'm sorry if we've distressed you."

The woman gave a waxy smile. "I had no idea the Arrojo

police had such broad-minded views about women being on the force."

Adele gave Nin a look. "You might be surprised, Mrs. Bain." As she smoothed down her skirt, she said, without looking up, "Miss Gibb wasn't looking for a monetary contribution to the children's home."

"No?"

"She was organizing a bazaar and wanted donations," Adele said.

"Well, that's hardly —"

"That's if she really was interested in the children's home."

"But you just said —"

"Which she wasn't," Nin added. "She thought all children were spoiled and insolent."

The woman fell silent. Then, in a thin voice, she said, "I am distressed, Miss Gossling."

Adele made a gesture of regret, knocking one of the daguerreotypes off the piano. She picked it up and arranged it neatly, glancing at it as she did so. The man in the photo looked like the Huey Bain she had seen except he was older and wore a curling mustache.

"I'm sorry I never met your husband," Adele remarked. "He looks like a fine man."

"He looks like he had an eye for the ladies," Nin murmured.

Mrs. Bain gave her a sharp look. "Why do you say that, Miss Branch?"

"I'm sorry," Nin said, blushing. "It was careless of me."

"I'm sure he was an extraordinary man," Adele said kindly. "When one has been a lion in your life —"

"Yes, that's exactly the right way to put it," said the woman with a little smile. "Some men just have that kind of personality. What is the word for it?"

"Magnetism," Adele supplied. "My father had it." She opened her reticule and slipped out the handkerchief with the initials

O.G. "You see, I have my mementoes too. My brother is always scolding me for it."

"He must have been a fine man also," said Mrs. Bain politely.

"He was a lawyer in San Francisco," said Adele. "Perhaps you heard of him — Otis Gossling?"

"Yes, of course." She became less high-toned. "If you had told me you were Otis Gossling's daughter —"

"You might not have been so standoffish?" Nin finished.

The woman glared. "Odd you should live now in a small country town."

"I wanted peace after he died," Adele said.

"Yes, I know what you mean," said Mrs. Bain. "San Francisco was always just a little too bustling for my taste."

Adele smiled as they stepped into the hall. "Yes, it is an exhausting place, isn't it?"

"Sacramento is much more even-tempered," said the woman. "Both its society and landscape." She laughed.

Adele peered into what looked like a large study with the kind of old-fashioned decor she had seen in Huey Bain's office. A pompous humidor perched at the edge of the desk, the black cigars standing out like twigs.

"My brother was very impressed with your son when we spoke to him," she remarked.

"I wasn't aware anybody had spoken to my son," Mrs. Bain echoed.

"Only a formality," Adele said. "My brother is Arrojo's deputy sheriff."

"I see," the woman said quietly.

"Jack thought him amiable and very serious about his business."

Mrs. Bain looked pleased. "Huey is a very serious boy. He always has been."

"He's not a boy," Nin reminded her.

The woman laughed. "I suppose every mother considers her son a boy, even when he's twenty-two."

"As young as that?" Adele asked. "He took on the business when he was twenty, then, after his father died."

"Yes, that's right."

"Quite a responsibility for a young man," she remarked.

"He has his father's ambition."

Adele stepped into the study and fingered the row of cigars for a moment. The round tip looked up at her like a blind eye. A flash of gold paper glared from the sun.

"Your son favors this brand of cigars," Adele commented. "I remember seeing a box in his office."

"You must have been there quite some time to see that." The woman's voice sounded small.

"Only a matter of routine." Adele smiled at the woman. "One of the salesmen stayed at the same boarding house where Miss Gibb lived not long before her death."

"I see," said Mrs. Bain.

"A Mr. Owen Burke," Adele said.

"I don't know my husband's employees," she said stiffly. "He had his world and I had mine."

"Yes, I'm sure," Adele said, remembering only too well the precious divide among the men and women in the well-to-do set of San Francisco. "Please don't think me rude, but might I take one of these cigars?"

"Cigars?" The woman looked confused.

"For my brother," she lied. "Jackson enjoys a good cigar. I'd like to get him a box of these for a present."

"Well." The woman shifted her handkerchief from one hand to the other. "Well, I suppose Huey wouldn't mind. He's always giving away his cigars. He considers smoking one of the greatest pleasures of life and he likes to see men enjoying themselves."

"Yes, I'm sure he does," Adele murmured as she slipped a cigar out of the humidor and put it in her purse.

CHAPTER 29

hey came out into the early afternoon sunlight with the sound of gulls cawing at the clouds.

"Let's go to The Blue Goat," Adele said.

"That awful man!" Nin shivered.

"He won't be there today," Adele promised.

"How do you know?"

"I rather fancy it," Adele said.

Nin shook out her shawl and put it around her shoulders. "She lied twice."

"Mrs. Bain has something to hide," Adele agreed.

"You've an idea of what it is?" Nin eyed her as they reached the streetcar station.

"What if I told you I don't think Millie led a blameless life?"

"Even saints have their follies," Nin remarked.

"We know Millie was unhappy with her work and had other ambitions," Adele said. "I think she was desperate."

"Desperate for what?"

"Money," Adele said. "A woman will do anything for her liberty. Money is all it takes."

280

"A teacher's salary is enough to avoid starvation," Nin said. "I don't imagine it was much more than that."

"Exactly," said Adele. "Her parents were long dead. She had no family other than this cousin who was himself trying to bleed her for money."

Nin's eyes widened. "You think she was trying to get it from the Bains?"

"Mrs. Bain admitted she asked for two hundred dollars," Adele said. "I doubt it was for charity."

"Blackmail, just like you said." Nin waved at the street car, which rang its bell and stopped. "Why didn't she tell us that?"

"It's hardly a pleasant thing to admit," Adele said as they climbed onto the car.

"Why would she try to blackmail Mrs. Bain?"

"That's what we've got to find out," Adele said. "We're going to The Blue Goat to hunt up a young woman whom I think can help us."

They rode the streetcar down to the main center of town and walked to the restaurant. The small room was crowded with people hurrying through lunch before heading back to work. At the bar was a young woman without a hair coiled out of place, a smart blue suit, and wide mouth laughing at some joke told in animated form by a young man standing at the doorway of the kitchen in a cook's uniform.

Adele approached her. "Good afternoon, Miss Taper."

The girl whirled around, the skirt nearly slipping down her very slim figure. "Oh! Miss — er, Miss —"

"Gossling," Adele reminded her. "What a pleasure it is to see you again."

"Pleasure's mine, miss." The girl was more at ease.

"Would you let two hard-working women buy another hard-working woman lunch?" she asked. "I believe that table over there has just been vacated."

"Oh, I shouldn't put you out, miss," she said.

"Call me Adele." She smiled. "This is my friend, Miss Branch."

"Pleased to meet you, Adele. Call me Annie, won't you?" She was now completely at ease at the thought of being invited to a meal, and she flicked her head back at the cook. "Marty, three specials. And mind you bring plenty of French-fried potatoes."

"Yes, madame," the young man said a little mockingly with a salute and retreated to the kitchen.

"Don't mind him," said Annie. "He's a good sort, but he's a little fresh sometimes."

"So that's your young man?" Adele asked as they settled in.

"Oh, he ain't my young man," she said. "We grew up together, that's all."

"Mr. Bain seems to think he is."

"I don't care a hoot what Mr. Bain thinks!" This came out razor-sharp. "He's always getting into my business."

"He did seem a little too attentive," Adele said gently.

"He fancies you," Nin suggested.

"Just like his father," the young lady snorted as she drank half a glass of beer. "Only his father wasn't all work and no play like Mr. Bain, if you know what I mean."

"I think I do." Adele leaned forward. "Did you work with Bain Publishing in San Francisco too?"

"Oh, yes," she said. "I started there when I was sixteen. Mr. Bain Senior was a rather jolly man. Always had a joke on him and one not always fit for Sunday church." She winked. "He had a kind heart and he was generous with bonuses." She gave a satisfied smile."

"And the younger Mr. Bain?" Adele asked. "Less generous with the jokes and bonuses?"

"Pooh!" The woman scoffed. "Wouldn't give you a nickel if he don't have to. And I don't think he even knows what a joke is."

"He's a studious young man," Nin echoed Mrs. Bain words.

"Not that I don't like working for him," the girl admitted. "But a little less machine and a little more human, that's what I say."

"A little more open and a little less secretive too?" Adele eyed her.

"What do you mean?" The girl looked up from the shrimp and fried potatoes she was thoroughly enjoying which, Adele noted, was the most expensive item sold.

"I saw the look on your face when my brother mentioned Owen Burke," Adele said.

"Oh, that was your brother, was it?" The girl grinned. "A nice-looking man."

"Yes, he's very nice." Adele smiled. "Why were you surprised when you heard Mr. Burke's name? I imagine if he was sent to the Arizona territory to train salesmen, he must have been with the company at least as long as you have."

"If he has, I never heard of him," said the girl. "The salesmen, they're in and out, but they still get their calls through me."

"So you know of no Mr. Owen Burke with the company."

"None, Adele." She leaned back, lifting her hand. "I see what you mean by secrets. Well, I never thought of that. A secret employee!" She sat with her mouth open. "But why?"

"I can't imagine," Adele said.

"I always knew he had plans well beyond what Mr. Bain — the senior Mr. Bain —knew, mind you." The waiter brought her another helping of chips, and she dove into them.

"Did they get on?" Adele asked.

"Oh, they got on all right, but the younger Mr. Bain wasn't much in the office while the elder was there," said the girl. "He was a salesman then, you see."

"Yes, he told us," Adele said. "What was his territory, do you know?"

"Between here and Wagley," said the woman.

"That would include Arrojo, wouldn't it?" Adele asked.

"Oh, yes," she said. "He used to grumble about how the red dirt ruined his shoes. He called it a dusty little town."

"It *was*," Nin said. "It has more character now." She glanced at her friend, smiling shyly.

Adele pressed her hand. "Mr. Bain told us he'd never been to Arrojo."

"Well, maybe he didn't remember," said Annie. "He's happy to forget his days as a salesman. Though he's as slick as any of them." The last was said with a snort.

"Tell me, Annie." Adele leaned forward. "What's your employer *really* like? I mean, under the machine?"

The girl considered this, chewing slowly on the last of the shrimp. "I suppose he's more like his father than he would admit. In some things, that is."

"He has an eye for the ladies?" Nin guessed.

"In a different way." The girl grinned. "He doesn't want to have fun with them. He wants — He thinks —"

"He's above all ladies," Adele finished.

The girl nodded. "Oh, and how he hates those educated women! He used to complain about them something *awful* when he was selling to them. He can talk with words that could melt butter. All flattery and smiles. But, oh, he hated them!"

"A boy learns about women from his father," Nin remarked.

"Oh, no, Miss Branch, that ain't it," said the girl. A waiter passed by with a large slice of lemon pie on a plate, and she looked at it with longing eyes. Adele motioned to the boy and ordered one for her. "You're so good, miss. I haven't had sweets in, oh, I don't know how long! Reducing, you know." She patted her non-existent stomach. Adele guessed the "reducing" had more to do with her purse than her figure.

"You don't think Mr. Bain learned about women from his father?"

"Well, not that part of it, anyway," said the girl.

"I take it you mean Mr. Bain Senior had more than just an eye for the ladies," Adele said

The girl hesitated. "They were only rumors, mind you, but you know how rumors can take awful hold of people."

"Yes, I know," Adele said dryly, thinking of Mrs. Faderman and her brood.

"Oh, not anybody in the office," she said quickly. "We're only stenographers and the like. But as I said, there were plenty of educated women who came by, and, well, Mr. Bain Senior insisted on seeing to them himself. He used to say it was good business."

"I understand Mr. Bain Senior was also very active with charities."

"Oh, yes," said the woman. "That was his kind heart. He asked me to go with him sometimes when they didn't have a stenographer." She sat up with pride. "I got training as a secretary, you know."

"So Mr. Bain Senior liked his flirtations to be educated women."

"Oh, I don't mean to imply —" She dropped the fork in her plate.

"Of course not," Adele said. "We're just talking gossip. Was there any woman in particular to whom you noticed Mr. Bain Senior showed an unusual regard?"

She had leaned forward, lowering her voice. The young woman fell for it, pushing the empty pie plate aside.

"There were a few," she said, her voice loud even in a whisper now that the crowd had thinned. "I don't remember their names. One young lady had dark red hair. That I remember. Another was as pale as a ghost. And there were a few rather scragglylooking ladies. You'd think they were crows!"

"All educated women?" Adele asked.

"Oh, certainly," she said. "School administrators and teachers, mostly."

Nin leaned forward and whispered, "Did Mrs. Bain know?"

"Oh, I expect so. Don't the wives always know?" She gave her a knowing look.

"Most do, even if they pretend they don't," Adele agreed.

"You mean they keep their mouths shut?" Nin stared at her.

"Why wreck a good think when you've got it?" Annie asked. "Pots of money and social position, right? Who cares if his eyes go roving once in a while?"

Adele called over the waiter and paid the check. "One more question, Annie. Does Mr. Bain Junior travel for business?"

"Not much." She gathered her coat. "He goes to some convention once in a while, but he hasn't gone anywhere lately." She became thoughtful. "Well, that's not really so. He did go away, quite recently, in fact."

"How recently?"

"Well, it wasn't really that even." She put her hand on her chin. "What I mean is, he was coming and going."

"Coming and going? Like the salesmen come and go?" Adele asked.

"Yes, odd, that is," said the girl. "He don't usually do that. He likes to stay put, like a bird feathering his nest." She giggled as she cast her eye toward the cook, who looked at her through the glass window of the closed door as they passed. Adele saw her wink at him.

"When was this?" Adele asked. "A week ago? A month ago?"

"More like a few weeks," she said. "I remember because Marty — that's the gentleman who brought us the specials — took me to the square dance in Rosa Gris, and I was late. Mr. Bain kept me on to do some work for him before he left for the train."

"Thank you, Annie." Adele pressed her arm. "You've been a great help."

"Thank *you*, Adele." She grinned. "I haven't had that good a meal in a long time. Oh, I must run!" She glanced at the watch chain swinging from Adele's neck. "They get awful cross if I'm so much as five minutes late." She rushed across the street, waving at them.

"A square dance!" Nin snorted. "That sounds like a beau to me."

"And Mr. Bain kept her at work until late," Adele remarked as she hailed a cab. "He keeps a tight rein on his female employees."

"Your mind is somewhere else, isn't it?" Nin asked as they settled into the cab.

Adele nodded. "Right now, it's at the post office."

"Funny. It was there all this business with Millie started," Nin remarked.

"And there it will end." Adele called up to the cab driver, "The nearest post office, please. And hurry."

At the post office, she dispatched a hurried telegram to Sheriff Horatio Hatfield of the Arrojo Police: *You and Jack come down at once to Sacramento. Need to reopen Millie Gibb case. Will explain when you arrive. Take 6:10 train this evening. Will meet you at the station. Adele.*

"Reopen the case?" Nin looked over her shoulder.

"Yes, dear," said Adele as she handed the telegram form to the operator. "The links in the chain have come together."

~

*A*dele could see the fury on her brother's face as he and Hatfield stepped off the train that evening. Jackson looked like a charging bull, his pleasant features gathered and eyes narrowed so their light brown shade looked almost black.

"It would have been gracious of you to phone, Del," he barked. "Tomas and I were up half the night waiting for you."

"I'm sorry, dearest." Adele gave him a warm peck on the cheek.

"Does she have to report her whereabouts to you every minute, Mr. Gossling?" Nin asked archly.

287

"Being away all night is a little more than a minute, Miss Branch," he said in an icy voice. "We had no idea what had happened to you."

"It couldn't be helped, Jack," Adele insisted. "You needn't be concerned we were sleeping in the street. Oda was very kind to put us up."

"Oda?" Hatfield adjusted his hat over his curly hair. Several people passed by, looking at the imposingly tall man.

"Our host." Adele smiled. "You'll meet her."

"We haven't time to socialize," Jackson snapped.

"What's all this about reopening the Gibb case?" Hatfield asked as they made their way out of the station.

"I have reason to believe it ought to be opened again," she said.

"Reason is not evidence," the sheriff pointed out.

"Then why are you here?" Nin asked.

"I was intrigued by Adele's telegram," Hatfield said simply.

"I'm sure you were," Nin mumbled.

"I'm glad you're not pigheaded like my brother," Adele said. "You really ought to learn to keep an open mind, Jack."

Oda and her sisters welcomed them. Adele had a feeling they didn't often see many men. The two girls stared in awe at the sheriff, and he gave them a wink, sending them giggling out to the yard.

"All right, Del, what's all this about?" Her brother settled in a hard-backed chair, looking even more rigid than usual.

"I thought you and the sheriff would be interested to know a few things Nin and I discovered." Adele crossed her legs.

"A few things you believe warrant reopening the case." The sheriff rested his elbows on his knees.

"You know I would never ask you down here unless I was sure," Adele said.

"Sure of what?" Jackson demanded.

"Millie did not commit suicide." Her voice was firm. "She was killed."

"Really, Del —"

"Why don't you hush and listen for once?" Nin growled.

The sheriff held up his hand. "Let's hear her out, Jackson."

Jackson sighed and leaned back, playing with his watch chain in the way that annoyed Adele. It was a sign he was being terribly tolerant of what he considered her well-intended but misguided womanly whims.

She proceeded with a staunch determination. She laid the letter fragment, envelope, and papers from the Wrigley girls on the table.

"So you took evidence out of the station — again." Hatfield was less than pleased.

Jackson snarled, "Sheriff, I think Edison needs more disciplining."

"Don't blame the poor boy," Adele said. "He was only trying to help."

"I have no doubt," the sheriff said. "You know how I feel about that, Adele."

"She had good reason," Nin insisted. "Just as she had good reason with Lucy Blackstone's letter."

"I was only borrowing it," Adele insisted. "To show Dr. Blessings."

"Again?" Jackson raised an eyebrow.

"I had a theory, Jack," she said. "I believed it was correct."

"What was your theory?" the sheriff asked.

"You and Jack assumed the letter was from Millie's uncle," Adele said. "Nin and I found this." She pushed the envelope toward them. "Look at the writing, Sheriff. Does that look like a man's handwriting to you?"

Hatfield examined it closely. "I can't say about the writing, as I'm not an expert like Dr. Blessings. But I can't imagine a man using that sort of envelope."

"Exactly," Adele said. "The letter was inconclusive, as you said. But paired with the envelope, it didn't fit."

"You found this in Millie's room?" her brother questioned.

"When we went back to search it," Nin said.

Jackson grimaced at the sheriff. "Assistant Deputy Dooland's sharp eye." To his sister, he growled, "You're taking too many liberties with the police, Del."

"We closed the case, Jackson." The sheriff put the envelope back on the table. "I can't see the ladies broke any laws, as long as Mrs. Taylor didn't object."

"She held back evidence!" Jackson stared at him. "That's against the law, isn't it?"

"That's for me to decide, Deputy." The sheriff's voice was stoic. "I'd like to hear the rest of what your sister has to say."

Adele gave her brother a satisfied look. "These papers," she tapped the stack on the table, "are from the girls at the Wrigley School. They have Millie's handwriting on them. I wanted Dr. Blessings to compare the handwriting to the letter and envelope and tell me if they could have been written by the same person."

"With the pen," Nin reminded her.

"Yes, with this fountain pen we found in Millie's desk at the school."

"And what did he say?"

"He can't commit himself," Nin said with a grimace.

"He won't commit himself," Adele admitted, "but he's as sure the letter and envelope were written in Millie's handwriting as he was sure about Lucy's letter."

"And you know how *that* turned out," Nin said with a grin.

"In other words, he thinks they were the same handwriting," Sheriff Hatfield concluded.

Jackson was sitting up. "But why would Millie have in her possession a letter she wrote to someone else?"

"Because that someone else brought it with him or her when he or she came to see Millie," Adele said. "And that someone tried to burn them."

"Now you're going to say that same someone killed Millie?" Jackson asked.

Adele sat back, threading her hands together. "I believe that person did."

"Based on?" The sheriff was interested but still skeptical.

"Based on the fact the letter was a blackmail letter."

Both men stared at her.

"Blackmail whom? And why?" her brother asked.

"I suspect when we know that, we'll know who killed her," Sheriff Hatfield said.

Adele leaned forward. "Then you're willing to consider it was murder?"

The sheriff rubbed the edge of his hat, making the brown leather stand up like the hairs on a cat's back. "I'll reserve judgment until I hear everything you have to say. I assume you have more to tell us?"

"We know the answer to one of your questions, Jack," Adele said. "The who."

"You mean who Millie was blackmailing?"

"I think it was Mrs. Carrie Bain."

Now the sheriff did not hide his surprise. "The wife of the young man for whom Owen Burke works?"

"His mother," Adele said.

"That's quite a wild guess, Del," said her brother.

"Mrs. Bain almost admitted it." Nin glared at him. "We don't go on wild guesses, Mr. Gossling."

"Neither do the police, Miss Branch," he snapped.

"Mrs. Bain admitted she received the letter from Millie but claimed Millie was asking for a donation to some charity," Adele said.

"A barefaced lie," Nin snorted. "Millie didn't give a hang about anybody's charity but her own."

"If that's true, why didn't Mrs. Bain go to the police about it?" Hatfield asked. "Blackmail is a serious matter."

"I've a feeling it was something so explosive, she was afraid it would come out," Adele said. "The Bains are Sacramento high society. You know how they are when it comes to publicity."

"Yes, I know," said Hatfield in a wary tone. "But it seems rather incredible."

"There's one more piece of the puzzle," Adele said. "Jack, you remember that telephone operator in whom Mr. Bain took an unusual personal interest?"

"Miss Taper." He nodded.

"We had an interesting chat with her," Adele said.

The sheriff grinned. "You might be better than Edison and the lads after all, Adele. It seems you track down the most interesting witnesses."

"I wanted information, Sheriff," Adele insisted. "She's not a witness to anything."

"What was the information you were interested in?"

"She confirmed some of my suspicions," Adele said. "For a start, she said she had never heard of an Owen Burke working for the company."

Oda chose that time to slip into the parlor with a tea tray. Seeing the grave look on their faces, she set it down gently on the side table and withdrew from the room.

"That wouldn't be unusual if he's a salesman," Hatfield said.

Adele smiled. "You clearly never worked in an office, Sheriff."

"No, I'm rather the roaming type," he admitted.

"I've had dealings with office girls in the city," said Adele. "They always know everyone. Even the file clerk sitting in the basement knows every employee by name."

"Perhaps Miss Taper was an exception." Her brother eyed her.

"She's a telephone operator, Jack," said Adele. "Even salesmen get calls to their office. There is no way she wouldn't know who he was."

"And the fact that she doesn't?" Hatfield asked. "What does that tell you?"

"It tells me Miss Taper doesn't know Owen Burke because there is no Owen Burke."

"This is too much, Del," said her brother. "Everyone at Mrs. Taylor's boarding house saw and spoke to him."

"So did we," Nin said.

The sheriff stared at Adele. "You spoke to Owen Burke?"

Adele couldn't help but feel a little ashamed. "I sent him a telegram in Jack's name asking for an interview."

"You did what?" Her brother sprang from his chair. "Del, you ought to be kept in a locked room!"

"Maybe you're the one who needs the locked room, Mr. Gossling," said Nin in a prim voice. "You had no use for him anyway, so why shouldn't we see him?"

"What use did you have?" Jackson snarled.

"I wanted to meet the man and see him with my own eyes," Adele said. "It was rather a good performance."

"I don't follow," said the sheriff.

"The way Mr. Walsh described Mr. Burke. Do you remember, Jack?" She turned to him.

Her brother took out his small leather pad. "Thin, light on his feet. Red hair, red beard, and thick eyeglasses. Wore flannel checkered suits."

"Doesn't that strike you as rather theatrical?" she asked.

"Perhaps," he admitted. "But I met many salesmen when I was in Chicago. They lean toward the theatrical in their dress and manner. One of them once told me it was one way to make them unforgettable to their customers."

"Mr. Burke insisted he barely knew Millie," Adele continued. "He tried to insinuate she had made more of him than he of her."

"And that this was the usual scheme of things in his profession," Nin added. "He was rather pompous about it."

"That is odd," Sheriff Hatfield admitted. "There should be no reason for him to deny having met Millie, as it would be easy to prove he sold her some of his wares."

"Perhaps he was embarrassed a spinster was taking such an interest in him," Jackson suggested.

Both women glared at him.

"Even if Owen Burke knew Millie, there is no evidence Mrs. Bain did," Jackson pointed out. "She would hardly have met with the owner of the company."

"I think Mr. Bain Senior knew her," she said quietly. "Rather intimately."

The sheriff gave her an incredulous look. "That's a little far-fetched, don't you think?"

"Is it?" Adele asked. "Why would Millie ask Mrs. Lynn a lot of questions about Sacramento's prominent families, including the Bains? Why would she insist on getting their address even after Mrs. Lynn told her the Bains were in mourning?"

"You may have a point." Now the sheriff was interested.

"And," Adele continued, "Miss Taper told us Mr. Bains Senior was overly friendly with some of the women on the committees he served."

"Did she mention Millie by name?" Jackson asked.

"Not exactly."

"But he favored educated women," Nin put in.

"Even if he knew Millie," said the sheriff, "there's nothing to show they were on intimate terms."

Adele pressed her hands together. "Miss Taper also said Mr. Bain Junior had some mysterious absences from the office a few weeks ago. He was in and out — like the salesmen." She eyed Hatfield.

"That wouldn't be unusual," Jackson pointed out. "I'm sure in his position, he would have made several trips out of state."

"According to Miss Taper, he liked to remain close to home," Adele said. "With all his books in front of him. Remember, Jack?" She looked pointedly at him.

"What of it?" her brother asked.

"I think he was away being Mr. Owen Burke."

"That's absurd!" Jackson growled. He glanced at the sheriff. "You're not buying all this, are you?"

Hatfield sighed. "Anything else, Adele?"

"Just one more thing." She took the cigar Mrs. Bain had given her out of her reticule and handed it to him. "Jack ought to recognize these."

"They look like Mr. Bain's brand of cigars," Jackson agreed.

"They are," Adele said. "His mother was kind enough to give me one. After I told her my brother was anxious to get hold of just that brand for himself." She smiled while Jackson gave a snort.

"I suppose you're going to imply this cigar will match the one Assistant Deputy Dooland found in Mrs. Taylor's shrubbery?" Hatfield asked.

"I recognized the gold seal," she said. "I didn't think of it when we were interviewing Mr. Bain, but when I saw it again —"

"Why don't you be frank with us, Del?" Her brother folded his hands. "You've taken on the role of lady detective, so why not go all the way?"

"Mind your manners, Jackson." For the first time, Hatfield sounded genuinely annoyed. "Your sister had some good theories regarding the Blackstone case. We wouldn't have solved it so quickly otherwise."

Adele rose and wandered around the room. She could see the two girls playing in the garden. They picked daisies from the cluster in the corner and attempted to weave them into a chain. But their clumsy, small hands kept slipping over the stems. They giggled, putting their heads together. Oda sat on a straw chair, her hands folded in her lap, looking at them with a maternal smile. Her eyes wandered toward the house, and she caught Adele's glance. She gave her a sedate smile, the sort Adele would have expected from a tolerant queen.

She grasped the back of a chair. "I'll say it very plainly, Jack. I believe Huey Bain had something to do with Millie's death."

"I knew it!" Jackson tapped his foot.

"You think Mr. Bain killed Miss Gibb?" the sheriff asked in a quiet voice.

"That or hired someone to do it."

"Why do you believe that?"

"Isn't it obvious?" Nin asked, not without a little superiority. "She was blackmailing his mother."

"I think it more likely, if Mr. Bain Junior had known about the blackmail letter, he would have gone to the police," Hatfield said.

"For his mother's sake, he would have wanted to avoid any publicity," Adele said. "Murder is more discreet, if done in the right way."

"Wild guesses," Jackson mumbled.

"Then why don't you prove I'm wrong?" she challenged. "Pay the Bains a visit."

"And do what?" Hatfield asked. "Accuse Mr. Bain of killing Millie Gibb because she was blackmailing his mother?"

"I think Mrs. Bain will talk to us," Adele said.

"You're asking us to go on evidence that wouldn't convict a clown," Jackson snarled. "A cigar stub, a half-burned letter, and your intense dislike of a man who's a little too big for his britches but nothing more."

"I think he's much more than that," Adele insisted. "I think he wouldn't hesitate to kill if he thought he had a good reason."

"And if he thought the person he was killing was so beneath him, her life didn't matter to anyone anyway," Nin added.

"You're taking a rather cavalier approach to murder, aren't you, Miss Branch?" Jackson remarked.

"Is she, Jack?" Adele glanced at him. "Mr. Huey Bain doesn't have much regard for women as equals. He hates educated women. Annie told us that."

Hatfield studied her with his too-exacting gaze. "Adele, why are you so anxious to prove him guilty? Do you really despise him as much as your brother says?"

"It has nothing to do with him!" Adele snapped. "It's about Millie — about being trapped in her youth, destined to the take care of others — her parents, her students — wanting something else for herself and being desperate enough to get it."

"Desperate enough to blackmail an innocent woman?" Hatfield suggested.

"She may not be innocent," Nin pointed out.

"I don't justify what she did, Sheriff," Adele said. "But that doesn't mean anyone had a right to kill her." She returned the exacting gaze. "I thought you were as determined to do justice as I am."

"She was a victim of her own greed!" Jackson insisted.

"And that makes her deserving of murder?" Adele looked at him steadily. "I can believe that from the Anspaches but not from you, Jack."

He looked down at the carpet, studying its zigzagging pattern.

"I can hardly believe you would feel sympathy for a blackmailer, Adele," Sheriff Hatfield said quietly.

"But there's a story behind her greed," Adele lamented. "There's always a story. There can't be justice without a story." She looked at the sheriff.

Jackson looked at him too. Nin stared ahead at the dry roses in the vase sitting on the table.

Hatfield rose and put his hand on her shoulder. It felt light and soothing. "I've connections with the Sacramento police. I can contact them about this blackmail business—if there is blackmail involved—and suggest it might have something to do with our case."

"It hardly seems likely they'll want to pursue it," Jackson pointed out. "If the Bains have influence —"

"Sheriff Hill is a rather ornery fellow," Hatfield said with a smile. "Once he has a bee up his bonnet, he's not likely to let go, even if it means some discomfort in his job." He turned to Adele.

"I think you and Miss Branch ought to come with us. I gather the woman has some trust in you."

"And it's always good to have a woman about when questioning other women," Nin said, quoting what the sheriff had once told them.

"I don't suppose Miss —"

"Kriska," said Adele.

"I don't suppose Miss Kriska has a telephone?" He glanced at the modest surroundings. "I saw a box down the street."

Adele grasped his arm. "Thank you, Sheriff."

"For what?" he asked.

"For not letting any silly ideas of pride stand in the way of your fairness," she said.

He gave her a sheepish grin, then stuck his hat on his head, making it lean into his face.

CHAPTER 30

*O*da insisted they have dinner first and put out an elaborate spread of cold meats, cheeses, and a dense, dark bread she had baked herself. Elsie came in just as they were about to begin with two other ladies, both looking as determined as she.

"Elsie, dear, you remember my brother Jack?"

"I'm not likely to forget him," Elsie said with a little wariness. There had once been some question of affection between them until Elsie had become more interested in the city politics than courting.

"Miss Blessings." He bowed.

"Such airs!" Adele heard one of the ladies murmur.

But Elsie was surprisingly defensive. "Mr. Gossling is a gentleman. He's old-fashioned but not one of the oppressors."

"Thank you kindly," Jackson said dryly. "Your father is well?"

"He's been tired this entire trip, I'm afraid," Elsie said, wrinkles appearing on her brow.

"I won't disturb him, then." He turned to the sheriff. "Sheriff Hatfield, Miss Elsie Blessings."

"At last we meet." The sheriff gave her a winning smile. "I've heard much about you, Miss Blessings. Your father was a great help to us in our last case."

"So he is again." She eyed Adele.

"If only he would commit himself," Nin said in a hollow tone.

The three ladies joined them for dinner, and there was some conversation about trite subjects. Adele noticed Elsie carefully avoided mentioning the suffragists or the fact her two friends where there to take her to the rally in front of the governor's mansion that night. In fact, she spoke in a shrill tone Adele knew came from feeling unsettled at having two lawmen in the house.

Oda played the hostess, refilling cold tea in everyone's glasses without their asking, shooing her younger sisters from their position near the fireplace into the kitchen to help with the dishes, and serving a splendid cake with icing.

All the while, Adele felt as if ants were crawling inside her bones. She wanted to scream the sheriff out of his mild banter, to remind him they had a duty to perform and a very unpleasant one.

Oda took her arm. "You're nervous, no?"

Adele did not answer for a moment. She felt the heat from the fire Oda had lit, the yellow flames sending red sparks onto the floor. "Oda, what do you think of a woman who did wrong to gain her liberty?"

"You mean a criminal wrong," said the woman in a grated tone.

"Perhaps," Adele said.

The woman led her to the couch. "In my country, women commit many crimes because they are not free. You heard of the pogroms, no?"

"I heard something," Adele said softly.

"When one has no space to breathe — it is like clawing at walls. But one can tear down a wall, brick by brick if necessary. Yes, one can behave like an animal!" This last was said with a vicious growl.

"I'm sorry," Adele said softly.

"Oh, but we are friends now, aren't we?" The woman smiled. "Friends ask one another dangerous questions."

"And don't always get answers," Adele reminded her. "That's a friend's right."

There was a knock on the door, and Oda's two younger sisters, excited to have their quiet home filled with so many people, bounced up to answer it. They came back leading a balding man of medium height, smartly dressed with a beard. The vest beneath his coat parted to show a shiny sheriff's badge.

The sight of him put the ladies Elsie had brought on their guard. They took their friend into a corner, whispering in her ear. The doorbell rang again and two more women arrived with folded banners under their arms. They, too, stopped short when they saw the two sheriffs and slinked to the corner where Elsie stood with her friends.

Hatfield, observing all of this but in his nonchalant way, shook the other man's hand and introduced him as Sheriff Edward Hill. "We rode the Wells Fargo carriages together quite a while ago."

This calmed the ladies somewhat. Sheriff Hill glanced at them, then at Hatfield, and the knowing look between them let Adele know Hatfield had already made his friend aware of the nature of Elsie's business in Sacramento.

"The streetcar downtown will be leaving in five minutes, ladies," said the man, his tone almost jovial. "Give the governor my regards when you see him."

The ladies grumbled at the sheriff's mockery but were happy to escape. Adele was surprised to see Oda not going with them. "We thought we might leave Susie and Amy with Dr. Blessings," she said in a low voice to Adele as they both watched the women hurry across the street to the waiting car. "But he is ill, so I must stay with the children."

"Perhaps it's better," Adele said.

"They will not make trouble," Oda said firmly. "We have Elsie's word, remember. For her father's sake."

"Her word is her bond," Adele agreed.

Sheriff Hill declined coffee. "I understand you're here to stir up trouble." He threw a glance at Adele.

"That's not my intention, I assure you," Adele said. "Blackmail is a serious offense, no matter to whom it happens."

"If there is blackmail involved," said Sheriff Hill.

"It's true, Sheriff," she insisted.

"Adele doesn't lie," said Nin fiercely.

"I wasn't implying she was, miss," said Sheriff Hill. "But I rather doubt Mr. or Mrs. Bain will own up to it if there is. The swells here are apt to hush up matters."

"This is one matter they might not be able to hush up," said Sheriff Hatfield. "The blackmailer was our murder victim, and that makes it our business to investigate the matter. Remaining as discreet as possible, of course," he added.

"We'll be very discreet," Jackson promised.

They rode in the police wagon, which Sheriff Hill ordered to be left at the end of the street. "They don't welcome the police here," he admitted as they trudged down the road. "Only wore this for impression." He pounded the silver star.

The same maid who admitted Adele and Nin the day before answered the door. She seemed a little frightened at the sight of so many people wanting to see "madame," and had them wait in the hall while she went to see "if madame is in." Adele noticed the study door was closed.

Mrs. Bain appeared wearing the same gray dress and carrying a fan, though it was chilly that evening. Her face showed signs of distress when she saw Sheriff Hill and even more so when she saw Adele. But her voice was composed as she invited them all into the parlor and closed the doors.

"I believe you know why we're here, Mrs. Bain," Sheriff Hill began.

"I don't believe I do," she said, but her eyes swept toward Adele.

"We've been informed you have received a blackmail letter —"

"Blackmail?" The woman jumped. "Don't be absurd, Sheriff. Who would be blackmailing me?"

"That's what we'd like to find out, ma'am," said the man respectfully. "Blackmailers are usually repeat offenders."

"What do you mean?" she asked.

Jackson leaned forward and intervened in a kind tone, "If they've blackmailed one person, they likely will blackmail more."

"I see." The woman crossed her legs. "I'm guessing this young lady told you I was being blackmailed." She glared at Adele. "I can't imagine how I gave you that impression the other day."

"It was more than an impression, Mrs. Bain," said Adele. "It's the truth."

"That's absurd!" The woman's voice rose a pitch but then became subdued. "You asked me if I received a letter from Miss Millie Gibb. As I explained to this young lady and her friend," she turned back to Sheriff Hill, "the letter was from a former acquaintance of my husband's. She is — was, as I understand — a teacher working with an educational charity, and she asked me for a contribution."

"A contribution of two hundred dollars," Adele said. "A rather large sum."

"As I told you, Miss Gossling, that's not a large sum in our circle," the woman said stoically.

Adele softened her voice. "Mrs. Bain, we want to help. If you or your son received a blackmail letter, please tell us."

"I don't know what you mean." The woman's voice was more unsure now.

"It might have had something to do with Miss Gibb's death," she said.

Sheriff Hatfield leaned forward. "People believe blackmailers stop once they get what they're after. But most don't. Just as

Deputy Sheriff Gossling said, they go on blackmailing until they bleed their victim dry."

"Well," said the woman, her face tight. "Well, then, it looks as if your Miss Gibb deserved her fate, doesn't it?"

"That's a rather callous attitude, Mrs. Bain," Adele said. "Millie Gibb was a woman just the same as you or I."

"She was nothing like me!" the woman thundered. "That insolent little —" She bit her lip, staring down at her hands in her lap.

There was silence for a moment, and Sheriff Hatfield spoke in his mild tone. "There is more to it than just a letter asking for a contribution, isn't there, Mrs. Bain?"

Something about the commanding tone in his voice made the woman sway. Adele caught her by the shoulders, then nodded at the maid standing just inside the door. The girl rushed out and returned with a glass of water.

"Won't you tell us now?" Adele asked gently.

The woman stared at her. Then, she burst out laughing, a hysterical laugh that made Adele shiver. "Yes, yes, she was a blackmailer!" She collapsed with her face in her hands.

Sheriff Hill had withdrawn to the corner of the room. Hatfield gave Adele the go ahead.

"She knew your husband died," Adele said.

"She heard about it," the woman said. "Oh, to come to me at a time like that — it was inhuman!"

"We make no excuses for her, Mrs. Bain," Hatfield said.

"Why was Millie trying to blackmail you?" Adele asked.

When the woman didn't answer, Hatfield said, "She knew something she thought you would pay her to keep quiet."

The woman wiped her eyes and face. "Yes, I would have paid to keep it quiet."

"Is it — does it have anything to do with your husband?" Adele asked.

The woman looked at her. "You're the daughter of Otis Gossling. You know what it's like with our society. Men work so hard and must have their fun. Some wives suffer, oh, they have illusions. But I was never like that." She sounded proud. "I was above that. I knew Huey would always return to me. He never loved anyone but me."

"I'm sure he didn't." Nin knelt beside her and took Mrs. Bain's hand in the strange way she had of showing warmth at the oddest times.

"He returned to you after he and Miss Gibb —"

"Naturally." The woman sniffed. "He was never taken in by that dried-up scarecrow. The others, well, they were charming, and some were even lovely, but Miss Gibb was so plain!" She almost laughed. "I wondered what he ever saw in her."

"Ambition, perhaps," Adele said softly.

"Yes," said Mrs. Bain. "Yes, he admired ambition, especially in a woman. He told me once, 'Miss Gibb, she won't be one of those who surrenders to life. She shall shine like a star!'" Her eyes filled with tears.

"Did she tell you her ambition in the letter?" Adele asked.

"She only said she had even more ambitions now than she had twenty years ago," the woman scoffed.

"She wanted to study etymology with a professor at the university in Rosa Gris," said Adele. "She believed words were powerful, and she wanted to bring that message to the world."

The woman glared at her. "You won't make me feel sorry for her, Miss Gossling. She knew something very precious to me, and she threatened to expose it."

"What was that precious thing, Mrs. Bain?" Jackson intervened in a professional but respectful tone.

"Oh, but if it should get out —"

"We'll be as silent as possible," Sheriff Hatfield assured.

The woman's face relaxed. "My husband had an intimacy with Miss Gibb some twenty years ago. There was a child."

"A child," Adele lamented. "You mean your son."

The woman turned pale. "I couldn't have children, and Huey

so wanted a son and heir to his fortune. All men do, don't they?"
She stared at Jackson.

"Some men," Jackson said softly.

"She wanted money to keep silent," Nin guessed.

"It's not the newspapers. I don't care about that anymore." The
woman looked at Adele with appealing eyes. "My son doesn't
know."

"You don't want him to know you're not his mother," Adele
said.

"He's such a loyal and devoted boy." Her voice broke. "He
loved his father. He thought the world of him. It would devastate
him."

"Mrs. Bain." Adele took the woman's hand and held it
tightly. "Did you ever consider perhaps your son already
knows?"

The woman blinked. "How could he? His father never
breathed a word, and heaven knows I didn't." Then, her face went
from pale to white. "You don't think that awful woman told him
after all!"

"No," said Adele. "I don't think Millie told him. I think he
found out on his own."

"I don't understand."

Jackson leaned forward. "Did you tell your son about
receiving a letter from Miss Gibb?"

"Certainly not!" Her lip curled with distaste.

"You told me you received condolence calls from young ladies
your husband worked with on his committees," Adele said. "Did
you receive letters as well?"

"Yes, a few," she said. "But I don't see what that has to do
with it."

"Did your son help you with the condolence letters?"

"Well, no, not really. I hired a secretary to help me."

"And yet, they were probably lying about where he could see
them."

"Miss Gossling, you're confusing me." She put her hand on her head.

"I think what Miss Gossling is trying to say is you might have left Miss Gibb's letter with the others," Sheriff Hatfield intervened, "or your son might have seen it and, thinking it was just another condolence letter, read it."

"He would have told me!" The woman was horrified. "We never hide anything from one another."

"Mrs. Bain," Jackson said, "I'm afraid we must ask this question. Can you give us more specifics as to the contents of Miss Gibb's letter?"

Her face grew sour. "It's not the sort of thing I care to recall, Deputy Sheriff."

"It's very important," Adele said. "It might give us a clue as to what Miss Gibb's state of mind was when she wrote it and why she died."

"It was a demand for money," Mrs. Bain said. "Two thousand dollars."

"Two thousand dollars!" Adele stared at her.

"Yes," she admitted. "I don't know why the letter read two hundred."

"The other zero might have been burned off," said Sheriff Hatfield. Adele produced the fragment from her bag. "'Pride and j' must be 'pride and joy.'"

"She said the money was a small sum to keep the truth from my 'pride and joy,'" the woman snarled. "And it was a paltry sum to insure everyone would continue to think of my husband as a martyr. Oh, that volatile woman!"

"If your son would have found the letter, he would have known exactly what it was about," Adele said.

"Yes," she said, "he would."

"Mrs. Bain, is your son home?" Adele asked.

"He had to work late," she said. "I expect him back at eight o'clock, though."

"Then he should be back soon," said Sheriff Hatfield. "We'd like to wait if we may, ma'am." He glanced at Sheriff Hill. "I think we can take it from here, Ed."

The woman's face froze. "Is that necessary, Sheriff?"

"We have a few questions to ask him about an employee of his named Owen Burke."

"You mentioned that man to me before." Mrs. Bain glanced at Adele. "Do you think he might have been involved?"

"I think he was very much involved," Adele said. "I think he's the key to the whole mystery."

"Well, then, I'm sure my son will want to help." She returned to her composed self, putting away her handkerchief. "I suppose I ought to ring for coffee."

"Don't trouble," Hatfield said.

"It's no trouble, Sheriff." She rang the bell cord, and the maid came in. "Coffee, please, Matilda."

"The cook's out, ma'am," said the girl.

"Oh, dear!" Mrs. Bain fiddled with her rings. "Well, isn't there *someone* in the kitchen who can make it?"

"Well, ma'am, Beth went with Mrs. Clark, you see, and —"

Adele rose, taking Nin's hand. "Miss Branch and I would be happy to make some coffee. My brother always says I make a very good coffee."

Jackson nodded. "Hot and strong."

"I think we all need that right now," Hatfield agreed.

They had no more gotten the coffee pot on the stove, and Nin had stuck her head in the ice box to search for cream, when a lady of about fifty with a perfectly placed bun on her head came in through the back door, followed by a scraggly-looking young woman carrying a large basket with both hands. The older woman regarded them with annoyance.

"Tilda, I won't have your friends bustling around my kitchen," she declared.

"Thought you'd be out for a while," came the grumbling reply.

"Whether I am or not, you're not to bring them here."

"We've come to see Mrs. and Mr. Bain," Adele said.

"Oh!" The woman's voice immediately changed. "I beg your pardon. What can I do for you, miss?"

"You're Mrs. Clark?"

"Yes, miss."

"We were rather hoping to do for you," she said. "Mrs. Bain would like coffee, and I told her we would make it."

A shadow of the annoyance appeared on her face. "There's no need, miss. I can make it."

"Mrs. Bain asked particularly for Miss Gossling to make it," Nin announced. "*She* will make the coffee." She spoke in an authoritative tone with a hint of haughtiness Adele had never heard before.

"Yes, miss." Mrs. Clark took the basket from the scraggly girl's hands.

Nin looked at her with hollow eyes Adele had seen many times. "The pantry —"

"Pantry, miss?" The cook stared at her.

"My friend means it's so nice and cozy here," Adele said quickly.

"Thank you, miss." Mrs. Clark was clearly pleased. "I try to keep it nice and tidy."

"You do an excellent job," Adele complimented.

The woman smiled. "Young Mr. Bain liked to poke around here as a boy. Looked in all the cabinets and asked questions. He never upset nothing either. He was a good boy."

Nin continued to hover near the pantry.

"Don't bother to set the tray, Mrs. Clark," Adele said. "I'll get it."

"Oh, well, I must admit, I wouldn't mind a rest, what with my feet and all." The woman eased herself into a chair, clearly happy not to have to add one more task to her plate.

Adele filled the pitcher with cream from the icebox. While

Mrs. Clark was fanning herself, she poured most of the sugar from the sugar bowl into the sink. "I see you're out of sugar."

"Well, I never!" The woman stared. "Filled it only yesterday night."

"Don't fret, Mrs. Clark," said Adele. "I know where sugar is kept."

She hurried to the pantry and cast a quick eye on the boxes sitting on the shelves. One caught her eye: *Rough on Rats*.

She filled the bowl, and as she set it down on the tray, she asked in a light tone, "Mrs. Clark, does Mr. Bain still poke about the kitchen?"

"Well —" The woman's eyes half closed.

"It's all right. We won't tell his mother," she promised.

"He does like to come in and glance about now and then," she admitted. "Usually finds the cake I hide from Matilda, the rascal." She laughed.

"Is the cake usually in the pantry?" she asked.

"Oh, no, miss, in the icebox." The woman heaved herself up. "I've a nice lemon sponge sitting there right now."

"Please don't bother." Adele made her sit down again. "Do you keep any sweets in the pantry?"

"Well, he has some strange tastes, Mr. Bain," the woman admitted. "Spent some time in the Orient, you see. He has this odd tea he likes in the evening, some sort of flower, I think."

Adele peered in the pantry. "Jasmine tea?"

"Yes, miss, that's it!" Mrs. Clark's eyes lit up. "My but you're a smart one, ain't you?"

"So he makes himself tea every evening?" Adele asked.

"Sometimes I make it," she said. "But Mr. Bain is a thoughtful one. Comes in and says, 'Don't you interrupt yourself, Mrs. Clark. I can make my own tea.' And bless me, he can! He used to take his own electric pot with him when he was traveling around so he could have a bit of home, as he put it, in those hotel rooms and boardinghouses."

"You mean when he was a salesman." Adele felt her heart pounding.

"Oh, the madame told you," she said. "That was a long time ago."

"And more recently?" Adele asked. She felt her friend's eyes watching her with their cat-like gaze, though Nin remained standing against the wall.

"Well, now, funny you should ask," said the cook. "Just a few weeks ago, he was asking me where I put that electric kettle. Said he had some convention he had to attend in the east. He spent some time in the pantry, like he was looking for something special."

"He was," Adele murmured. "He was looking for poison."

In the doorway, still with his hat and coat, was Huey Bain. He looked like a caricature of the businessman with his case in one hand and his umbrella in the other. But he had neither the serious nor sedate look of a businessman. He looked, indeed, like a man stricken with terror. His eyes were fixated in Nin's direction, but Adele realized it wasn't her friend he was gazing at but the open cupboard door.

With a flash of black silk, Mr. Bain was gone. She rushed out in time to see the back door slam.

She darted up the stairs and burst into the parlor. "Sheriff, Huey Bain just ran out into the street!"

Despite the sheriff's slow speech and calmness, he reacted so quickly, it was almost like a gust of wind escaped the room. Jackson ran after him. Whistles and shouts came from outside, and Mrs. Bain rushed to the window.

About ten minutes later, Hatfield and Jackson entered, each clasping Huey Bain by the arm.

CHAPTER 31

A half hour later, Adele was serving her hot and strong coffee while Huey Bain sat on the couch, holding his mother's hand, and, in a wary voice, telling the story of how he killed Millie Gibb.

"I suppose my mother told you about the letter?"

"We found a fragment of it in Miss Gibb's fireplace," Jackson said. "Along with an envelope with your address." He put them on the table.

The lines on the man's face deepened. "I'm not very good at lighting a fire."

"Why did you bring the letter with you, Mr. Bain?" the sheriff asked. "Did Miss Gibb ask you to bring it when you brought her the money?"

"She knew me as someone else," he said. "I wasn't sure she would believe me, so I knew the letter would convince her who I was." He pressed his hands together. "I suppose it won't do much good to say I didn't intend to kill her at first."

"Whether you intended it or not, you *did* kill her," Jackson pointed out.

"If you begin at the beginning, we might be able to do something for you." Hatfield nodded at Jackson, and he took out his pad.

"I suppose it began a month or so ago." He turned to Mrs. Bain. "You remember that night at dinner, Mother?"

The woman, whose face was buried in her handkerchief, nodded.

"Mother was distressed," he said to the others. "I thought at first it was because of Father's death, but she'd been so happy lately, getting back into society and her friends."

"And then she told you about the letter," Adele said.

Mr. Bain gave her a withering look. "Pardon me, Sheriff, but must there be ladies present? Except for my mother, of course."

"These ladies have more right to be here than we do," said the sheriff in a harsh tone. "You may find yourself glad in the end that they're here."

The man shrugged as Nin gave him a wary look.

"Mother tried to tell me she was just tired from some luncheon she had helped organize for the working girls that day." He looked at Mrs. Bain's hand affectionately. "You could never hide anything from me, Mother, you know that." The woman gave a dull smile. "Mother told me she received a letter from one of my father's 'lady acquaintances.'"

"You knew about them?" Jackson looked a little horrified.

"But naturally." Mr. Bain gave him an odd look. "You're the son of Otis Gossling, I've been told. Surely, you must know men in our society and how they are with women, married or not."

Jackson's face went rigid, and his lips turned white, but he said nothing.

"Father told me about some of them," Mr. Bain continued. "Oh, not in a shoddy way. He was always respectful. When I was older, I suppose he wanted me to know how things stood."

"How things stood," Adele repeated, feeling sick inside.

"Weren't you alarmed about the letter?" Sheriff Hatfield asked.

"Not at first," he said. "They wrote Father from time to time, though usually at his office. No, it wasn't the letter. It was Mother's distress." He pressed her hand. "I had to find out what was in it, of course. It was my duty."

"Your duty to pry into your mother's private correspondences?" Nin snarled.

He gave her a vacant look. "I don't suppose women really understand the devotion a son has to his mother."

"So you went looking for it," Jackson prompted.

"I didn't have to look," he said. "I knew where it was. Locked in Mother's jewelry box." He gave a soft smile. "I've seen her lock things in there since I was a boy, and I knew where the key was." Mr. Bain put his arm around her. "I know I shouldn't have read it, Mother, but curiosity got the better of me."

"I wish it hadn't. God, I wish it hadn't!" His mother let out a choking sound.

"Don't fret, dear," he said soothingly. "There was nothing in it I didn't already know."

She turned pale, staring at him.

"Father told me everything before he died." He smiled. "You didn't think he would keep something like that a secret from me, do you?"

"He told you about Miss Gibb and his relationship with her?" Adele asked.

"It's rather a sordid story," he said. "Not one I wish to repeat in front of ladies."

"We're not china dolls, Mr. Bain," Nin growled.

"Perhaps it wasn't as sordid as you think." Adele reached into her reticule and brought out the pen. "This was found in Miss Gibb's desk at the Wrigley School. I trust the inscription 'H. with love, M' means 'Huey, with love, Millie.'"

"A mere token!" the man scoffed.

"A woman doesn't give a man an expensive gift she can ill

afford on a teacher's salary as a token, Mr. Bain," said Adele. "Two gifts, in fact."

"Two?" Jackson eyed her.

"Mr. Bain's lighter," she reminded him. "It had the same inscription."

The young man's lip curled. "Suffice it to say I knew about Millicent Gibb and all he did for her."

"So you weren't shocked to read Miss Gibb was your mother." Adele sat in the chair opposite him.

"But she wasn't my mother, Miss Gossling," he said without much emotion. "Mrs. Carrie Bain is my mother."

"Huey." The woman leaned against his shoulder.

"The demand for money shocked me," he said. "After all my father did for her. I thought it in very bad taste."

Adele studied this young man whose good looks froze like wax. There was glassiness in his eyes.

"A woman my father knew twenty years ago suddenly asks for two thousand dollars," he lamented, "I suppose ladies like you call that gumption."

"We call it blackmail, Mr. Bain," she snapped.

"Yes," he said. "Yes, that too." His voice trailed off as he looked out the window.

"It was then you conceived of the idea of killing Miss Gibb?" asked Jackson.

"Oh, no!" The man looked horrified. "That would have been cheap."

"But you wanted to protect your mother," guessed Sheriff Hatfield.

"I thought if I could speak to her — explain — reason with her, even — She was an educated woman, and educated women are supposed to listen to reason." He sounded unconvinced.

"Is that why you disguised yourself as a salesman for your company?" Jackson asked.

"I knew Miss Gibb was a teacher," he said. "I thought if I could approach her as a professional, it might make her more amenable to reason."

"You certainly softened her," Adele remarked. "According to the boarders at Mrs. Taylor's."

He chuckled. "When I was younger, I used to go into these little towns and register as Owen Burke. For a lark, you know."

"Complete with red wig and spectacles and plaid suit," Jackson guessed.

"You would be surprised how many ladies in boardinghouses and hotels cast their eye on me," he said. "They wouldn't have looked twice at me as Huey Bain. They would have thought me too refined for their tastes." Adele couldn't help but shoot Nin a look of amusement. "But Owen Burke had something — well, a little seedy about him. A challenge to their propriety, perhaps?" He glanced at Adele.

"I wouldn't know, Mr. Bain," she said coldly. "I've never met a man I considered too refined for me."

"You had no doubt Owen Burke would appeal to Miss Gibb, then?" Jackson asked.

"None whatsoever," said the young man. "I never intended it to be a flirtation. And I never flirted with her, no matter what those people at Mrs. Taylor's say. But I knew my appearance and profession would make her warm to me."

"Your confidence in yourself is far superior than any I've seen in a young man," Sheriff Hatfield said dryly. "And I've met many young seamen whose egos could hold a candle to a whale."

"But they never got eaten by the whale, did they?" Mr. Bain challenged.

"No, sir," he said. "They were defeated by their own presumption." Adele bit back a smile.

"Well, I wasn't," Mr. Bain said with a stubborn lip. "Miss Gibb fell right into my hands."

Adele peered at him. "What did you *really* think of her, Mr. Bain?"

"I thought she was a spinster looking for excitement, like the rest of them," the young man said. "Rather disgusting the way she poured her soul out to me. She told me her entire life's story."

"She thought you were her friend," Adele said softly.

"Friend?" he scoffed. "She was trying to trap me into sympathizing with her, just like she did my father. Do you know how they became involved?" He turned to her. "Her parents had just died. They forced her to give up her life to them because of her plainness, and yet, she played the martyr, the grieving daughter, to the hilt. My father was a kind man who couldn't stand to see a woman upset. She took advantage of that."

"She was alone, Mr. Bain," Adele said. "It's not easy for a woman who's been taking care of others all her life to suddenly be alone."

But he wasn't listening. "She sobbed all over my shoulder about how she wasted her entire youth fetching and doing only to be constantly reminded that her marriage prospects were dismal. She wailed about the tragic consequences of having been taken by an older man — as if it were a melodrama!"

"You said your father did much for her," Jackson reminded him.

"My father agreed to take her baby — me — and give him the proper home he deserved." His voice was growing righteous. "He vowed not to let her fall into disgrace since her parents left her nothing. He got her a job as a schoolteacher in San Francisco. And all that wasn't enough for her!" He gave a devilish grin. "How sad my mother should have been such an ugly person inside and out."

"You just said she wasn't your mother." Nin reminded him.

He stared at her, then went on, "I saw no harm in doing some business on the side." Adele caught the incredulous look in her brother's eyes. "I didn't know then my sales acumen would serve a purpose later on."

"I gather you couldn't reason with her," Adele said dryly.

He gave the devilish smile. "I didn't even try, Miss Gossling. I realized it would be useless. Damned obstinate woman!"

"Much like her son," Nin growled.

He blinked, but when on, "There was something else. Something in my favor, Sheriff."

The sheriff folded his hands.

"I learned Miss Gibb was going to ask my mother for three thousand dollars instead of two." His mother gasped, and he put his arm around her shoulders.

"How did you find this out, sir?" Jackson asked.

"I prompted her to take sherry after dinner, and she rather took to it," he said, almost amused. "A woman's tongue loosens on too much sherry, as I'm sure you know."

Again, Jackson's figure went rigid. "You are impertinent, sir."

"She needed it for room and board," Adele murmured, thinking of what Dr. McCabe had told them.

"I don't care what she needed it for!" Mr. Bain growled. "I knew she would continue to be a threat to my mother, and I couldn't have that."

"So you put arsenic in her hot toddy that night?" Jackson asked.

The man gave him a seething look. "That would have been clumsy. No, Deputy Sheriff, I did not kill her that night. I waited my chance. I planned it all out very carefully."

"Sir," Sheriff Hatfield leaned forward," did you never think of going to the police with this blackmail letter?"

"Certainly not!" The man looked horrified. "Subject my mother to a scandal on account of that cheap spinster?"

The sheriff closed his eyes and leaned back. "When exactly did you decide to kill your mother?"

"She was *not* my mother!"

"Mr. Bain, we're wasting time," Jackson snarled.

"A week or so into my stay at Mrs. Taylor's."

"Miss Gibb never suspected who you were for a moment?"

Mr. Bain rose and took one of the daguerreotypes from the piano, looking at it with longing. "I wondered about that too. My father and I look quite alike, you see." He handed Jackson the picture. "I rather think it was a matter of guilt."

"Did your father send her daisies?" Adele asked.

He stared at her. "How did you know?"

"And he used to read her poetry?"

"Yes, some such nonsense like that."

"Mrs. Taylor's guests told us she had violent reactions to both," said Adele. "When one is trying to forget a past hurt, anything that brings it up again is painful."

"Why didn't you withdraw from Mrs. Taylor's when you realized you couldn't reason with Miss Gibb?" asked Jackson.

"I suppose I wanted an idea," he said simply. "I thought remaining close to her and discovering her habits and weaknesses, I could see my way through."

"And you did," Adele said, "with the hot toddy."

He smiled. "That rather fell into my lap."

"Fell into your lap?" Sheriff Hatfield stared at him.

"She asked me to make it for her one night," he said. "She was very particular about it. Two ounces of whiskey, four ounces of hot water, unless Mrs. Taylor had some cider in the house, two teaspoons of dark sugar — none of that white powder, mind you — two teaspoons of lemon juice, and don't forget the cinnamon stick. Oh, and lemon slices, lots of lemon slices. And don't take them with your fingers, that's quite unsanitary. Take them with a fork." He grinned, as if he were a schoolboy ticking off his lesson.

"You have a good memory," Jackson mumbled.

"Of course, I didn't put the poison in then," he said. "I was waiting."

"Waiting for what?"

"You forget, Deputy Sheriff, I had done some business with her," he said. "I knew she ordered a subscription to *American*

Language Origins and *Fundamentals of English In Our Time*. I knew when they would arrive."

"And you knew Miss Gibb had a tendency to sit up all night reading when she received a new book she was excited about," Adele said.

The man glanced at her. "I didn't trust that. I armed myself with some insurance she would do so that night."

"I see what you mean when you say you had it all carefully planned," Sheriff Hatfield remarked.

"The trick to success is to not only make a plan, but follow through on it to the letter," Mr. Bain's eyes narrowed as if he were giving a business lecture. "My father taught me that. If one wanes from one's plan, one is liable to get into trouble."

"Even when one does not wane, one may get into trouble," Sheriff Hatfield said dryly.

"Tell us about your plan, Mr. Bain." Jackson's tone sounded encouraging in a way Adele did not expect, but she realized he was using one of his tricks from the Anspach Agency.

Mr. Bain's eyes widened and his face grew damp with excitement. "I'm sure you'll find it rather ingenious, Deputy Sheriff. It was a few weeks after I sold Miss Gibb the subscription and book. They showed up on my desk one morning. I knew they were hers, and I called the shipping department to get the exact date when they would arrive at the post office."

"You conveyed that to Miss Gibb?" Adele asked.

"And made her promise to read it that night." He chuckled. "She didn't need much prompting. She said she already planned to stay up all night and call in sick at work the next morning if need be."

"You must have done your work well for her to have been so excited about it," Nin remarked.

"I was a good salesman, Miss Branch," he said. "Even my father said I was the best he ever had."

"Go on with your ingenious plan, sir," Jackson said. "I'd like to hear the rest of it."

The man leaned forward with shining eyes. "I left Mrs. Taylor's for good and came home that night. Mother, you remember. I called to say I would have dinner at the club, as I promised to join some of the men for a card game that night."

His mother drew a little away from him, her face calm and tear-stained. She closed her eyes and nodded.

"I didn't play cards, of course." He sounded almost ashamed. "I came back here at about four o'clock through the back door. I wanted to get into the pantry, and I knew Mrs. Clark and Matilda would be resting before they started dinner."

"That was when you took the Rough on Rats," Nin guessed.

He glanced at her. "Exactly, Miss Branch."

She looked away.

"Why did you choose arsenic?" asked the sheriff.

"What does it matter?" This scream came from Mrs. Bain. "Oh, it's all so horrible!" She rose and retreated to the window. Nin went to her, whispering soothing words.

"I wanted her to suffer, Mother," he said. "For all she'd done to us. She *had* to suffer. I read in one of our books years ago about arsenic. It seemed the only way."

"Only way," Adele murmured.

"I knew Mrs. Clark kept the stuff in the pantry," he said. "You see, my plan shows not only intelligence but ease."

"I see," Jackson mumbled. "Go on."

"Then it was a time of routine," he said. "I went to my club, getting there at about five. I stayed long enough to have dinner and make sure some acquaintances I knew saw me. I joked with them about a rendezvous with a lady I didn't want my mother to know about, so if they were asked, I played cards with them all evening. They naturally were happy to oblige."

"Naturally." Adele eyed him.

"I had arranged with a friend earlier to borrow his car, and I drove to Arrojo," he continued. "I left the car far enough away so nobody would see it. You know those fields not far from Mrs. Taylor's?" Jackson nodded. "I timed it to the last minute, if you care to hear it. Or will that bore you?"

"On the contrary," her brother answered. "I would be intrigued."

Adele was amazed how Mr. Bain now spoke as if only he and Jackson were in the room. Her eyes slid toward Hatfield. The sheriff sat back with his hands threaded, content to have his deputy sheriff take the lead.

"At about twenty minutes to eleven," Mr. Bain dictated, "I arrived at Mrs. Taylor's boardinghouse and concealed myself in the overgrown shrubbery. As I had a little time to wait until Lilly the maid had her nightly chat with that scraggly-looking assistant deputy —" Here the sheriff choked back a laugh. "— I saw no harm in smoking a cigar I had in my pocket ."

"Assistant Deputy Dooland's prize find," Adele whispered to the sheriff.

"Exactly at eleven, Lilly ventured out to the gate and conversed with Assistant Deputy —"

"Edison," Sheriff Hatfield said quietly.

"Edison," said the man. "They spoke in hushed tones." He looked up. "Lilly isn't a flighty girl really. She just needs some attention."

"Please don't editorialize, Mr. Bain," Jackson said. "We'd like to wrap this up and get home as soon as possible."

"Of course," said the man, going back to his story. "While Lilly's back was turned, I ducked into the open door and dove into the kitchen pantry."

"Why?" asked Adele.

He looked at her warily. "To hide, of course. I had to get into the house *some* way."

"Sally's open and closed door." She nodded at Sheriff Hatfield.

"Lilly finished chatting with Assistant Deputy Edison and

locked the back door, then locked the front door, and went to bed. You see, I studied the habits of the house exactly to the last letter. It was about eleven-fifteen."

"And then?"

"I extracted the lemon slices from the icebox and covered them with the rat poison I had placed in the cavity of my lighter." He gave Adele a sheepish look. "I trust you noticed the lighter was hollow when you examined it in my office?"

"I didn't have time since you wrenched it out of my hand," said Adele in a defiant voice.

"Weren't you afraid of getting it on your hands, Mr. Bain?" Sheriff Hatfield asked.

"I wore gloves, just like the villains in the cheap detective novels." He grinned.

"I wouldn't think you would stoop to reading cheap novels," Adele snarled.

"I don't, Miss Gossling," he said. "I know a publisher who does and told me all about them."

Jackson nodded for him to continue.

"Then it was just a matter of waiting." He sighed. "I knew Miss Gibb would come down eventually and make her hot toddy. And, of course, she did."

"When?"

"A little after midnight," said the man. "She made it exactly as she had instructed me. My, but you spinsters stick with your routines." He gave Adele a knowing look.

"My sister is not a spinster, sir," Jackson said in a rough tone.

"I suppose not," said the man. "She is far too young and pretty."

Sheriff Hatfield looked displeased. "As Deputy Sheriff Gossling said, Mr. Bain, we would appreciate it if you would go on with your story without interruptions."

"While Miss Gibb was in the kitchen, I took the opportunity

of stealing up the stairs — I believe that's how you put it — and hiding in her closet."

"Another gem from the cheap detective novels?" Jackson asked warily.

"I thought it was rather daring," said the young man, not without a little pride. Adele caught a glimpse of his mother looking at him with a pitying gaze.

"Murderers usually choose to leave the scene of the crime as quickly as possible," Adele remarked.

"I had no fear of being caught," said the young man. "No one knew me as Huey Bain in Arrojo. Owen Burke had disappeared. They would be hard-pressed to find any connection other than he said he was employed with Bain Publishing." He gave Jackson a wary look. "Or so I thought."

"Why did you hide in Miss Gibb's room?" the sheriff asked.

The young man's face became as hard and cold as ice. "I wanted to see her suffer. I wanted to see this woman who had given birth to me and given me up so easily, and who had made my mother so distressed, suffer."

There was silence in the room. Adele realized Nin and Mrs. Bain were gone. She guessed her friend had taken the woman to her room to lie down and was thankful for Nin's foresight. Sheriff Hatfield was having a difficult time keeping his composure. His even lips quivered, and his eyes knitted together like a bull.

"You had no reason to revere her," said her brother carefully.

"Revere!" the young man growled. "I hated her!"

"Yes, yes," said Jackson.

"At about one a.m., Miss Gibb finished her hot toddy — the liquid part, that is — with no ill effects, I observed. And then she ate the lemons." He shivered as if tasting their bitter sourness.

"As you expected," Adele remarked.

"Naturally, I expected it." He gave her a patronizing look. "I wouldn't have put the rat poison on them otherwise. I also knew she would throw the rind in the fire after she finished, as I had seen her do that before. No evidence, you see."

"Except there was," Adele said. "We found rinds among the coals."

His face turned red with anger. "By 'we' I can only assume you mean you and possibly Miss Branch. Judging from the trick you played on Owen Burke, I see you're not above meddling in other people's business."

"Sometimes a woman's eye is sharper than the entire police force, Mr. Bain," said Sheriff Hatfield. Adele felt grateful for his kind words.

"When did Miss Gibb begin to feel the effects of the arsenic?" Jackson asked.

"At about one-thirty or so," he said. "It was dark in the closet, you see, and I couldn't see the time on my watch. I believe it wouldn't have been more than half an hour."

"Yes, that fits," Hatfield murmured.

"I couldn't see much, of course, though the half open doorway," he said. "But I heard it all. Things smashing about, glass falling, furniture shaking. I rather feared she would bring the entire house in."

"But she didn't," Adele said softly.

"She died in less time than I expected," he admitted. "I didn't realize arsenic worked that way. I've never seen a rat die of it, you see."

"Miss Gibb was not a rat," Adele snapped. "She was a woman, the woman who gave you life."

"Please, Miss Gossling," he snorted. "Let's not get sentimental."

"Finish your story, Mr. Bain," said Jackson.

"All was silent fifteen minutes later. I know that because I came out of the closet and checked my watch in the light. She was slumped over the desk. Odd seeing her that way." A note of remorse crept in his voice, but he went on as evenly as before. "I set to work hiding the evidence."

"The evidence?" Jackson asked.

"The letter, for one. I wanted no trace of it anywhere. That was the one connection between Miss Gibb and me. And it devastated Mother so."

"A boy takes care of his mother." Jackson nodded.

"I got quite a fright when I heard footsteps outside the door," he admitted. "I think that was the only moment of fear I had."

"Iona Hoddle was in the hall," Adele said.

"I gathered it was one of the ladies," he said. "I shut off the light on the desk so it would look as if Miss Gibb had gone to bed."

"One of your mistakes," said Sheriff Hatfield. "A dead woman would hardly turn off the light."

His confidence was, for the first time, pierced. "My God, I didn't think of that!"

"Murderers don't think of everything," Adele said.

"I thought of everything else," he insisted. "The glass, the lemon peel, the cinnamon stick." He looked sheepish. "I did rather a careless job, it seems. But the footsteps alarmed me, and I wanted to get out of the house as quickly as I could."

"And then?"

"And then, nothing." Mr. Bain sat back. "I snuck out of the house, walked back to the car and drove to Sacramento."

The sheriff rose and stretched. "You have all that, Jackson?" His deputy sheriff nodded.

Adele rose too, more slowly. She studied the young man sitting with his elbows on his knees and his hands thrust out, ready to be handcuffed. "Mr. Bain, how did you feel when you saw your mother dead?"

"Eh?" He looked at her.

"When you saw Miss Gibb slumped over the desk, and you knew she was dead," she said. "How did you feel?"

He blinked, his eyes looking like bluebells. "I felt fine. Why shouldn't I?"

"Why shouldn't you?" Adele murmured. "Millie Gibb almost committed a crime because she had no space to breathe. But you had no right to take what little breath she had left away from her."

The young man looked away, but there was no sign of remorse on his face.

CHAPTER 32

A few nights later, there was a dinner party at Mrs. Taylor's boardinghouse. The usual boarders were joined by the Gosslings, Sheriff Hatfield and his mother, Lady Augusta, and Nin. They laughed and sang toasts to everyone's health, and Mr. Walsh told riddles no one found amusing.

And yet, the subject of Millie Gibb was unavoidable.

"It's a horror to think a murderer was staying in my house!" Mrs. Taylor said with a shiver. "We could all have been killed in our beds!"

"Not really, Mrs. Taylor." Mr. Lyman sniffed. "Owen Burke was only interested in murdering one person."

"He wasn't a homicidal maniac," Jackson agreed. "He had one single endeavor in mind."

"And he wasn't Owen Burke," Adele reminded him.

"Still, I can't help but wonder if he wasn't at least partially justified in what he did," Mr. Walsh remarked.

This began a lively discussion that continued until they retired to the parlor for coffee.

"This Bain fellow ought to have gone to the police," Mr. Stoker insisted. "That's all I can see in it."

"She was a terrible woman," Miss Craig agreed. "She demanded money from innocent people. She ought to have been punished for what she did."

"I wouldn't like to think killing one's own mother, whatever the reason, deserves less than a hanging," Lady Augusta said. She tapped at the side of her son's leg with her stick. "Horatio! The man will hang, won't he?"

"I expect so, Ma," he said.

"'Whoever makes a practice of sinning is of the devil, for the devil has been sinning from the beginning,'" Mrs. Taylor quoted.

"Still, I can't help see his side of things." Mr. Lyman rubbed his chin with his hand.

"So can I," said Mr. Walsh. "Once a blackmailer, always a blackmailer. Isn't that the truth, Sheriff?"

"Not all blackmailers, sir." Sheriff Hatfield accepted another cup of coffee from Mrs. Taylor.

"None of us really liked the woman," Mr. Lyman pointed out. "Is it a stretch to think she wouldn't have continued her demands for money even after the first payment? I heard the Bains were awful rich."

Adele had been on the couch with Nin, listening quietly, but now she spoke up. "That wasn't the reason Mr. Bain killed her."

"Oh?" Jackson looked at her.

"It wasn't money," said Adele. "It was vengeance."

"Isn't that a little far-fetched?" Mr. Stoker asked. "After all, it happened twenty years ago."

"His father told him about Miss Gibb on his deathbed," said Adele. "Imagine the father to whom one had been so close, to telling you a story like that just before he dies."

"I should think resentment and rage would have been eating away at him," Nin agreed.

"His mother died a horrible death at his hands," Adele said. "When he told us the story, he was almost proud of it. As if he had done right by his father."

"He was unbalanced, Del," said her brother. "There are criminals who don't know what they're doing."

"But the man planned it all very carefully down to the last minute," Lady Augusta pointed out. "I hardly think that's the mind of a man who didn't know what he was doing."

"Ma's right, Jackson," said Sheriff Hatfield. "I remember one time when I was deputy to Sheriff Nealy, we had a case down in Rosa Gris. A man tarred and feathered his neighbor. The neighbor planted onions, which went bad and stunk to high heaven. His neighbor behaved in much the same way as Mr. Bain. He even pounded his fist like a gavel." Hatfield demonstrated with such an expression of fierceness on his face that everyone laughed.

Adele rose and wandered to the window. It was a bright evening, and the moon looked like an egg in the sky. She felt a light hand on her shoulder and turned to find Miss Hoddle smiling with sadness.

"Thank you for keeping your promise, Miss Gossling," she said.

"It's my promise to all victims," Adele said. "Justice."

"It's a shame it turned out this way. But if you had known Miss Gibb — well, I don't say she was right in what she did, but —"

"She had her reasons." Adele patted the woman's hand. "Yes, I know. She felt she was trapped, and her only way out was to do what she did."

"Others used her," Miss Hoddle insisted. "There were so many things I didn't know about her that were in the newspaper. About her mother and father and Mr. Bain, the elder, I mean. What can a woman do?"

"Yes," Adele said softly. "What can a woman do?"

~~~~~

Author's Note
~~~~~

Hi there! I'm so glad you've reached the end of this book. I hope you enjoyed the surprising story of Millie Gibb and Adele's fight to get justice for her death, even though she wasn't what you would call a very nice person.

*M*illie's love of words was inspired by my increasing fascination with etymology. Since I began writing historical fiction in 2019, words have become much more of a big deal to me. Historical fiction uses words differently than contemporary fiction, as I quickly found out when I was editing my first historical women's fiction book, *The Specter*.

*W*hy? Because some words we might take for granted as having always been around were actually not always around. Some are obvious 21st century inventions ("selfie," anyone?) But others aren't so obvious. For example, did you know the word "sleuth" came into the English language in the 1870s but the verb "sleuthing" didn't until 30 years later?

*N*ow, that might not sound like a big deal. But when I wrote a mystery set in 1903 (the first book of this series), I couldn't have Jackson accuse Adele's "sleuthing interfering with police business" because the word hadn't been invented yet! I could, however, have him accuse his sister of "playing sleuth again," since that word was in the language and could have been used.

*I*f you're a fan of Scrabble or Wordle, the word game that seems to have taken Facebook by storm, you know playing with words is super fun. That's sort of what I do with the title of Book 3 of this series, *Death At Will*. The "will" isn't willpower but an actual will and testament. There's a family death involved too. Like to find out more? Turn the page!

*H*appy reading!
Tam

Can Adele Gossling prove a son didn't kill his mother?

Teddy Roosevelt has just been elected president and even Arrojo can't deny progressive reform is here to stay. Rebecca Gold, one of the era's New Women, comes to Arrojo to start her own law practice and lands the affluent Thea Marsh as her first client.

Thea dies unexpectedly and the trail of suspects leads to her own family. In particular, her beloved eldest son, Theo, is accused of the crime. Mild-mannered and somewhat of a mama's boy, could he really be guilty of such a heinous crime?

The police think so. So Rebecca turns to her new friend in town: stationary shop owner Adele Gossling. Adele has already proven herself to be adept in helping the local police solve crimes, much to the shock and chagrin of her more conservative neighbors. Despite promises never to involve herself in crime detection again, how can she refuse a friend in need?

Will Adele make a case against Theo for the police out of a stained teacup, a fountain pen nib, ashes that should have been in the fireplace, and daisies that should have been fresh? Or will Theo go to the gallows and the real murderer escape justice?

Find out in this third installment of the Adele Gossling Mysteries, the compelling early 20th century series spearheaded by Adele Gossling and her spiritual sidekick, Nin Branch, as they set out to prove women can be crime busters too!

Read on for an excerpt from this book!

Within fifteen minutes, her brother sauntered into the shop, the silver deputy sheriff's badge shining in the sunlight. "All right, Del, why the hush-hush?"

"Does the sheriff know you're here?"

"I told him I was going to the Bush farm to check on that stolen horse," he said, amused. "Those girls of yours insist you have a murderer locked in your storeroom."

Adele laughed. "I'm afraid they let their imaginations run away with them. No, no murderer, Jack."

"Not yet," Nin said.

"Are we playing guessing games now, Miss Branch?" he asked in a stiff tone.

"I never guess, Mr. Gossling," she answered. "I take evil and death in any way it comes."

He crossed his arms, looking at his sister. "Well?"

She told him all Rebecca had said about her employer's death as the woman sat silently with her hands in her lap. It was as if Jackson's badge made her nervous again.

He looked at Rebecca. "It would be better, Miss Gold, if you would tell the sheriff of your suspicions, just as my sister suggested."

"I promised Theo I wouldn't," she insisted. "I promised him there wouldn't be any scandal."

"But if Thea Marsh didn't die of natural causes —"

"I didn't say that wasn't true!" she insisted. "I merely said I had a feeling about it."

He sighed. "I understand your trepidation. But there's a procedure to these things, you know."

"Fiddlesticks!" Nin burst out. "Don't you believe in helping a friend?" Rebecca gave her a grateful look.

"When there's no crime involved, I'm the first to help anybody," Jackson's tone was crusty. "But if there is a crime—"

Adele took his arm. "We need your professional and astute eye, Jack. If there is nothing in it, no harm done. If there is something, Rebecca will convince the family to go through the proper channels."

"They won't have much of a choice," he remarked.

"Then you have no reason to object a look around Mrs. Marsh's room, do you?" She gave him a sharp look.

"I have no objection as long as there is a method to it," he insisted. "One simply can't go bursting into a room with a magnifying glass hollering 'murder afoot!'"

"Don't tell me the Anspatches never entered a room permission." She eyed him.

He looked away and she was sorry she had spoken. But then, he said, "I suppose it can't do any harm to look around as long as the family consents, and we're very careful. But *only* if we have their full consent, Del."

"That you have, deputy," Rebecca said in a relieved tone.

"*And* I have your full promise if there is anything in the least suspicious, you go to the sheriff."

"You have my promise." She bowed.

What do Adele, Nin, and Jackson find in Thea Marsh's room? Is it enough to holler "murder afoot"? You won't know until you read *Death At Will*, the third book in the Adele Gossling Mysteries. Copies are available at your favorite online book-store <u>here</u> https://tammayauthor.com/books-2/the-adele-gossling-mysteries/death-at-will-book-3.

How about a little more of the Adele Gossling Mysteries, right here, right now? Read on for how to get hold of my free novella, *The Missing Ruby Necklace*.

When a jewel and a girl go missing on New Year's Eve...

Eleanor McCarthy, a lovely though somewhat flighty debutante, has graced the tiny town of Arrojo, California, with her presence. One of Arrojo's prominent ladies throws a New Year's Eve shindig to introduce her to Arrojo's high society — whatever little of it there is. Naturally, the daughter and son of one of San

Francisco's influential lawyers, Adele and Jackson Gossling, are invited.

But screams replace popping champagne corks when Eleanor's priceless ruby necklace is discovered missing. And soon, so is Eleanor!

In this historical cozy mystery set in the early 20th century, follow Adele Gossling, stationary store owner and amateur sleuth, and her clairvoyant sidekick Nin Branch as they search for a ruby necklace that may or may not have been stolen and a young woman who may or may not have run away.

Want to read an excerpt from this book? I got you covered!
    Turn the page.

"Coffee!" Miss McCarthy laughed. "Heavens, no! I haven't had my first taste of champagne yet." She flung her hand out to her brother. "Bring me a bottle of champagne, my good man."

"I don't mind," he said.

Before he could saunter out the door, Mrs. Abberton jumped up. "I'll get it."

"I really think we ought to get coffee," Mr. Abberton mumbled.

"She wants champagne," Mrs. Abberton was almost stern. "It's a celebration, after all!" She practically fled from the room.

Adele followed her and caught her arm. She spoke in a soft tone. "Mrs. Abberton, why did Miss McCarthy faint?"

"She just told you, didn't she?" The woman gave a shrill laugh. "Albert said we ought to open some windows, but it was such a windy night, I —"

"It wasn't the windows," said Adele. "Or the corset."

"Of course it was!" The woman examined some bottles on the floor. "I never could read these labels."

"You were staring at Miss McCarthy as if something that wasn't there."

"What an imagination you have, dear." The woman said.

"Miss McCarthy had her hands on her throat when she fell," Adele continued. "You kept looking at her throat."

"Nonsense," the woman hissed.

"Miss McCarthy wasn't wearing her ruby necklace," Adele declared.

Mrs. Abberton tore through a row of bottles lying on a table. One rolled onto the floor with a crack and the bubbly drink spilled across the marble. She sunk into one of the chairs. "You're too observant, Miss Gossling."

"You saw it too."

"Just before the lights went out," she said. "But Eleanor is one of those girls who gets easily flustered with her jewelry. She says it weighs her down."

"If that's true, why were you so alarmed just now?" Adele said.

"I wasn't," the woman insisted. "She locks that necklace in a box. Albert tried to persuade her to put it in our safe at the finance company, but she refused."

"That's rather unusual," Adele said.

"Eleanor's a lovely girl, but rather flighty," The woman said in a harsh tone. "I expect Celestine spoils her."

"If the necklace is missing, there might be a theft involved," Adele suggested.

Jewelry goes missing all the time. But does that mean theft? And why is Mrs. Abberton so nervous?

How can you get your hands on a copy of *The Missing Ruby Necklace*, not available in any bookstore? Simple. Go to this link: https://landing.mailerlite.com/webforms/landing/ 12u0c3. What else will you get when you get this novella? How about fun facts about women in history and true crime classic mysteries, which are just as fascinating, if not more so, as contemporary true crimes?

As soon as Tam May started her first novel at the age of fourteen, writing became her voice. She writes engaging, fun-to-solve historical cozy mysteries featuring sassy suffragist Adele Gossling. Her mysteries empower readers with a sense of "justice is done" for women, both dead and alive. Her fiction is set in the San Francisco Bay Area because she adores sourdough bread, Ghirardelli chocolate, and San Francisco history.

Tam is the author of the Adele Gossling Mysteries which take place in the early 20th century and feature amateur sleuth and epistolary expert Adele Gossling, a forward-thinking young woman whose talent for solving crimes doesn't sit well with her town's Victorian ideas about women's place in society.

Tam has also written historical women's fiction. Her post-World War II short story collection, *Lessons From My Mother's Life*, debuted at #1 in its category on Amazon, and the first book of her Gilded Age family saga, the Waxwood Series, *The Specter*, remains in the top 10 in its category.

Although Tam left her heart in San Francisco, she lives in Texas because it's cheaper. When she's not writing, she's devouring everything classic (books, films, art, music) and concocting vegetarian dishes in her kitchen.

Tam May can be reached at:
WEBSITE: http://tammayauthor.com/
EMAIL: tammay70@tammayauthor.com
FACEBOOK: https://www.facebook.com/tammayauthor
INSTAGRAM: https://www.instagram.com/tammayauthor/